URSULA ORANGE
BEGIN AGAIN

URSULA MARGUERITE DOROTHEA ORANGE was born in Simla in 1909, the daughter of the Director General of Education in India, Sir Hugh Orange. But when she was four the family returned to England. She was later 'finished' in Paris, and then went up to Lady Margaret Hall, Oxford in 1928. It was there that she and Tim Tindall met. They won a substantial sum of money on a horse, enough to provide the couple with the financial independence to marry, which they did in 1934.

Ursula Orange's first novel, *Begin Again*, was published with success in 1936, followed by *To Sea in a Sieve* in 1937. In 1938 her daughter, the writer Gillian Tindall, was born, and the next year the war changed their lives completely. Their London home was badly damaged and, as her husband left for the army, Ursula settled in the country with Gillian, where she had ample opportunity to observe the comic, occasionally tragic, effects of evacuation: the subject of her biggest success, *Tom Tiddler's Ground* (1941). Three more novels followed, continuing to deal with the indirect effects of war: conflicts of attitude, class and the generations, wherever disparate characters are thrown together.

The end of the war saw the family reunited and in 1947 the birth of her son Nicholas. But Ursula Orange's literary career foundered, and the years that followed saw her succumb to severe depression and periods of hospital treatment. In 1955 she died aged 46.

By Ursula Orange

Begin Again (1936)

To Sea in a Sieve (1937)

Tom Tiddler's Ground
(1941, published in the U.S. as *Ask Me No Questions*)

Have Your Cake (1942)

Company in the Evening (1944)

Portrait of Adrian (1945)

URSULA ORANGE

BEGIN AGAIN

With an introduction
by Stacy Marking

DEAN STREET PRESS

A Furrowed Middlebrow Book
FM11

Published by Dean Street Press 2017

First published in 1936 by Michael Joseph

Cover by DSP

ISBN 978 1 911579 27 4

www.deanstreetpress.co.uk

INTRODUCTION

ON THE FIRST page of a notebook filled with carefully pasted press cuttings, Ursula Orange has inscribed, in touchingly school girlish handwriting: *Begin Again, Published February 13th 1936.* Later she adds: *American Publication Aug 7th 1936,* and then a pencilled note: *Total sales 1221.*

She was 26, a young married woman, and this was her first novel. There are plentiful reviews from major publications in Britain, Australia and America. *Begin Again* by Ursula Orange is included in the *Washington Herald*'s Bestsellers' list for August 1936, where it comes higher than *Whither France?* by Leon Trotsky. The *Daily Telegraph* praises her insight into "the strange ways of the New Young, their loves, their standards, their shibboleths, and their manners ... An unusually good first novel, in a decade of good first novels."

To be greeted as the voice of the new generation must have been thrilling for a young writer, and a year later her second novel was published. *To Sea in a Sieve* opens with the heroine Sandra being sent down from Lady Margaret Hall, Oxford, the college which Ursula herself had so recently left. Rebellious and in pursuit of freedom, Sandra rejects convention, marries an 'advanced' and penniless lover, and the novel lightheartedly recounts the consequences of her contrariness.

But despite her light tone, Ursula Orange takes on serious themes in all her work. She explores the conflicts between generations, between classes, between men and women. Her characters embrace new and modern attitudes to morality, sex and marriage, and take adultery and divorce with surprising frivolity. She understands young women's yearning for independence, their need to express themselves and to escape the limitations of domesticity – though she often mocks the results.

In 1938 she had her first child, Gillian, and by 1941 when her third and most successful novel, *Tom Tiddler's Ground*, was published, the chaos of war had overshadowed the brittle 'modern' world of her generation. With her husband now away in the army, Ursula and her small daughter left London to take refuge in the country, where she could observe firsthand the impact of evacuation on a small English village (just as her heroine Caroline does in the novel).

Tom Tiddler's Ground is set in 1939-40, the months later known as the "phoney war." The evacuation of London is under way, but the horrors of the Blitz have not yet begun. The clash between rustic villagers and London evacuees, the misunderstandings between upper and lower classes, differing approaches to love and children, the strains of war and separation on relationships and marriage: all these indirect effects of war provide great material for the novel. The *Sunday Times* describes it as "taking a delectably unusual course of its own, and for all the gas-masks hiding in the background, [it] is the gayest of comedies." It's a delightful read to this day, and includes an astonishing number of elements, ingeniously interwoven – bigamy, adultery, seduction, fraud, theft, embezzlement, the agonies of a childless marriage and the guilt of a frivolously undertaken love affair.

The book reveals a real talent for dialogue and structure. As Caroline arrives for the first time at her new home in a Kentish village, the scene, the plots and sub-plots, the major characters and the themes are all established on a single page, almost entirely in dialogue.

> "Red car," said Marguerite ecstatically as Lavinia's Hulton sports model, with Alfred in the driving seat, drew up alongside.
>
> "Excuse me," said Caroline, leaning out, "but can you tell me where a house called The Larches is?"
>
> "The Larches!" Alfred was out of his seat in a minute, and advancing with outstretched hand: "Have I the pleasure of addressing Mrs. Cameron?"
>
> "Good God!" said Caroline, taken aback. "So you're – are you Constance's husband by any chance, or what?" (It might be. About forty. Not bad-looking, I will say that for Constance. That slick, smart, take-me-for-an-ex-public-schoolboy type. Eyes a bit close together.)
>
> "Yes, I'm Captain Smith." (Caroline found her hand firmly taken and shaken.) "And Constance and I are very very pleased to welcome you to Chesterford."

"But that isn't Constance," said Caroline, feebly
indicating Lavinia. Alfred gave an easy laugh.

"Oh no! Constance is home waiting for you." (Or I hope
she is and not hanging round after that slum-mother and
her brat, curse them.) "This is Miss Lavinia Conway," he
said, taking her in a proprietary way by the elbow to help
her out of the car.

"How do you do?" said Caroline, recovering herself. (....
Who is this girl? Good God even I didn't put it on quite so
thick at her age. Can't be Alfred's little bit, surely?)

Part of the entertainment throughout the novel is the contrast
between the perfect politeness of everything expressed aloud, and
the bracketed thoughts that are left unsaid. Ursula Orange uses
the device not to convey complex interior monologue, in the way
of Virginia Woolf or Joyce, but as a comic, sometimes cynical,
commentary on her characters' evasions and self-deception.

The notices and sales for *Tom Tiddler's Ground* were good, but
Ursula must have been disconcerted to receive a personal letter
from her new publisher, Michael Joseph himself. He had been away
at the wars, he explains, and has been reading the novel in hospital.
He writes that he was "immensely entertained" and predicts "that
it is only a question of time – and the always necessary slice of
good luck – before you become a really big seller ..." But then he
adds: "The only criticism that I venture to offer is that Caroline's
unorthodox behaviour ... may have prevented the book from having
a bigger sale. I think it is still true, even in these days, that the public
likes its heroines pure."

Whether influenced by Michael Joseph's strictures or no, in
her next novel, *Have Your Cake*, the clashes of moral values, of
hidden motives, of snobbery and class distinction, are not taken
so lightly. Published in August 1942, it features an ex-Communist
writer who (in the words of *The Times*) "is one of those devastating
people who go through life pursuing laudable ends but breaking
hearts and ruining lives at almost every turn." But lives and hearts
are not ultimately broken: the notices are good; sales figures top
2500 – evidently "the Boots Family Public", and her publisher,
were pleased.

By 1944 when *Company In the Evening* was published, Ursula Orange's crisp dialogue-driven style has altered. Told in the first person, with greater awareness and self-analysis, it is the story of Vicky, a divorcee whose marriage had been abandoned almost carelessly (and somehow without her ex-husband discovering that she's having their child). Vicky finds herself coping single handedly in a household of disparate and incompatible characters thrown together by war. Less engaging than Ursula Orange's earlier heroines, Vicky seems particularly hard on her very young and widowed sister-in-law, who is "just so hopelessly not my sort of person", in other words what her mother would have called common.

The novel is full of the taken-for-granted snobbery of the era – hard for the modern reader to stomach. In fact Vicky raises the issue, though somewhat equivocally, herself.

> "When I was about 19 and suffering from a terrific anti-snob complex (one had to make *some* protest against the extraordinary smugness and arrogance of the wealthy retired inhabitants ...) I practically forbade Mother to use the word 'common' ... "Don't you see, Mother, it isn't a question of phraseology, it's your whole *attitude* I object to."

But just as one starts to feel sympathetic, she adds:

> "Goodness, what mothers of semi-intellectual daughters of nineteen have to put up with!"

As the novel progresses, Vicky's faults are acknowledged, her mistakes rectified, her marriage repaired. She returns contentedly "to ordinary married life in the middle of the worst war ever known to history."

Perhaps this context is the point. The *New York Times* praises Ursula for her admirably stiff upper lip: "Ursula Orange, calmly ignoring as negligible all that Hitler has done, ... has written a novel that is a wet towel slapped nonchalantly across the face of the aggressor. " Her light and entertaining novels were indeed helping the nation to carry on.

At last in 1945 war came to an end. English life returned to a difficult peace of deprivation and scarcity. Tim Tindall, Ursula's husband, had been almost entirely absent for 5 years, a total stranger to their young daughter. He had had – in that odd English phrase – a 'good war', seeing action in North Africa, Salerno and France. After his return, the family opted for country life; Tim picked up the reins of the family's publishing firm, commuting daily to London and an independent existence, while Ursula passed her time in Sussex with Gillian and her new baby son. That year she published one more novel, *Portrait of Adrian*, which escapes to an earlier period and the happier existence of young girls sharing a flat together in London.

Ursula's horizons seem gradually to narrow. She had been the smart, modern voice of a young and careless generation that no longer existed, and she did not find a new place in the post-war world. Severe depression set in, leading to suicide attempts and hospital treatments. Her literary life had virtually come to an end. She undertook two projects but these were never realized, perhaps because they were well before their time: an illustrated anthology of poetry for teenagers, a category as yet unnamed; and a play about Shelley's as yet unheralded wives.

In *Footprints in Paris*, (2009) their daughter, the writer Gillian Tindall, describes her mother's decline as she becomes "someone who has failed at the enterprise of living.... London now began to figure on her mental map as the place she might find again her true self." But the hope of finding a fresh life when the family moved to a new house in Hampstead, proved illusory. "Six days later, having by the move severed further the ties that had held her to life ... she made another suicide attempt which, this time, was fatal. She was not found for two days."

But we cannot let this sad ending define the whole of Ursula Orange. It should not detract from our enjoyment of her work, which at its entertaining best, gives us a picture of a sparkling generation, of intelligent and audacious women surviving against the odds, with wit as well as stoicism, with courage in the face of deprivation and loss.

Stacy Marking

PROLOGUE

"YOU ARE LISTENING, aren't you, mummy?" said Leslie Fisher anxiously.

"Yes, dear, of course."

This was true. Mrs. Fisher always listened to what her only daughter had to say. It was only because it was ten o'clock on a Saturday morning with the breakfast not yet cleared away that a lurking consciousness of Cook to be interviewed and the grocer to be phoned showed occasionally through her interest.

"It's not," continued Leslie, patiently, "that it's not a very nice life here. But you see I can't help feeling that I'm not getting anywhere."

Mrs. Fisher did not agree or disagree. To her daughter's annoyance she simply reverted to the dull subject of money.

"I'm sure you would be sorry if you went and spent Grandfather's hundred pounds straight off. Now I'm quite willing to let you have a year in London at an art-school if you think that's what you'd really like."

"I *know* that's what I need now," corrected Leslie, "if I'm ever to do anything with my painting."

"I told you Miss Wilkinson was giving some local classes here this summer, didn't I, Leslie? I thought you might be interested."

Leslie sighed. She had been afraid her mother had not understood.

"That wouldn't be the slightest use," she said quickly, "Miss Wilkinson's sort of classes would never lead on to anything. Besides, I'm not interested in landscape at the moment. I want to study fashion drawing and poster work."

She paused expectantly, but her mother did not ask her to what this would lead. She merely reiterated:

"I really wouldn't advise you to dash up to London and spend Grandfather's hundred pounds on a studio straight away. Now why not try living with Aunt Sybil? You'd be very comfortable there—"

Comfortable! Leslie shuddered at the epithet. She had lived in comfort at home for nearly five years; she believed now that it was not a thing she valued in the least. She stared gloomily at the breakfast table, at the June sunlight dancing on the well-polished silver kettle and tea-pot, through the window at the border, now a blaze of tulips and lupins, much admired by her mother's visitors; and reflected with a touch of regret that she did not care at all for silver tea-pots and tulips, a comfortable house, a large garden and all the placid leisurely routine of life in her Berkshire home. No. It was the precarious, the dangerous, the colourful that would really appeal to her. She would like to live in an attic with an enormous skylight and canvases stacked all round the walls; she would like to cook sausages and kippers over a gas-ring and share them with her artist friends. She would like to stay up all night and sleep all day. She would like to have a frying pan and a loaf of bread and an alarm clock of her own. She would like to wear trousers and a bright yellow sweater and paint her front door a vivid green. She would like to cut off her hair and sleep on a divan and live her own life.

She tried very hard to be patient with her mother.

"I think if I'm to get on," she said, "it's rather important to have the right atmosphere."

"Yes? Of course, dear, I only want you to be happy. I'm quite willing to give you a year in town."

Leslie sighed. She did not in the least want her mother only to want her to be happy; she did not want to be given a year in town on her mother's money. She wanted it to be acknowledged that there might (indeed almost certainly would) be a future for her in the world of art. She wanted to make a gesture, to believe in herself, to sink her small capital and gamble on her own ability: and of course to find out that she had been right. From her mother she wanted nothing but comprehension. Not, no, most certainly not, indulgence.

"I wish I could make you understand, mummy."

"I'm afraid I don't quite see what it is I'm to understand, Leslie."

"Well, you see, mummy, it isn't that I'm exactly asking you for anything. I really want just to *tell* you that I've decided to spend Grandfather's money on just this thing."

There was a moment's silence and Leslie hoped, a little anxiously, that her mother was not offended.

Mrs. Fisher was not. The slight frown on her forehead was due to the strain of financial calculations. She said slowly:

"But, Leslie dear, I don't see how your food can possibly cost you less than—"

At this point a diversion was created by Alice, the maid, who came in and said: "Please, madam, Robinson says did you know the new chicken-house has arrived and shall he put it up in the lower field with the others?"

"Tell him I'll come and see him about it in ten minutes," said Mrs. Fisher. "Leslie, I was just going to say—there *is* Robinson crossing the lawn. Is that one of the sides, I wonder? Good gracious, it doesn't look to me at *all* like the one I ordered from the catalogue. I wanted the one with the little windows. Perhaps he'd better not unpack any more until I've made sure. . . ." Mrs. Fisher hurried out of the room.

And that, thought Leslie disgustedly, is the event of the day. The arrival of a new chicken-house!

When her mother returned, reassured (it was only the back wall that was windowless), Leslie had found material for a new argument against living at home.

"You see, mummy, I haven't really any part in this sort of life, have I? I mean new chicken-houses and all that sort of thing are very nice, but—well, it isn't even as if the chickens were mine, is it?"

"But I thought you didn't like chickens, Leslie?"

"I don't," said Leslie instantly. "I'm just explaining that chickens and gardens aren't the sort of thing I care about."

"No, dear, I know you don't. It's really very seldom I ask you to feed them, isn't it?"

"No, no, I know." Leslie paused. An exasperating sense of being at cross-purposes assailed her. They seemed to be agreeing; and this, she felt sure, must be wrong. "It's not only that I'm not interested in the sort of things people do here," she continued, "it's the way they talk too."

"Talk?" said her mother, surprised.

"Well, you see, they don't talk really, do they?" explained Leslie. "The sort of people who live down here never seem to me to talk about anything. Not even the girls my own age. Sylvia Perry and I were discussing it the other day. We were listening to the people at a tennis-party, and we agreed afterwards that nobody said anything in the least remarkable the whole afternoon. But you don't like Sylvia, do you?"

Sylvia was an old school-friend of Leslie's, and the Perry family lived not far from Leslie's home.

"I think she's so rude to her mother. And Mrs. Perry is such a nice woman—oh, that reminds me. . . ."

"What?" said Leslie, instantly curious.

"Nothing that would interest you, dear," replied her mother with a twinkle of amusement, "only about some cuttings Mrs. Perry promised me."

Leslie's curiosity died an immediate death.

"Sylvia is rather like me," she said, "in feeling that, living in the country as we do, we're getting more and more out of touch with things."

"I hope you won't begin to show it quite so plainly as she does," said Mrs. Fisher, remembering a recent tea-party at which Sylvia had been peculiarly ungracious. "Mrs. Clarke was horrified at the way Sylvia talked about St. Ethelburga's. You know I asked Mrs. Perry and Sylvia to meet her because I thought she'd be interested. She's sending her little girl there next term. But the things Sylvia said about her old school! And the way she snapped up poor Mrs. Perry when she tried to smooth things over by telling Mrs. Clarke that Sylvia was really very happy there! I don't suppose Sylvia really meant it all, but it was very tactless."

Mrs. Fisher knew that she was an indulgent mother, but she flattered herself that she would never permit Leslie to behave as Sylvia sometimes did.

"Oh, tactless," said Leslie airily. "When Sylvia's interested in a thing I don't suppose she bothers about being tactful." Leslie, who was herself both by training and by temperament a polite person, had recently begun to find Sylvia's ruthlessness rather admirable.

"Evidently not," said Mrs. Fisher, with some asperity. (It had been difficult to bring the tea-party to an amiable close.)

"That's just it, mummy," pursued Leslie, "that's what I mean about people never talking here. If anybody ever gets off safe topics like—like chicken-houses—well, then people don't understand and get annoyed. It isn't like that with people who live in London. I mean people like Jane and Florence," said Leslie, mentioning two more of her old school-friends. Jane and Florence had been up at Oxford. Now they were sharing a flat in Maida Vale and went off cheerfully to their typewriters every morning.

Mrs. Fisher resented Leslie's choice of a chicken-house as symbolic of the neighbourhood's conversational resources. She said, "What do Jane and Florence talk about, then, that's so interesting?"

"Oh—just everything," said Leslie grandly. "Just—" She searched for something more explicit but found it eluded her. "Everything," she concluded.

She knew, not only from Jane and Florence's conversation (it had been some time since she had had a really good talk with them) but also from the pages of modern novels exactly the way in which young people living their own lives in London talk together—an attractive mixture of an extreme intensity and a quite remarkable casualness. "Henri says Marcovitch's new poems are the finest things he's ever read—will certainly found a school of their own. By the way—hand me the marmalade—Elissa is living with Henri now. He says he needs her for his work at present." Clearly the sort of person who talked like this lived a much freer, a much wider, a much *better* life than the sort of person who merely said, "Good morning, mummy. Did you sleep well? When Alice brought my tea this morning she said a tree was blown down in the orchard last night."

It was impossible to put into words this feeling that somewhere, waiting for her, almost expectant of her, was a life into which she would plunge as into her natural element. Leaving home would be like jumping into the river and swimming with the stream instead of lingering stupidly on the bank. Leaving home would be like stepping into a gaily painted bus which would rattle briskly off to some destination infinitely alluring if not precisely specified.

"I feel," said Leslie inadequately, "as though Jane and Florence were *getting* somewhere. And I'm not."

"Oh, yes, tell me about Florence," said Mrs. Fisher. She felt a motherly affection for this old school-friend of Leslie's. Although she had not seen her for some years she had followed her career, as reported by Leslie, with interest. "You say she's getting on? Does she like her job any better then?"

Leslie was a little disconcerted by her mother's passion for the concrete.

"I'm not sure that she's exactly 'getting on' at her job. As a matter of fact, I think she's probably rather wasted there. But she has an interesting sort of life, you know. I believe she's nearly finished her novel. She's always wanted to write. Just as I've always wanted to work at art," said Leslie, neatly bringing the conversation round to herself again.

Mrs. Fisher looked a little surprised, and Leslie, oversensitive about herself, fancied that her mother was silently holding the word "always" up to ridicule. She rushed into speech again.

"Yes, I know I said when I left school that I wanted to stay at home. But that was years ago. Besides, what I really meant was that I thought it was landscape I was interested in. I couldn't tell, could I? But now I find it isn't." Leslie shook her head, remembering regretfully the few unfinished canvases in the attic, the odd water-colours pinned experimentally on the walls. "And now I believe I should do well in something quite different. I've been finding out about poster work and fashion drawing and magazine illustration. Have you ever noticed how bad most illustrations are, mummy? I know I could do better than that. There's a course I could take—a place near Baker Street—I believe I could make something of it. I really believe that's what my line is." Leslie gazed at her mother enthusiastically.

"Well, dear, if that's what you've set your heart on—certainly . . ."

It was a pity that mummy's kindness was so infinitely more damping than any opposition could be. Set your heart on! The phrase had all the associations of an indulged childhood, of toys clamoured for, of "treats" demanded and given. Leslie, who liked to think of herself, artistically speaking, as an apostle responding to a call that could not be ignored, replied, "I can't help feeling that if I don't do something about it now I shall never do anything with my art at all."

Mrs. Fisher, apparently unmoved by this prospect of ultimate unfulfillment, merely gazed thoughtfully at her daughter's flushed face. Leslie, nervously afraid that she was going to talk about money again, rushed on, "And you see the *whole* point is that if I'm really to get on I *know* I must have the right sort of life. It wouldn't be the least good living with Aunt Sybil. It really wouldn't. You do understand, don't you, mummy?"

"That you don't want to live with Aunt Sybil?"

"It's not exactly not wanting. It's just that it would be no good."

"Well, where would you like to live then, dear?"

"That's just it. I want to find out everything like that for myself. I don't want you to bother about it at all." Leslie paused, drawing solid comfort from the thought of Grandfather's hundred pounds. "I want to experiment on my own."

Mrs. Fisher realized that her daughter was secretly yearning not for sympathy, not for kindness, but for opposition; for opposition, so that she could have an excuse for breaking away, flaunting her independence and Grandfather's hundred pounds; for opposition, to snap the ties which had bound their lives together so happily and which now were beginning to fret the child. Perhaps it was only natural—but it was hard to accept the implication suggested, probably unconsciously, by Leslie's absurd insistence on her hundred pounds—that her obligations to her mother rested only on a financial basis.

"I want this to be absolutely *my* affair," reiterated Leslie.

"Very well, dear," said Mrs. Fisher resignedly, thinking that for the life of her she would not be able to prevent herself from taking a passionate interest in all the details of her only child's existence.

"Of course when I'm living in town," said Leslie, a stray pang of compunction suddenly assailing her, "I'll see you often—come down here—and you must come up and see me. You mustn't be lonely. . . ."

Leslie had grown up accepting her mother's widowhood almost as a matter of course. It was only recently, since she had begun to think about leaving home, that she had found cause to regret that there were only the two of them in the family. It had always seemed to her quite natural that all her mother's affection and a great part of her interests should be centred in herself. Now it occurred to her for the first time that this was somehow wrong.

Fortunately Mrs. Fisher was too practical-minded to sentimentalize over the prospect of losing Leslie.

"Oh, you needn't worry about that, dear. I know I can't expect to have you always with me. I have all my interests here, you know—the garden and my friends." (Mrs. Fisher looked out of the window as she spoke, noticing with automatic concern that the peonies in the bed by the laburnums seemed in need of water, and that Robinson was just carrying down the perches and nesting-boxes of the despised chicken-house.) "But I *should* like to feel that—well, that you weren't short of money and were looking after yourself properly." (It really was too much to ask of her that she should immediately stifle all maternal solicitude.)

"You really haven't any need to worry about all that," said Leslie earnestly. "As a matter of fact, I want you to have a talk with Jane and Florence when they come down next Saturday. You know that's really why I wanted to ask all my London friends to a party here. I want you to meet them. I want you to talk to them, so that you can see for yourself that they're different from the girls who just do nothing down here. They—they seem to me to be making something out of their lives. They—they make me feel purposeless. Whenever I—"

"How many exactly are coming, Leslie?"

"Well. There's Jane and Florence. You know Florence."

"Yes," said Mrs. Fisher, remembering a long-legged school-girl with untidy hair, awkward movements and a tendency to become suddenly intense. "A nice child—I liked her," she added kindly.

"I hope you'll like Jane too. They live together, you know. Jane always seems to me to be typically modern. In the best sense, I mean," added Leslie hastily, "not like that silly film last night."

"No, no, of course not," said Mrs. Fisher reassuringly, recalling some of the more startling incidents in the drama in question.

"And then Henry," continued Leslie, "he's Jane's fiancé, you know. They were up at Oxford together. That's where they met."

"I see," said Mrs. Fisher, thinking that the university must have changed considerably since her husband was at Christ Church. His reminiscences of Oxford, she remembered, had always been exclusively male.

"And Sylvia is motoring over—of course she's not really a London friend, but she's a friend of Jane and Florence's, and she'll fit in all right because she's not at all the sort of girl who just stays at home really—is she? Although she doesn't actually do anything else."

"No, I always think she'd be *much* happier away from home," agreed Mrs. Fisher, sympathetically recalling poor Mrs. Perry's face at the tea-party.

"And then there's Claud," continued Leslie. "Sylvia is bringing him over. He's a friend of hers. I've only met him once. He's very nice."

"I wonder if that's the young man Mrs. Perry was mentioning the other day," said Mrs. Fisher interestedly. "She said he was such a nice boy and she'd never known Sylvia faithful to any one else."

Leslie was faintly shocked at this glimpse of maternal interest.

"I don't believe there's the slightest idea of an engagement between them," she said, "and I think it's rather hard on Sylvia if her mother goes about talking like that. As a matter of fact, Sylvia was saying to me the other day that she didn't think she'd ever want to marry. She doesn't really believe in it."

"Oh, I see," said Mrs. Fisher, instantly deciding that Sylvia's love-affair must have suffered some slight setback. Probably this also accounted for her ill humour the other day.

"And then to make up the numbers," concluded Leslie, rather apologetically, "I've asked Bert and Bill Anderson. They're rather dull, and I'm afraid they won't mix very well. But I knew they were both going to be home this week-end and it seemed convenient one way and another."

"A very nice party, dear," said Mrs. Fisher. "How many do you think will stay to supper?"

"You know," said Leslie eagerly, "I'm sure you'll notice it as soon as you meet Jane and Florence. The *difference*, I mean. It's not only the way they talk. It's their whole attitude to life. It's—"

"Yes, I'm sure I shall be interested to meet them. How many—"

"So you honestly won't need to bother wondering whether being short of money and living a quite different sort of life will be hurting me. You'll be able to see that it hasn't hurt Jane and Florence. I tell you what, mummy. I won't bother you any more about it till after you've seen and talked to them for yourself. That's fair, isn't it?" concluded Leslie, hoping that by this means Aunt Sybil would be at any rate temporarily forgotten.

"Very well, dear," said Mrs. Fisher. (It really was time she went and saw about that chicken-house.) She turned at the door. "It's not that I'm opposing the idea, Leslie," she repeated. "It's just that I'd like to help you to—"

"I know, I know," said Leslie, a little impatiently. The last thing on earth she wanted was to be helped. "But, mummy—" Her glance wandered critically round the sunfilled breakfast-room, over the Axminster carpet, the Sheraton bookcases, the corner-cabinet that held the Crown Derby china. "Mummy. Don't you think it's good for people to do without things for a bit?"

"I dare say," said Mrs. Fisher. She smiled at Leslie, and thought how delightful she looked in her new pale green summer costume, with the sun catching all the golden lights in her prettily-waved hair. As she went down the garden she found herself ruthlessly qualifying her last remark. She could not bring herself to want Leslie to do without anything—ever.

Leslie, rising thoughtfully from the table, reflected that her mother, even if she couldn't understand some things, was really extraordinarily sweet. In some ways this was, of course, a disadvantage. It gave Leslie so very little justification for behaving in the way she wanted to behave. She would have liked to have avoided all this fuss by keeping her plans secret until the last moment; she would have liked something much more dramatic in the way of an escape. A quarrel, perhaps, bitter reproaches hurled against an unswerving purpose, a final slam of the door, a letter, simple and dignified, posted from London. "I hope you are not thinking I have failed in my duty to you in recognizing, as I must, another duty to myself. . . ." For a moment Leslie yearned for the stern parent she had never had. "You say that you want never to see me again, and my only answer can be—"

"May I clear away now, Miss Leslie?"

"What? Oh—yes, Alice. I have finished."

Leslie picked up the *Daily Mirror* and stepped through the open French windows into the garden. She would read the paper in the cool of the summer-house until it was time to go out with mummy in the car. As she crossed the lawn the morning sun struck warm on her face. She could feel the hardness of the ground through her thin clippers, although in the shade of the copper beeches the dew still glinted on the grass. The garden sloped gently to a little river that meandered along at the bottom. Leslie got a deck-chair from the summer-house on the lower lawn, arranged it so that her feet should be in the sun and her head in the shade, sprawled into it and lit a cigarette. A bee hummed round her head, the reeds whispered, the sunshine danced on the water and lay warm on the rising sweep of the hill beyond. It was a peaceful and lovely scene; and it afflicted Leslie with a sense of the most frightful impatience. If only she could be leaving here tomorrow! If only everything could be settled! How lovely this garden would seem if only she knew she wouldn't have to stay in it any longer! She shifted restlessly in her chair, picked a daisy, fingered it idly, and then suddenly flung it crossly away, resenting the patient placidity of its upturned face. She cast her paper on the ground and gave full rein to her impatience. If only the party were today instead of next Saturday! She had a feeling that this party was going to be a great help to her, to mark the beginning of her new independence. Jane and Florence should join forces with her in persuading her mother, they should demonstrate (as indeed they would not be able to help doing) the naturalness, the healthfulness, the absolute necessity of having a life of one's own away from one's family. They would settle it all up quickly on the spot. Jane should assure Mrs. Fisher that money mattered little as compared to spiritual freedom; and if her mother still seemed inclined to think in terms of hygiene rather than in terms of self-expression, Florence (who was, Leslie remembered, rather good with mothers) should tell her that their life in London was a peculiarly healthy one; that they ate a good mixed diet and kept free from colds and chilblains. She did not want them exactly to persuade her mother; she merely wanted them to help convince Mrs. Fisher that she, Leslie, was only behaving rightly, and that her plans to leave home were prompted not by selfishness or discontent, but by a sudden recognition of her duty to herself.

Fortunately she would be seeing Jane and Florence before the party next Saturday. She was having supper with them on Wednesday, after a day's shopping in town. It was the one incident she was looking forward to in a week that promised nothing more intellectually stimulating than a meeting of the fête committee (probably she would be asked to take the Hoop-la stall again) and a picnic with the Clarkes' children. Of course, even if Jane and Florence knew nothing of the situation, their very presence at the party would be a moral support. Still, she would take the opportunity of telling them about her plans on Wednesday. It would be interesting for them to know.

For oh! thought Leslie, as another surge of impatience shook her, if only I could be sure that everything was going to be settled properly. If only this week would come and go more quickly, if only the party would be a complete success, if only I could really look forward definitely to beginning again. Beginning again! The very idea caused Leslie to wriggle in her chair with excitement and impatience. At the thought, the whole of her past life paled into insignificance. At last, reflected Leslie, dismissing her childhood, her school-days, and nearly five years of her subsequent life at home, at last I shall be able to begin properly. At last I shall be able to do what I want. At last I shall be living a life that is really—how could she describe it? Really—

"Leslie! Are you ready, dear? You know I promised to give old Mrs. Jones a lift, so I think we ought to be—"

"Coming, mummy."

Worth-while! That was the word that she was looking for. Worth-while! Leslie left the deck-chair for somebody else to put away and ran hurriedly to her room to change her shoes. Mrs. Fisher got into the car and waited patiently.

CHAPTER I

ALARM CLOCKS and frying pans and divan beds were not, to Jane and Florence, romantic symbols of escape and independence. They were simply things which you had to have in a flat. Necessary, of course, but a nuisance. According to their kind they needed perpetual winding, cleaning, or remaking.

On this particular Saturday morning, at about the same time as Leslie was changing her shoes, Jane's alarm clock went off with such energy that it whirred itself right over the edge of the painted chest-of-drawers and clattered on to the floor. The shrill metallic ringing changed to a croaking rasp. Then silence. The clock lay on its back with its ugly moon face staring at the ceiling, ticking in an offensive and deliberate manner. Beyond pulling the bed-clothes of the divan bed a little further over her head Jane took absolutely no notice. The clock, its three tin legs sticking out sharply, continued to tick. It had the sulky and obstinate air of one who performs a duty, however unpleasant, with extreme thoroughness. It was a cheap clock (five-and-sixpence, bargain basement, and You can depend on the alarm to wake you up, madam) and it had fallen on to the trailing sleeve of a new and expensive squirrel fur coat which was sprawling half off and half on the bed, just where Jane had flung it down on returning to her flat late the night before.

The cheapness of the clock, the expensiveness of the coat, and the fact that their owner continued to sleep on were all typical of Jane.

It was Saturday anyway, and she and Florence had both got the morning off from the office. The alarm had only been set in order to be luxuriously neglected. Jane was not awake enough actually

to formulate this thought, but a dreamy sense of satisfaction slowly stole across her mind. No hurry—beautifully warm. A blurred
and velvet oblivion re-engulfed her. A lorry clattering by below
jarred the window-frame. Some one in the flat above turned on the
bath-water. A little breeze blew in at the window, and though it was
a London breeze it yet carried with it a sweet damp earthy smell,
an early summer smell of wet ground growing warm again and
flowers opening to the sun. Jane slept on and on, not composedly
and serenely as people sleep in pictures illustrating patent food or
nerve-restorers, but defiantly, hoggishly, with little wuffling noises
and an occasional snort, nose screwed into the pillow, bed-clothes
a tumbled heap. She opened her eyes only once and then, seeing
the disorder of the room—evening dress cast off anyhow, two pairs
of shoes kicked into one corner, chest-of-drawers loaded with bottles, gloves, handkerchiefs, odd jewellery—seeing all this disorder
she murmured "My God" and hastily shut her eyes again. All these
things cast so wildly about the room reminded her of the night before, and from the thought of the night before she shied away. She
did not want to think about Henry and Henry's accusations and
Henry's demands and the unpleasant squabbling evening they had
spent with Claud and Sylvia. Poor Claud and Sylvia! It could not
have been much fun for them to have Henry and her snapping at
each other all the time. Well, let it be a warning to them not to get
engaged. Although, as a matter of fact, she didn't think there was
any idea of an engagement between them. As a matter of fact—The
words modern and sensible and why not? drifted into Jane's mind.
If I were twenty years older, thought Jane, for she was now awake
enough to think (although not to think yet about getting up), supposing I were twenty years older and had a daughter, I should any
to her, I should say, "I don't care what you do, my dear, as long as
you make up your own mind, and as long so you get some pleasure
out of it and don't make other people miserable and don't come
and say you wish you hadn't afterwards." I should tell her it's never any good regretting anything because—because it isn't. I should
say, "Do what you like, my dear. Every one has to make up his own
mind about everything in the end." And if she said, "But won't you
advise me?" I should say, "No, I won't advise you at all. . . ." (It was
pleasant to dwell on this original portrait of herself as a mother,
kindly refusing advice to a more dimly-conceived daughter. It kept

her thoughts off the present and Henry and the sad muddle of her engagement to him that had already lasted three years and looked like lasting another thirty.)

Presently sounds began to come from the other room in the flat, the only other room besides the small bathroom and the still smaller kitchen. Sounds of a kettle being filled, gas lighting with a pop, crockery rattling. It was Florence getting her breakfast. A hiss from the kettle. A clank from the lid of the bin. A dull clatter from the bread-board falling over. Jane turned over, wriggling her toes luxuriously in the warm sheets. Presently the telephone rang, and immediately the kettle boiled over. Florence's voice.

"Yes. . . . Oh, hullo, Henry!" (How awake Florence sounded!) "Yes, she's asleep still. I'll wake her up. What? No, I don't suppose she'll mind it, it's nearly ten. Did you have a good party last night? Oh—er—good. I'll call her."

Brisk footsteps. The door opened.

"All right, don't tell me," said Jane hurriedly, "I heard." She yawned, and made a half-hearted attempt at putting on her dressing-gown without getting out of bed. Florence, a little quenched, stumbled over a shoe, and then picked it up and gazed at it thoughtfully. Jane got out of bed and trod on the alarm clock. At the other end of the line Henry waited patiently.

"Damn," said Jane, "how did that get there?" She showed no inclination to answer the telephone, but picked up a comb and began to run it thoughtfully through her short fair hair.

"I wish you'd said I'd already gone out, Florence."

Florence looked worried. "What's the matter?"

"I *don't* want to go out with Henry this week-end. I honestly don't. I suppose I'd better answer that blasted phone."

"Sorry, Jane. I didn't know you didn't want to speak to him."

"It wouldn't have done any good if you had. He'd have rung up later. Fidelity! Spaniels aren't in it! Henry would have made a beautiful spaniel, wouldn't he, Florence?" Jane giggled. Her spirits were beginning to rise. "A nice golden-brown colour and ever so willing to say he was sorry."

"You are a funny girl," said Florence. Jane's resilience, her buoyancy of spirit, her extraordinary capacity for evading unpleasantness by flippancy never failed to astonish her.

Jane was answering the telephone as Florence went into the bathroom, conscientiously turning on both taps so that she could not hear much of the conversation.

"Hullo, Henry."

"Hullo, darling." Henry's voice was tender and full of solicitude. "Darling, I'm terribly sorry about last night. It was all my fault."

"What?"

Henry raised his voice.

"I said it was all my fault about last night."

"I'm sorry, Henry. I simply can't hear a thing. It's because Florence is running the bath-water. I'll go and turn it off."

A pause, and then, "That's better," from Jane.

For the third time Henry braced himself for a manly apology.

"Listen, darling. I want to apologize about last night. I really am frightfully sorry—" He stopped suddenly. Jane appeared to be laughing into the telephone. Some very odd noises were gurgling in his receiver. Or could it be—ah, could it really be—that she was crying? Henry's heart gave a bound. Perhaps she was miserable because of all the dreadful things he had said to her. Perhaps she had been lying awake all night worrying, as he had. Ah, but he would comfort her. What a brute he was to make her cry!

Jane's clear little voice sounded again in his ear.

"Sorry, Henry darling. It's horrid of me to laugh. But you did shout so! It nearly broke my ear-drum."

"Sorry," said Henry flatly. It was no good. He could never make Jane really care. He could never make her suffer a tenth of what he himself suffered whenever they quarrelled. She was so dear to him, so painfully dear. And so sweet to him too, except when they quarrelled, and said bitter things to each other; and even then there was no malice in what she said, none of the pent-up resentment that drove him to wound himself savagely in saying cruel things to her.

"It's just that I'm not your type really, Henry," Jane had said yesterday, calmly, pleasantly even, in the tone she might have said it was raining or asked for the marmalade.

"I could never love any one but you," said Henry desperately. If only he could make her feel something of the rapturous torment that shook him! But Jane was persistently agreeable. When Henry apologized she would protest that there was nothing to forgive. It was true that she remembered very few of the bitter things Henry said to her when they quarrelled. There was nothing to forgive because all was so quickly forgotten. She was even rather sorry for Henry because he said such funny things when he was cross.

"Listen, darling. I hope I didn't wake you up?"

"Not exactly."

"You were such a long time coming I was beginning to think you must be asleep."

"Only sort of."

"I must see you, Jane dear. Can you meet me for lunch?"

"Oh—not for lunch, darling. I mean it's awfully late already, and I've got such a lot I must do."

"Why, what time do you make it? Perhaps my watch is slow?" Henry was always so ready to believe himself mistaken.

"I don't know. I trod on the clock."

"Darling, you are sweet."

"Darling, you are a nuisance. I honestly can't meet you this morning. I've such a lot to do."

"What?"

"Oh, sort of stockings and coffee and tinned beans and blue frock and scent-spray."

"I can't imagine what all that means, but will it really take all the morning?"

"Yes. Besides I must wash my hair."

Henry did a rapid calculation. If he fetched her in a taxi and then went to Victoria himself afterwards in a taxi—

"Listen, Jane. I must catch the 2.35 from Victoria. I forgot to tell you yesterday that I'm going to Aunt Alice's for the week-end. I'll fetch you in a taxi, and we'll have a quick lunch. Do. Please."

So Henry was going to Aunt Alice's for the week-end! Splendid! She wouldn't have to bother about him tomorrow then! All right, she would meet him for lunch. Poor darling, he sounded so desperately faithful. . . .

"It doesn't matter really about doing those things," said Jane. "You needn't fetch me in a taxi. I'll come by bus."

Florence, soaping her neck in the bath, felt a pang of disappointment. She would have liked to see Henry that morning, even if it had only been for a moment. She was very fond of Henry, and she was always touched by his cordial greeting of her whenever he came to the flat. As if it were somehow a delightful surprise to find her there, whereas, she thought humbly, I should have thought I would have been rather in the way. Florence had a fixed idea that engaged couples preferred to be left entirely alone, but somehow this did not seem to apply to Henry and Jane. Henry often tried to detain her when she would have made her escape into the other room, and once, when Jane was unexpectedly out, he had stayed and talked to her a long time. That evening remained very clear in Florence's mind.

"Henry is a dear," she had told Jane the next morning. "He was awfully nice to me last night, and I thought he'd be so sick at finding you out."

"Henry," said Jane, rather unkindly, "is the sort of man who's awfully good at looking at other people's snap-shots."

"Well, it would be very nice of him if he did," said Florence rather crossly.

After washing herself very thoroughly, she put on a clean vest, pinned a broken shoulder-strap with a small gold safety-pin, tied her dressing-gown round her, and went into the sitting-room to have breakfast. Jane and she took it in turns to sleep on a divan in this room. It was not so nice as sleeping in the bedroom, especially if there had been sausages or kippers for supper, and Florence, who suffered from a positively ferocious sense of "fairness" saw to it that the change-over was strictly observed. When you were sharing a flat with some one, thought Florence, it was necessary for neither to be under the slightest obligation to the other, and accordingly Jane and Florence, like most young women who have agreed to live together, took care to preserve a rigid independence of action. Jane liked china tea, toast (hard) and an orange for breakfast. Every morning she prepared this slightly anaemic meal for herself, while Florence firmly cooked an egg and made more toast (soft). This unswerving adherence to personal tastes governed every moment of Jane and Florence's domestic life together. Each was convinced that any compromise would have immediately imperilled the success of their friendship. The thought of a debt of gratitude was utterly abhorrent to both. Gratitude, it must be realized, was destroying to one's self-respect—hence, thought Florence, the extreme difficulty of getting on with one's parents, to whom one was continually obliged to feel this nauseating sentiment. Jane and Florence, when deciding to take the flat, had agreed that a communal life based on unselfishness and a measure of self-sacrifice was not to be tolerated for an instant.

"That's why most marriages are such ghastly failures," said Florence.

"Luckily we're neither of us unselfish, so we ought to get on all right," agreed Jane. In practice this so necessary independence of spirit worked out in terms of buying different tins of soup for supper, using two sorts of marmalade, and, to prevent any sort of obligation, engaging a woman to come in to do all the cleaning. Florence, however, nursed a shameful secret. She might religiously refrain from inquiring whether Jane would be in to supper; she might restrain her twitching fingers from rescuing an evening frock of Jane's from the cupboard floor; she would never, never wash Jane's hair-brush—but in her heart of hearts she could not help confessing to herself that she was desperately fond of Jane, far fonder, alas, than Jane was of her. There was nothing to be done about this sorry truth but to conceal it. The rush of warm affection that would flow through her at the sight of Jane's yellow head, the nagging anxiety that occasionally assailed her when Jane seemed in a mood to be particularly reckless of her neck or reputation (as the time when Jane insisted on trying out somebody's new Bentley after a particularly merry cocktail party, or the occasion of the mixed sleeping-out party on the roof)—both of these feelings were equally false and despicable. Jane, thought Florence, enviously and truly, never worried for an instant about other people. This was the high ideal at which she herself must aim. Although her efforts met with considerable non-success, Florence must at any rate be congratulated on the way in which she hid her lapses. There was nothing in her attitude this particular morning to suggest that Jane's quarrels with Henry induced in her a single moment of melancholy misgiving.

Nor, indeed, did Jane, who was now making toast by the gasfire, look at all depressed. On the contrary she appeared to be in the highest of spirits. She wore a pair of expensive pink satin pyjamas of cunning and sophisticated cut. (A Christmas present from an indulgent brother.) Her feet were thrust into Woolworth slippers (6d. each, 1/- the pair. Jane had been indignant on discovering this artful evasion). Over the pyjamas she wore an old white sports sweater of Henry's. The pink stripe in it, as Jane carefully pointed out, exactly matched the pink of her pyjamas. As usual, by some lucky trick of her own, she contrived to make this odd ensemble appear attractive. Florence in pyjamas at breakfast would look simply as if she had just got up; but Jane, Jane would manage to look ravishing in a high-necked jersey, put on with a swagger, a pair of grey-flannel trousers, an old scarlet blazer, or (if it was very hot) a handkerchief and shorts. Florence, who was accustomed to choose her clothes with a dull sense of knowing her limitations, sometimes wondered whether it was Jane's figure or her personality that caused skirts to hang so blithely down her long, slim legs, coats to fit so snugly and yet so jauntily on the shoulders, hats to perch with such a gay self-confidence on her yellow head. There was about her a suggestion of bright colours, of banners waving, of preparations for merrymaking in the air—or so thought Florence, wandering round the room while her egg was boiling, and tripping over the book she had been reading in bed the night before, which had tumbled onto the floor as she fell asleep. Jane had made three bits of toast at once, and was now lying on her back reading the *Daily Telegraph*, Woolworth slippers waving in the air, fair hair flopping into a pool of sunlight that lay across the stained boards. Florence looked at her and one of those unbidden secret thoughts popped into her head. How horrid it would be to live with any one else. She did not of course say this. It was a recognized thing that they were bound to each other by ties of convenience, not of affection. Instead she remarked, "Damn, neither of us has put the milk-bottles out for weeks," and wandered back into the kitchen to discover that her egg had annoyingly cracked in the boiling.

While they ate breakfast, happily, untidily, marmalade in a pleasant sticky pot and cigarette ash on the floor, Jane gave Florence a slightly touched-up account of her quarrel with Henry the evening before.

"So after Claud and Sylvia went off Henry was still so furious that he called a taxi and put me into it and then slammed the door and hissed the address at the driver and marched straight off."

"Had you any money?" inquired Florence, knowing the usual state of Jane's finances.

"No. Not nearly enough to pay. I told the driver to wait—I don't know why, it was very silly—and plunged after Henry. I ran all the way down the street after him, bleating, 'Henry! Henry!'" Jane giggled. "By the time I got to the underground station there was a string of about six Henrys after me."

"All right. I don't believe a word of this."

"Quite true. Then I saw Henry at the booking-office rapping down tuppence, still looking very cross. In my eagerness I fell down the stairs from the top to the bottom. Henry inquired coldly if I was hurt, and a porter retrieved my shoe which was just disappearing on its own down an escalator to Waterloo."

"Liar. Go on."

"I asked Henry for some money. He said, 'Good Lord!' in a disgusted kind of way. What was really rather nice—" Jane chuckled—"was that the porter who had fetched back my shoe like a well-trained terrier, was hanging round listening. He gave Henry the most marvellous look as if to say, 'You're no gentleman, give the lady back her purse.' And then, of course, with all the waiting the taxi came to pounds. Really, you know," concluded Jane, happily, with a hearty bite of toast and marmalade, "it was all completely my fault."

"I'm sure it was," said Florence, amiably.

"Thank you, darling. You're quite right—it was. In fact, the only person who's wrong is Henry because he now thinks it's his fault. The poor brute is writhing in agonies of self-remorse. Unfortunately he wants to writhe in front of me. I shall have to be oh! so sweet and comforting. Henry would like me to say,—'Darling, I am most terribly wounded and hurt by all the dreadful terrible things you said to me last night—do, do, dear Henry, tell me you don't mean them,' and then Henry with enormous fervour would tell me he didn't mean any of them. Then I should cry with relief—on his shoulder—and we should all enjoy ourselves enormously. You might do it, Florence," said Jane, scanning absently the headlines of the *Daily Telegraph*, "but it isn't my style at all. I'm not a bit hurt, and although I forget quite how it all started, I'm sure it was me that annoyed Henry first, and I expect most of the things he said to me were quite true. Query. Is truth an insult? Answer. In some cases, evidently yes."

Jane began to eat her orange, and losing interest in the subject of Henry, began instead, with great elation, to tell Florence all about a wonderful new economy scheme she had thought out. Apparently this was to be put into force immediately.

"You see, Florence, other people's economies are no damn good. But I simply must cut down. At the moment I'm using my screw as pocket money and my dress allowance to live on, and my odd dividends as dress allowance, and that won't work any more because—" (with indignation) "I'm not going to get a dividend this half-year. Now when people tell me how to economize they always suggest something absolutely impossible like buying three pairs of woollen stockings all the same colour and washing them every evening."

"Yes. Or else there's the helpful aunt who advises one always to buy the very best butter or something because it saves doctor's bills in the end."

"Which it doesn't, because supposing one had any doctor's bills, which one doesn't, one would use the panel."

"Yes, quite. Well, what's your great five-year plan?"

"All the things I call essentials other people call luxuries," explained Jane. "That's point number one. It must often have struck you."

"Often," said Florence, with feeling.

"I mean things like oranges every day and sherry and taxis when you're in evening dress. If you have three pounds a week they're not really the sort of things you ought to have but, of course, you simply must."

"Where does the great economy come in, then?"

"That's just the clever part. You see, there's a compensating side too. *Heaps* of things other people call necessities *I* call luxuries."

"Such as? . . ."

"Well—toothpaste, for instance."

"Aren't you going to clean your teeth?"

"Yes, with salt. It's much cheaper and I believe it's excellent."

"What else?"

"Oh, heaps else. I shan't buy any more stamps. Most of the letters one writes are quite unnecessary and, anyway, I can always ring up from the office. Then I shall cut off the milk and newspaper bills. I can easily drink tea without milk and you can always find a newspaper if you want one."

"Don't go and find some one's before they've lost it."

"Then, another thing. I'm getting too fat. One day a week I shan't eat anything."

"I'm sure you won't keep to that."

"Yes, I shall. It will be very good for me. Whenever I feel hungry, I shall have a cigarette."

"That will cost something."

"Well, a peppermint, then. I expect as time goes on I shall think of more and more things," said Jane cheerfully.

"I like to think of you riding about in taxis all day with a bottle of sherry under one arm and a bag of peppermints under the other," said Florence. Another of Jane's intricate schemes for economy. At one time it had been a complicated system depending on a row of brightly-painted tin moneyboxes. Then it had been never taking a bus anywhere but walking instead. (This had been abandoned as costing too much in darning-silk and resoling.) Lately it had merely been spend your weekly screw as you liked and see if it happened to last till next Friday. (Smoked salmon and new stockings on Friday, bread and potted meat for supper on Thursday. Jane had rather enjoyed the contrast.) Now it was a new idea. Anything topsy-turvy always attracted Jane. Florence suspected that the toothpaste and newspaper economies would hardly balance the sherry and taxis. But odd as their way of living undoubtedly was, thought Florence, as she pulled on her stockings (which had been hastily washed the previous evening and were not quite dry), queer and uncomfortable as her parents might, and did indeed, consider it, it was yet the only possible way. In theory it might be possible, even at times faintly desirable, to live at home. In practice it most definitely was not, not, at least, if you had spent three years at Oxford, three years which might be regarded as either intellectualizing or unsettling—the latter effect had been most apparent during the few months Florence had spent at home before coming to London to share the flat with Jane. Oxford, it appeared, if it did not seem to have fitted her for any precise occupation, had at least unfitted her for a great many things. Impossible to stay at home. True, one could read and write as much as one liked; but experience proved that one did, in fact, read very little but novels, and found writing impossible without further stimulus. What kind of job can I get? Florence had soon asked herself, and bought a book on careers for women. The introductory chapter was encouraging. All careers, the author informed her grandly, were now open to women; but when the careers were enumerated in alphabetical order, all (with the possible exception of angora rabbit farming) appeared to need from one to five years' further training. In no profession except teaching did an Oxford honours degree appear to be a necessity, or even an advantage. All careers are open to women, thought Florence a little bitterly, but a good speller can get a scholarship in a shorthand and typing school. The discouraging decision was taken. Florence's spelling, however, proved to be below scholarship standard, and her parents paid a hundred guineas for their daughter to attain the speed of sixty words a minute on the typewriter and one hundred and twenty (failed one hundred and thirty) in Pitman's shorthand. At the brief interview with her future employer, Florence, on mentioning apologetically her degree, got the impression that this could probably be lived down in course of time.

And yet it was the only life! Look how restless Sylvia was at home. Florence privately thought Sylvia's affair with Claud a pity—(although she approved in theory, she had an odd feeling that Claud was too nice for that sort of thing)—and she had come very near to the truth, nearer than Sylvia would admit, in suggesting to her once that the reason she didn't get on with her family was that she couldn't quite rid herself of a lurking sensation of guilt. Nobody, thought Florence, ought to live at home. It might be dull to "take down" and type and index and "take down" and type again from nine-thirty to five-thirty. It might be humiliating to find oneself considerably less competent than the girls who had left school at seventeen and had now been at work for four years. It might be a little absurd to feel so elated at occasional instructions to compose an unimportant note oneself—You know what to say, Miss Somerset, the usual—but not for one moment did Florence doubt that this was infinitely, vastly preferable to remaining with one's parents. "She lives at home"—it was difficult to speak the damning words without an accent of pitying scorn in the voice. The girl who lived at home was usually what one's mother would call a "nice girl." To escape this frightful fate Florence was prepared to type till her back ached for seven hours a day and to come home cheerfully to the comforts of a gas-fire and a hastily prepared meal of baked beans. She had gone into her first job (a publisher's office) reassuring herself that brains would count in the end, that typing errors and minor inaccuracies would weigh as nothing in the balance against mental acumen. Unfortunately, at the moment, routine accuracy appeared to be more in demand than mental acumen. After nine months Florence still hoped that brains would count "in the end," but the "end" thus vaguely specified seemed so far off as to be almost inapprehensible. In the meantime Florence knew that typing errors mattered terribly. Like many other young women similarly placed she began to write a novel.

CHAPTER II

I

WHILE JANE AND Florence were up at Oxford, Sylvia Perry often visited them, staying a day or two in the college. On these occasions they would all sit up late at night exchanging ideas. Towards midnight the conversation would usually veer towards either sex or religion, and, as the night wore on, the business of reconstructing the world continued with more and more enthusiasm. Sylvia enjoyed these talks enormously, and would go back to her home in Berkshire feeling that she had really assisted in the intellectual revolt of youth, a little regretful that she had never tried to go to the university herself, and more than a little dissatisfied with her home. For nowhere but in Oxford, thought Sylvia, listening scornfully to the gentle platitudes on the garden and the weather uttered by her mother's friends (she had returned on one occasion to find a tea-party in progress and the contrast was bitter)—nowhere but in Oxford was conversation worthy of the name.

How stimulating to live in a place where the exchange of ideas was the material of everyday talk! Even if Jane and Florence did have to sign in a funny little book when they went out in the evenings, even if they couldn't go to late dances or up to London during term-time, from the conversational point of view Oxford was ideal. Ideal, thought Sylvia, because here were interesting people with interesting ideas to exchange. Two more powerful reasons might have, but did not, occur to her; that nowhere but among young students at a university is the opportunity of doing work stimulating to the mind so happily coupled with an entire lack of any necessity for doing it at any given moment. Hence, one might sit up putting the world to rights till four o'clock in the morning with an easy mind. There would be no nine-fifteen train to catch to work the following morning. Moreover, conversation is enormously stimulated by a lack of any practical experience whatever; and this condition of course applied ideally to Jane and Florence and their friends.

When, in the course of time, Jane and Florence came down from Oxford and settled into a flat in Maida Vale, Sylvia began to find their companionship a little less amusing. They tended, regrettably, to spend the evening talking about methods of economy, or even actually doing things—like washing stockings—instead of gathering round the fire in the old way to discuss the affairs of the world. Moreover, about this time, Sylvia met and fell in love with Claud. After gaining some practical experience of a subject which she had been discussing for years, she could not help feeling slightly superior toward Jane and Florence, particularly Florence, who was not, it must be admitted, attractive to men. Occasionally she envied them their independence, but she knew herself too well to think that she would really like regular office hours and getting her own breakfast. The way she expressed this to herself was that she didn't think it would be fair for her to take paid employment when there was absolutely no necessity.

So she continued to stay at home and made much use of the family car for day-trips to London; and, although one could not, of course, really have any conversation with one's family, she was nevertheless accustomed from time to time to give them the benefit of her views upon various subjects. Most of these, particularly her opinions on the value of the family and on marriage, met with a consistently poor reception from her father and mother, but Sylvia rather enjoyed provoking these indignant rejections, beginning with a scandalized "I never heard anything more disgusting in my life" from Mrs. Perry and a brusque "Nonsense, nonsense," from her father. Sometimes Mrs. Perry wondered, a little bewilderedly, what she had done to deserve a daughter with quite so many views on so many subjects. She could not remember that she had ever been like that as a young girl herself. But Sylvia, it appeared, believed that if you didn't think things out for yourself (and the conclusions to these thoughts were inevitably in direct opposition to what Mrs. Perry called ordinary decency and Sylvia alluded to as middle-class morality) then you were an unfulfilled person, and consequently an unhappy one. "Well, anyway, *I'm* not unhappy," said Mrs. Perry, emphatically. Here at last was something that was a matter of fact, something to be triumphantly contradicted. And, although she could not help feeling a little impressed by Sylvia's odd passion for argument, believing it, quite humbly, to derive from the brains she must have inherited from her father, nevertheless it was often intensely irritating, and she congratulated herself secretly on the fact that Henrietta, her younger daughter, seemed to take after her.

"I'd much rather you didn't keep my breakfast hot for me, mother," said Sylvia, coming into the sunlit breakfast-room of her home in the Chilterns about the same time as Jane and Florence were making toast in Maida Vale.

"Why, darling? Don't you like fish-cakes?"

"Oh, yes, I *like* fish-cakes," said Sylvia, taking two, "but I don't think you ought to on principle. If I'm late for breakfast that ought to be my look-out."

"Well, I know you were late last night, dear. Did you have a good evening?"

"Yes, thanks," Sylvia said, automatically. Then she reflected that, what with Jane and Henry's quarrellings, it had been rather a horrid evening. Forgetting that her mother would be interested to hear what theatre they had been to, she lapsed into an abstracted silence, pondering that Jane-Henry situation. It was quite obvious what the trouble was. Henry was too possessive. He made demands on Jane which she could never fulfil. No relationship, Sylvia believed, ought to be subjected to such a strain. It was, she decided, absolutely Henry's own fault if he was miserable. Heartlessly she dismissed the remembrance of his gloomy, puzzled face. She was not going to be sorry for him.

Henrietta, Sylvia's younger sister, came into the room, embraced her mother affectionately, and exclaimed, "Oh, mummy, you are an angel! Did you keep it back for me? I was afraid everything would have vanished."

Mrs. Perry shot a glance of subdued triumph at her elder daughter. After the snub of Sylvia's "principles" Henrietta's enthusiasm was particularly welcome.

"I heard good-bys on the porch at some very late hour last night," she said indulgently, "and Sylvia was back from town even later, so I thought to myself that I shouldn't see either of you till about ten this morning."

"It was sweet of you to salvage a fish-cake," said Henrietta, her mouth full. Although she had not been asleep till three that morning she looked radiant. Her mother met with affection her bright, laughing gaze, and contemplated, with maternal satisfaction, the hearty mouthfuls of fishcake disappearing between her red lips.

It was unkind of Sylvia to spoil this pleasant atmosphere of indulgence and affection by saying in her most "reasonable" voice, "If you don't get to bed till three it seems to me only sensible not to get up till ten."

This was too much for Mrs. Perry. Arguments with her elder daughter had long ago convinced her of only one thing—that an excuse was preferable to a principle any day, and far less upsetting to the servants.

"That's what you never understand, Sylvia. In a decently-run household you *can't* have people just behaving like that."

For the hundredth time she was protesting against the thing that she most objected to in her daughter, something that Sylvia called "the right of the individual" and most annoyingly persisted in championing. From Mrs. Perry's point of view it was worse than believing in Soviet Russia or divorce by mutual consent or even legalized abortion. Disgusting as Sylvia's other opinions might be they did not at least disorganize so completely domestic routine.

"It depends what you call a 'decently-run' household," said Sylvia. (Of all her methods of argument—and alas! this morning she seemed to be in an argumentative mood—her mother found this habit of suddenly querying the meaning of some perfectly-well-established word the most trying.) "You'd probably say that you must have some sort of regularity, wouldn't you?"

"Certainly," said Mrs. Perry, suspecting a trap, but nevertheless staunch.

"You mean, in fact, that every one has got, to a certain extent, to be sacrificed to an idea?"

At this point, to Sylvia's disappointment and her mother's relief the door opened and Mr. Perry walked in, cutting short a promising argument on one of Sylvia's favourite themes—that adjustment to other people was not a virtue but a positive defect in character. This theory was so opposed to the whole of Mrs. Perry's personality as to be absolutely unintelligible to her. Nevertheless, Sylvia, naturally taking a keen delight in anything so completely at variance with the principles of her upbringing at home and at school, had recently pressed it continually upon her family.

"Did I leave my paper here just now?" inquired Mr. Perry.

"Daddy, can I have the car today?" countered Henrietta. "Sylvia doesn't want it."

"Yes, but don't forget I want it next Saturday for Leslie's party," put in Sylvia warningly.

"How do you know, young woman, that your mother and I don't want it today?" said Mr. Perry teasingly.

"Darling—you don't, do you?"

Father and mother looked at each other with indulgent smiles. Mrs. Perry shook her head.

"You take it and enjoy yourself, my dear," said her father, stooping to bestow a good-morning kiss on her cheek. "*Have* any of you seen my paper here?"

This was almost a daily question. Although none of his family ever opened his *Times* at breakfast, Mr. Perry relied on them to tell him where he had left it. Sylvia was never very helpful, but Henrietta was clever at remembering she had seen it on the morning-room table or on the hall hat-stand. She pointed it out to him now, lying quite obviously on the window-sill. He said, with the familiar accent of reproach, as though it had been purposely hidden from him, "Oh, *there* it is," and, tucking it under his arm, left the room. Henrietta and her mother exchanged secret glances of amusement. Both enjoyed this little daily ritual.

"Will you be in to lunch today, Sylvia?" said Mrs. Perry, her thoughts taking their usual after-breakfast trend.

"No," said Sylvia, adding after a moment, "Claud is coming down in his car. We're going out in my boat."

"Will you bring him back to supper here, dear?"

"No—no, I don't think we'll be back in time," said Sylvia. For some reason which she always shied away from analyzing, she avoided bringing Claud to the house more than was necessary.

"I shan't be back to supper, either," said Henrietta.

"Will you want to take any lunch with you? Whereabouts will you be?" said Mrs. Perry, who, being a well-trained mother, never inquired more than in the most general way as to her daughters' plans, but was always ready to provide picnic lunches if required.

"Oh, Mary and people," replied Henrietta, giving the information in such a bright and willing voice that it struck nobody as a little vague.

"You've got a lovely day for it," said Mrs. Perry.

Sylvia glanced out of the big French windows over the green lawn and the belt of trees to the blue sky and the rising sweep of the Chiltern Hills, and suddenly her heart lightened. It was such a very perfect morning. The air that blew in at the window was an exhilarating cordial, charged with promise laden with a thousand secret fragrances of the warm sweet earth. The early summer sunlight danced over the dew-spangled grass. A cuckoo called from the hedge and the rhythmic whirr of a grass-cutting machine thrummed from across the way. Everything in this green and crystal morning, everything from the blue distant line of the hills to the wasp humming against the window-pane seemed in joyous and perfect attunement to the secret promise the day held. A thousand memories of other summers thronged Sylvia's mind—the heady nutty scent of gorse on the wind, the squelchiness of river mud, warm under bare toes, the sharp sting of tossing salt water, the sensation of utter surrender that comes from lying in the hot sun. . . . How could one bear to be old, not to be in love, to stay quietly in the house and garden on such a day? Sylvia glanced at her mother and suddenly marvelled at the tranquillity which could rejoice wholeheartedly in a fine day for other people.

"Oh! My new dress! Why *didn't* you tell me," cried Henrietta suddenly as she caught sight of a big cardboard box on a chair by the door. Pouncing on it she attacked the string with a fish-knife, tore off the wrappings, and finally pulled something that looked like a handful of red chiffon lovingly from the careful layers of tissue paper.

"Isn't it a divine colour, mummy?"

"There doesn't seem to be very much of it," said Mrs. Perry, doubtfully looking over her spectacles and the *Daily Mirror* at her daughter, who was holding the frock against herself in evident delight.

"Oh, mother! There's masses! Look at all the wee frills on the skirt!" Henrietta held up a foaming red armful.

"I was thinking about the top, not the skirt. Surely it's cut unusually low?"

"Low!" cried Henrietta. "Oh, look. I'll put it on and you can see for yourself it was made for me."

Two waving arms, a stamp and a wriggle. Henrietta flung her discarded dress aside and shook back her ruffled curls.

"Doris will be shocked if she comes in and finds you in pink cami-knickers," said Mrs. Perry. "Do hurry up, dear."

"This dress needs very careful getting into," explained Henrietta from beneath folds of chiffon. A hand appeared and then was withdrawn. "Damn, that's wrong. Wait a moment."

"Let me help," said Mrs. Perry, giving a mild tug to the skirt.

"Oh, mother, be *careful*," shrieked Henrietta, "You must be frightfully careful. It fits so marvellously that I have to absolutely *ooze* myself into it."

"Must you have it quite so tight, darling?"

"Yes, that's the *whole* point." The oozing process accomplished, Henrietta confronted them with delight.

"Don't I look as if I'd been born in it?" she cried.

"Turn round," said Mrs. Perry doubtfully—"Oh, my dear child! Must you have a completely backless frock?"

"But I have such a very nice back!" cried Henrietta exultantly, wriggling in her efforts to contemplate it.

"My dear, you're only eighteen. Wouldn't white be more suitable?"

"Suitable!" cried Henrietta disgustedly, "Suitable!" A coaxing note came into her voice. "Oh, mummy. I've got the most divine pair of long earrings to wear with it. Oh, mummy. I shall look marvellous—you know I will!"

Half mollified, Mrs. Perry yet stuck to her point. Perhaps Sylvia would support her. Sylvia was a funny girl. You never knew what she would think.

"Sylvia, dear, don't you agree with me that Henrietta's a little young for that sort of dress? She's only a baby."

"Sylvia," cried Henrietta, making a face at the word "baby," "Tell mother—"

Sylvia contemplated her sister quizzically and returned to her newspaper. "Maternal jealousy, mother. Henrietta isn't a baby any longer, but your instinct is to refuse to acknowledge it. She's a right to wear what she likes, I suppose."

This impartial analysis of the situation had the effect of making both parties cross.

"Jealousy!" cried Mrs. Perry indignantly. "As if any one in their senses could accuse me of being jealous of my daughters!"

"Most mothers feel a sort of hidden sexual jealousy towards their daughters," explained Sylvia calmly.

"Don't be so horrid to poor mummy," said Henrietta, half indignant and half amused, slipping her arm affectionately into Mrs. Perry's.

"I shall go and see Cook," said that much injured lady, and left the room with considerable dignity.

There was a moment's silence between the two sisters.

"I'm sorry," said Sylvia finally, "I forgot."

"Forgot what?"

"Oh, just that nobody ever likes the truth about anything." With an air of complete disillusionment she poured out another cup of coffee for herself.

"Do you think it would be better if they did?" asked Henrietta interestedly. She bore her sister no malice for the quarrel, guessing rightly that her mother would voice no further objections to the frock. She was always ready to listen to Sylvia's theories, and believed wholeheartedly that it was very clever of her sister to think everything out so thoroughly. She also reflected from time to time that it was a pity her mother and Sylvia did not get on better together.

"Yes, of course it would be better," said Sylvia, who in her turn always enjoyed an opportunity of expounding her views to a sympathetic listener (during the last year, Henrietta had filled this rôle most excellently). "It would mean a higher standard of morality all round."

"How do you work that out?"

Sylvia embarked on a brief lecture on her favourite topic—intellectual honesty. She pointed out to her sister that the ordinary middle-class conventions of right and wrong were false, because they were based not on what you think of yourself, but on what other people think of you.

"Yes?" said Henrietta encouragingly. She had heard Sylvia say this before, without taking very much notice. But recently she had become more interested, started borrowing Sylvia's books, and begun to wonder whether people really applied these theories to everyday life.

"So that if the ordinary inhibitions and sex-taboos and—and things," continued Sylvia sweepingly, "were discredited—well, it would end in a far higher standard of morality all round." Feeling uneasily that she had got to this fine conclusion a little too soon, and regretting that consequently it seemed to lack the magnificent ring of conviction she had in imagination accorded it, she added, "That's the idea very briefly, of course. I'll lend you some more books about it if you like. There's an awfully interesting one about the bringing-up of children I've been reading. I wanted to make mummy read it, but she wouldn't—not properly."

"Thank you," said Henrietta. She was standing by the window, twiddling with the catch. "Do you *really* not believe in—in *any* of the things mummy believes in?" she asked.

"I certainly don't believe in any of the usual mumbo-jumbo of the conventions," replied Sylvia with satisfaction. "Mumbo-jumbo" was a phrase she always enjoyed.

"Then you don't think it would matter doing something mummy would disapprove of very much if—if you wanted to?"

"Not exactly 'if you wanted to,'" corrected Sylvia. "But as long as you didn't disapprove of yourself for doing it there would be no reason for not—would there?"

It was a reasonable conclusion to a reasonable discussion and therefore it is odd to record that Henrietta's answer suddenly spoilt all Sylvia's pleasure in the argument. "I think that's very interesting," was all that she said. But something in the tone of her voice caused Sylvia to look sharply at her, and to forget immediately the convincing point she had been about to bring forward next. A vague anxiety assailed her; and suddenly she surprised both herself and her sister by saying, "I shouldn't think about it too much, if I were you."

It was a caution that sprang, not from reason, but from pure impulse. It had nothing to do with what she had been saying before, nor indeed with what she had intended to say at all. It was somehow connected with an emotion roused by the young curve of her sister's cheek as she stood by the window, by the sunlight on her hair, an emotion obscurely and a little absurdly mixed up with thoughts of roses that faded and time that spoilt everything. It had the effect of changing the whole feeling of their conversation, so that what had been a matter for interesting speculation became suddenly charged with an undercurrent of emotion. When Henrietta faced round, surprised, and said, "Why? Don't you believe in what you're saying?" Sylvia sensed behind the words a defiance that alarmed her. An obscure feeling that somehow, in some way, she was fencing with her sister, made her response slow and awkward.

"Yes. But that's different."

"Why is it different? Why shouldn't I believe in things that you believe in?"

"You're—you're so young," said Sylvia, lamely—ill-chosen words, conveying only an unintended sense of superiority and nothing at all of the protective tenderness that had prompted them.

"I don't *feel* young," said Henrietta, absurdly. She added defiantly, "Anyway I'm old enough for people to fall in love with."

Sylvia, remaining outwardly unmoved, felt within her mind little scurryings to and fro of an odd panic.

"You're the sort of person lots of people will fall in love with," she said hastily, hoping thus to discount sufficiently whoever it might be that was occupying too large a share of Henrietta's thoughts at the moment.

"But I may not fall in love with a lot of people," retorted Henrietta.

Sylvia's feeling that she was fencing with her sister, that the real point at issue lay unexpressed between them, increased.

"Oh, I expect you will," she said heartily.

"May I ask you something about yourself?" said Henrietta.

A violent mental recoil urged Sylvia to cry out "No! No!" A love of expounding theories of conduct ran in her side by side with a deep reticence as to her private emotions, so that even to Henrietta, and especially to her parents, she never spoke of Claud except when necessary, never referred to him in more than the most casual manner. She would have preferred for them not to know him at all, and since this was not possible she ignored as far as possible the fact that they had met him, liked him, and would have been glad to entertain him more often at the house. That Claud and her parents should be on friendly terms outraged her sense of the fitting, and, in keeping him away from the house, she acted on impulse and hid from herself her own irrationality. Henrietta's question made her feel as if in this strange duel between them she was about to be disarmed. Not daring to refuse the challenge, she said, "What is it?"

It was an enormous, an absurdly enormous relief, to hear Henrietta merely ask if she were going to marry Claud.

"I don't know," said Sylvia. Marriage was a civil contract, useful in the case of children, superfluous otherwise; but, for once, she was not anxious to take an opportunity of expounding her views. She was eager to put an end to the whole discussion, which now filled her both with nervousness and distaste. She was afraid of what Henrietta would say next, afraid of what she dared not say herself; and strung-up by emotions which should have no place in a discussion of the sort, a protective love for her sister, a desire, which was all of the heart and nothing of the mind, to shield so much loveliness, so much youth. She made an effort to round the scene off lightly, saying that she must go and get things ready for the picnic, and went out into the sunlit garden puzzled and vaguely apprehensive, feeling that Henrietta had asked something of her which she had refused. Rightly, she believed. But she had given her nothing in its stead. Sylvia shook her head and tried to think that she was letting her imagination run away with her. In any case every one, she knew, must decide everything for themselves. The principle was clear enough. In such a bold, clear, triumphant scheme of living tenderness, pity, anxiety for another, the desire to protect, had little significance. Nevertheless, while she went across the garden to collect her collapsible boat from its shed, she found herself wondering where Henrietta spent all her time. "Mary and people." The vague explanation was typical. Who were these people she had been so constantly with of late? When I was eighteen, thought Sylvia with uncharacteristic severity, and had just left school, mummy knew a lot more about my doings than she does about Henrietta's. Casting her mind back it seemed to her that she was much younger for her age at eighteen than Henrietta. She remembered dimly awkwardness at dances, hesitation over clothes, shyness—Sylvia smiled at the incongruity of associating such things with Henrietta. Child she might be; awkward adolescent never. "I don't know," said Sylvia aloud to a pear-tree, "I simply don't know." She carried her boat carefully to the porch and went off to collect her belongings.

Claud had insisted that this time it was his turn to supply food; but Sylvia's pile on the hall floor soon included several cushions, a camera, an extra thermos, a bathing-dress and cap and towel, a book of poetry and a rug.

"Moving, I see," said Claud as he entered the hall. Sylvia giggled. She picked up her bathing-towel, and a comb and a powder-box fell out. Suddenly, absurdly, she felt happy. It was going to be the sort of day when an accident like a broken cup would be exquisitely funny.

"Darling—I can't *not* take any of these, can I? I mean the cushions are special picnic cushions. I bought them specially. They've got mackintosh behinds. Look. And then I must bring Marvell's poems because I know I shall feel an urge to be read aloud to. And I must have the camera because I want you to take a snap of me diving so that I can see whether I look like what I feel like. And I must have the rug because of ants and sleeping after lunch. . . ."

"But, Sylvia darling, you haven't got nearly enough things." Claud's voice was full of a tender solicitude. "Supposing you suddenly felt an urge to play the piano? Why, you haven't even included a musical-box. And how do you know you're going to want Marvell particularly read aloud to you? It might just as easily be Gibbon's *Decline and Fall*. Why, there are all sorts of things you've forgotten. What about your skates?"

"Perhaps I'd better make a list, Claud dear. The little housewife always makes a list, doesn't she?"

"The trouble about a list is that paper and pencil are so far more difficult to find than anything else."

"Oh, dear! And now I've forgotten my goloshes!"

Several minutes passed thus pleasantly. Claud insisted on a telescope. Sylvia was inclined to think a set of saucepans more vital. Henrietta, dressed very smartly in a red and white outfit, passed them as they wrangled happily in the hall. She was glad to be able to slip by unquestioned. Mother had left her a picnic-basket of food on the chest. She took it and went round to the garage to get the car. Before starting she investigated the contents, and then put it on the back seat with a sigh. Potted-meat sandwiches, seed cake, bananas, chocolate, lemonade. Two strawberry tartlets, carefully wrapped up in grease-proof paper—because she knows I like them, thought Henrietta with a pang. Captain Fortescue—John (it was absurd to think of him as Captain Fortescue still) would probably think of picnic food in terms of hampers from Fortnum and Mason. Well! They would probably go to a hotel anyway. Feeling a beast, Henrietta backed the car out of the garage, reversed, and sped away along the drive to the gate. Mrs. Perry waved to her from an upstairs window. Henrietta tooted back. In the drive Claud and Sylvia were carefully stacking Sylvia's boat into the back of Claud's car. Sylvia smiled and waved a paddle. Every trace of her earlier moodiness had disappeared. She is a funny girl, thought Henrietta. I wonder what she really thinks about Claud. I wonder if they—The gravel crunched under her wheels and the car bounded forward on to the road. There was a humming in the telephone wires, a light breeze fanned her face, the dark-blue road uncoiled enchantingly before her. It felt as though the sea ought to be just round the next corner. Useless to try to decide anything on such a day. Round this bend lay a further bend and round that one another. There was adventure in every twist, a mounting excitement in every mile. Singing softly to herself, Henrietta trod on the accelerator.

II

"Darling, l am overwhelmed by the most utterly suitable emotions," said Sylvia, sitting by Claud's side in his open low-bodied car. "I look at your hands on the wheel and the adjectives 'big, brown, capable' immediately flash into my mind. I very nearly think of them as 'toiling for me.'"

"Shall I call you 'little woman'?" inquired Claud obligingly.

"Yes. And would you now and again please express a desire to protect me?"

"If any one hurts a hair of your head—"

"That's exactly right!" They laughed, a little superior in their absurd happiness. Presently, for no reason, they became a middle-aged couple with several progeny and, on their way to the river where the boat would be launched, Claud and Sylvia sustained an animated conversation on the relative merits of English seaside places for a suppositious summer holiday.

"Margate would be good for little Paul's tonsils," said Sylvia anxiously, "and you know the doctor said—"

"Pshaugh! The boy's a mollycoddle. Tonsils! When I was his age—"

"I know, dear. But then Paul is rather an exceptional boy. So highly-strung—"

"Highly-strung fiddlesticks! What he wants is the corners rubbed off him."

"I think this would be a very good game to play in a railway carriage, don't you, Claud? You could watch every one taking sides."

"Yes, and whoever made any one interrupt first would win."

"All the same I think you're rather hard on Paul," resumed Sylvia. "Paul is so *sweet*. He came to me the other day and said, 'Mummy, where *do* babies come from?'"

"I hope you didn't put any filthy ideas into his head," rejoined Claud sternly.

"Oh, no, dear! Of course I didn't tell him the truth!"

They giggled, enraptured by the summer morning and by their own silliness.

They left the car presently by the roadside and, panting, carried the boat across some fields to the river, marked by a distant line of willows. The ground was squelchy under Sylvia's sandalled feet, the sun struck hot on the nape of her neck. Beads of sweat stood out on Claud's forehead. The boat jogging between them they padded longingly towards the water.

The bathe was perfect. River-bathing has an enchantment of its own. River-mud is naturally and rightly slimy. River-water is not tainted with chemical purifiers. Human bodies, slipping into its limpid embrace become part of the river, part of the landscape of willows and grass, part of the shadowed green and silvery cool of the water. Claud and Sylvia dived directly in from the bank. The grass, coarse and springy under their bare feet, gave them a firmer foothold than the sodden matting of a spring-board. Under the shadow of the trees the water was almost black. Riverweeds, strained gently, incessantly by the current, floated against their bodies with sudden soft little touches. Water-boatmen skimmed busily to and fro. Sylvia swam upstream, fighting the pushing current. The taste of the water was faintly brackish, not unpleasing. Exhausted she floated back downstream, a white body surrendered to the river's force, one with the bending reeds or the logs and branches that drifted past. Claud was standing ankle-deep in mud.

"It's heavenly stuff," he said. "Softer than anything I know." He wriggled his toes voluptuously.

"Liquid velvet," suggested Sylvia.

"Come and stand here, darling. It's beautifully squidgy."

"I can't quite bring myself to like actually standing in it, Claud. I'm hypercivilized, I expect. Darling, what about that last dive?"

"Your ankles were about three inches apart as you went in."

"Oh, Claud! Isn't it extraordinary what will-power can't do?"

"I know. You think and think and think about your legs and it doesn't seem to make any difference."

"Listen. Shall we tie my ankles together?"

They tied Sylvia's ankles together with some string from the picnic-basket and she executed several extremely flat and painful dives.

"That was a better one," said Claud eventually.

Sylvia, paddling furiously with her hands, looked at him suspiciously.

"I don't believe it was. It hurt frightfully. I believe you simply want your lunch."

"No. I said it to encourage you," replied Claud annoyingly.

"You don't think you'll get patronizing when you get old, do you, darling?"

"No," said Claud, beginning to undo the picnic-basket, "I shall always be a boy at heart. You know, ready for anything. I shall wear a paper cap and join in the frolics and laugh uproariously at practical jokes."

"Thank God I shan't know you then," said Sylvia, wrestling with the string round her ankles.

"What did you say?"

"I said, 'Thank God I shan't know you then.'" (It did not sound quite so casual this time.)

Claud came over to her.

"Here, let me help." He knelt down and began to unknot the wet string. As always when doing some job with his fingers he seemed completely absorbed. Sylvia put out a hand and stroked gently his rough wet hair. It was funny. The atmosphere was suddenly tense. A moment ago she had been dreamily conscious of everything round her—the sun and the lapping water and the shimmer of heat over the distant grass; and now all her awareness was fixed on Claud's wet bent head. Claud—Claud. A thousand memories bound up in one meaningless monosyllable. She used to think it rather a silly name; but now she couldn't think of it as just a name at all. She studied with extraordinary concentration a lock of hair that had strayed across his forehead. Her own voice echoed foolishly in her ears—"Thank God I shan't know you then."

Claud flung away the string.

"I wouldn't be too sure of that," he said. Picking up her foot he kissed it gravely. Then he smiled at her and gently bit a toe. The tension, not surprisingly, immediately relaxed. The green fields and river and sunshine rushed back upon them. They were enormously hungry.

"Darling, I adore you," said Claud. "Tomato or egg?"

"How many are there of each?" inquired Sylvia greedily.

Claud put the sandwiches out in piles on the grass. There was tomato, appetizingly red, and hard-boiled egg, yellow and white, and lettuce, crisply green. Buttered rolls and cheese. A packet of chocolate and two bottles of lager beer.

They began to eat hungrily.

"Darling. You look like a rabbit in a hutch with all your food spread round you like that," said Claud.

"My rabbit burst," said Sylvia through tomato sandwich.

"Rabbits do."

"If I lie on my front my elbows get sore, and if I lie on my back bits of sandwich keep on falling down my neck."

"You're what is technically known as 'a dirty feeder.'"

"'Dear Mrs. Jim,'" said Sylvia, "'My boy seems to be fond of me and yet he says I am a "dirty feeder." What can I do? I feel rather hurt about it. Perplexed.'"

"'Dear Perplexed,'" said Claud. "'I expect it is just his fun. Have a quiet talk with him some time and tell him that it makes you unhappy when he finds fault with you. Be careful to wipe your mouth between every mouthful, particularly in the case of egg.'"

"Not *every* mouthful, surely?"

"Certainly, *every* mouthful. Are you going to sleep after lunch for long?"

"Not *very* long."

"Good. I've got a brilliant idea."

"What?"

"I'll tell you when you wake up," said Claud cunningly.

"You've got egg on your mouth," retorted Sylvia.

"Quite the little mother, aren't you? Go to sleep."

Sylvia rolled over luxuriously on the warm grass. Pillowing her head in her arms she fell fast asleep. The sun, falling full on her bare legs and shoulders cooked them to a delicate pink. Claud thoughtfully arranged his bath-towel over her head. He lit a pipe and drowsily contemplated Sylvia's sprawling form. She was a darling. "I am a lucky man," he thought, and forgot to be repelled by the commonplaceness of the sentiment. Sylvia was sweet to him. "We'll be good experience for each other," she said. "Darling. Honestly, it's what I want. I should simply hate to be married." They had agreed, solemnly, that marriage was a frightful risk. "It's definitely anti-social to go and get married just because you happen to have fallen in love," she had said, and had spoken with scorn of the girls who remained "technically virtuous" because they were afraid of not getting married otherwise. "Technically virtuous"—Claud and Sylvia used the phrase with the maximum of sarcastic disparagement. Since then they had not talked of marriage. Orange-blossom and a white veil and "The voice that breathed o'er Eden" were too obscene to be mentioned. "It seems to me that a love-affair ought to be absolutely spontaneous," said Claud.

"Spontaneous and experimental," agreed Sylvia.

It was funny how lately they had got into the habit of thinking of themselves as permanently together.

"Adorable darling," thought Claud, contemplating through eyes half shut against the sun Sylvia's sprawling relaxed grace; and he added to himself, secretly, "I want you—always." It was the last thought in his mind before the sun and the beer he had drunk and the fragrance of the crushed grass blurred together into a tremendous drowsiness. A secret forbidden thought. Because no one had a right to claim anyone forever. Every one must be free, every one must. . . . It was more comfortable to lie right back in the grass and close one's eyes. Darling Sylvia—so sleepy.

Sylvia, womanlike, was even more conscientious about her thoughts than Claud. So that when she woke up and saw Claud asleep, his eyes screwed up against the sun, his hair ruffled, she immediately suppressed the wave of maternal tenderness that swept over her unawares, "Darling Claud. He's just my little boy. He looks about twelve asleep"—and busied herself instead with strapping up the picnic-basket. Then she made a daisy-chain and hung it on his ear. He did not wake up, so she picked more daisies and stuck them between his toes. Still he slept. It was silly to be touched by this, but nevertheless Sylvia was touched. She kissed him gently on the nose. He opened his eyes and smiled.

"Darling Sylvia," he said.

Chapter III

I

JANE, HAVING HAD the whole morning to get ready in, was terribly rushed.

The hem of her skirt was coming down. Had Florence any safety-pins? No? Well, yesterday or the day before she had noticed a large safety-pin on the mantelpiece. What could have happened to it? She ran about in her knickers looking for the safety-pin.

"Why not sew it?" said Florence.

"Oh, my dear, that would take far too long!"

Florence restrained herself from offering to do it for her.

Eventually Jane wore another skirt.

"I shall be late again," she said, leaving the flat. A few minutes later the bell rang furiously. Florence opened the door. Jane, it appeared, had forgotten her latch-key.

"Henry is so damned punctual," said Jane, disappearing for the second time. She banged the door behind her. A photograph on the mantelpiece fell over.

Florence suppressed the slight qualm of depression that sometimes welled up in her when Jane went off and left her alone in the flat. "There's lots I must do," she thought briskly. "Stockings to wash, some shopping, an egg for lunch." It was nearly lunch-time now. These leisurely mornings were lovely. Florence contemplated her unmade bed and the litter of breakfast things on the table. Lovely, she thought vaguely.

This afternoon she would have a nice long time for writing her novel.

Sometimes Florence, after reading the reviews of new books in the Sunday newspapers, would imagine the terms in which the critics would acclaim her book. These notices of new novels, she had remarked, were often highly enthusiastic. "Quite out of the ordi-

nary run." The phrase was a commonplace. "Startlingly original."
"An author who merits close attention." You could not read through
the reviews without stumbling across one or more of these phrases. Would the critics be equally perspicacious in her case? "A study
of the mind of a child of extraordinary subtlety and sensitiveness."
That would be fair enough. "Miss Somerset," improvised Florence,
"has had the courage not to distort, not to minimize, not to—falsify?
ameliorate?—the emotions of a sensitive high-spirited child in the
most uncongenial of surroundings. 'Rubbing off the Corners' is a
powerful indictment of a certain type of school." Or perhaps an especially perceptive critic might write, "The reader is so carried away
by this ruthlessly penetrating study of school life and manners that
he lays the book down with the feeling that he has undergone some
intense emotional experience. It is only in considering the book later that he realizes with something of a shock that very little in actual
point of fact has happened within its pages."

Of course much of the effect was lost when the book was read in
extracts. Florence had quite given up reading it to Jane, chapter by
chapter, because Jane seemed persistently to miss the point.

"I think it's terribly clever, Florence. But oughtn't something
to—sort of—well—*happen* soon?"

"Happen!" cried Florence, deeply wounded. "What do you
mean?"

"Well, you might make her do something awful and be expelled.
Or have a fire, or she could elope with the head mistress's chauffeur
or the riding-master or something like that."

"I don't remember anything in the least like that happening at
St. Ethelburga's," said Florence coldly.

"No. But it would have been much more amusing if it had.
School was so ghastly dull."

"Amusing!" cried Florence scornfully, "amusing! Good God, I'm
not *trying* to be amusing. I want to paint an absolutely sincere picture of school life."

"Oh, of course, from that point of view, I think it's terribly
good," said Jane hastily.

Leslie, into whose sympathetic ears Florence still enjoyed pouring her literary aspirations, was kind but a little obtuse.

"Darling, it's absolutely agonizing." (Florence had just read the chapter in which Celia, the new girl, had her poetry books confiscated by the house-mistress.) "Now read me a funny bit."

"Funny bit? There aren't any funny bits. There's plenty of irony, of course."

"But school was awfully funny sometimes, wasn't it?"

"Not to Celia. You see everything is seen through her eyes, and it's part of the tragedy that she's utterly humourless. A sense of humour is usually defensive, you know."

"Do you mean Celia's as miserable as that all through the book?" cried Leslie, appalled.

Afterwards, when asking after the progress of the novel, which she usually remembered to do, she would inquire after Celia's state of mind with sympathetic anxiety.

"Do make her cheer up a little, Florence. I should think the poor child would go off her head soon."

"I'm not sure she isn't going to," said Florence seriously. "I did think at one time I'd make her try to commit suicide in the last chapter. But I think perhaps it would be a little inartistic. Perhaps it would be better just to indicate subtly that she was never quite the same again. What do you think?"

"I think I should make her cheer up and get popular and win a match for the school and get chaired round the quad."

Disgusted at these suggestions, Florence wondered why even quite intelligent people sometimes missed the point. She was so disheartened by this widespread lack of perceptive power that "Rubbing off the Corners" had been quite neglected lately. Spring was a restless time of the year. She had not felt like settling down to her writing in the long light evenings when Jane and Henry would go off with a picnic supper, and the sound of bouncing balls and players' voices drifted in from the public tennis-courts below. Spring, the sweet spring, is the year's pleasant king. . . . The silly, joyous words rang in Florence's head. Funny how restless she felt. The sight of her typewriter repelled her. Carbon-papers and filing cabinets were the dullest things in the world. She bought a bright green spotted scarf and had her hair waved. The pear-blossom was forgotten and in the country the cuckoo's note mocked from every tree. May slipped into June. "Rubbing off the Corners" was getting a bit dusty, tied up with string on the bottom shelf of the bookcase.

Today, however, would be a suitable opportunity for taking it up again. The story was approaching its climax. It would be a pity not to continue as quickly as possible. Florence wanted something today to occupy her mind. The office had been so disagreeable lately that she felt in need of some definite distraction. Yesterday she had not been able to read her shorthand and had, moreover, forgotten about a telephone message. The indexing was getting behindhand. She had been nervous and distraught—and was it getting her anywhere? At thirty, forty, fifty, thought Florence wildly, would she be where she was now? If she were an inaccurate and forgetful typist would any one ever believe she could do more difficult work? Those vague and tantalizing phrases—"lead to something," "an opening," "make a position for yourself"—could it really all analyze down to nothing but a maximum three pounds a week and dull office routine? Florence could not accept this. At any rate, she had escaped the awful fate of living at home. That much must be counted as achievement. And for the rest—something would turn up. It was, of course, intolerable to think of herself as waiting to get married; but it was permissible to hope vaguely that something would turn up. She would have the offer of a marvellous new job. She would travel and meet interesting people. She would—(Spring, the sweet spring, is the year's pleasant king)—Damn that doggerel. She scrubbed the cover of "Rubbing off the Corners" with her handkerchief. Surprising how dirty things got in London. (Then blooms each thing, then maids dance in a ring.) "Shut up," said Florence aloud. "Shut up and get down to work." Where had she got to? Ah, yes! The homesick and wretched Celia had for the last three chapters been composing a lyric for the school play. The time had come to hand in the entries, and Celia, too smitten in soul to follow instructions, had placed her poem, together with such shreds of hope and self-confidence as remained to her, in the wrong pigeon-hole. By a stroke of brilliant cynicism the climax of the book lay in a gigantic anti-climax. "You must try and be a little more careful, Celia," said Miss Coventry, handing back the child's poem unread.

Spurred to a furious indignation by the injustice she had invented, Florence took up her pen and began to write quickly.

II

"Did you manage to get the things done you wanted to?" inquired Henry.

"Yes, thank you. At least I forget what they were, but I believe I did, some of them."

"Will you take soup, sir?" said the waitress. Henry and Jane were facing each other across a little blue-painted table, neatly spread with orange raffia mats and a cottage cruet-set. The table was too small and too low for comfort, and the basket-chairs in which they sat were hard and creaked. You could, however, have a three-course lunch for 1s. 6d. and three courses, as Henry and Jane knew well, cost more often 1s. 9d. or 2s.

"Will you have soup, Jane?"

"What's the choice?"

Henry studied the menu.

"There isn't a choice."

"Two soups," said the waitress tactfully, and disappeared.

"Darling," said Henry, leaning across the table and taking Jane's hand, "I *do* wish you'd let me apologize about last night." He knocked over the salt.

"Henry dear. You have no sense of atmosphere."

Henry moved the water-jug (painted earthenware) to a safer position.

"It's the only chance I have of seeing you today," he pointed out.

"I know. Don't let's spoil it by beastly apologies."

"I wish you'd let me just explain."

"Oh, honestly, darling, there's nothing to explain. Don't worry about it."

Henry began to drink his pea-soup gloomily. It was always like this. She called him "darling" and said there was nothing to worry about. She was sweet and flippant and unattainable, and every day she got further and further away from him. There was nothing he could do to make her care. And she said that absolutely nothing was the matter.

"You're going to Leslie's party next Saturday, aren't you, Henry?"

"I suppose so," said Henry, and then brightened and suggested that they should drive down together. His family were going away for the week-end, and wouldn't want the car.

"It will be like those lovely days at Oxford," said Henry, his eyes shining with reminiscent sentiment, "you remember, when we—"

"What will you have to follow, sir?"

"Oh, bother. What will you have, Jane? Steak-and kidney pie, calves' liver and bacon, roast mutton and onion sauce or macaroni cheese?"

"I'll have roast mutton. No, I won't, I don't like onion sauce. Let me see, I'll have—isn't there something *quite* different?"

An unhelpful look stole across the waitress's face.

"Have you any salads?" suggested Jane.

"French, potato or beetroot—9d."

"I think I'll have a French salad," said Jane, repelled by the thought of beetroot or potato.

"It's not included in the lunch," said the waitress reprovingly.

"It won't be nearly enough for you, darling. I do wish you'd eat a bit more."

"Don't be silly, Henry. Salad is frightfully good for you. What are you going to have?"

"Steak-and-kidney pie," said Henry stoutly.

"Thank God I'm an Englishman," muttered Jane.

"I was just going to say," continued Henry, "What? Oh—er—fried and mashed parsnips—that having the car and you and going off into the country together will be just like those marvellous days at Oxford two years ago. Do you remember, darling?"

Jane did. Those picnics in the country round Oxford. Bablock Hythe, Wytham Woods, Marston Ferry. The very names held an enchantment never since recaptured. Instead of attending lectures she had spent the mornings making sandwiches in the pantry. A crumbly loaf and tomatoes in a brown paper bag. Then waiting in the hall for Henry to drive up to the college gates in his disreputable old Morris, sniffing the summer air, watching the conscientious set off on bicycles, lecture-bound, their black caps pulled forward on their earnest foreheads. Then Henry, Henry bare-headed and laughing, a gayer, younger Henry. Had she really felt that absurd rush of elation at seeing him for the first time each day? She could recall only the ghost of the emotion. Memory told her it had been so, but memory could never recreate the magic and potency of that brief-lived enchantment. It had been so, and now it was so no longer. There was really nothing more to say.

"It's marvellous to think we haven't changed a bit," said Henry.

"We have changed. Of course we've changed."

"What do you mean?" Henry laid down his knife and fork and studied Jane's face anxiously.

"Here's my salad!"

Henry, with a shrug of hopelessness, resumed his steak-and-kidney pie. He was always being taken aback by the offhand way in which Jane would let drop the most appalling statements. To reassure himself he said, "I think we've grown closer to each other since then."

"Do you? Oh, Henry, I've thought of such a marvellous new economy scheme!" She rushed into an account of her new plans. Her eyes lit up with laughter. She took off her hat and shook her fair hair back from her face with an arrogant grace. She was utterly adorable and completely elusive. And she could hurt most damnably.

"Do you really think we've changed much, Jane?"

"Darling! Everything always changes. It would be horrid if it didn't."

"I don't think my love for you will ever change."

"Oh, darling! I wish you wouldn't talk about 'my love for you' as though it were a sort of overcoat, guaranteed not to wear out."

"You only talk like that because it's fashionable to pretend not to be serious about anything."

"Is it fashionable? I suppose the newspapers say so. I didn't know."

There was a silence. Henry picked up the menu and decided on apple-fritters. Everything seemed equally beastly. The hot sunshine poured into the room. Another summer was here and Jane was right. Things were absolutely different.

His gloomy face filled Jane with a sort of irritated pity.

"Henry. Henry darling. You really agree with me, you know. 'My love for you' is—well, pompous and masculine and possessive. 'Our love for each other,' if you like. Don't you think so?"

"You're so funny, Jane. You seem to mind about such odd things."

"I can't bear it when you're a typical Englishman."

"I think that's a pose."

"Yes. I know you do. Oh, Henry, you are funny. You just refuse to believe in the bits of me you don't like. You have an idea of what I ought to be like and you can't help knowing (rather uncomfortably) that I'm really rather different. It's worrying for you. So the best way out is to say, 'Oh, that's just a pose,' and go on shutting your eyes and shutting your eyes."

Henry took this rather well. It hurt, of course, but not so much as Jane's flippancy or indifference could hurt. Prodding his apple-fritter, he replied, as casually as he could manage:

"Perhaps there's something in what you say. But, Jane—it never used to be like this. You've changed. You—evade me. You don't like my kissing you any more. Don't you remember how we used to—" But in the presence of the stranger facing him across the table he could not bear to put into words the swift succession of remembered moments that rushed into his mind. The silly tenderness of that first summer of their engagement. They had driven the car holding hands. He remembered clearly the feel of her slim little fingers beneath his as he changed gear. And that absurd game of trying to kiss the other in public when no one was looking. Once in a cigarette shop, he remembered, Jane had tried to plant a surreptitious kiss on his ear when the assistant's back was turned. The assistant had moved and seen her. Jane and Henry had caught each other's eye, and all three had suddenly burst out laughing. Terribly silly, terribly sweet memories. He could not bear to remind her of them.

"That's exactly it," said Jane. "When you want to make love to me nowadays you always say 'Don't you remember how we used to—' and so on. Or else you drag in the future and say, 'My love for you will never change,' or something improbable like that. Darling, I can't live in the past or the future. Why talk about how we used to love each other, or will one day love each other? Everything changes. We may, or may not have a future together. Let's love each other without thinking of that."

These suggestions of change and impermanence, touched on so cheerfully, so lightly, sent a cold breath of foreboding down Henry's spine.

"Perhaps that's all right for you, Jane," he said desperately, mechanically pursuing a portion of apple-fritter round and round the plate with his fork, "but I'm not like that. I couldn't be happy unless I thought I was always going to have you. When you talk like that you frighten me. Oh, darling! You *do* love me, don't you?"

He had tried to keep it back, but a desperate need for comfort and reassurance forced the silly pointless question from his lips. Let her at least say it! Even if she didn't mean it let her say it!

For one mad moment Jane, the avowed advocate of complete honesty, contemplated the rashness of an absolutely sincere reply. (I don't love you as I used to. I'm still rather fond of you and I like the way your hair grows and if I never saw you again I should miss you rather badly for a week.) Then compassion defeated principle and she replied hastily:

"Of course I do."

Sighing with relief, Henry relapsed into platitude.

"A long engagement is rather a strain."

"Let's get married," said Jane obligingly.

"Oh, darling! If only we could!"

"We could."

"How do you mean—we could?"

"Well, we could, couldn't we? We each earn three pounds a week."

"Jane, darling. I wish I could believe it would work. But you know it wouldn't. It would be so awful for you having to work all day."

"I don't see why it would be any more awful for me than it is now," said Jane reasonably.

"All the married couples I know who are short of money squabble all the time and are perfectly miserable," said Henry.

"Yes. But Florence and I aren't perfectly miserable, are we? And you and I wouldn't need to be perfectly miserable. You could live on your three pounds a week and I could live on mine. Just like we do now, only we could share a flat. We might stay on in my flat. I dare say Florence wouldn't mind turning out. There wouldn't be anything to squabble over. We should go on being perfectly self-supporting." Growing entranced by this vision of married independence, she waxed more and more enthusiastic. They would not, she pointed out to Henry, need to consider each other's convenience in the least. There would be no foolish pretences to keep up. They would have different friends and separate interests. They would not get on each other's nerves because they would not see too much of each other—

"I think it sounds perfectly bloody," said Henry.

"You won't then?"

"No, I won't." He glowered at his coffee. "If absolute financial and moral independence is your idea of a perfect marriage—"

"It's better than your idea—"

"You don't know what my idea is—"

"Yes, I do. I know what your ideas are about *everything*," cried Jane wildly, "just hopelessly typically middle-class Englishman. You think one English tommy is worth six frog-eating Frenchmen—"

"No, I don't."

"Yes, and you think the sun never sets on the British Empire—"

"No, I don't."

"Well, I don't know why you don't, because it doesn't. And you think—"

"Don't be silly, you know what I meant."

"And you think Russia must be an awful place now and English policemen are so splendid, and you don't approve of wives being financially independent because it hurts your beastly masculine pride and you think the lower classes are very well off where they are and too much education is a mistake—"

"And I suppose you think," retorted Henry as Jane paused for breath, "that every one should wear sandals and eat nuts and children should be brought up to do exactly as they please. . . ."

But Jane was too quick for him.

"And you believe in the 'sanctity of the home,'" she countered, "and in the 'decent thing to do,' and you probably really think sex is thoroughly nasty."

She drank her coffee at a gulp and, good humour completely restored, smiled bewitchingly at Henry.

"Well, anyway that last accusation isn't true," said Henry. (It was the only one which had the slightest power to hurt.)

"Well, you believe in the purity of women anyway," countered Jane accusingly.

"So do you, if it comes to that."

"No, I don't." With a lofty conviction Jane voiced the creed of her age and generation. "I believe it's entirely a matter for personal preference."

"You mean if you wanted to go off with a man without marrying him you would?"

"Yes. Of course I should. If I wanted to."

"Oh. Have you—er—been off with many people recently?"

"Don't be silly, darling. You know I haven't been in love with any one but you—yet."

"Darling," said Henry fondly, "I don't believe for one second that you'd live up to your principles."

"Oh, yes, I should. People do. Claud and Sylvia do, I believe."

"Well, if you really think that," said Henry reasonably, "why aren't we lovers too?"

"Because you think sex is nasty," said Jane triumphantly.

Henry thoughtfully stirred his coffee round and round. His eyes on his cup he said slowly, "Would you really—come away with me for a week-end—some time?"

He did not look at Jane as he waited for the answer. He wanted her desperately both to refuse and to accept, and at her answer a double pang of joy and despair pierced him.

"As an experiment—yes."

Henry laid his hand over hers as it lay on the table.

"Oh—darling." Too deeply moved for words he stroked her hand. The waitress, who had been hovering round with the bill, discreetly retired.

"Next week-end? After Leslie's party?" asked Henry at length in a low voice.

"All right." Jane strove to appear casual. Henry raised his head and she noticed with horror that there were tears in his eyes.

"Oh, Henry—please, darling. You mustn't take it too seriously. It's—it's an experiment, you know."

"I can't help its meaning rather a lot to me. Oh, Jane darling. I didn't force you into it, did I? It is because you care, isn't it?"

"Yes. Yes—of course it is. I mean I think it's right on principle too," said Jane, determined to vindicate theory at all costs.

"Darling. You don't understand how wonderful you are to me."

Jane became increasingly aware that Henry was not getting the situation right. This week-end ought to be regarded in the light of scientific experiment, a reasonable preliminary to any marriage. A sentimental point of view was completely out of place. Henry must be made to understand.

"I love you so terribly," said Henry humbly, "and I never dreamt I could ask you for—for so much. I wasn't sure you loved me enough."

Once again it did not seem the moment for complete honesty.

"Darling," said Jane, "what time did you say your train was? It's twenty past now. Darling, I'm sorry. But life is like that, isn't it?"

They hurried to Victoria in a taxi. Jane came with Henry out of maternal solicitude. She did not think he would succeed in getting himself and his suit-case on to the right train unless some one was there to help him. He was completely silent in the taxi, holding her hand and gazing out of the window with a rapt expression.

She put him into a corner seat and kissed him good-by affectionately.

For an hour and a half, until Aunt Alice, greeting him on the platform, interrupted his reverie, Henry thought of Jane and of nothing else.

Jane, suppressing an inclination to giggle, and a later one to burst into tears, bumped home to the flat on the front top seat of an empty bus. She thought about Florence and about Leslie's party and about the people in the streets and whether she could afford a new frock. A delicatessen shop reminded her to wonder whether they had anything in the flat for supper. She was just on the point of leaping off the bus to buy eggs and spaghetti when she remembered suddenly that she had accepted an invitation for that evening to dine with a young man she had met the previous week. It was all right, then. She needn't bother about the eggs.

CHAPTER IV

I

CLAUD'S PLAN turned out to be a scheme for paddling up the river in their boat as far as the Punt-Stop. This was a new riverside restaurant, just becoming popular, not particularly with boat-owners but with car-owners. In fact, it was the ingenuity of arriving actually by boat that appealed to Claud and Sylvia. They could have supper there and dance and return later in the boat back to the car.

"We shall have to paddle up in bathing-dresses," said Sylvia, "and change before we get there. They won't let us into the restaurant unless we're dressed."

"Good Lord! People do have filthy minds, don't they?"

"Yes. Funny, isn't it?"

Amicably they contemplated the filthiness of people's minds.

"It will need courage," said Claud, "because we shall have to change back into wet bathing-dresses to come home in."

It was only half-past four in the afternoon, and still broilingly hot. They agreed instantly that that wouldn't matter at all. Sylvia said that it would be rather nice, after getting hot dancing, to have something cool to change into.

"We'll put our clothes in the front, rolled up, on the way there. We'll roll your trousers round everything."

"Thank you, darling."

"I'm a woman of action," explained Sylvia, tucking a pair of pink silk knickers into Claud's trouser-pocket.

"I suppose the picnic-basket had better go back to the car," said Claud.

"All right, darling," said Sylvia. "Throw me your shirt."

"Toss you for the job of taking it back," suggested Claud. Sylvia looked up surprised.

"Darling! Don't be lazy. It won't take you long."

"It wouldn't take you long either."

"It would take me rather longer than it would you."

"I doubt if that's true. Women have greater powers of endurance than men. I should probably have to sit down for a rest half-way through that very large second field. I might have to rest for quite a long time."

Claud lay back and lit a cigarette. He seemed to be preparing for a long and pleasant argument.

"Don't be silly, darling." Sylvia was half amused and half annoyed. "Why have you suddenly gone like this?"

"You ought to like me better like this. I've stopped being Public-School. You don't like the public-school type, do you?"

"Not the *type*. But I never said there wasn't *some* good in them," conceded Sylvia generously.

"Convenience, you mean. It must be rather nice to have parcels carried and doors opened and things fetched and all that. But I've decided," said Claud aggravatingly, his *eyes* gleaming with amusement, "that it's really rather insulting for you to give you preferential treatment. I have too much respect for your intelligence, my dear Sylvia—"

Sylvia threw a cushion at him. He was joking, of course. But how serious was he underneath? He had always seemed to agree with her views on absolute sex-equality. Was it just barely possible that her militant independence had left a rankling itch of wounded pride? Curiously enough, the thought filled her with a mild elation.

"Beastly masculine conceit." She flung the insult at him triumphantly. "You're trying to pay me out because you know I don't believe in your wonderful male superiority."

"Beastly feminine pride," countered Claud, "you don't like it when I take you at your word and treat you as an equal because it doesn't flatter your sex."

Sylvia decided that a dignified capitulation was perhaps best.

"I expect you'll lose the toss anyway," she said.

They tossed up with the nearest thing to hand, one of the paddles of the boat.

"Clean or muddy side?"

"Muddy," said Sylvia primly.

It came down clean.

"Of course the real truth is you're just plain lazy," said Sylvia over her shoulder to the lounging, grinning Claud.

"Don't hurry, darling. I shall be quite comfortable here till you come back."

Sylvia set off, the picnic-basket under one arm. It was not really very heavy, but it was a nuisance. The ground was very rough and the sun still very hot. A field, a stile, another long field, a stile, a path and a gate. The car must be quite a quarter of a mile away. Never mind. She would have thought out a good answer for Claud by the time she came back. She was sure there was a fallacy in his argument if she could think of it. Chivalry must be admitted to be disgusting, but still—This rough grass was poking through her sandals and tickling her feet. Her ankle twisted in a rut. She staggered slightly and then took a firmer grip of the basket and impatiently slapped at a fly on her hot wet forehead. Male patronage was, of course, revolting. The behaviour of young men at dances, for instance! Why shouldn't the girls ask the men to dance with them instead of meekly sitting there awaiting some spotty-faced boy's condescension? Spotty-faced boy, thought Sylvia savagely, shifting the basket over to her other arm. Darling Claud, thank God he isn't spotty. She resisted a temptation to look back at him. It was rather horrid of him suddenly to behave like this. Horrid, but interesting. It was very difficult to think properly in this heat. She felt sure there was a perfectly good reason why Claud ought to have taken the basket. Given that men and women were intellectual equals, then—here was the first stile. Thankfully she plumped the basket on the top and clambered over. Panting slightly, she pushed crossly at a lock of hair which persisted in tickling her nose.

"Lovely weather, isn't it?" said a cheerful voice behind her.

"Claud!"

"You looked so purposeful, darling. Never looking back once, though I was only a little way behind you."

He was dressed absurdly in bathing-dress and walking-shoes. He seemed disgustingly pleased with himself. Sylvia wanted to slap him.

"Don't let me keep you if you're going for a walk," she said.

"Not at all I assure you." Claud became unnecessarily polite. "For the pleasure of your company, dear Sylvia, I would forgo even the delights of a ramble over a ploughed field on the hottest day of the year."

"Well, you needn't forgo it, because I'm going on." She picked up the basket.

"Oh! Allow me!" With enormous protestation and deference he seized the basket from her. "That I could not permit. Women aren't strong enough to carry heavy weights. I must insist. . . ."

Sylvia fought down a growing desire to giggle.

"If you will allow me to offer you my company and—shall I say protection?" suggested Claud.

"No, thank you!"

"No? Oh, Sylvia, why are you so cold to me?" Claud dropped the picnic-basket and fell on his knees, gazing up into her face with pathetic entreaty. "You must have guessed something of my feelings for you. Surely you must realize, my dear young lady, that my only desire is to protect you, to keep you—dear God—in merciful ignorance of the harsh realities of this wicked world. I as a man—" (he struck his breast)—"must perforce learn to live unsheltered. But you, dear Sylvia, you as a woman—"

He was not being funny, Sylvia told herself. He was being perfectly maddening, and showing off like a child of three. Her mouth quivered at the corners. It would never do to encourage him. The best thing to do would be to take absolutely no notice. She picked up the basket and marched off. Anyway she hadn't laughed. She quickened her pace.

"Sylvia!"

No, she wasn't going to take any notice.

"Sylvia!"

Damn! He was following her. She began to run. The basket dug painfully into her ribs. Of all the silly ways of spending an afternoon! His footsteps were close behind her. With the sudden nightmare panic of the hunted she dropped the basket and began to race as fast as she could. She could hear him panting behind her. Idiotically frightened she tried to run faster still. Her foot caught in a tuft of grass and she fell sprawling on her face. Immediately Claud's arms were round her. He knelt beside her.

"Darling sweet! You haven't hurt yourself?"

"No," Sylvia giggled weakly and hid her flushed face on his shoulder.

"Sweetheart. I can run faster than you, can't I? Can't I?" Kissing her, he demanded an answer.

"Yes, Claud."

"And I'm stronger than you, aren't I? Aren't I?"

"Oh, darling! Stop kissing me a moment."

"Aren't I?"

"I suppose so. In a sort of coarse way."

"And you love me more than any one else in the world, don't you?"

"I never said so."

"Yes, but you do, don't you?"

"Perhaps. You're hurting me."

"And you like me hurting you, don't you, and you wouldn't love me if I was weaker than you, would you?"

"I might."

"No, you wouldn't. You know you wouldn't. My own sweet silly-billy. Stop giggling, woman."

But Sylvia couldn't stop giggling. It was so silly and so pleasant to lie there on the grass in the sun, laughing foolishly up at Claud's tender mocking face and feeling his adoring kisses on her lips and forehead and neck.

"Darling Sylvia, you *know* you love me more than any one."

"Conceited."

"Yes—*terribly* conceited because of you. You haven't thought of an answer to that, have you, darling? Never mind. I'll be tactful and kiss you instead."

It was awful to let him have the last of the argument after all. Sylvia tried to stifle her giggles on his shoulder. She simply would not have Claud beginning to lord it over her. His hair was still wet from the bathe. She loved the clipped feel of it on his neck.

"Claud, I think you're—Claud, don't kiss me just when I'm going to say—Oh, Claud, you are maddening. Oh, darling! Do stop! I'll say anything you like. I've got such a pain from laughing. Please stop, darling. What do you want me to say?"

"Nothing at all," said Claud firmly, pulling her to her feet and encircling her with his arms, "you can just listen while I tell you that I adore you and I don't care about any one in the world but you, because you're the most wonderful, beautiful, lovely thing on earth. So there." He released her, breathless from laughing and surprise.

"Even if you have got mud on your cheek," he added, and ran away, picked up the picnic-basket and made off in the direction of the road.

Sylvia, exhausted, sauntered back towards the river in a state of elated bewilderment.

II

It became cooler as Claud and Sylvia paddled steadily downstream. Disregarding their aching arms, they followed patiently the wriggling stream to the point where it debouched into the River Thames. By seven o'clock the sun's rays came low, dusty gold, and slanting over the level meadows. Pools of shadow lay at the foot of the hedges. The river-water, by contrast with the cooling air, struck warm to the touch. The skin on Sylvia's back and arms felt tight and stretched. They inquired tenderly after each other's sunburn.

"Tired, sweetheart?" asked Claud, as Sylvia stopped paddling and stretched out her arms with a sigh.

"No. Where is this place?"

"Just round the next bend. I think we'll have a lovely meal when we get there, don't you, darling? Salmon mayonnaise and lager, do you think?"

This subtle encouragement gave fresh energy to Sylvia's paddling. Round the bend the river-bank was lined with bungalows. Bright-cushioned punts were tethered to the mooring-stages. A bored-looking young man in immaculate flannels was punting along just ahead. The girl with him was dressed in a chiffon frock and a large hat. Sylvia would not admit that she was beginning to feel a little conspicuous, cross-legged on the floor of a rubber boat in a bathing-dress, but she agreed with Claud's suggestion that they should land, dress, and complete the journey on foot.

"They *have* spoilt the river here, haven't they?" said Sylvia, sparing a moment from her hasty toilet behind a large willow-tree to cast a look of scorn on the docile domesticated stream, flowing tidily between lines of neat huts, labelled on their brightly-painted gates with appropriately facetious names.

"Disgusting," said Claud cheerfully, his thoughts on dinner. He shook out his bathing-dress and suspended it to dry from a bough. Sylvia wrestled with a comb. This woodland toilet had its difficulties. She dabbed some powder on her face and hunted for a lipstick. Claud, whistling softly, hung her bathing-dress behind his. Looking absurdly small, they flapped companionably together in the breeze.

Leaving the boat tied to the bank, they struck across a field into a lane, and followed the lane to the door of the Punt-Stop. A blare of music greeted them as they entered. It was both shocking and enlivening to find such a place set down in the midst of the dusty lanes and dew-wet fields from which they came. It appeared to be some sort of a gala night. Nearly all the tables were already full, and more people were driving up to the door every moment. The small band played furiously, and couples were already jammed on the limited floor-space. The tinkle of knives and forks made a scraping undertone to the music, and whenever the band stopped the roar of conversation rose on an upward swell. It was hot and brightly lit, and crowded and noisy, and Sylvia, taking in a general confused impression, at once became self-conscious about her appearance. From river-bank to restaurant was a sudden jolt. She must immediately compose herself by repowdering her nose.

She bolted upstairs and spent a long time before the mirror, aiming at a smart and sophisticated effect by means of a beret very much on one side and plenty of lipstick. The result was surprisingly successful, and, mind at peace, she went down to rejoin Claud, who had succeeded in getting a table outside.

Pleasantly weary, they lay back in comfortable cushioned basket-chairs. The cool tide of evening air flowed round them. The tang of a cigarette was pleasant in the mouth. Fish jumped in the river with little plopping sounds. Claud and Sylvia smoked in companionable silence. It had been a lovely day and they were together. Together—what a lot of happiness the word covered. (At evening these silly thoughts come unbidden into the mind.) Darling Claud, thought Sylvia. And darling Sylvia, thought Claud. The salmon mayonnaise arrived and was delicious—firm pink flakes, laced with smooth-textured creamy yellow sauce and garnished by the crinkly leaves of crisp green lettuce. Lager beer in long glasses, crowned with amber froth. Strawberry ices, soft and cold to the tongue, melting in the mouth into little trickles of deliciousness. The golden glow that the sinking sun had left in the air slowly thickened and darkened to a bluish twilight. The lighted lantern over their table rocked gently on its wire with a faint creaking. The band, muted by distance to enchantment, fiddled away the dying light. A water-rat on the far side of the river splashed suddenly into the stream. The waiter brought them coffee in gay yellow cups.

"Darling," said Sylvia, softly.

"What?"

"Nothing really. I can't express it."

"Nor can I," said Claud and regrettably they held hands under the table.

They were often very silly together. Sylvia sometimes reflected that it was odd that two intelligent adults should find pleasure in absurd nicknames, holding hands, private jokes and pulling each other's hair. She apologized to herself by saying that if she realized she was being silly she wasn't being quite so silly after all.

Just at first they had been a little intense about their love. They had thought and talked a good deal about it, and discussed, as reasonable intelligent adults should, the wisdom and rightness of the step they proposed to take. Sylvia pointed out it would be very unnatural not to become lovers. It would, she said, be wrong and unfair to each other. Claud said it was marvellous of her to think like that; but she wasn't to unless she really wanted to.

They had been lovers now for nearly a year, and although Sylvia tried very hard she had not yet succeeded in entirely suppressing a sensation of guilt whenever she talked to Claud's landlady. She could not help shuddering a little at respectable Mrs. Wilkins's romantic interest in her favourite lodger's "fiancée," at her readiness to cook extra dishes for Sylvia when she came to spend the evening with Claud, at the kindness which prompted her to charge Sylvia the very minimum for another room in her lodging-house when, as occasionally happened, Sylvia came to London to stay for a few days, after murmuring to her family something about a camp-bed in Jane and Florence's flat. It was really owing to Mrs. Wilkins that they had stopped being intense and begun to be silly together. Once, almost at the beginning of it all, Claud had come back from work to find Sylvia, who was coming to supper, waiting for him in his room. For no reason that he could possibly divine she was sobbing into the sofa-cushions.

"Don't ask me. I can't explain it," gulped Sylvia.

He found her a clean handkerchief and implored her to tell him.

"It's so silly. You wouldn't understand." She sniffed. "I don't understand it myself."

Finally, because he looked so miserable and puzzled, she told him.

It was merely that Mrs. Wilkins had been talking to her and saying how fond she was of Claud and how she was so glad to think he was going to have a nice home of his own soon and how much he liked marmalade pudding.

"I simply can't tell you why it made me want to cry, Claud. I think I must be a bit tired or something."

Not for worlds would she have admitted that their situation involved a certain nerve-strain; nor her silly obscure feeling that if only everything didn't end by having to go home, if only she could have stayed and perhaps done something rather domestic for Claud, like cooking his breakfast or darning his socks, it would have relieved the intensity of everything rather comfortably.

Claud mopped tenderly at her tear-streaked face. It was true that he did not quite understand, but he did realize that, for that evening at any rate, Sylvia did not want to be treated as an intelligent enlightened adult. She wanted to be petted, comforted, teased a little; she wanted not passion but tenderness.

Sylvia never forgot how sweet he had been to her. When it was time to go, although he had had a tiring day, he had accompanied her all the way back to Paddington. He had stopped on the way and bought her a large box of marrons glacés. He had said he liked her to be unreasonable sometimes.

It was soon after this that they began to get less intense and more silly. They stopped being self-conscious about themselves. Sylvia ceased to think of Claud as her partner in a mutual experiment. In the happiest, most natural way, they began to act clean against their principles. They began to take each other for granted.

The only friction that existed occurred between Sylvia and her family.

"I wish I wasn't so horrid to mummy, sometimes," she said once to Claud in a rare mood of penitence.

"Are you?" said Claud, surprised. "What are you like when you're being horrid?"

"Oh—argumentative and horrid. Family life is so difficult. It's all wrong."

"Yes, I expect it is," agreed Claud cheerfully. Both his parents were dead. He had always been accustomed to being more or less on his own. And because he knew very little of family matters it did not occur to him that he complicated considerably Sylvia's life at home; not only in practical details, but in subtler ways. He would have been astonished to learn that he was the chief, if unwitting, cause of a great part of the confused antagonism that existed between Sylvia and her mother.

"It's all so natural and lovely between us, isn't it, Claud darling?" Sylvia would exclaim sometimes, rapturously.

They would agree that it was perfect. Then Sylvia would go home and snap at her mother.

The last dregs of light drained away and the river became only a murmur in the dark beyond the lawn. Most of the diners had finished and gone inside to dance; but Claud and Sylvia continued to sit on in a sort of trance of companionship.

"Oh, darling," sighed Sylvia, "it is marvellous to think I can say absolutely anything to you and be understood. Which makes it so completely unnecessary to say anything at all."

They played with each other's hands. Claud waggled each of Sylvia's fingers in turn and then Sylvia waggled each of Claud's. They did not notice how wet the grass was becoming beneath their feet.

"Darling, you're so divinely silly," said Claud.

"You've got it wrong. I was merely humouring you. A woman should always humour her man. She manages him, you see, without his knowing it. Sick-making, isn't it?"

"Yes. Am I easy to manage?"

"Oh, yes! As easy as a child of two," said Sylvia airily.

"How nice for you, darling. Shall we dance?"

They went in to join the stamping wriggling crowd. It was very gay and very hot.

"Let's fling ourselves into the spirit of the party and order drinks," said Claud.

They ordered drinks and danced again. Claud is the nicest-looking man in the room, thought Sylvia, but I shan't tell him so because he might get conceited.

"What are you giggling at, Sylvia?"

"I'm just laughing at the way I'm 'managing' you. What are you giggling at, Claud?"

"Oh, just at not being annoyed by your laughing."

"Please, Claud, I want another drink."

"You're very expensive tonight. No more after this one."

"Mean. That's it."

"No. But I know what sort of a head you've got. Last time I took you out, you got roaring screaming drunk on cider-cup."

"You must try to conquer your habit of telling occasional untruths, dear. I'll help you as much as I can."

"Thank you, darling. And I'll try to fight with you against this horrible tendency to drunkenness. I believe I can give you spiritual strength."

Holding her away from him as they waltzed round the room he contemplated her with a triumphant smile. Sylvia opened her mouth to reply just as Claud planted a surreptitious kiss on her nose. She laughed, forgot what she had meant to say, and looking up caught the gaze of his shining adoring eyes on her face. It was one of those moments when the rest of the world falls away. Sylvia sighed and Claud's arm tightened around her. The music stopped. Absurdly Sylvia felt tears pricking the back of her eyes.

They sat down and the drinks arrived.

"Make the most of yours," teased Claud.

It was rather awful to think he really would refuse to get another. They had often agreed together that no one should ever be responsible for any one else. On the other hand it was comforting to be looked after (although she would not admit this to Claud).

"I feel so happy, don't you, darling?" (Claud always became affectionate after getting his own way.)

"Yes," admitted Sylvia. "Oh, Claud! I'm sure we're so terribly *right*, aren't you? Just think, darling, if I was spending the whole time wondering if I could induce you to propose!"

"Do you think girls really went on like that?"

"Oh, *yes!*" cried Sylvia, emphatically, "and so they do still. Honestly, darling, it's frightful the way they behave. It's absolutely disgusting—and they have such filthy minds that they'd probably be shocked at a perfectly honest, straightforward love-affair like ours."

Claud agreed that they probably would. It was in fact a little worrying to think *how* shocked actually people like—say Sylvia's parents—would be. But then one must keep on remembering that it was wrong to mind about other people's opinions.

"Darling," said Claud, diffidently, "you'll probably laugh at me, but I can't help sometimes wondering whether it isn't just a shade hard on you. I mean—" His voice faltered. He was obviously experiencing a familiar difficulty—that of trying to say something and at the same time trying not to say it.

"Hard on me! It's *exactly* the same for me as for you."

"Well, not in a sense, because—"

"Well, if it isn't it ought to be," interrupted Sylvia firmly. "Why *should* there be this utterly artificial distinction between men and women? Oh, darling, you *know* we agreed. . . ." Her voice suddenly died away as her attention became fixed on two figures who had just appeared at a table at the far end of the room.

"Good Lord! There's Henrietta." Her voice was curiously deadened.

"Where?"

"Over there—in the corner—next to the wall."

Claud looked and saw Henrietta, a little flushed, a little over-animated, twiddling restlessly the stem of her wineglass and laughing, laughing a little too gayly up into the face of a middle-aged man whose eyes were fixed on her young form in a manner at once proprietary and sentimental.

"Who's she with, Sylvia?"

"A man called Captain Fortescue. Lives near us. Lots of money. Semi-invalid wife."

It was a casual enough answer to a casual-sounding question. It is curious to record therefore that Claud, stroking Sylvia's hand, said softly and seriously to her, "Darling, don't be upset."

"She's so young, Claud."

"I don't suppose there's anything in it."

"He's telling her dirty stories," said Sylvia, in tones of gloomy intensity. Watching them, Claud agreed that it seemed probable. Not a word could be heard of their conversation, but it was clear from their expressions and regularly-spaced bursts of laughter that Captain Fortescue was regaling his escort with a string of anecdotes.

"He's got a nasty mouth," said Claud.

"He's got a bad reputation, too." (This was the sort of remark that ordinarily called for derision. At the moment, however, it was not funny.)

Claud tried consolation.

"Don't worry, darling. She's got to meet different kinds of people. And since she's the sort of person she is—I mean so pretty and all that—I should think the sooner she gets used to all sorts of people falling in love with her, the better. It's all experience for her."

The words rang hollow, devoid of reassurance, and Sylvia's only reply was a gloomy, "She *is* pretty, isn't she?"

Claud tried another line.

"Besides, there's probably nothing in it. Why shouldn't they—"

"I believe she's drunk," interrupted Sylvia. Henrietta rising to dance, had staggered and clutched at Captain Fortescue's arm.

"I expect she's just—er—carefree," said Claud, glancing at Henrietta with some anxiety. "After all, we've all—"

"I know. But that's different. Where do you think she's been all the evening?"

"God knows. Cheer up, darling. In a minute you'll be talking about 'worse than death.' She's all right. Do you want to speak to her? She'll be dancing round here in a minute."

"No," said Sylvia with considerable vehemence. "Let's get out quick."

The gruesome and damp journey home was accomplished. When they reached the place where they had left the boat it was found that Sylvia's bathing-dress was still soaking wet.

It had fallen down into a bed of nettles. With a gesture of extreme chivalry Claud offered to exchange, and Sylvia had too little spirit left to refuse. Claud indeed continued to behave with truly remarkable restraint and good humour. By skill and coolness he several times averted the shipwreck that Sylvia's savage and intermittent paddling threatened to bring about, and he was as firm as a family Nanny about the necessity of changing back into dry things again on reaching the car. And all the time Sylvia, deeply conscious that she was being irritating and yet unable to help herself, continued to talk about Henrietta.

"Mother never asks where she's going."

"Good Lord! I should hope not," said Claud, serenely changing into top.

"She's probably been going about with him for months."

"Think so? Well, after all—"

"And his wife's a great friend of mother's," said Sylvia, becoming more and more horrifyingly conventional. Forgotten were her declarations of a profound belief in married independence, her assertions that any man had a right to a complete and fulfilled existence. Or not perhaps quite forgotten, and not exactly disproved. It was merely quite clear that the present situation had nothing to do with this eminently reasonable theory of living.

"Sylvia, my sweet, please don't worry. You're being so funny about this. I should never have expected you to mind so much. You're leaping to conclusions in the most violent way. You don't want me to offer to horsewhip the cad, do you?"

Sylvia summoned the ghost of a smile, and then put out a contrite hand and patted Claud's knee.

"Sorry, darling. It's just that she's so young."

"I know," said Claud, comfortingly.

They drove on in silence, their headlamps boring a yellow tunnel down the dark leafy lanes. Both were busy with their thoughts.

Sylvia was telling herself that she was being silly. Again and again she assured herself of this. Desperately she caught hold of the stock phrases of reassurance—making a mountain out of a molehill, mare's nest, false alarm—using them as weapons with which to belabour her tired brain whenever her thoughts began again to scuttle off down forbidden ways. At the back of her mind was the query that that morning had translated itself merely into a vague anxiety, and that she still obstinately refused to recognize. Suppressing it before it became articulate, it remained as a lurking sense of responsibility. The query was, "Does Henrietta know about Claud and me?"

Claud was thinking that it was sweet and silly of Sylvia to be so upset about Henrietta. She wasn't anything to worry over. Sylvia was worth two of her. His mind was also vaguely occupied with an idea that had been mysteriously growing on him in the course of the last few weeks. The idea—it had hardly yet reached the stage of a conscious wish—was that he and Sylvia should get married. As soon as this idea had occurred to him an unaccountable shyness began to restrain him from mentioning it to Sylvia. And yet they could— and did—discuss anything with each other. Anything, that is to say, except this. There had been a moment that afternoon when they had come near to it. It had been strange and sweet and—frightening, and they had run away from it. Then the river and the twilight and the evening had been drawing them closer to each other—the idea had begun to lose its strangeness, becoming natural and simple and sweet—and then it had all been spoilt by Henrietta, jarring and intruding on a mood that might be difficult to recapture. Claud crashed his gears and decided gloomily that it would be in the worst possible taste to propose to Sylvia now.

CHAPTER V

I

WEDNESDAY WAS a busy day at the office. Jolting home in the bus on Wednesday evening, Florence disgustedly squeezed carbon-stained fingers into her gloves. The typists had no hot water to wash in. You left your hat and coat in a nasty little cupboard and waited your turn for a look in the glass, politely insincere.

"No—after you. I'm really not in a hurry." (Bother the woman, what an age she's taking.)

What with the insufficient light and the London dust, reflected Florence savagely, it was really necessary to come straight home and have a bath. She looked out of the window and the phrase "straight home" immediately took on a bitter sarcasm. The bus had spent the last ten minutes perfectly stationary in a block that appeared to stretch the whole way down Oxford Street. Florence began to read the *Evening Standard* of the woman next to her. Tiresomely, the woman turned over to the next page. Disheartened, Florence began to chew her bus-ticket. It was a habit of which she sincerely believed herself to be incurable, and one which had caused her many embarrassing moments owing to the inopportune arrival of inspectors. On this occasion Florence had rolled it up into a little scroll and was biting the end when the woman next to her said, "Excuse me." Florence clutching her belongings to her, and leaving the ticket revoltingly between her teeth, stood up to let her pass.

"What a nuisance she is," thought Florence unfairly.

She was in a very bad temper; but there was no doubt that it had been a trying day at the office. A day of almost nightmare frightfulness. The telephone had rung incessantly. Nearly all the callers had been partially or wholly inaudible. She had been three deep in interruptions. There was a great pile of work left over till tomorrow, without any particular prospect of having any more time to cope with it then. The day had been full of minor trivial absurd happenings, each of which had appeared so absolutely maddening at the time that Florence could not think of them now without a deep sense of raging injustice.

There had been the incident of the shorthand note. Florence had taken down a letter thanking for a book which some one had sent to Miss Locke, the woman Florence worked under. It was not even a business letter. ("If you wouldn't mind just doing this personal note for me, Miss Somerset—it won't take you a moment.") But for the fact that Florence afterwards found herself wholly unable to read her shorthand transcript of the title of the book, it would have been quickly enough done. As it was she puzzled over it for twenty minutes, occasionally pausing to look in horror at the amount that still remained to be got through. Eventually she went out to lunch with the problem still unresolved. The Something Attempt. Did that odd middle hieroglyph begin with a p or b? Or even with a t or d? Was there perhaps a vowel before? She had never seen a funnier-looking outline. She was ready to swear she had not perpetrated it. The Something Attempt. She had asked Miss Con-

way, who worked in the same room, and Miss Conway, uninterest-
ed if not exactly unkind, had said it might be anything. She would
hurry through lunch and go back and worry at it again, and if she
couldn't get it she would jolly well have to ask. If she just left out the
title Miss Locke would be sure to notice. Florence reflected sadly on
her own deficiencies as a shorthand-typist. It was the humiliating
truth that one mistake makes others, and Florence was so often in a
state of being violently distracted over some trifle that she had little
scope to develop that calmly efficient air that made, she believed,
the successful secretary. Half-past one saw her back at her study of
the indecipherable hieroglyph. She had invented a new technique,
glancing away from the page and then back suddenly in the hope
that the meaning might thus suddenly break gloriously upon her.
The hope died a lingering and painful death, and at a quarter to two
Florence knocked at Miss Locke's door.

"I'm so sorry, Miss Locke, I can't quite read the title of this
book."

"What book?" said Miss Locke brusquely.

"The one you asked me to write and thank for. I'm afraid I—"

Miss Locke sighed and Florence observed with alarm more than
a trace of impatience in her manner.

"I sent a special message through Miss Conway to say you
needn't do that letter. I've been on to my friend on the telephone
since."

"Oh, I'm sorry," said Florence, adding humbly, "Miss Conway
hasn't come back from lunch yet."

There was no response to this and Florence closed the door
quite sick with irritation and mortification.

There was the incident of the telephone call.

The telephone had been behaving badly all day, and at about
four o'clock it developed an intermittent and disturbing twitter. It
stood on a table some distance from Florence's typing-desk and
twittered maddeningly at her for half an hour. Miss Conway was out
of the room, and Florence was goaded into getting up three times
to answer it. Each time there was a faint buzz, a tentative click, and
the cool brisk voice of the switchboard clerk, "What number, pliss?"

"No number," said Florence wearily on each occasion. "You
rang through to me."

"Sorry, Miss Somerset. There's no call come through for you," was the invariable response.

With a harassed glance at the clock Florence went back to her typewriter for the third time. Let the beastly thing twitter. Let it ring its head off. She had plenty to do without getting up every minute to fuss over it.

"Dear Sir," typed Florence (double space, indent), "I should like to have and opportunity of discussing—" Damn. "And" was always turning up instead of "an." Was it best to rub out (always a messy business with two carbons in the machine) or to correct in ink, a procedure frowned upon by Miss Locke, or to begin again, wasting paper, temper and time? Better perhaps go on and see if she made many more mistakes. . . . "Of discussing your suggestion that—" The telephone was twittering again. Let it. Florence's fingers, damp with sweat, pounded the keys furiously. The telephone's twitter shrilled into an insistent ring. With a groan Florence pushed back her chair and lifted the receiver. There was a faint buzz.

"Hello. Hello. Hello." The first hello was subdued, the second emphatic and the third distinctly irritable.

The faint buzzing continued.

"I can't hear a word you're saying," said Florence, and her tone suggested anything but the calm efficiency of the perfect secretary. As she did not really believe any one was at the other end of the line her manner was perhaps excusable. There was, however, an instant and appalling response to this piece of bad humour. Miss Locke's icily-clear voice suddenly sounded in Florence's appalled ear.

"I am sorry you can't hear, Miss Somerset. I am speaking as distinctly as possible from the ground office. Can you come down a moment please?"

Miss Locke, quite naturally, was not particularly interested in Florence's confused apologies. She said, with truth, that the behaviour of Florence's telephone was not her concern; and added briefly that she had a few more letters which were rather important and should go off that evening. Florence was left with the conviction that Miss Locke believed that her secretary spoke to everybody in an irritable whine.

The evening sunshine flooded the packed street, winking on the polished radiators of the close-jammed cars. A delicious whiff of strawberries came from a fruiterer at the corner. Girls in dainty summer clothes, hatless men, older people from whose faces the sun seemed to have melted some of that London expression of guarded respectability, were strolling along the pavements, in whose grey stones the glow of the day's heat still lingered. It was an enchanting hour, an enchanting time of year, and Florence regarded it all with a mixture of irritation and distaste. Her worried mind, churning over her anxieties, cast up desires and thoughts of the unworthiest description. I wish I were very rich, with a Rolls and a lady's maid to do my hair every day. (Oh, dear, I must go to the hairdresser in my lunch-hour one day this week.) I wish I were extremely decorative and completely useless. I wish I were in love. I wish (with a sudden descent to realities) that I could type quicker and more accurately. I wish I had taken up medicine instead of going to Oxford. No, I wish I were in Oxford now, in a punt on the Cher, writing—no, having just written—a clever essay. (And my essays *were* clever, all my tutors said so.) I wish, concluded Florence unhospitably, thinking longingly as she got off the bus of warm water and cool linen, I wish Leslie weren't coming to supper.

II

Leslie was standing on the doormat, looking exquisitely cool and dainty in a white pique suit with a blue and white blouse, high-heeled shoes and small smartly-perched white hat.

"Darling!" she cried. "How nice to see you again."

Florence wondered whether this enthusiasm was due to a prolonged wait on the doormat, and decided that it was probably quite genuine. Leslie always greeted her friends with rapture and took leave of them with expressions of reluctance. She had never acquired the casualness over social encounters that Oxford had implanted in Jane and Florence and an independent working life in London deepened. Jane and Florence were capable of telling some one to their face, quite pleasantly, that they did not like them. Leslie, overhearing this once, had been at the same time admiring and appalled. In the same way Leslie's politeness had occasionally been the source of some slight social embarrassment to Jane and Florence. They were accustomed to introduce her to their Oxford friends with a friendly hint given in advance that one must not be put off at first by her manner. "It's only her way, you know, and she's really awfully genuine." Jane and Florence's friends, reassured by a promise of this most necessary characteristic, extended a kindly tolerance towards Leslie's idiosyncrasies. They understood perfectly that it was because—poor girl—she had never had a life of her own. She hadn't had their advantages, and one must make allowances for her in consequence.

"I'm *so* hot and filthy," said Florence, fumbling for her latch-key. Leslie's politeness always made her feel a little inadequate. "I'm sorry you had to wait, Leslie."

"It didn't matter a bit. Oh, Florence! Every time I come here I think what a *sweet* little flat it is!"

"Good God! How frightful," said Florence, staring aghast at the unmade bed in the sitting-room and the litter of breakfast things on the table, "Mrs. Thing can't have come."

"Oh, do you have a *maid*?" cried Leslie, apparently delighted at the ingenuity of the idea.

"We have a char. She should come every day and clear this up—" Florence distastefully picked up a suspender-belt and a toasting-fork from the hearthrug.

"What fun!" cried Leslie, to whom the idea of engaging a char appeared in all its pristine enchantment. "What's she *like*, Florence?"

"I haven't the least idea," said Florence briefly, "I've never seen her."

"Why not?"

"Because I'm never in, of course. If you work in an office from nine-thirty to five-thirty (and usually much later) you never are in."

"I never thought of that. What do you do then?"

"We write each other notes."

"What fun!"

"Yes. Only we can never find a pencil," said Florence, beginning to clear the breakfast things away. Leslie offered to wash up. Florence, taking the offer more or less for granted, explained that they would wash up everything after supper.

"Then I'll make the bed," said Leslie, determined to be useful.

"Thanks. Don't air it or anything silly like that, you know. Just pull the things up and shove the cover on. I can't think why Jane's so late."

"Poor Florence, you're tired. Do sit down and rest. I'm sure you've had a hard day at the office."

"I must start getting the supper."

"It's so sweet of you to bother about supper. Please don't worry about it because of me, will you? It's so hot, isn't it? Something cold would do, wouldn't it, to save trouble. Sort of salmon mayonnaise. . . ."

"I haven't got anything cold," said Florence, keeping a tight hold on herself, "and it's not sweet of me to bother because I should be doing it for myself anyway. I didn't know it was going to be so hot and can't have salmon mayonnaise" (salmon mayonnaise, indeed!) "because I haven't got any salmon or any salad or any—"

It was perhaps fortunate that at this moment Jane's latch-key was heard in the door.

"Darling," cried Leslie, "how nice you're looking!"

"Mrs. Thing hasn't come," said Florence, simultaneously.

Jane, looking tired, but still jaunty, greeted Leslie, took off her hat, and inquired of Florence whether she had brought the asparagus with her.

"Damn, I forgot," said Florence, "at least, anyway, I worked late and the shops were shut."

"Never mind," said Jane, "there's some sweetcorn in the cupboard."

Leslie thought how nice of Jane to take it like that. She was wrong. Jane was always nice about everything, firstly because she disliked above all things unpleasantness, and secondly because she never really cared.

"Poor Florence is so tired," Leslie said to Jane, "and I do want to help her but she's being so obstinate."

"The best thing you can do, Leslie," said Jane with a bewitching smile, "is to sit absolutely motionless in this arm-chair and entertain us with your charming prattle while we get the supper ready."

Leslie, disappointed but docile, obeyed, and Florence, heaving a sigh of relief, went off to wash her face and hands and put on a pair of bedroom slippers.

"There's soup," said Jane, "and then there's a choice."

"Darling, how exciting!" cried Leslie.

"You can either have poached egg on sweetcorn, or scrambled egg *with* sweetcorn or sweetcorn omelette."

Leslie, enchanted by these variations, said enthusiastically how *much* she preferred this sort of meal to ordinary home fare.

"I don't," said Florence, reappearing with a towel in her hands. "What I really like is a hot joint and two veg."

"But joints are terribly simple to cook, aren't they?"

"Oh, terribly," said Florence. "All you've got to do is to leave the office about four o'clock in the afternoon to put the joint in the oven."

"Florence is embittered tonight," said Jane, "but as a matter of fact you do get rather tired of the sort of food you can cook in ten minutes."

"There's always sausages," suggested Leslie.

"Yes, but you do so smell them the next morning," said Florence reminiscently.

"You'd never believe the horrors of being a bachelor girl," said Jane, watching the other two with secret amusement.

"I think it must be *heavenly*," said Leslie, settling herself delightedly at the rather small and rocky gate-legged table. "As a matter of fact I want to talk to you about—"

"Sorry! I'll get the spoons. Don't try to eat your soup with a knife and fork, Leslie," interrupted Jane. She reappeared from the kitchen with three rather doubtful-looking spoons in her hand and announced that she had put the coffee on.

"Will any one who hears it bubble over please rush? Sorry, Leslie, you were going to say—?"

"It's about living in London," said Leslie. "I'm frightfully keen to come and live here too. I want to have a studio." She gazed expectantly at her friends' faces.

"I've finished so I'll go and make the omelette," said Florence. "Why a studio, Leslie?"

"She paints," said Jane. "Don't you remember she paints?"

"The last six novels I read have all been about people with studios," said Florence and disappeared into the kitchen. Leslie felt that her bombshell had been disappointingly received.

"Darling, I want you to help me because you *know* about these things," she said pleadingly to Jane.

"Darling, I know absolutely nothing about painting."

"Yes, but you know about living in London and the cost of things and that sort of thing."

"Oh, I know all about that."

"Well then." Leslie paused impressively. "I've got a hundred pounds of my own."

"Darling, how terribly rich of you."

"I could easily rent a studio and live in London on that for a year, couldn't I?"

"No," said Jane agreeably. "Not possibly."

Leslie looked taken aback, and a diversion was created by Florence appearing with the omelette.

"You're giving me more than my share," said Leslie with her usual politeness.

"No, I'm not," replied Florence truthfully. "I'm giving you exactly a third."

"But Jane," said Leslie, returning to the attack, "the rent of the studio I'm thinking of is only one pound a week. It's a marvellous room with an enormous skylight. It's in Chelsea."

"Too perfect," agreed Jane.

"Yes, that was one of the ones I read about," said Florence, rather annoyingly.

"You see that would leave me a whole pound a week to live on. After all, everything's frightfully cheap in London, isn't it? I mean, you can have a marvellous meal for about 5d."

"Yes, and an extremely long bus-ride for 6d."

"Well, the studio wouldn't be very far from the place near Baker Street where I want to go for lessons."

"Wouldn't it? I always thought Chelsea and Baker Street were rather far apart. How would you go?"

"Darling Jane, how do I know? I thought you'd know *all* about that sort of thing. As a matter of fact, I expect I should walk most days."

Jane and Florence exchanged looks. They knew all about walking in London.

"But, Leslie," said Florence, "if you're going to be at an art-school all day why do you want a studio? You could get a room much cheaper."

Leslie sighed. "That's what mummy couldn't understand. Perhaps if you don't paint yourself you can't. I couldn't bear to live in a beastly club or boarding-house. I must have somewhere to myself."

"Well, couldn't you at least share a studio or something with some one?"

"I'd much rather be alone. I don't think I'm a very easy person to live with."

Jane was reminded vividly of her first term at Oxford, and how six of them, all freshers, had sat up in her room the whole of one night explaining how they all felt an urge towards physical and spiritual solitude.

"I don't think your hundred pounds will last very long," said Jane.

"How long?"

"A few months. I suppose you have to buy paints and canvases and things, don't you?"

"Yes, and they *are* pretty expensive. But you see I should be *frightfully* economical in other ways."

"However economical you were you'd have stamps and laundry and bus-fares and stockings and shoe-repairs. Is the studio furnished?"

"No. But there's such lots of furniture in our house. Too much, I always think. I'm sure I could have some of it."

"Don't forget the saucepans and bed-clothes and china and cleaning materials," said Jane. "Could you have some of those?"

"I expect so," said Leslie airily.

"Have you ever lived alone?" asked Florence suddenly.

"No. Actually not. But I've always wanted to. Why?"

"Oh, I just thought you might be lonely," said Florence.

"Oh, no! I'm sure I shouldn't."

"Oh. I'll get the coffee."

"And what does mamma say to the great scheme?" inquired Jane.

"Well, she doesn't really understand. She says it's a pity to spend my hundred pounds, and why can't I live with Aunt Sybil and attend the school from there?"

"Would you pay Aunt Sybil then?" Leslie wondered at Jane's insistence on money.

"Oh, I believe mummy said something about standing me a year in town with her."

"Why not, then?"

"Oh, Jane! I thought *you'd* understand. I want to be on my *own*. Like you and Florence."

"Yes, but we're earning," said Jane crudely.

"I know, and I think it's frightfully clever of you both. But every one has to be trained, don't they? Oh, Florence! *You* wouldn't like to live at home, would you?"

"No. I should hate to."

"There you are, you see," cried Leslie triumphantly.

"Black or white, Leslie?" asked Florence.

"White, please."

Florence put the coffee-pot down on the table and went back into the kitchen. Jane prudently shifted the pot on to Florence's plate and mopped up the wet ring on the table with her pocket-handkerchief.

Florence reappeared, sniffing forlornly at the curdled remains of milk in a milk-bottle.

"How sour do you think this is, Leslie?"

Leslie sniffed and replied politely that she really liked black coffee just as well.

"We ought to have a refrigerator," said Jane.

"Yes, why not?" said Leslie.

"Oh, my dear, they cost pounds and pounds," said Florence, handing Leslie her black coffee.

It was funny, thought Leslie, how the conversation circled round and round the question of expense. Surely Jane and Florence used not to talk such a lot about money? At school and afterwards at home one took money more or less for granted. Of course mummy sometimes said she couldn't afford something. She had said that at first about the new car they had recently got, but she had decided to buy it in the end, saying that it would probably be more expensive after all to run the old one for another year. "Can't afford" had always seemed to Leslie a figure of speech, a convenient excuse for not buying something one didn't very much want. It was odd to reflect that "can't afford" to Jane and Florence meant that they had quite simply not got the money.

"What's Aunt Sybil like?" asked Jane.

"She's terribly kind," replied Leslie cautiously. "And she has a very nice house and it would be frightfully comfortable and all that. But you know I *do* feel that to really get down to it I must be quite on my own. Just paint and paint and paint without interference."

"Do you think she'd interfere with your free time then?"

"No, not exactly," said Leslie doubtfully, "but it would be so awful to have to waste time over dinner and that sort of thing."

"It wastes much more time buying things and cooking them for yourself," said Florence discouragingly.

"My dear, I think it would be marvellous to have dinner every night, and stockings washed for you and your laundry done and that sort of thing," cried Jane, adding mischievously, "Do you think Aunt Sybil would have me instead?"

"You *are* extraordinary," said Leslie, deeply disappointed by this misplaced enthusiasm for Aunt Sybil. "I thought you loved living on your own?"

"We do," said Jane and Florence, without hesitation.

"After all, it's fun giving up things, isn't it?" pleaded Leslie.

Jane and Florence, contemplating the chaste perfection of Leslie's white suit, expensive hat and tasteful handbag, promptly disagreed.

"No," said Florence simply.

"It's much more fun *not* having to," said Jane.

III

"Do you think we were rather horrid to her, Jane?" said Florence when the door had finally closed upon Leslie's slightly chastened enthusiasm.

"No. After all, we did promise to tackle mummy for her on Saturday. I believe Leslie means the party to turn into a mummy-tackling entertainment, you know."

"I rather like Mrs. Fisher. I stayed with them once years ago, you know. I didn't think she was at all the assertive mamma. I think Leslie is silly about not being understood. Funny. I used to like Leslie so much, and now I don't seem to get on with her very well."

"Understood only too well, I should say," remarked Jane, yawning and kicking off her shoes. She continued to comment in jerks on Leslie's character, while clearing away the slightly ghoulish remains of supper. "Trouble with Leslie is she thinks life in London is a perfect orgy of self-expression. . . . Is this all the bread we've got for tomorrow's breakfast? . . . Didn't she remind you of our first year at Oxford? All that about the home atmosphere being cluttered up with non-essentials. Non-essentials! It was a lovely expression.

I haven't used it for years. Don't you remember—damn! Sorry, I'll wipe it up. . . . It's funny her going like this, isn't it? I always thought her the perfect daughter. She used to do it beautifully."

"She wants to 'live her own life'," said Florence, gingerly fishing a cigarette end out of a coffee-cup.

"Yes. So did I once. Well, of course you and I do—in a sense. Only Leslie wants it both ways."

"Oh, well! It is rather bad luck on her having to live in the country with her mother if she wants to be up here. Only I should think the country must be lovely in this weather, wouldn't you? Still, I don't mind having a quiet word with Mrs. Fisher on the subject."

"The worst of self-expression is that it's so damned expensive," said Jane.

"I don't express myself very well by banging a beastly typewriter all day," said Florence, the anxieties and drudgery of the day flooding back into her mind, so that she suddenly felt very tired.

"It's funny how *young* Leslie seems now," said Jane, and dismissed the subject by turning on the bath-water. "Shall I be quick or don't you want one tonight?"

"No. I can't be bothered." How horribly close tomorrow's work loomed! Florence took off her stockings and noticed a large hole in one heel. Oh, dear! She was too tired to mend it tonight and tomorrow morning there wouldn't be time. Time! There was never time for anything if you had a job in London. No time to darn stockings, no time to shop, no time to have your hair done, no time to write letters, worst of all no time to do nothing. Such an enormous amount of effort was needed to do the simplest thing. Even packing a week-end case was a nuisance, something to be put off till the last moment and then done hurriedly. There was Leslie's party on Saturday and she hadn't had time to think about what she was going to wear; but even if she did think about her clothes she wouldn't have time to *do* anything about them.

"Jane," shouted Florence, "how are you going to get down to Leslie's party?"

Jane turned off the bath-taps and said, "What?"

"How are you going to get down to Leslie's party?"

"In Henry's car," said Jane, and added candidly, "We'll take you down in the back if you like, but we can't take you home again because Henry and I are going off for the week-end afterwards."

"Oh," said Florence, her immediate reaction being one of annoyance at having to make her own arrangements for getting back to town.

"I expect Leslie could put you up, or motor you to a station, or something."

"You might have told me before so that I could have asked her," said Florence wearily, thinking of further letters to write.

"I did remember this evening. But I thought Leslie might be shocked," said Jane.

Florence suddenly realized what had hardly penetrated before—the implications of Jane's remark. In theory of course she was not shocked; but the idea did seem a little odd when actually arranged. Had Henry suggested it or Jane? Her speculations were answered by a cheerful voice from the bathroom.

"It was really my idea," said Jane shamelessly.

"What did Henry say?" inquired Florence.

"Oh, he was awfully pleased," said Jane vigorously soaping her toes.

"Oh," said Florence. There did not seem to be very much else to say. She did not know whether Jane wanted to talk about it or not. Moreover, she felt dimly that too much display of interest would be in bad taste. Of course these affairs were the merest conversational commonplaces. It just happened that she hadn't known any one well before who had actually put theory into practice—except, of course, Sylvia. But then she hadn't seen much of Sylvia lately and anyway she didn't know her nearly as well as Jane. There was nobody in the world she knew as well as Jane. Of course if a thing was theoretically right it should make no difference how well you knew the person who did it. "Muddled thinking," said Florence firmly to herself, stripping the day-cover off her divan-bed. Somehow this sensation of regret about Jane's decision, this silly unhappy feeling that it was all rather a pity had got muddled up in her mind with her own tiredness and feeling of futility. Something was making her feel extraordinarily depressed. Florence tossed about and listened to the snatches of song that floated in from the bathroom. Jane was singing bits of that old thing, "My heart is saying—"

> "My heart is saying
> He loves you very dearly,

The way he kissed you he was clearly
In love. Pom. Pom. Pom."

(She was probably doing it on purpose, for Florence's benefit.)

"My head is saying
That men are gay deceivers ever,
They fool themselves, but they are never
In love."

The bath-water began to gurgle away and Jane sang, "Oh, sell no more drink to my father." She seemed to be in the best of spirits. Probably she had stopped thinking of Henry already, reflected Florence. Well, whoever got hurt it wouldn't be Jane anyway. She hadn't lived all this time with Jane without finding out it was never Jane who got hurt. . . . Florence was suddenly shocked at her own savageness. I am in a beastly temper, she thought, and sat up in bed and turned over her pillow. Why should she be so angry at Jane's invulnerability? It suddenly occurred to her that she was probably envious. So many things could hurt her, so very few Jane. Envy, thought Florence, is at the root of everything. She reached out a hand and drank a whole tooth-glass full of water. How cunningly the mind disguised its base motives! When she had been so discouraging to Leslie this evening she had believed she was doing it for Leslie's good, to save her disappointment later. But of course no one ever really did anything for other people's good. It was simply because she had been jealous of Leslie looking so pretty and so untired when she herself had had such an awful day. And now she was jealous of Jane. Jealous because Henry wanted Jane and no one had ever wanted Florence; still more jealous because if things went wrong Jane wouldn't suffer. A clock outside struck twelve. Just fancy, in four hours it would be getting light again. Sleep seemed further off than ever. Of course envy was at the root of all (so-called) moral condemnation. That was why women were so hard on girls who despised the sex-conventions, because they wouldn't dare to themselves. It wasn't so bad if the girl "got into trouble" and had a baby and was deserted. Then people would be kind to her because they weren't jealous any longer. She had been paid out and could be used as an object of pity. And people always got pleasure out of pitying others. . . . During the course of the next two hours Florence drank three glasses of water, took two aspirins and found the motives of human behaviour ever increasingly base.

In the next room Jane slept as calmly as a healthy baby.

CHAPTER VI

I

"I CAN'T EAT in this blasted hot weather," said Florence fretfully. It was Friday, the day before Leslie's party, a perfect summer morning. A morning when the air was all a-shimmer with a golden warmth; a haze of heat in the blue of the distance; walls already warm to the touch and a triumphant giant sun riding up a deep-blue sky. But also a morning when everything was sticky; when hot hands smeared carbon smudges across clean letter-paper. A penance to be squashed close to another sweating being in a bus. A constant irritation at becoming more crumpled, more dirty. Finally crossness and exhaustion—and in the evening the melancholy prospect of another perfect summer day to follow.

"Wouldn't it be lovely on the Cher?" said Jane, and added wearily, "Damn, the butter's melting."

"Everything's melting," said Florence, her thoughts turning away from summer memories of trees and the river and a punt of books and fixing themselves distastefully on melting butter and perspiring hands and softening tar on the roads.

"I wish those curtains would pull properly in the bedroom, Florence. The blasted sun woke me up at six o'clock this morning. Absolutely streaming in."

"We ought to get a new curtain-rod or something."

"Yes."

But they both of them knew that this little matter of the curtains was one of the odd jobs that inevitably does not get done in a household where both parties go out to work. The curtains had not pulled properly all last summer. They would not pull properly all this. There would be occasional suggestions about a new rod, but of course nothing would ever really get mended.

"I honestly think I shall try for a new job soon," said Florence.

"You won't get more than you do now."

"I shall be more experienced." (As soon as the words left Florence's lips she was struck by their hollowness.)

"Will Miss Tiddleypush give you a good reference?"

"I shouldn't think so," said Florence in a burst of candour.

"I think you'd be silly to leave, then."

"Well, I can't stay on forever just because I don't think I should get a good reference if I left." There was a hysterical note in Florence's voice.

"The best agencies won't find you a new job until you've definitely left the old."

Unwelcome truths. Florence decided that Jane was not being helpful.

"I'm so tired of doing—of being—"

"'Chained to an office-stool,' is the correct phrase, I believe."

"I only wish I was chained to it. Some days I do nothing but run up and down stairs all day chasing flies. Honestly, Jane, it is a bit silly. I should be much happier—and incidentally much better—at my job if I'd left school at sixteen and done a secretarial training straight away and never gone to Oxford or anything."

"It is a bit silly, isn't it? But I don't see what else one can do now."

"Well, I don't believe I can do this much longer. I don't like it and I'm not good at it."

"It's this awful heat. Do you feel a call to teach or nurse or anything?"

"No, I don't. And even if I did it would mean years more training. Oh, hell! The only thing I want to do is write. I could do that all day and be perfectly happy—"

"Have you written anything lately?" inquired Jane, applying lipstick.

"Well, there's my novel—of course it's only about three-quarters finished. And I wrote a short story a little time ago and sent it to an agent, but they sent it back."

"Why? Wasn't it good enough?"

"They said they only read typed manuscripts. I keep on meaning to type it at the office, but there never seems time."

"Why didn't you read it to me? What was it about?"

"Oh, it was rather subtle—have you seen a card of darning-silk?—No, all right, I've got it. It was just about what some one thought in a bus."

"Oh, I see. Damn, I shall be late. Look here, I shan't be in tonight, so don't wait."

"All right. I shall buy ice-cream and eat it in the bath, like we did the other day. It's the only thing to do in this weather."

"You're right. It is," said Jane, banging the door behind her.

Florence, who was not obliged to leave the flat till about twenty minutes later than Jane, looked at her watch. Damn! It had stopped. She shook her wrist violently. The hands still pointed stupidly to ten minutes to three. Perhaps it wasn't wound up? Yes, it was. Bother! Should she run after Jane and ask her the time? Her imagination took her rapidly out of the flat door, along the passage, two flights of stairs, the landing where the carpet was loose, more stairs—no. It was too much fag. It was rather slack of them really never to bother to wind up the clock, which now said three minutes to six. What a pity it wasn't three minutes to six that evening! Perhaps there was some one in the corridor who could tell her the time. No, there was no one there. Why hadn't the boy taken away those dirty milk-bottles though? They looked awful sitting there on the doorstep. Florence shut the door on their awfulness and her eye fell idly on the telephone. Brilliant inspiration! She would ring up the telephone exchange and ask them the time. She took off the receiver.

"Number, pliss?"

"Er—I don't want a number. I could, could you tell me the time?"

"What is your number, pliss?"

Bother! They counted it as a call, did they? How mean! She gave the information a little resentfully.

"The time by the exchange clock is eight-fifty-two," replied the clear pinched voice.

Resisting an impulse to say, "Sorry you've been troubled," Florence replied meekly, "Thank you," replaced the receiver and wandered back into the sitting-room. Eight-fifty-two. Twelve minutes to nine, she thought comfortably and incorrectly. Needn't start for another ten minutes or so. Another cup of tea and a cigarette. She sat down on the arm of a chair, and picked up a copy of her old school magazine which had arrived that morning. Fancy it's being still so much the same. Fancy it's going on and on like that! Fancy her having pressed her unfortunate parents to pay some enormous sum like five guineas in order that she might become a life-member of the Old Girls' Association. Fancy, thought Florence ungratefully and unkindly, fancy their being idiots enough to do so. Now the magazine would go on and on and on arriving. One never read it. One was not ruthless enough to put it into the waste-paper basket immediately. It hung about the flat, collecting dust. It found its way into that funny sort of heap (one could hardly call it a pile) on the bottom shelf of the bookcase, doubled up under a book of snapshots, mostly loose (last summer's holiday, never yet pasted in) and some copies of *Vogue*, extravagantly bought and economically hoarded.

Perhaps it would be more sensible to read this copy at once and then throw it away. After all, it might possibly suggest to her some fresh ironical touch for her novel. Florence flicked over the pages hopefully. News of Old Girls (B. Smith is helping two mornings a week in a Girls' Club in Brixton—G. Robinson has been staying in India with a married sister), the contribution page (a poem about fairies by a precocious child in the Lower IV, an essay entitled "Learning to Skate"—good clean fun from the school humourist—some windy blank verse from the Upper VI), reports of house-matches, extracts from letters—Florence was disappointed to find the magazine so apparently innocuous. Convinced as she was of the evils of "artificial segregation" she had expected to disagree most strongly with the whole tenor of the paper. But (apart from a possibly slighting reference to the Soviet Union on page 16) there didn't seem to be very much in this particular issue on which to fasten her expectant disapproval. And yet it was a subject about which she felt most deeply. Otherwise why was she writing "Rubbing off the Corners"? Florence turned over another page and comforted herself with the discovery of at least one typical bit of hypocrisy. Nightingale House wanted to say how grateful it was to Miss Simpson for so kindly coming one Saturday evening to give them such an interesting talk on Greece. Saturday evening indeed! Gosh, how they must have hated it, thought Florence, flinging the magazine on to the floor. Jerking herself away from a contemplation of past Saturday evenings irretrievably ruined by lectures on Greece or the League of Nations or the Children's Country Holiday Fund, Florence realized with annoyance that she had forgotten to put the clock going and was once again completely ignorant of the time. Oh, well! Better go, anyway. She picked up a white straw hat and put it on; took it off again to see whether it was really so dirty as it looked; decided for the hundredth time that it was silly to wear white in London, and put it on again because anyway it was only for the office. Gloves, bag. The bag didn't really match, but she simply couldn't be bothered to change everything over into another. She banged the flat door behind her, leaving with some satisfaction the unmade beds and dirty breakfast things. It would be frightful if Mrs. Thing didn't turn up again today to clean the place, but surely she would!

It was funny. She hadn't thought about school for ages, and now all the way to the office in the crawling red bus she couldn't stop thinking about it. What *was* I like in those days, mused Florence, and succeeded in conjuring up an image of a lanky figure in a too short gym-tunic, straight bobbed hair held back from the face by a large slide, and long thin legs in black woollen stockings. Her suspenders were always breaking, she remembered, and the seams of her stockings were always going into holes at the heels. A hole in your stocking meant a bad mark for your dormitory. It was all part of the great game of not "letting down the house." Curious as it now seemed, this was terribly important. There was no sort of punishment attached to this crime. The mere fact of having done so was so dreadful that punishment would have been superfluous. Sometimes one cried in one's cubicle at night. For it is wrong to suppose that youth is carefree and gay and irresponsible. Florence knew that youth is anxious and intense and desperately conscientious—perhaps particularly in her case, because school had encouraged these natural traits of adolescence. It was all—from the house-mistresses' point of view—most excellent and satisfactory. Conscientious adolescents were more easily controlled than carefree gay irresponsibles. "You have been naughty. You have let down the house" sounded a far more impressive charge than "You have been naughty and a nuisance to me." Team-spirit, thought Florence, automatically showing a crumpled ticket to the bus-inspector, is a labour-saving device for house-mistresses. I should like to tell them so.

For some reason the fact that she had been so normal, so gullible, so impressionable at school, annoyed Florence very much, even though it had, of course, contributed largely to her happiness. It annoyed her more and more as she thought about it, until, by the time the bus was jolting down Regent Street, she was longing to go back to school and be as strikingly individual as possible. It would be fun, thought Florence regretfully, to be a problem to the house-mistress, an articulate problem, who argued about everything, and accepted nothing on trust. "You don't like me, Miss Bates, because I have individuality, which is very awkward for you. I rather sympathize but you can't expect me to fall in with your ideas to suit your convenience." Delightful picture! Or, when she was sent to the head mistress, as surely she would be, "No, I am afraid I can't agree to be a conscientious prig." Conscientious prig—Florence rolled the offensive phrase lovingly round her tongue. For a moment Florence played with the idea of rewriting her novel along those lines, of transforming the downtrodden Celia into a rebel spirit. Then she decided that her present method of portraying the evils of school life was perhaps subtler. To become more and more miserable was a deeper degradation for a child's spirit than open rebellion.

It was really rather odd that she had taken neither course herself.

The education of the young was an absorbing subject, thought Florence, stepping off the bus into the gutter, and catching sight of a clock. She suddenly saw that instead of being rather early, as she had comfortably imagined, she was in reality distinctly late. It was much more absorbing than tapping a typewriter. Perhaps she would have done well to be a school-mistress. Almost immediately she admitted to herself that she would have loathed it. The actual teaching would have been all right. She knew she had some natural gifts in that direction and plenty of communicable enthusiasm. But the atmosphere of a school! The appalling silliness of the girls! Well, perhaps it would be all right if one were a head mistress and not in too close contact with them. Florence entertained herself with a vision of herself, aged forty, poised, charming and humorous, welcoming a new girl. "Don't be exactly like the others, my dear. Cultivate individual tastes and don't believe anything is important unless it seems so to you. Always test the truth of anything people tell you for yourself. Never believe your elders simply because they are your elders." Well, perhaps it would be a funny school, but all the same she would be a very stimulating head mistress—and a very queer under-mistress, admitted Florence to herself with a sigh, turning in (ten minutes later) at the office door. Anyway these speculations had kept her mind off that horrible pile of yesterday's work sitting waiting to be done by the side of her typewriter. She cast a look of disgust at the filing-basket and one of impatience at her machine, and, trying unsuccessfully to look and feel like the perfect secretary, went off to collect her morning's mail.

II

Jane worked for a man, to Florence's secret envy, and managed both him and her job with an airy competence. Because she amused him and because she never appeared harassed, Mr. Earnshaw thought her a good secretary. She was, at any rate, a very pleasant one, and it was both unjust and natural that she should succeed where Florence failed.

"It's too hot to read half these letters and far too hot to answer them," had been her employer's amiable greeting that morning.

"A deck-chair in the shade and a copy of the *Rainbow* is about my intellectual level for today," said Jane. She was looking very brown and pretty in a striped yellow and white frock.

"The *Rainbow*? Oh, yes, of course. I read that too once," said Mr. Earnshaw reminiscently.

He dictated a few letters and gave her a pile more that required formal acknowledgment, and then retired to his room. Jane suspected that he was reading the *Morning Post*, but bore him no grudge for it as she tapped merrily away on her typewriter. The other girl was away on holiday. Business was fairly slack. Probably she would get away about five. Presently the telephone rang. It was Henry, tender and solicitous, and anxious to know if she were alone.

"Yes, of course I'm alone," said Jane. "Why, what do you want?"

Henry, it appeared, wanted to tell her he loved her.

"Oh, is that all," said Jane, gayly wounding him for the thousandth time, "I thought at least you wanted to make some dishonourable proposal."

She doesn't mean it, thought Henry, manfully resisting the instantaneous pang that this suggestion sent through him, she doesn't mean to hurt me, but, oh God, I wish she wouldn't talk like that. I don't know about next weekend, after all, I'm a man, it will be my fault if she's sorry afterwards. . . .

"Do you want anything special, darling?" inquired Jane casually.

"Just a moment. You're not sorry about next week-end, are you, darling? I mean I feel rather a cad when I think—" His voice trailed solemnly away.

"I shouldn't think then," said Jane, glancing at the pile of letters she had to work through.

"You're sure you're not sorry?"

"I'm never sorry about anything," said Jane with devastating truthfulness.

It was not very satisfactory, but at least it was reassurance of a sort, and Henry, who had lain awake most of the previous night torturing himself with uncertainty, recognized that it was all the comfort he would get.

"Where would you like to go this evening, darling?" he asked.

"Oh, I don't know. Anywhere."

"Isn't there something you'd like to do?"

Irritated, alas, as always by Henry's indecisive humility, Jane replied rather crossly that after working all day in the office in such frightful heat she thought she'd probably like to lie prostrate in the shade and be fed with ices.

"Shall I come to the flat then?" said Henry, pathetically eager to respond to any suggestion.

"All right. We'll have a picnic on the roof," said Jane, vaguely wishing she had suggested dinner at a restaurant and a theatre afterwards.

"Just us," said Henry, his voice thrilling with emotion. (How *could* he get like that just after breakfast?)

"Well, Florence will be in, I believe, but she said she was going to spend the evening in the bath."

"She can't spend the whole evening there."

"Yes, she can. We often do." (What *had* it got to do with Henry anyway?) "Eating ice-cream," added Jane as an explanatory afterthought.

"Oh, darling, it does sound frightfully bad for you."

"No, it's marvellous," said Jane patiently, "you try."

"Promise me you won't do it too often."

"I say, Henry. Have you got an awful lot more to say?"

"No. Why?"

"Well, it's just that I've got an awful pile of work here . . ."

"I'm terribly sorry." (It was maddening how one could always tell what the effect of any remark one made would be. If only he wouldn't always be so penitent.)

"Good-by, my darling." (Thank goodness he was ringing off.) "It will be marvellous this evening."

"Good-by."

Jane went back to her typewriter, but Henry, after replacing the receiver, stood for some moments before the telephone in a sort of trance. It was extraordinary the effect just her voice had on him. That sort of hidden chuckle in it sometimes. . . .

When she came back from lunch Jane found a copy of the *Rainbow*, neatly folded, lying beside her typewriter. The habit of fifteen years back immediately asserted itself. She turned at once to the last page and perused with every symptom of eager interest the coloured adventures of Peter and Pauline.

"Marzipan the Magician was my favourite," said Mr. Earnshaw, coming in while she was still intent on the paper.

"Let's see if he's still here," said Jane, reluctantly tearing her eyes from Peter and Pauline and turning over the pages in search of the versatile wizard. He was. Everything was, in fact, precisely the same from the green, red and yellow Bruin Boys on the cover (how those boys did laugh when Mrs. Bruin fell right into the bath!) to Bonnie Bluebell as irritatingly pat with her answers to riddles as ever. (Ha! Ha! laughed Bluebell, I guessed that one, didn't I? Now, can *you* guess this?) Jane and Mr. Earnshaw found themselves particularly appreciating the breezy enthusiasm of the Editor's Chat. "Well, now I must get on with my post-bag, mustn't I? What clever boys and girls the *Rainbow* readers are! Here is such a good trick to try on your chums. . . . Ha! Ha! How surprised they will be when they see how simple it is after all! Mabel will receive a splendid prize for sending me this smart catch!"

"Yes, *I* won a prize once," said Jane bitterly. "It was for 'Dolly's Birthday Cake.' You got a potted meat jar, one of the flat china kind, and stuck matches on it to represent candles and sealing wax for icing. Very clever. And do you know what happened to the filthy prize? It got lost in the post and never arrived at all! Of all the sickening swindles!"

"Ha! Ha!" said Mr. Earnshaw gravely, "the Post-Office gets the prize for *that* smart catch."

"Oh, look at this, isn't it clever?" said Jane, forgetting her grievance as her eye fell on the Editor's concluding paragraph. "'Well, kiddies, before I stop don't let me forget to remind you to ask daddy to buy you Tiger Tim's lovely Painting Books. They are selling out very quickly, so hurry up, boys and girls, and look out for my exciting news next week.'"

"M'm," said Mr. Earnshaw. Jane looked at him sharply. He was not really listening. He was turning another sheet round and round in his hands, scrutinizing it carefully. Apparently he was trying to find Wippity Woppety's fine catch—six fat fish, concealed somewhere in the picture.

"I know the one you haven't seen," said Jane, "look—there. In between his boot and the tree. That's the only tricky one."

"I saw that first of all," said Mr. Earnshaw proudly. "But look how many do you make altogether? One, two, three—"

It was past three o'clock before Jane settled down to the typewriter again. Some urgent letters came in by the afternoon post. People rang up to speak to Mr. Earnshaw, who insisted that he was out. Long and complicated messages were then taken by Jane; and Mr. Earnshaw, on receiving them, remarked annoyingly that he would have liked to have spoken to old So-and-so himself. After this he began to stand behind Jane as she telephoned, listening to her replies and trying to divine by this unsatisfactory means the relative importance of the callers. Jane, who found this the most maddening of all habits, bore everything patiently. After all, he had bought her the *Rainbow*. He was rather a lamb on the whole. If the work couldn't get finished, well, it was jolly well his fault. "Yes—yes—yes—quite, I'll tell Mr. Earnshaw," she cooed into the mouthpiece in a soothing and noncommittal voice. There were sounds of impatience behind her. I should like to slap him, thought Jane, and said politely, "Excuse me one moment, I believe I hear Mr. Earnshaw just coming in." She handed him the receiver with a winning smile, and successfully blackmailed him into doing his own work.

She got back to the flat later than usual and found Henry patiently waiting on the doorstep. He had a cardboard box under his arm.

"You didn't get off punctually, did you?" said Henry. He was prepared to be sympathetic, but Jane perversely refused to have a grievance.

"My fault," she said. "We spent half the afternoon reading the *Rainbow*. I've brought it back for you. Oh, Henry, it's *marvellous*. Exactly the same as ever."

"Never read it," said Henry. It was rather hard that he had not been given a chance of being noble about being kept waiting.

"Oh, if you've never read it—"

"Are you all alone with Mr. What's-his-Name now in the office?"

"Yes. Highly immoral, isn't it?"

"Is he in love with you?" inquired Henry gloomily.

"Oh! Passionately! Look out, Henry, that box you've got is dripping."

"I don't see how any one could be with you all day and not fall in love with you," said Henry, putting the offending box down on the table.

"Oh, darling! It's run all down your trouser-leg."

"Never mind. Oh, Jane, it is marvellous to see you again!"

"What is it in the box?" inquired Jane, postponing an imminent embrace.

"Lobster mayonnaise. I *do* love you."

Florence's key was heard in the lock and the embrace was again postponed.

"Hello, Henry."

"Hello, Florence."

"I thought you were going to be out," said Florence, trying not to sound inhospitable.

"We're going for a picnic on the roof," said Jane. (There wasn't enough lobster mayonnaise for three, was there?)

"Oh. Well, I've got an egg. God, I am hot." Florence disappeared abruptly into the bathroom, where she could be heard divesting herself vigorously of her clothes. Jane and Henry gazed silently at the mayonnaise and felt secretly both greedy and unkind.

"I say, Florence. Do you want the bread and butter?"

"Yes."

"Oh. Well, you don't want all of it, do you?"

"There isn't much. If I'd known you were going to be in—"

"Oh, no, you're right, there isn't much. I say, Henry, would you mind frightfully—that little baker at the corner stays open quite late."

"Let's go together, darling," said Henry.

"Well—wouldn't it be better if I took things up to the roof while you were out? I mean, it's fairly late already."

"All right," said Henry heroically, and added compassionately, "I expect you're tired."

"Well, it seems silly two of us going, doesn't it?"

Henry, who never found it silly to perform the most trivial errand in Jane's company, departed obediently, and Jane, with much effort and sweating, carried up rugs and cushion and plates to the roof and laid them out in the shadow of a chimney-stack.

The roof was a little grimy, but the air was beginning to get cooler now and the view over miles of London roofs was exhilarating. She piled all the cushions under her fair head, stretched herself full length, and hoped ungratefully that Henry wouldn't be *too* quick. Henry, however, seemed to take practically no time. He appeared round the corner of the chimney-stack with a large loaf under his arm and a beaming smile on his honest perspiring face.

"I haven't been long, have I, darling?"

"Very quick," said Jane, and felt suddenly touched. Touched by his devotion, by his obvious need of her, by the sight of his fingers unwrapping the loaf, by the thought that the poor pet had evidently bought the largest in the shop. She sat up and arranged the cushions and made it comfortable for him to sit beside her, leaning against the chimney-stack in great content. There were still moments like this for them. Suddenly, now and again, it would be as if they had never quarrelled; as if the Henry and Jane of three years ago, instead of retreating like ghosts into a dimming past, had slipped back, warm-blooded and alive, into their old bodies. At such times the Oxford days seemed only a short while ago, not a long way off in another world. Was it yesterday that they lay together in a punt, blinking at the patterned fronds of green above, each finding in the other the secret of utter contentment? "I didn't know falling in love was like this." The thrilled murmur of Henry's voice. The sound of a punt-pole on a gritty bottom, the swish of a paddle, the warmth of the sun on their faces. "Oh, Henry, darling—darling. . . ." The shyness and wonder of their first kisses. "Just to be near you, Jane, is so marvellous. . . ." A gramophone in the distance playing a tune that no one played now. The gurgling whispering river-water.

The lobster mayonnaise lay untouched, while Jane, remembering suddenly these things, stroked Henry's head and said, "Darling, you're sweet to me."

"You see, I love you so," said Henry simply.

"I know, I know," murmured Jane. The little short hairs on his neck were bristly to the touch. It was rather sweet the way his hair grew. "Darling Henry, I love you too. In my own way. You mustn't mind its being my own way, darling. You do see, don't you?"

"Yes," said Henry, wanting only to keep Jane a moment longer as she was, seizing her hand and kissing it, ridiculous tears pricking at the back of his eyes, "Yes, darling, I see." Lying with his head in Jane's lap he gave a long sigh. With one finger Jane gently ruffled his eyebrows. It was an old trick of hers, unbearably dear to him. He closed his eyes. The sharp pattern of the sky and chimneypots etched itself for a second, dancing, inside his eyelids. Jane's hand caressed his cheek, then lay on his mouth. She offered him each finger in turn, and he gently bit each one. Terribly silly, terribly sweet. Why should she suddenly choose this moment to remember these dear things? "This is just like Oxford," said Henry softly.

"We never sat on roofs at Oxford."

"No. But you know what I mean."

"Yes," said Jane, understanding. But we can't go back, she thought sadly. That's what Henry never understands. We must change. We must go on. Oxford was lovely, but it's over. It's over.

If only people could leave us alone, thought Henry vaguely and desperately, it would all be just the same as it used to be. We haven't changed really, sometimes it's as wonderful as ever. It's just that things come between us. I shall never love any one else.

Their moment passed. Neither had the power to snatch the other for more than a few minutes out of time and place and the implacable march of everyday events. The charmed circle in which they had once loved so securely now dissolved at a single breath.

Jane could not help noticing that the lobster mayonnaise was lying in the sun. Perhaps she should not have cared, but she did care. Lobster mayonnaise was expensive. It was impossible not to think of that.

They ate it with tea-spoons and bread and butter, and Henry was very obliging and went all the way down in the middle of the meal to fetch Jane up a glass of water, because she felt thirsty.

"Florence feeding?" inquired Jane, when he came back. Poor Florence! A pity there hadn't been enough mayonnaise for her.

"She was having a boiled egg," said Henry, and added as an afterthought, "out of a wineglass."

"I know. The egg-cup got broken."

"Florence looks tired," said Henry, who had a funny habit of noticing how people were looking.

"She's fed up with her job. The only thing is I don't think she's much chance of anything better."

"It's rotten how hard you have to work."

"Oh, I don't know. Not awfully. Come to that I suppose we needn't work at all if we don't want to."

"I can't think why you do."

"Can't you? Why, what do you suppose I should do all day at home? It isn't only that either. It's—it's one's whole attitude to life. Living up here in London I have a right to my own friends, my own opinions. I'm not accountable to any one for anything I do. I can't hurt any one but myself. Oh, Henry! You must see it's the only possible—the only decent way of living!"

"You talk as if your family were difficult to live with, but I think they're awfully sweet. They've always been terribly nice to me when I've been down there anyway."

"No, they're not difficult," admitted Jane kindly. "But of course if they knew what I was really like they'd disapprove."

"Nonsense."

"It isn't nonsense. I don't suppose we should agree on a single important subject."

"I don't suppose you'd talk about that sort of thing," said Henry, and then looked puzzled at this remark being greeted with delighted laughter.

"Oh, Henry, you *are* perfect. Darling, you're almost too perfect to be true."

"But, Jane darling, you do say such silly things. As if any one could disapprove of you!"

"Why, what do you suppose they'd say if they knew about next week-end?" said Jane, and then immediately cursed herself for a blundering fool. That stricken look on Henry's face! Oh, Henry, why are you so hopelessly sensitive? Hurriedly she tried to repair the damage her thoughtless remark had caused; not only, or even chiefly, because she was sorry at hurting him, but because she felt too tired, yes, literally physically too tired, to cope with the outburst of conscience she had unwittingly provoked.

"But they won't know and it's nothing to do with any one else anyway—oh, Henry, for God's sake, don't look like that."

"Oh, Jane. Jane, darling. *Promise* me it's all right."

"Of course it's all right. Oh, Henry, please! If you don't want to—don't! But if we do, at least let's be cheerful about it. By the way, I must get a wedding-ring, mustn't I? Oh, dear, what's the matter?"

"Oh, Jane—it hurts when you talk like that. . . . Darling, if only I could tell you what it means to me. So sacred and lovely."

Well, whatever it is or isn't, though Jane, it's not sacred. If Henry's going on like this I honestly don't think I can go through with it. Sacred! I wanted it to be fun, to bring us closer, to stop our quarrelling. I've said I will, and I will, but I must stop his going on like this or I shall go mad.

"Will you get the wedding-ring or shall I?" said Jane. She did not really mean to be so brutally practical, but she felt that if Henry did not become less sentimental she would slap him.

"You can leave all that to me," said Henry shortly, and he added in a low, hurt voice, "I don't know how you can think of such things just now."

Perhaps if Jane had not been so tired, if it had not been such a long and hot day, she would have let this protest go by with a mental shrug; but Henry's ill-timed fit of conscience had played on her nerves. He was trying to put too much on to her. Why couldn't he stand on his own feet instead of demanding from her a moral support she could not give? All this about "meaning such a lot to him" was a sort of way of trying to stifle his conscience. He wanted her to bear with him the burden of this sickly load. Well, she wasn't going to. She wasn't going to pretend any more. Jane, resentment seething in her mind, burst into an impassioned self-defence.

"You're just a muddle of sentiment, Henry. Of *course* you can think of 'such things' now, or at any other time. You can think of *anything* at any time," cried Jane wildly, "only you won't admit to yourself you can. You simply won't see that the whole point about a love-affair is that it's natural—not the muddle of second-hand emotion that you try to make it. Oh, God, I wish I could explain to you what I mean!" She battled fiercely among her jostling thoughts for words to express a conviction that sprang from the very essence of her personality and that the stimulus of anger was bringing to the forefront of her mind. "If you're genuine about things, *nothing* is incongruous. *Nothing* can shock you. Think of Shakespeare," cried Jane (meaning to explain, but the urgency of her thoughts carried her on), "think of all great creators. Oh, Henry, I wish I could make you see how important that is. It's only people who shut their eyes and pretend who can talk as stupidly as you do. If you were honest to yourself about loving and wanting me you wouldn't go on like you do. You think I shock you. Well, I can tell you you shock me far more and far worse. . . ."

At this point Jane stopped for breath, and seeing that Henry had gone quite white, faltered and said suddenly, "Oh, well—never mind. It doesn't matter." He would never understand, so what was the good? And it was really rather awful when he looked like that. She stretched out a tentative hand. Henry averted his face and immediately a final spasm of irritation ran through her.

"It's just that we're—different," she concluded hopelessly.

"We needn't be."

"What do you mean, we needn't be?"

The quarrel was dying away into a gloomy and hopeless interchange of perfectly meaningless accusations.

"I mean you aren't a bit like the real Jane these days."

"Yes, I am. I mean this *is* the real me." (The futility of it!)

"No, it's not. It's this beastly life is spoiling you. It's—it's working so hard and eating ice-cream in the bath and eggs out of wine-cups and—and that sort of thing."

"Well, I think it's much more natural to eat ice-cream in the bath than to sit at an idiotic dinner-table mouthing platitudes at the best type of English people."

"I don't. I think it's a pose."

"How *can* eating ice-cream in the bath be a pose? I suppose you'd like to think of me gathering roses in a linen overall in a Sussex garden."

"No, I shouldn't," said Henry, to whom this picture made a strong and immediate appeal.

"That's your type, really. Looks fragile, but a good little sportswoman. Standing on the terrace of a large country house in breeches saying 'Down, sir!' to a beastly spaniel."

"Don't be silly. You know I like you as you are."

"You've just said you didn't."

"No, I didn't."

"Didn't you? I thought you did." (Lord, what depths of idiocy!)

"I like you," said Henry heavily, "as you *could* be."

"I know. Ever so winning. Jumping up and flinging my arms impetuously round your neck when you come in. Half-darned sock falls to the floor."

"It would be better than having to wait twenty minutes on the doormat."

(Oh, this picking-over of the past for idiotic grievances, this resuscitating of wrongs barely felt at the time, these loathsome dragged-up accusations.)

"If you sit here much longer telling me how long you were kept waiting on the doormat you won't be home in time to see your sister before she goes."

It was a shot at random, as Jane had no idea of the time, but it was a lucky one. Henry, who had promised to be back by half-past ten to see his married sister and her husband who were dining with his family, looked at his watch guiltily, got up, and stood uncertainly among the remnants of lobster mayonnaise and dirty plates. He ought really to have been at home tonight. His family weren't too pleased at his going out anyway. But he had wanted so badly to see Jane again, to hold her in his arms, to learn from her lips that she really loved him. And even now, for one of Jane's kisses he would miss a thousand sisters. But nothing, he thought, neither quarrel nor kiss, ever came to a dignified end in his life. There was a thwarting spirit abroad which turned awry all things before their proper conclusion. He saw this spirit as something tangible, something with an evil grinning mouth and a spider-like body. Their anger would in time have dulled down, turned to remorse, been transmuted into tenderness; but a spidery hand had stopped the circling wheel. There was another appointment to be kept. Love should not die before it had flowered into passion, possession. The wheel was slowing—but if he could shout defiance at the spider-spirit just for a few brief hours, snatch away those thwarting clinging fingers, clasp his love to him. . . .

"You'd better hurry," said Jane. "There aren't so many buses at this hour."

III

Florence's novel did not go well that evening. She was working on a difficult chapter. Celia was by now to have reached a stage
of utter apathy. She no longer cried herself to sleep in bed every
evening. She no longer locked herself into the bathroom and wrote
poetry. She no longer implored her mother to remove her instantly
from school. She no longer, in fact, did anything at all. This is the
subtle part, thought Florence, and gazed thoughtfully at the half-
page of writing, scored with crossings-out. "'Get up, Celia,' shouted
the dormitory head. 'Yes,' said Celia. 'Have you stripped your bed?'
'No,' said Celia. 'I say, Celia,' shouted another, 'what answer did
you get to that sum about the two trains?' 'I don't remember,' said
Celia." It was all extraordinarily true to life, but was the subtlety of
it quite effective on paper? And yet how else but by pages and pages
of this was one to indicate Celia's mental apathy? Moreover, herein
lay the artistic climax of the novel, and the ultimate denunciation
of the girls' public-school régime—that Celia, who had spent the
earlier part of the book in protesting, imploring, and weeping, was
now so utterly cowed that she accepted everything with the mute
resignation of despair. Florence read the last half-page over again,
and wondered if there were too many "saids" in it. And yet there
was a subtle emphasis in this too. The monotonous repetition of the
word "said" might be intended to accentuate the contrast between
the child's mind and her mechanical actions. Or would the reader
miss this? Florence read it through once more, and decided that as
this was to be an especially significant chapter she would leave it for
this evening. The effect was intended to be cumulative, and cumulative effects involved a lot of careful writing. She was feeling tired,
and when she was tired her thoughts were apt to get out of control,
shifting about in her head, suggesting strange things to her. She
closed her eyes and immediately an imaginary picture sprang up in
her mind like a jack-in-the-box (but who had touched the spring?),
of herself seated before a luxurious dressing-table. She was exam-
ining a pearl necklace, while a lady's maid brushed out her hair.
Florence opened her eyes quickly. It would be so dull to be rich,
so dull to be rich. Now she was stepping down an old oak stair-
case, holding her long white satin train carefully to one side. Some
one was standing waiting for her in the hall. He took her hand and

kissed it—Good God! This time Florence was genuinely shocked at herself. *This is the only life I could live. This is the sort of thing I like.* She opened her eyes on the table littered with the pages of her novel. She picked up a piece of egg-shell off the carpet, and threw it at the waste-paper basket. It fell short. *How awful to live in a house full of servants! I am tired. I think I'll go to bed.*

But instead of doing so she picked up a hand-mirror and scrutinized her face.

When you look into a mirror the strangest thoughts come into your head. Florence believed that she was ashamed of nothing; but there was a little rankling core of feeling buried deep down in her mind of which she was ashamed and whose existence she therefore denied. All sorts of defences and barricades guarded this secret place. Scorn of "society butterflies" who "do nothing but chase after men." Avowal of independence. ("I don't think I could stand being married.") The expression of "advanced" views. ("Of *course* sex-experience is good for every one.") It was comforting to talk thus of sex as something every one knew all about, something one could experiment with at any moment if one cared to. Thinking like this, one built up more securely the barriers round that secret place. ("I couldn't possibly make a career of just being married." "A series of affairs probably suits some women much better." "'Some of this season's prettiest *débutantes*'—isn't it *disgusting*, Jane?")

Think, talk, say anything. Anything as long as you hide from yourself the shame in the innermost parts of your mind. The secret rankle and itch of humiliation. The cold ashy voice that suggests, "Has any man ever desired you? Will any man ever desire you?"

There is something hypnotic about looking into a mirror. As if something had suddenly frightened her, Florence flung the glass down and began to undress as fast as she could. Apparently the barriers were not so secure after all; something in the concentrated gaze of her own reflected eyes, greenish-hazel under their heavy dark eyebrows, had pierced through her defences, almost caused the barriers to crumble away. For one moment, terrifying in its suggestion of ultimate loneliness, those eyes in the mirror, mercilessly scrutinizing, had almost bored their way into the secret place. Florence left her clothes lying in a heap on the floor and scrambled into bed. *I must go to sleep quickly. I'm tired, it's late. I'm tired, it's late. I must go to sleep quickly.*

Chapter VII

"Fear," explained Sylvia to her parents as the soup went out and the fish came in, "is due entirely to an association of ideas."

"Is it really, darling?" said her mother. (The plates weren't very hot, were they?)

"For instance," said Sylvia, "you can teach a baby to be absolutely terrified of its food." She paused impressively. She was prepared to talk on the subject indefinitely.

"How?" asked Henrietta amiably.

"Baby?" said Mrs. Perry, her attention suddenly arrested. "Terrified? Nonsense. Poor little thing."

"There have been experiments in America. Whenever you give it its bottle you let off a pistol behind its head. In time the baby screams with terror whenever it sees its bottle whether you let off the pistol or not. Association of ideas, you see."

"Whoever would want to do such a cruel thing?" exclaimed Mrs. Perry, her attention now thoroughly aroused.

"And the proper way to treat fear is to find out the association, you see, and break it down—or rather replace it by a nice one. I mean you could give a baby a golliwog or something to play with when it had its bottle—build up a *pleasant* association of ideas for it."

"A baby young enough for a bottle wouldn't care for a golliwog."

"Oh, well, mummy, you know what I *mean*."

"But where would you be after you'd finished all this pistol and golliwog business?"

Sylvia was very patient with her mother. "What do you mean, where would you *be*?"

"I mean what *good* would you have done the child?"

"Oh—*good*! You don't understand. This was a scientific experiment."

"Oh, I see," said Mrs. Perry, mystified.

"Where do you get all these queer ideas from, Sylvia?" inquired her father.

"Oh, daddy! They aren't queer. Absolutely every one knows a little elementary psychology these days."

"Do they really? I had no idea I was so ill-informed." He was chaffing her in the kindest way, as sceptical, as indulgent, as generous and as *infuriating* as ever.

"You're absolutely bottom of the class, daddy," said Henrietta.

"Yes, but Sylvia will take me in hand. She'll coach me privately till I surprise you all."

Sylvia smiled automatically at her father and ate her excellent fish. If only one's family could treat one as a *person*. One must humour daddy, the poor sweet, but it was rather pathetic the way one's parents laughed at anything they couldn't understand.

No one would have guessed that Henrietta was trying so hard to say something. She laughed. She talked. Words were such easy things. Something came into your mind and you said it. You could say anything you wanted to, couldn't you? After all, it wasn't anything difficult she wanted to say. Nothing to be afraid of. Fear is due to the association of ideas. What ideas? No, that's wrong—build up a *pleasant* association. Ask mummy to hand me a golliwog as I say it. Have I laughed out loud? No, I only laughed in my mind. Nobody heard. I'm saying something else out loud. I can hear myself asking daddy about his golf. Go on, say it now. Say it while you're thinking about something else. It's easier that way. As if you had just remembered. Oh, mummy, Phyllis rang up while you were out and asked me to stay with her this week-end. I said I would. Go on, say it.

"Oh, and do you know who I met at the club-house?" continued Mr. Perry, placidly helping himself to mustard, "a fellow who's just moved near here—no, no cauliflower for me, thank you—name of Atkins. Has a daughter about your age, Henrietta. Awfully nice girl. Came to fetch him in the car. Wants us all to go over to tea and tennis next Sunday."

Next Sunday! Now I shall have to say it, now I shall have to say something. Oh, I can't, Phyllis rang up and—

"No, wait a minute," continued Mr. Perry. "It wasn't next Sunday. It was Sunday week. Were you going to say something, Henrietta?"

"Me? No, nothing."

"Bella Atkins," said Sylvia. "I met her a week ago at tennis with the Robinsons." (Poor daddy. Did he really think the Atkins girl a nice type?)

"That will be quite possible, dear, I think. What about you two? That's very nice, then. Did you accept, Charles?"

"Yes. No, I said you'd phone when I got back," said Mr. Perry, reproducing, without intending to, the sequence of his replies. He had been carefully trained by his family never to accept invitations without leaving a possible loop-hole, but he usually remembered this after he had already accepted.

"I'll write a note," said Mrs. Perry. (It was a little awkward phoning a strange house.)

"I wish my tennis hadn't gone off so this season," said Henrietta. (Oh, mummy, by the way, Phyllis rang up—by the way, mummy, Phyllis rang up—while you were out—Phyllis rang up. . . .)

"You play very well dear."

"You try to do too much," said Mr. Perry, who was of the good old British back-line school of tennis-players. "It's no good running up to the net the whole time until you've got a sound drive. I'll give you a bit of coaching now and then, my dear, if you like. You want to stand square to the ball and—"

"Sideways," said Sylvia.

"You know," said Mrs. Perry, pursuing a train of thought of her own, "Mrs. Robinson was telling me the other day that they won't *allow* her little girl to serve underhand at school. I think that's such a mistake. An underhand serve is often surprisingly effective. I know I nearly always win my service anyway."

"Yes, you do, mummy." (We're nearly through dinner, I *must* say it before dinner's over. Anybody can say anything if they try. Oh, mummy, Phyllis—)

"You wouldn't in good tennis," said Sylvia.

"I think we sometimes have some *very* good tennis here, dear," said Mrs. Perry gently. She had always enjoyed the week-end tennis parties. Her husband, she believed firmly, had been considered a very good player in his day. He had taught the children to play when they were quite little things. Sylvia and Henrietta in cotton frocks and sun-hats. "I've got a grown-up racket, mummy, it weighs *twelve* ounces." "Please send me one of your *really* hard ones, daddy." Now they were bigger they didn't seem so keen on those family games. Of course it was sometimes a little awkward— Charles did like to win, and Sylvia would play net the whole time. One way and another they hadn't played so much this summer.

The week-ends got so booked up. Sylvia and Henrietta were out such a lot. Sometimes they hardly seemed to be in for a meal for days together. But anyway here they all were tonight, all in good tempers and discussing nice plans for the week-end. It would be quite like the old days to have every one at home tonight. The family circle complete.

It was a little disappointing that immediately after dinner, the family circle promptly dispersed, Mr. Perry to water his roses and Sylvia and Henrietta presumably to their rooms, each muttering something about letters to write.

Henrietta, panting from running all the way upstairs locked the door of her room. She sat down on her bed and ran fingers damp with nervous sweat through her short curly hair. I'm a coward, a coward. I haven't said it. I *must* say it tonight. There's nothing to be afraid of. Fear is an association of ideas. I mustn't think of being afraid when I think of John. I must think of something *pleasant*. Pleasant. The word suggested nice ordinary things. Strawberries and cream in summer, the shaded coolness of the veranda, her own room, coming home for the holidays, mummy's voice calling to daddy now across the garden. A jumbled confusion of happy thoughts, all bound up with the past, all associated with home. Pleasant! She couldn't think of John as pleasant! Fascinating, thrilling, compelling—but not pleasant.

Sylvia wouldn't be frightened, thought Henrietta, and picked up a book she had borrowed from her sister's bookcase. It was the sort of book she had recently taken to reading; the sort of book that made her feel sane and sensible and enlightened, and just a little sorry for her parents. She opened it at random and read, "The motives of female virtue in the past were chiefly the fear of hell-fire and the fear of pregnancy; the one was removed by the decay of theological orthodoxy, the other by contraceptives. For some time traditional morality managed to hold out through the force of custom and mental inertia, but the shock of the War caused these barriers to fall." It was all so reasonable, thought Henrietta. One had only to give a little thought to the matter to be convinced; although it was difficult to believe that the faintest repercussion of the "shock" of which the author spoke had shaken even momentarily her parents. Family life was, however, notoriously difficult and most rightly referred to throughout the book as a problem. Were mummy and daddy very much in love when they got married? Pondering why this idea appeared to her as faintly indecent, Henrietta flipped over the leaves and read: "The importance of the family, as it exists at present, in the psychology of mothers is very difficult to estimate. I think that during pregnancy and lactation a woman has, as a rule, a certain instinctive tendency to desire a man's protection—a feeling, no doubt, inherited from the anthropoid apes." Well, yes. Probably. But of course it would be no good telling mummy about the anthropoid ape bit. As a matter of fact, it was rather difficult to imagine her grasping any of the real argument of the book. Sylvia did of course occasionally regale her parents with choice snippets from what the author alluded to throughout as the "new morality," once indeed going so far as to remark in front of Aunt Agatha that female chastity was the direct cause of prostitution. It had not been well received. So far, alas, the new morality had gained remarkably little foothold among the older members of the Perry household.

Troubled by these thoughts of her parents, Henrietta flung down the book. It was very sensible, but wasn't it just perhaps a trifle—cold? A little remote from a world in which one's mother said, "Darling, why don't you ask that nice young man to dinner with us?" All that about anthropoid apes and things, thought Henrietta, doesn't help really very much. After all, I'm in love with John. In love, in love. I'd rather think of it like that, and she picked up a copy of a woman's paper in which she was following with interest the serial story. The human heart is capable of a limited range of emotions, but of an almost unlimited variety of expression, and Henrietta, it must be admitted, felt more at home among the language of popular romance than among the Latin sonorities of classical prose. The plot dealt, not for the first time in the annals of this and similar papers, with a situation universally and delicately referred to as a Marriage in Name Only. The editress of the paper was always sympathetically inclined to stories turning on this romantic (if improbable) state of affairs. The conclusion to such a story, while always eminently satisfactory, had the advantage of being morally sound. Without any suggestion of impropriety the hero and heroine could, in the popular phrase, Deny each other Nothing; and the solid satisfaction afforded by this proper and natural conclusion outweighed, in her opinion, the less respectable attractions of illicit love. "Women are Like That'" was still, however, only in its initial stages. In the last week's instalment the necessary misunderstanding had been manoeuvered between the heroine and her newly-married husband, and this, Henrietta knew from experience, would probably persist until the last instalment but one. "'I assure you I shall not trouble you again,' he said with a slight bow. 'Thank you,' said Jasmine coldly. He left the room, his shoulders square." Now, having satisfactorily quarrelled with her husband, Jasmine was going off to meet Robin, Robin of the persuasive tongue and "dare-devil" smile. Because this was a June issue of the paper she was going to bathe with him. (Had it been December she would have gone skating.) As it was, they swam out to an island together. "'I've been looking forward to this afternoon,' murmured Robin. 'You mustn't talk like that. You forget I'm married,' protested Jasmine. 'I can hardly believe that, it seems too—' 'Too what?' said Jasmine (obligingly). 'Too bad to be true,' muttered Robin, with a scowl disfiguring his handsome face." Time passed rapidly in pleasant chat of this sort, and Henrietta was not nearly as surprised as Jasmine on discovering that the tide had come up and cut them off from the land. "'I can't possibly swim all that way,' said Jasmine, sudden panic clutching at her heart. 'Don't be frightened, darling. Look, there's a sort of cottage over there. They might be able to help us.'" A boat perhaps? No, thought Henrietta, surely the authoress wouldn't be such a spoil-sport as to allow a boat on the island. She read on and learnt with relief that the only boat was out fishing and not expected in till the next morning. "'You'll have to bide till the tide goes down,' said the old woman," speaking in the dialect old women do speak in popular fiction. "'I could gie you a room for the night.' Jasmine stood as one in a dream. 'What do they call this island?' she heard Robin ask. 'They call it the Ile d'Amour round about these parts,' replied the old woman. Robin's eyes met Jasmine's in a long look. *Another fine instalment next week.*"

Bother! Probably, however, next week's instalment would be disappointing. It wasn't very likely that Jasmine and Robin would Deny each other Nothing so early on in the story—as a matter of fact, Henrietta thought regretfully, it wasn't very likely that they would at all. After all, the paper only cost 2d. You couldn't usually have the heroine Denying the hero Nothing under 6d.

However, it was all rather comforting, although of course it wasn't really terribly like real life. What would John say if he knew how stupidly she was behaving? Hiding in her room because she was frightened of her family, trying to bolster up her courage with silly stories, not daring, simply not daring, to go down and tell them she was going away for the week-end to a friend. ("They don't make a fuss about exactly where you'll be?" "Oh no!" [airily], "I'm just tell them I'm going to Phyllis. I often do.") I must be brave, thought Henrietta feebly, think of John, he's a soldier, he would admire bravery. She conjured up a picture of John, dressed (for her ideas of the army were a little vague) in the costume of the Life Guards, repeatedly repulsing the attacks of a ferocious enemy. I must be brave; she opened a drawer. Her hand knew the exact spot to find his photograph, behind the trinket-box under the handkerchiefs. It was, she thought, looking at the fixed gaze of the eyes, a strong face; and yet the lips (rather full under a small moustache) showed, she thought, tenderness. It was, reflected Henrietta proudly, the face of a man, not that of a mere boy; and it was rather wonderful to think that a man like Captain Fortescue—John—should admire her so very much. ("What I like is your spirit! I don't believe a girl like you is afraid of anything." "I'm not," she had replied untruthfully.) It was difficult to recapture the same fine bravado feeling when you were sitting alone in your room, surrounded by silly home-like things like teddy-bears and books you had at school and old presents from the family—things that reminded you unnecessarily of the past. Suddenly Henrietta burst into tears. It wasn't like it ought to be. It wasn't fair. It wasn't like in the books. Sobbing, she crouched on the bed, her face buried in the pillows, and her tears fell bitterly on the nightdress-case she had treasured for many years because Sylvia had worked it for her long ago for her birthday. Typical, she thought angrily. Fresh tears fell on the innocent embroidered rabbits.

Mrs. Perry, knitting and rocking gently in the hammock, allowed her thoughts to dwell pleasantly on her family. Henrietta, dear child, was so gay, so pretty. Other mothers might boast of their daughters' cleverness, of the jobs they obtained and held, of the wonderful opportunities afforded to girls in these days; but Mrs. Perry, while she lent a sympathetic ear to such prattle, rejoiced in her own heart at her secret superiority. Mrs. Robinson's Nancy might be doing so well with her house-decorating, Mrs. Clarke's Joan might be appointed private secretary to a director, Mrs.

Wood's Cynthia might be cataloguing a Manchester library; but Mrs. Perry's Sylvia and Mrs. Perry's Henrietta stayed at home—the most triumphant, the most silencing brag of all. There was, there could be, no higher trump in the maternal hand, and Mrs. Perry was accustomed to her quiet enjoyment of the envy either frank ("How lovely for you to have them *both*!"), or spitefully disguised ("But isn't it a little *dull* for them?") that the production of this card invariably provoked. By virtue of two daughters at home, Mrs. Perry, not unnaturally, considered herself daughter-bragging champion of the neighbourhood. ("But haven't you ever wanted them to take up some work, Mrs. Perry?" "No, I can't say I have. I don't consider office-work a real life for a girl. Of course Sylvia's head mistress was *very* anxious for Sylvia to get a scholarship to Oxford. She said she was perfectly sure of one. But I said, 'Well, where will it lead to?'") Mrs. Perry mused over that distant and satisfactory interview between herself and Sylvia's head mistress, the more satisfactory, in fact, the more distant it became. What an abrupt woman she had been, iron-grey hair, tailor-mades, horn-rimmed spectacles. Such efficiency of voice and manner was alarming. ("So I said, 'I don't think Sylvia is quite the type who *needs* a college training,' and in the end she agreed with me.")

Musing thus pleasantly, Mrs. Perry swung gently to and fro, creaking slightly. Brett, the gardener, must oil the hammock tomorrow. She lifted her eyes and saw her husband approaching her across the lawn. He wore an old green square-crowned hat and carried a watering-can in one hand. Dear Charles, she thought, and then, I must hurry up and finish these socks for him—for in such channels her affections naturally ran.

"Those Golden Emblem roses have got a touch of black spot," he said, and then, "Where's Henrietta? She usually helps me water."

"She's writing letters in her room, dear."

"Oh," said her husband, and sat down a trifle heavily in the hammock beside her and made several comments on the beauty of the evening and the state of the garden (rain was badly needed) to all of which his wife made the appropriate or soothing reply. And then,

"Where's Sylvia?" he asked.

"Sylvia? Oh, she's—she's writing letters too, I think."

"Who do they write to?" queried Mr. Perry, idly curious.

"Oh, my dear, I don't know. Naturally, I don't ask. Young men, I expect."

"Young men? Do you think they write as well as telephone? Ah, well, it's cheaper." Mr. Perry had almost given up drawing his daughters' attention to the quarterly telephone bill. It seemed to make little difference. Indeed, since Henrietta had been home as well as Sylvia, the account had soared to such proportions as to make a further deposit necessary. Curiously enough, his wife gave him little support in this matter. "You can't expect them not to ring up their friends, dear." Mr. Perry did not, of course, expect them not to ring up their friends, but he did expect a few of their friends to live nearer than forty miles away. But this apparently was not so. Nor, it seemed, was it possible to ring up during the cheaper times, after seven o'clock in the evening for instance. It was explained to him that Sylvia and Henrietta's friends were never in after seven o'clock in the evening. The only time, in fact, when one could be sure of finding them in was before they got up in the morning. It was unfortunate that this was also the most expensive time of the day. Unfortunate, but obviously nobody's fault.

"I want to speak to Sylvia some time about those arrangements I told you about, dear. Do you think she'll be writing letters all the evening? Shall I go up and ask her?"

"*Call* up and ask her, dear," suggested Mrs. Perry tactfully. (It was never very wise to go into Sylvia's room while she was engaged there. She had the most disconcerting habit of covering up her writing with blotting-paper.)

Walking round to the back of the house, Mr. Perry dutifully addressed his daughter's window.

"Sylvia! Sylvia!"

Her head appeared and a non-committal "Hullo?" wafted down to him.

"Have you nearly finished your letters?"

"Letters? Oh—er—yes. Well, yes, sort of. Well, actually not quite."

"Well, when you have, will you spare me a few minutes? There's a little matter I want to go into with you."

Surely there had been nothing in his tone to alarm her? Perhaps it was only because her face was partly in shade that he fancied he discerned a faint look of apprehension at his words. He felt prompted to reassure her.

"Something nice," he called up genially. A little surprise he had planned. It would be as well for her to understand how she stood financially, and fortunately he was in a position to be fairly generous.

"I won't be long," she said and vanished from the window. He strolled round the side of the house, whistling gently. The garden, the tennis-lawn, his rose-trees, his orchard—each of his possessions impressed him favourably with the solid comfortable pride of ownership, the gentle durable satisfaction that replaced the ambition of youth and was on the whole so much more satisfactory than that heady urge. He bent to pick up a leaf from the lawn and, straightening his back, took a deep breath of the evening air, seeming to draw into himself with it a sensation of permanence, of durability. A house, a garden, children—these are the things a man works for, he thought, these are the things that remain. He heard a footstep, and, turning, saw his daughter coming across the lawn towards him.

"Oh, there you are, Sylvia. Just come for a little stroll round the garden with me. I want to explain a little matter to you—a financial arrangement that concerns you."

"Me, daddy?"

"Yes, you. Sure you won't be cold in that thin frock?"

"Cold? Good Lord, no."

"Very well. The position is this, my dear. When a man comes to my age he likes to think that his family is adequately provided for in all circumstances." He paused for Sylvia to express surprise at such a premature anxiety. She did not.

"Now neither your mother nor myself is in the least anxious for you to get married. We hope to have you with us for many years yet. On the other hand, we think it right that you should know that in the event of your marriage you would not be entirely unprovided for. A father has a certain duty to his children. . . ."

This is very slow, thought Sylvia, I wonder what daddy is working up to.

Mr. Perry, who was enjoying this little conversation, continued in a leisurely, amiable voice to tell his daughter of a father's duty. Of the necessity for not underrating through ignorance the value of money. Of his conviction that married life was on the whole the best, in fact the only "career" for a woman. Of the satisfaction that wise spending gave, of the security that wise saving afforded. While he talked a secret satisfaction swelled gently within him. It was only just, it was only his due that he should speak with authority on this subject. He *knew*. This was a right that he had earned, and as he talked it began to seem to him important that he should speak out and let people know of the danger that lay in slipshod thinking on this vital subject.

"Even though I would be the first to admit that money is not everything, Sylvia, I should like to feel sure that my family realizes that it is a thing to be treated with respect."

"Yes, daddy," said Sylvia, and thought—Polonius!

"Never trust any one, Sylvia, who is careless of his own or another's money. I am not trying to lay down the law to you but I would impress on you—"

"That you don't believe in 'living on faith'!" suggested his daughter.

"'Living on faith!'" exclaimed Mr. Perry, "What in the name of God is 'living on faith'?"

"That's just what it is, daddy. In God's name, I mean. You know the Buchmanites do it. You trust in God and the money comes."

"That's nonsense and it's dangerous nonsense," said Mr. Perry, severely. "Don't listen to any one who talks like that. Every one ought to have their money affairs in proper order and be able to estimate, as far as possible, what their income should be. I hope you don't consider yourself a Buchmanite, or whatever they call themselves."

"No. But it's rather interesting. After all, Christ was, wasn't He?"

"That's neither here nor there," said Mr. Perry, rather startled at hearing this name on the lips of his daughter, who had for the past few years consistently refused to accompany her mother to church.

"And the first Christians were Communists, weren't they?" pursued Sylvia.

"All this has nothing to do with what we're discussing," declared Mr. Perry, firmly haling the argument back from the inappropriate ground whither it had so curiously strayed. "I want to explain to you where you yourself stand financially. Now in the event of your marriage I have decided to settle a certain sum of money upon you. I shall of course do the same for Henrietta, when the time comes, but she's still only a child. It is, of course, quite a usual procedure. But fortunately," (again that secret satisfaction) "fortunately I am in a position to be fairly generous to my children. Without being exactly a rich man I think I should describe myself as being comfortably off."

"I'm sure you are, daddy," agreed Sylvia amiably.

"There are expenses in keeping up a place like this that you wouldn't think of," returned her father.

"Are there?"

"There are, indeed. However, as I say, I do not consider myself a poor man." He paused impressively. "I propose to settle a sum of ten thousand pounds on you—that is, in the event of your marriage."

"It sounds a great deal," said Sylvia, thinking of ten thousand a year.

"Invested in British government securities—that, I may say, would be a condition—it would bring you in an income of rather more than three hundred pounds a year."

Oh, of course—income. Three hundred pounds. It sounded almost as much.

"It's awfully kind of you, daddy."

"It's a considerable sum," he told her, watching her face for the look of dawning surprise and gratitude that might be expected.

"Yes. Honestly, daddy, I think it's too much. I—I think I'd almost rather not."

Surprise dawned, but not on Sylvia's face.

"Rather not? Don't talk nonsense, Sylvia. Rather not! Why on earth not?"

"Well—you see, I'm afraid if I ever *do* marry—and as a matter of fact I don't really approve of marriage, you know—I'm afraid you'll simply hate my husband."

Completely taken aback by these astonishing assertions, Mr. Perry contemplated his daughter's slightly flushed face with amazement.

"My dear Sylvia! Why on earth this extraordinary idea! Tell me, my dear"—an illuminating idea occurred to him—"have you fallen in love with some one—some one not of your own class? Some one socially impossible? You needn't be afraid to tell me, you know." He glanced wildly round for inspiration. "The gardener, for instance?"

It was with some relief that he saw his daughter shake her head. For a nightmare instant he had seen himself warmly shaking Brett by the hand and waving him to a seat on the drawing-room sofa.

112 | URSULA ORANGE

"No, daddy. I don't mean anything like that. I'm not proposing to marry any one for ages, anyway. But if I ever *do*—I mean I don't suppose he'll be *socially* impossible—you don't meet many people like that, do you? At least, I don't—but I should think he'd almost certainly be, from *your* point of view, quite *intellectually* impossible."

Mr. Perry heaved a sigh of relief. Intellectually impossible. That was far less serious.

"Are you," he asked with restraint, "thinking of any one in particular?"

"Oh, no, I mean just any one I should like would think so differently about things, that—that—well, I mean that I should think you'd prefer not to help me to get married to him. Or are you only going to give me the money if you like him?"

"Don't raise such ridiculous questions, Sylvia. I should like you to marry some one who would make you really happy. Neither your mother nor I would expect to influence your decision in the least— that is to say, of course, so long as he was reasonably—well, you know what I mean. Not absolutely impossible in any way. Really, my dear, you talk as if I were a Victorian stern father. You ought to know me better than that."

"Sorry, daddy. I honestly don't mean to be ungrateful. Would you be terribly disappointed if I didn't take the money?"

Mr. Perry wished his daughter would not talk so crudely about "taking the money." It was not the correct phrase. "Settle an amount" were the words he had used. His disappointment made him speak sharply.

"I simply don't understand you, Sylvia. I wish you could be a little more explicit about exactly what we are going to object to in this utterly vague son-in-law."

"Oh, daddy, just *everything*. I mean he'd think differently about *everything*."

"Do you mean he'd want to live on faith? Have you got engaged to a Buchmanite?" inquired Mr. Perry resignedly.

"No. I tell you it's nobody in particular. And anyway I'm not at the moment a Christian, you know. More likely I should think he'd disapprove of marriage altogether."

"Well, if he disapproved of marriage altogether I shouldn't think the question would arise," said Mr. Perry, not without reason.

"We might want to get married—for convenience's sake," said Sylvia darkly. "I mean we *might* decide we wanted children."

"In that case I should think you'd be glad of the money—for convenience's sake," suggested Mr. Perry. It seemed to him madness that his daughter should stand on the lawn and calmly contemplate a course of conduct for which marriage would be merely, in the last extremity, a "convenience." However, there was apparently no immediate cause for alarm, and Heaven defend him from provoking his daughter to give him a fuller exposition of her views on marriage—he had, from time to time, heard enough of the "new morality" to be anxious to avoid at all costs further elucidation of this immoral rubbish.

"I don't think it would be fair to take your money under false pretences," said Sylvia.

There was no doubt that the idealism of youth could be extraordinarily irritating.

"There's no false pretences about it," he said. "Naturally—oh, my dear child, do talk sense. Of course I don't expect you young people to agree with me over a great many things. It wouldn't be natural if you did. Every generation," he continued more gently, "has a different point of view. You mustn't think I don't appreciate that. Why do you always think we can't understand? Perhaps we don't always agree. But at least we can understand that you want to think out things for yourself." He felt her softening and added unwisely, "Although, believe me, my dear, when you're a bit older you'll find that we aren't so wrong after all."

"I don't think I shall ever think the things important that you do," said Sylvia with a pathetic and provoking conviction. "You see, we—at least I mean me and the sort of person I care about—don't think tradition and property and money and that sort of thing matters at all. As a matter of fact, it's most of it wrong. It takes rather a long time to explain—"

"You needn't bother," said her father. He extracted a certain grim humour from the picture of Sylvia, clad in expensive simplicity, well-nourished from the excellent meals prepared in her father's household, standing in her pretty, unpractical high-heeled shoes on the lawn before him and assuring him of the utter unimportance of property and money. But beneath his amusement his baffled generosity irked him. Silly, silly little girl!

"I'm sorry, daddy," reiterated Sylvia. "Do you think me horribly ungrateful?"

"I think you're mad," said her father candidly.

"Do you? I was afraid you would," said Sylvia, with just the faintest trace of satisfaction in her voice. It is always a little gratifying to be thought mad because of one's convictions. The mantle of the martyr is not an unbecoming garment.

"Or rather," continued her father crushingly, "more likely, temporarily insane. I shan't consider that this conversation has come to any reasonable conclusion. We won't say any more about it for the present. . . . By the way, exactly how old *are* you?"

"Twenty-four, daddy."

"Twenty-four! Good gracious, I should have thought—well, never mind. Do you know, by the way, whether your sister shares in your very odd convictions as to the unimportance of money?"

"Henrietta? Oh, I shouldn't think so. She's hardly reached the stage of really thinking things out for herself yet, you know. She's awfully young in mind still."

"Let us hope that she will remain mentally arrested then. Good night, my dear."

"Good night, daddy. I do think it frightfully nice of you to have thought of it. It's just—well, you do understand I can't accept it, don't you?"

"I don't understand in the very least, my dear. It's the privilege of the old. Good night."

"Good night."

It was quite the most puzzling conversation he had ever had with her, and it continued to worry him even though he tried to dismiss it from his mind as merely the latest of Sylvia's fads. Of course, ever since she had left school she had expressed from time to time the most extraordinary opinions; but these, fortunately, had never, to his knowledge, had the slightest practical bearing on her own life. It was, he thought, the first time he had ever known one of her fads stand in the way of something she wanted to do—for, surely, little as she apparently realized the value of money, she should be glad of the prospect of three hundred a year of her own when married. As a matter of fact he had rather thought that the suggestion might have come at an opportune moment. Sylvia had always gone about with plenty of young men, but recently it had seemed to be this fellow

Claud most of the time. Although Sylvia never allowed the family more than a glimpse of him now and again, Mr. Perry had felt considerably drawn to this young man. He had apparently a job, and certainly a pleasant appearance and good manners—more than could be said for some of Sylvia's and Henrietta's young friends. Mr. Perry was quite alive to the difficulty of making a sufficient income for two these days, and had been prepared to be sympathetic to the point of positive helplessness over a marriage postponed through lack of funds—but no! Apparently not. Very odd. He had always understood from fiction and from the occasional confidences of other men that daughters could be very trying. But what in heaven's name had induced Sylvia to be trying in this particular way? Now if she had eloped with a handsome rogue or wanted to reform and marry an incurable drunkard—of course it would be extremely unpleasant—more unpleasant, in fact—but still distinctly more what one might have expected and not perhaps quite so difficult to cope with. Mr. Perry shook his head and went off to find his wife. Perhaps she could throw some light on the problem.

Sylvia, feeling a little of the exultation of the martyr, but rather more of the self-abasement of the cad, walked slowly upstairs. It was difficult to persuade herself that she had refused her father's offer out of very high motives. Really it had simply been a moment's impulse that afterwards, through obstinacy, she had stuck to. Suddenly, while her father had been talking about saving money for her and Henrietta, of his belief in the happiness of married life, suddenly the most awful feeling of caddishness had come over her. Poor daddy, making his little plans for her, arranging for her well-being, poor daddy who would disapprove so frightfully if he knew all about Claud and her. An inexplicable weight of shame had fastened on her, and, unthinking, selfishly not caring how she would hurt him, she had tried to throw it off her conscience by refusing his offer. Supposing—just supposing—Claud and she *did* ever decide to get married, well then, they must do it absolutely on their own. They mustn't be helped by her parents, because such an obligation made her feel guilty. That was what she had felt and what she still, to some extent, couldn't help feeling. But—poor daddy's face! That bewildered upset look! And yet one had to live up to one's private ideals, hadn't one? Even if it meant being a selfish beast? Dimly, glimmering faintly as yet on the horizon of Sylvia's mind rose the strangest of thoughts—were private ideals perhaps after all a bit of a luxury?

II

"I really shouldn't worry, dear," said Mrs. Perry, "I've always thought it best not to pay too much attention to Sylvia's fads."

"This is the funniest fad of all," grumbled her husband.

"She doesn't understand what money *is*," continued Mrs. Perry, who was naturally more concerned with restoring her husband's self-esteem than with investigating her daughter's odd opinions. "She's such a child, dear, still in so many ways. Don't worry. Leave it alone. In time she'll come to appreciate your generosity."

"It's not *that* I mind," said Mr. Perry, untruthfully, "it's just— oh, I don't know. The whole business is so funny."

But Mrs. Perry very properly continued to apply balm in the correct quarter.

"Living at home, as she's always done, she's never learnt to understand that money isn't so easily come by. She doesn't realize how hard you've worked for us all. She'll realize it later on when she has a home of her own."

"She doesn't talk as if she wanted any real sort of home of her own," said Mr. Perry, considerably comforted.

"Oh, Charles, dear, that's all just nonsense," said his wife with a kindly laugh. "Perhaps—we don't know, you know—perhaps she's had some kind of an absurd tiff with that nice young man—Claud, they call him. Probably it's simply that."

"He's not such a bad young fellow," said Mr. Perry cautiously.

"Oh, a very nice young man," said Mrs. Perry placidly. "He looks as if he could do with a little looking-after, too. Last time he came here half the buttons were off his coat and his trousers were filthy."

"They all wear filthy trousers nowadays."

"Sylvia is such a child at heart," reiterated Mrs. Perry (the thought was not an unpleasing one), "such funny little things upset her, you know. I'm sure it's best to take no notice. Now although Henrietta is so much younger in some ways she's much more *sensible*. I shouldn't expect her to do a silly thing like that."

"Here she comes," said Mr. Perry. Henrietta was advancing towards them across the lawn. "Well, miss? It's beginning to get a little cold out here."

"Oh, daddy! It's a frightfully warm evening," said Henrietta, who was lightly clad in a sleeveless white frock with bare legs and sandals.

"Glad to hear it," said Mr. Perry. "Reassure yourself, my dear. Henrietta assures us it is frightfully warm."

Henrietta, fiddling rather aimlessly with the hammock springs, gave her father a slightly mechanical smile. This was, of course, just daddy's way. He usually went on like this.

"Sit down, my dear," suggested her father.

"No—that is—I mean I just came out for a moment. Oh, by the way, mummy—Phyllis rang up. I—I forgot to tell you. She wants me to go there this week-end."

"Leaving us again?" inquired her father indulgently.

"Certainly, dear," said her mother, her attention concentrated rather more on the sock she was knitting than on her daughter. "Rather short notice, isn't it? Do you want the car? Will you be wanting the car, Charles? Can Henrietta have it?"

"Well, I don't know. Let me see. In the morning I promised—"

"Oh, it's all right about the car, daddy. You can have it. At least—as a matter of fact, I believe Sylvia thinks she's having it. She's going to this party of Leslie's, you know. I don't see how she can get there without it." (It was a relief to discuss Sylvia's plans.)

"Well, if she can't get there without it I suppose there's nothing more to be said," agreed her father amiably.

Charles *is* a good-tempered man, thought Mrs. Perry contentedly.

"Oh, daddy! Poor daddy! I believe she did tell you, you know—will you be able to get a lift to the club-house?"

"She told *me*," said Mrs. Perry, "and I must admit I had quite forgotten. I wouldn't have ordered chocolate ice for dinner tomorrow if I'd known neither of you was going to be in. Daddy likes cheesy things better."

"Sorry, darling. You know I think we ought to have two cars." (It was extraordinary what a good imitation of oneself one could give with hardly any effort.)

"Or one daughter," said Mr. Perry, affectionately patting her cheek.

A horrid pang shot through Henrietta.

"Good night, daddy," she said hastily. (Really, affection was more than one could bear in the circumstances.) "I—I must go. I—I've left the electric iron on."

"Good gracious me! I understood from your mother you were writing letters. Do you iron your letters before you send them?"

"Not usually," said Henrietta with a rather creditable effort at a laugh. "Good night. Good night, mummy."

"Good night, darling."

With pride and affection in their eyes they watched their younger daughter run gracefully and rapidly back to the house.

"Henrietta has rather sweet ways," said her father fondly. "She's more demonstrative than Sylvia. Sylvia would never leave what she's doing just to pop out and see us as Henry does."

"She's a dear baby," agreed Mrs. Perry.

Henrietta had made a discovery. If you run as fast as you can go, it stops you from crying.

Chapter VIII

I

SYLVIA AND HENRIETTA had always had a way of wandering into each other's rooms and talking late at night. "As if," said their mother, "there's wasn't time enough during the day."

But during the day one did not ask for reassurance, for comfort, and during the years when they had been growing up together there had been times when either Sylvia or Henrietta had been badly in need of such.

Sylvia, at fifteen, had pretended she didn't at all mind having her tonsils out. All through the day before the operation she had alluded to it with a dignified calm. "It will," she said, "be lovely anyway not to have to get up for breakfast." Mrs. Perry, much relieved at Sylvia's sensible attitude, had tucked her into bed at a suitably early hour and gone downstairs to tell her husband that the child didn't seem at all nervous and would be asleep in two winks. Henrietta, who knew better, had waited till her mother was safely downstairs, and then crept into Sylvia's room. With a tact beyond her years she had made no mention of the morrow's grewsome events. They had had a thoroughly jolly evening under the bed-clothes, reading by the aid of an electric torch a paper-covered book lent them by the housemaid, and eating a bag of peppermints. When Mrs. Perry had peeped in, on her way up to bed, to reassure herself that Sylvia was asleep, Henrietta had lain flat under the bed-clothes, stifling giggles. It was one o'clock before, yawning, she had eventually crept back to her own room. Sylvia out of sheer weariness had dropped asleep immediately and did not wake up until the nurse arrived the next morning. There was a pleasing taste of peppermint in her mouth, and not much time to be frightened.

On the day before Henrietta, aged thirteen, went to St. Ethelburga's, a frightful thing occurred. The shop sent the wrong kind of flannel blouses and there was no time to send them back. It seemed that Henrietta would be forced to appear at her new school, even to travel to her new school, in the wrong kind of blouse. How with such an appalling handicap was she to avoid the frightful blemish of conspicuousness, the worst sin in the whole gamut of a new girl's crimes?

"It doesn't matter in the least," said Mrs. Perry kindly. "You'll have to wear one, Henrietta, and I'll send the others back to the shop and tell them to send you the right ones. It won't take more than about a week."

A week!

"Are they *very* different, Sylvia?" inquired Henrietta mournfully. Sylvia had recently left St. Ethelburga's.

"Well, they are *rather*," replied her sister, obviously, thought Henrietta bitterly, trying to soften the blow. "They oughtn't to have these little pleats. The neck ought to be quite plain. I think they wear this kind at St. Hilda's."

St. Hilda's. The neighbouring and utterly despised St. Hilda's!

"Perhaps we'd better send you there instead," suggested Mr. Perry with a laugh. The joke was pathetically unsuccessful.

Before getting into bed Henrietta arranged her new school things on a chair in readiness for the morning. Black woollen stockings, black lace-up shoes, tunic, girdle, navy-blue coat and hat. The blouse she hid well out of sight underneath the coat. The thing was too frightful to contemplate. Don't think of it, don't think of it. Anyway, *tonight* it doesn't matter. She was still thinking of it when Sylvia, very grown-up in an evening dress, came up.

"I've brought you a marron glacé," said Sylvia and sat on the bed. Henrietta in striped flannel pyjamas looked incredibly young and awake.

"I've been talking to mummy," continued Sylvia casually, "and I thought if you'd like it too, I might drive you up to town tomorrow in the car to meet the school train that way. It would mean starting rather earlier, but it might be rather more fun than the train. Also we could go round by the shop and change those blouses. You could put on the right one straight away in the shop. I mean it would save all the bother of sending them back and that sort of things wouldn't it?"

"Oh, it *would*, wouldn't it?" said Henrietta, great waves of thankfulness and rapture breaking over her. "You *are* an angel, Sylvia."

"Oh, I rather want to go up to town anyway," said Sylvia. She stayed some time, talking amusingly of St. Ethelburga's.

"Old Pop, your house-mistress, is a dear. Funny nice forgetful old thing. You mustn't jump on her too much. If you're reasonably kind to her, she'll eat out of your hand."

It was enormously comforting. Sylvia left Henrietta quite cheerful. She went away, and let herself out of the front door. There wouldn't be time tomorrow to look up maps, so she must go to the garage now and see if she could find a map of London. She had never driven in London before. People said it was very easy, but what about the one-way streets? It would be as well to know where they were.

"Where have you been, Sylvia? You're shivering," said Mrs. Perry when she came back to the home.

"Oh, just around and about," said Sylvia.

"You're sure you don't mind taking Henrietta up tomorrow? It seems rather a hare-brained last-minute scheme."

"No, I should like to."

"Do you think she's enough experience to drive in London?" said Mr. Perry suddenly, "The traffic goes so fast and thick round Marble Arch and places like that. I wish there was room for you to go with her too. I don't like to think of her coming back alone."

"Oh, daddy, don't *fuss*," said Sylvia crossly. She added after a moment, "Anyway, I don't need to touch Marble Arch."

The best part of this sort of understanding was that both of them instinctively never alluded to it. Once Sylvia and Henrietta had overheard their mother telling a friend that her daughters "always confided in each other." Squirming with embarrassment, they had immediately been publicly rude to each other, greatly to their mother's bewilderment and her friend's disappointment. It was unthinkable that Sylvia should go to Henrietta and say, "I'm miserable. Cheer me up," or that Henrietta should say, "I want comforting." Nevertheless, on this Friday evening, Sylvia, after wandering rather aimlessly round her room, sharpening a pencil, combing unnecessarily her hair and reading through some letters preparatory to tearing them up and then deciding not to tear them up, gradually became convinced that her restlessness could best be dissolved by what she expressed to herself as "going and seeing how Henrietta was getting on"; and Henrietta, who was now furiously concentrating on her packing, a salt and soaking handkerchief flung angrily into the laundry basket, was vaguely conscious of the idea that if Sylvia should happen to come in for a moment before going to bed it would be rather nice and reassuring.

"Hello," said Sylvia, wandering into Henrietta's room and curling herself up in the window-seat. "Packing?"

"Yes. Week-end with Phyllis," replied Henrietta, wedging a pot of face cream in between two pairs of shoes. (This time the lie came quite easily.)

"Oh. You don't want the car, I hope?" Henrietta shook her head, and Sylvia wondered idly why her sister was apparently taking all her evening dresses to Phyllis's country home. "I've got this party of Leslie's on, you know. It ought to be quite a good show. Jane and Henry and—"

"I *like* Jane," said Henrietta with surprising emphasis. "I think it's wonderful the way she never seems to bother about anything."

"Well—yes. I mean I think it's very attractive up to a point. Of course, I suppose it's a bit selfish."

"I thought you thought people ought to be selfish."

"In a way—yes, I do."

"So do I," said Henrietta fervently.

"I mean the *right* sort of selfishness, of course," said Sylvia.

"Oh, yes—the right sort," echoed Henrietta.

There was a general feeling that an important distinction had been made.

"As a matter of fact," continued Sylvia, "I've been feeling a bit selfish myself this evening, and yet I can't help thinking I did the right thing. Daddy told me that if I marry a man he likes—at least, he didn't actually say so but that's obviously what he meant—he'd give me three thousand pounds. At least I think it was that. Or did it work out differently? Just a moment. It was an *income* of three thousand, I think. No, it wouldn't be as much as that, would it? Perhaps it was three hundred. Anyway, it was quite a lot. But of course I said no."

"Oh, did you? I don't think I should have."

"Well, I don't think I shall get married anyway, and certainly not to any one he likes."

"Daddy sometimes likes quite funny people," said Henrietta kindly.

"Well, anyway, I didn't think I could honestly accept it. I refused and the poor pet was awfully hurt."

"Poor sweet. Still, I expect you were right. I mean if you think you're right you *are*, aren't you? You've often said so."

"Well, I don't think I ever put it quite like that," said Sylvia, a little startled by this very potted form of the new morality. "What I've said is that it matters much more what you think of yourself than what other people think of you."

"Oh. It's the same idea, isn't it? I say, would you be an angel and fill this scent-spray up from the bottle?"

"You see," said Sylvia, gingerly tipping up the bottle, "that's why I think lying is wrong. Obviously lies in themselves don't do any particular harm. If a person finds out you've told him a lie he's no right to be angry. Why should he? You haven't hurt him. But almost certainly you've hurt yourself."

"Oh. Have you?" Henrietta felt a little disappointed in Sylvia as if somehow her sister was letting her down. "But surely lies are necessary sometimes, aren't they?"

"No. You ought to have the courage of your convictions. It's frightfully bad to be ashamed of anything you've done."

"Oh."

"You must never allow yourself to feel guilty, you know. It's frightfully bad for you."

"Is it?"

"Yes. Frightfully."

"Oh."

The point satisfactorily settled, Sylvia handed the scentspray back to her sister and leaned out of the window, sniffing up the early sweet smell of the twilight dew-drenched garden. The darkness which lay in opaque pools round about the trees thinned to a yellow veil in the open distance. Far off a train rumbled by. There was a flutter in the bushes under the window. Problems of conduct, thought Sylvia, dreamily inhaling long breaths of night-scented air, do not belong to out of doors. Or perhaps if we lived out of doors we should always think in tune with the world round us. Every morning we should feel vigorous and ready for work. Perhaps we might want to alter things up to midday. But in the afternoon we should gradually become more and more acquiescent, and in the evening there would be nothing left but peace and fulfilment. Every day, as the earth wheels, we'd be swept with it through a complete circle of human emotion. Light, twilight, darkness. Vigour, acceptance, repose. Light, darkness. Stimulation, rest. Perhaps if we were perfectly attuned to the universe we'd have sources of power we don't dream of, be able to draw strength from the sun, harness the tides to our will, ask the moon and stars to give us a harmony beyond our own striving. But we live in houses. We are excrescences on the face of the earth. The universe has disinherited us. Perhaps if we could ever get back again—Her thoughts ranged out in wider and wider circles of speculation. Perhaps the music of the spheres was more than a dead poet's dream. Perhaps an ultimate harmony might resolve all things. Perhaps. . . .

Caged in the small brightly-lit room behind her, Henrietta continued to pack in a slightly worried and distraught manner. Sylvia's casual condemnation of liars had upset her hardly-won, precarious peace of mind. Without thinking very much about it, Henrietta had more or less taken it for granted that in the interests of family peace disciples of the new morality were necessarily forced to a modicum of lying. It was a shock to hear Sylvia, Sylvia the proclaimed prophet and leader, insisting that this was not so, that lying was, in fact, definitely wrong. Just what mummy might have said, thought Henrietta disappointedly.

"I say, Sylvia! Surely you can't always tell the truth? I mean mummy would have a fit."

Sylvia, snatched back from her dreams of the wheeling world, replied casually, "Oh, well. . . . Let her have a fit. It might be good for her."

Perhaps it was good advice. It was obviously utterly un-takeable.

"Well, I think," said Henrietta, firmly closing the lid of her suitcase, "that if you want to keep on any sort of terms with your family, you *have* to tell lies."

"I think you're wrong, you know," said Sylvia, who, regarding the question from an academic point of view, had conveniently forgotten the lies she had occasionally been obliged to tell. (She had moreover become an adept at avoiding lying by quite simply not proffering any information.) "Although I would have rather agreed with you once. I say—look out. There's a bit of your red dress hanging out. You'll get it torn. The case is awfully full, isn't it? Why do you want so many things for Phyllis?"

There was a pause, at first casual, later tense. Henrietta faced her sister, defensively clutching the lid of the suitcase. A sharp panic suddenly leaped in Sylvia's mind. All this talk about lying to one's family—suit-case full of evening dresses. . . . Henrietta at supper talking such a lot Oh, let her say she's going to Phyllis. Please God, let me believe she's going to Phyllis.

"Well, since you don't believe in telling lies," said Henrietta in a terrifyingly casual voice, "I'm going away for the week-end—with John Fortescue."

There was a horrid pause. Never had a proclaimer of the new morality suffered so nauseating a shock at a disciple's conversion. For a moment Sylvia was physically incapable of speech. Henrietta turned her back and began relocking the suit-case.

"If you mean Captain Fortescue," said Sylvia at length in a strangled voice, "I wish you wouldn't call him John. It makes me feel quite—sick."

"Of course I mean Captain Fortescue," said Henrietta tonelessly.

She wouldn't, thought Sylvia desperately, show any emotion of any kind. Something must be done to shake her out of this frightful cold decision, this unnatural casualness.

"You mean the man with the invalid wife," said Sylvia brutally.

"I can't help that," muttered Henrietta.

There was another pause.

"I suppose," said Sylvia at length, "that he tells you that you've brought a new meaning into his life. That when he's with you he realizes what he's missed."

"No, he doesn't," said Henrietta, untruthfully.

"He's old enough to be your father."

"He's forty-six. That's not old."

"And you're eighteen. My God!"

"You've said yourself," retorted Henrietta, repressed indignation struggling with attempted calm, "that a man in the forties from the point of view of sex—"

"Don't talk nonsense," interrupted Sylvia rudely. "A man with a past like his—"

"What do you know about his past? Anyway, I thought you believed in people having lots of experience."

"I don't believe in a nasty old rip seducing a girl of eighteen."

"You're making it sound awful on purpose," said Henrietta, calm decision now thoroughly routed from her manner. "As a matter of fact it isn't at all like that. He's not 'seducing' me. I'm going away with him because I want to. I—I love him."

"No, you don't. He flatters you. I know. He tells you you're the most beautiful girl he's ever seen and he's proud of your courage and spirit."

For a horrid moment Henrietta wondered if Sylvia had by some extraordinary chance overheard some of their conversations.

"Anyway, what right have you got to criticize?" she cried passionately. "You've often said people must do as they like and experience is good for every one."

"I thought I was talking to some one who'd be sensible enough to realize that *all* old men who are unhappily married talk like that to pretty girls."

"He's *not* old. And if he is unhappily married—it's not his fault. You've often said people shouldn't be tied by their mistakes."

"I never said it was your job to console them, though."

A raging sense of injustice swept through Henrietta. That Sylvia, Sylvia who had first opened the door to her of an enchanting new freedom of thought, should now turn round and talk just as Mrs. Perry might talk of old rips seducing young girls. She felt as if her sister had suddenly and treacherously betrayed her, but indignation at this sudden withdrawal of support now ran in her veins like a flame, strengthening her resolution as sympathy would never have done.

"I think you're the most inconsistent person I've ever met."

"And I," said Sylvia, "think you're the most frightful little idiot; utterly incapable of distinguishing good from bad."

"I suppose what you do is good, and what I do is bad. You don't understand. I love John."

"Oh. Does he love you?"

"Yes, of course he does."

"Has he suggested divorcing his wife and marrying you?"

"I—I didn't ask him to. Why should I?"

"I shouldn't if I were you," said Sylvia nastily.

With every word her panic increased. At the same time it seemed to her that she had never loved her sister quite so much before. Poor darling obstinate Henrietta. Probably terrified to death, but facing it out. Not realizing in the least what she was doing. Poor darling baby, pretending to be so wise, so old. How could she save her from the touching silliness of her age? Only, thought Sylvia bitterly, by being beastlier and beastlier to her.

"Don't you see," she continued savagely, pity welling up strongly in her heart, "that silly little girls like you are just a godsend to Captain Fortescues?"

This shot had the effect of reducing the quarrel to a still lower level, to recrimination.

"Oh, go *away*," screamed Henrietta furiously. "I thought you'd understand. I thought you'd *like* the truth. I thought I needn't tell lies to you. But you don't understand about love. You don't know what it is. You don't know what we mean to each other."

"I do like the truth. It's just because I like the truth I'm saying this. I suppose you think this is a great romantic love-affair—"

"No, I don't."

"Twin souls calling to each other across the deep," continued Sylvia offensively.

"You know it's not—"

"The clarion-call of passionate love which defies all—"

Henrietta burst into tears of rage. Stabs of remorse tortured her sister.

"You've no *right*," sobbed Henrietta passionately, "you've no *right* to come and talk like this. Why, it was partly because of you"—sobs choked her voice—"why should you be so superior? After all, lots of people—you, for instance. Why, the way you used to talk you'd think—" She blew her nose miserably.

Sylvia realized with bitterness the truth of these tangled and incoherent accusations. She made a sudden decision.

"Listen, darling," she said firmly, "as a matter of fact, you've got it all wrong. Perhaps from the way I've talked you've got a wrong impression. I mean, we—that is, my friends and me—we rather sort of talk about anything, you know. But, as a matter of fact, there isn't *one* of my friends, not *one*," reiterated Sylvia solemnly, "who wouldn't be awfully shocked at the idea of you going off with Captain Fortescue like this."

"I thought your friends were never shocked at anything."

"There you are! I *knew* you'd got it all wrong. Of *course* we are *frightfully* shocked at lots of things," cried Sylvia triumphantly.

"Well, you never sounded as if you were," said Henrietta resentfully.

"Well, we are," repeated Sylvia firmly.

Was Henrietta wavering? Was the moment ripe for the suggestion dropped, ever so tactfully, that she, Sylvia, should ring up Captain Fortescue and intimate that there had been a mistake? Just a formal message perhaps: "Miss Perry is sorry—" Or a note from Henrietta? "Decided I have been behaving foolishly—sorry to have misled you." Sylvia swallowed nervously, glancing at Henrietta's tear-streaked face. Her throat was dry. She moistened her lips.

"I say—Henry. I'll—I'll ring him up for you. There needn't be any explanation. Or—or would you rather—"

"No," said Henrietta, and added, savagely because she had in fact been considerably shaken, "you needn't think you've persuaded me because you haven't."

"I'm not trying to persuade you," said Sylvia untruthfully. (It was pretty hopeless as a final effort, but anything was worth trying.) "I'm just trying to make sure you know what you're doing. Do you realize it will mean telling a lot of lies the whole time to daddy and mummy?"

"You said just now that I'd better tell them the truth and the shock would be good for them."

"I *didn't*," cried Sylvia indignantly. "What are you talking about? When?"

"Just now. Just before we started quarrelling."

"Oh—before!" The intensity of their dispute had blurred Sylvia's remembrance of her earlier mood of calm assurance. "Before! That doesn't count. At least—I mean I didn't know then what you were talking about."

"Well, anyway it's no good. You needn't treat me as if I was a child. I've said I'm going and I'm going."

(But you *are* a child, cried Sylvia's heart, a wilful, obstinate child, desperately lovable, pitifully in need of protection.)

"Well, don't say I didn't warn you." Hopeless bitter words, sealing forever the deadlock of their quarrel.

"I shan't say anything at all." Sylvia had a nightmare glimpse of the Henrietta of the future, tight-lipped, evasive, shrinking away from her sister's sympathy, coldly watching the understanding that had been between them shrivelling up, withering away.

"Oh, Henrietta! You—you *can't*," said Sylvia desperately.

"If you can—why can't I?" said Henrietta, suddenly facing round with a challenge in her eyes.

The question, terrifying in its suggestion of ultimate responsibility, had the effect of stirring up all the secret fears, all the carefully-concealed misgivings, all the unacknowledged doubts in Sylvia's mind into a surge of guilty panic. It was an extraordinary sensation—as if a river had been flowing along, smoothly, sweetly, open to the sunshine and the sky; and then, suddenly out of the disregarded ooze and slime of its bed grotesque monsters had reared horrible, stretching, threatening heads, blotting out the sunshine, thrashing the clear surface of the water into distorted ugliness. Sylvia, shuddering from her own imagination, found herself instinctively, fiercely, denying everything. She had tried to convince Henrietta on general terms and failed. Perhaps she could shake her sister's resolution by one terrific personal denial, a glorious triumphant burst of negation of all she had preached and practiced and believed in latterly.

"If you mean that you think you are following my example— you're wrong," said Sylvia. As the lie left her lips a glorious sense of freedom and exultation possessed her. The monsters, the writhing, hideous monsters, were sinking back, defeated. "I suppose you are thinking of Claud. Claud and I," said Sylvia deliberately, "are not lovers. I don't think that when one lives in one's parents' house one *can* decently have affairs with people." There was in her voice a ring of conviction which surprised Henrietta and even surprised herself.

"Good Lord!" exclaimed Henrietta, disappointed and startled by this unexpected confession.

"Of course you can do what you like," continued Sylvia (now that she had—surely?—convinced Henrietta that really she could do nothing of the sort, it seemed safe to open in such a way), "but I shouldn't think you'd like behaving like this while you're dependent on daddy and mummy—spending their money on dresses to wear with him, having to tell lies about where you've been. Why, think of poor daddy and mummy," cried Sylvia, who, to tell the truth, was not very much in the habit of considering her parents' feelings. "Think how awful they'd feel if they found out. Why, they'd never get over it!"

Henrietta not unnaturally resented her sister's assumption of the rôle of parent-interpreter.

"They won't find out. Do leave me alone, Sylvia. This is my own business. I shan't tell you any more about it."

Sylvia, who had really been seeing her parents' point of view for the first time as it regarded herself, and not Henrietta, realized she had been tactless.

Annoyed at her own blunder at a moment when she believed she had practically won Henrietta over to her side, she cried out sharply:

"Do you really mean you're going to be a perfect little fool after all?"

She was in reality cross with herself and not with Henrietta, but the tone was fatal.

"Yes! Yes! Now get out of my room," cried Henrietta, suddenly turning on her in a burst of nervy fury.

The rest of the quarrel was of the most undignified description. Sylvia, assisted by a vigorous push from her sister, turned to go. Repressing a violent impulse to push back, she got what satisfaction she could out of slamming the door violently behind her. Something in the sharp bang, the angry conclusion to so many nursery quarrels, reminded her of the oldest, the most potent of childhood threats. Sylvia opened the door again to say:

"If you don't promise me you won't, I'll tell mummy!"

"I don't care. Tell her!"

(Don't Care was drowned in a duck-pond, thought Sylvia automatically. It was degrading that a serious discussion between two adults should take such a regrettable turn.)

"I mean it, you know."

"I don't care *what* you mean."

The door was slammed again, this time by Henrietta. Sylvia, left on the mat outside, discovered she was trembling all over. She made her way wretchedly to her own room, undressed mechanically and got into bed; but as she did not succeed in getting to sleep until three o'clock the next morning she had plenty of time to realize that this was certainly the most miserable night of her life. Worse than the time she had had measles and been convinced she was going to die, worse even than the more recent occasion when she had heard that Claud had been involved in a motor-smash, but didn't know how serious it was. For as the sleepless minutes stretched themselves out into hours, and the hours dragged by to the muted chiming of the clock in the hall below, a torturing indecision harried more and more cruelly her tired brain. Sometimes she felt that she could not, she simply could not, betray Henrietta to her mother. At other times she felt that it was worth doing anything—anything—to save Henrietta from her own youth and silliness. The curtains flapped, the windowcatch creaked, Sylvia's bedclothes grew more and more disarranged with her tossings.

It would have been some consolation to her to have known that Henrietta was spending an equally wakeful, an equally miserable night.

II

Before eight o'clock the next morning Sylvia was standing outside Henrietta's door. She had woken up with a jerk at seven; and immediately discovered, rather to her own surprise, that her mind was most firmly made up.

She got out of bed and began to dress.

It was all very well to say that every one must do as they pleased. Well, in this case Henrietta just couldn't. Sylvia pulled on a stocking with determination. It might sound very convincing to say nobody should ever take the responsibility of interfering with any one. Well, in this case somebody was jolly well going to, declared Sylvia to her reflection in the mirror, slapping down the comb sharply on the dressing-table. People (she cast a scornful look at her bookshelf) people might talk as much as they liked about the freedom of the individual. Well, things (and by the word "things" Sylvia meant vaguely to include a sort of jumble of her parents, everybody's parents, mummy hating it when they went back to school, the whole of the social system, daddy having to have his *Times* found for him, her home-life, everybody's home-life)—things weren't as *easy* as that. Not nearly as easy.

It didn't *sound* much of a discovery. But Sylvia, as she went along the passage to Henrietta's room, had the idea that it might be worth thinking over some time.

She opened Henrietta's door and, coming straight to the point, delivered her ultimatum:

"Henrietta, if you don't promise me you'll give up this idea forever, I *swear* I'll tell mummy."

"I don't believe you," said Henrietta. She had lain awake the greater part of the night vowing to herself furiously over and over again that her mind was made up and that nothing would make her alter it. Moreover, she really did not believe her sister.

"I shall go and tell her now," said Sylvia.

Silence.

"You won't promise?"

"No, I won't."

"Very well, I'm going," said Sylvia,

It was quite the nastiest thing she had ever made herself do.

Immediately her sister closed the door Henrietta sprang out of bed and began feverishly dressing. She did not really believe that Sylvia would tell her mother—before breakfast too!—but she couldn't bear to stay in the house a moment longer. Everything suddenly seemed wildly repellent to her—her room, the ornaments on the dressing-table, those beastly rabbits on her crumpled tearstained nightdress-case, the picture over her bed (The Piper of Dreams), the revoltingly girlish white paint and chintz curtains.

She would hurry at once to the station and catch the earliest train to town that she could. They had arranged to meet in London in order to lend colour to Henrietta's story of a week-end with Phyllis. She was not supposed to be meeting him till three o'clock, but Henrietta now felt that if she stayed a moment more in her parents' house she would have hysterics.

Everything was altogether beastly, and she would never forgive Sylvia.

It was not perhaps the happiest of moods in which to fly to one's lover's arms.

Mrs. Perry was astonished when her elder daughter entered her room fully dressed at eight o'clock in the morning.

"Mother," said Sylvia without any delicate preamble, "will you please go to Henrietta's room at once and stop her running away with Captain Fortescue?"

"Captain Fortescue?" gasped Mrs. Perry. "I didn't know she knew him." It was a silly and inadequate thing to say, as she instantly realized. But what comment could be adequate when one's daughter practically woke one up in the morning with such an extraordinary statement? It was lucky, thought Mrs. Perry, her thoughts automatically flying to her husband, it was lucky that Charles had elected to shave in the bathroom that morning.

Sylvia saw that surprise had stricken her mother dumb. She was sitting up in bed, goggle-eyed, in a pink quilted dressing-gown, holding a cup of tea. Poor mummy! She couldn't even think to put the tea down.

"Hurry, mother," said Sylvia. "I expect after what I said she's dressing to go now."

An absurd picture of Henrietta, hurrying from her window down a ladder into the arms of Captain Fortescue, flashed into Mrs. Perry's mind.

"Good heavens! Are you—do you really—? All right, Sylvia. I'll go at once." Mrs. Perry, getting hastily out of bed, thrust her feet automatically into lamb's-wool bedroom slippers. (My chilblains— every winter.) It needed more, apparently, than the impending seduction of her youngest daughter to break the force of habit. "But what an *extraordinary*—are you sure, Sylvia?"

"Yes—quite. Of course, mummy—of course, I mean she doesn't really understand. You won't be too furious?"

"My baby!" cried Mrs. Perry, hurrying across the room, jerking furiously at a trailing dressing-gown girdle. "Of *course* she doesn't understand. But I'd like to tell that horrible old man—" She disappeared.

Sylvia, marvelling at the maternal heart, went slowly to the garage and backed out the car. She too felt that she could not stay an instant longer in the house. A sort of profoundly wretched relief filled her mind. Probably it would never be the same between Henrietta and herself again.

Mr. Perry, entering the breakfast-room in jovial weekend humour, waited some little time for some one to appear. Nobody did; and eventually he was obliged to help himself, a little forlornly, to his solitary bacon and eggs. He turned for consolation to the crossword in the morning-paper. Immediately the patterned black squares began to exercise their soothing effect. "Obstacle of old seems to give advice to a fish." Absorbed, he cut up his bacon, munched toast and drank coffee. Presently he drew a silver pencil out of his waistcoat pocket, laid the folded paper on the table and wrote in large triumphant letters—TURNPIKE.

CHAPTER IX

I

ON SATURDAY MORNING Florence woke up with a dry mouth. She swallowed, took a drink of water, and swallowed again. That wasn't a sore throat, was it? Just that rather tight, dry, stretched feeling at the back of her nose. She blew her nose resolutely and turned over on to her other side. Another hour to sleep before she need get up. How lovely!

She lay awake in bed, blowing her nose at intervals.

It was difficult not to think of all the things that had to be done in the course of getting herself to Leslie's party that afternoon. If only she hadn't to go to the office that morning! She could have spent the time profitably in having her hair done (it certainly needed it), turning herself out decently and getting herself to the station in a leisurely way. As it was, she didn't know the times of the trains, nor how long it would take, and lunch would almost certainly be a railway bun. She couldn't wear any respectable party dress to the office and would consequently have to change at some point. (Probably in the lavatory of the ladies' waiting-room at Paddington.) It was tempting to think of Jane's offer of a seat in Henry's car, but of course one couldn't really butt in on a couple like that. Besides—an even more powerful argument—, Jane and he would be off at half-past twelve, whereas with all that pile of work waiting for her she'd be lucky if she got off by one.

After thinking in this strain for half an hour Florence felt so restless that she was impelled to get up and start getting breakfast. She discovered almost immediately that there was no marmalade left; and a little later that the milkman had left nothing but a bill for 7s. 5¾d. on the doorstep. Excessively irritated, she rang up the dairy, who would only repeat that it was their rule not to leave milk unless the account was paid weekly.

"Well, you don't keep to your rule," said Florence, "because you've been leaving it for weeks and weeks. I don't see why you should suddenly stop now without warning."

"I'm sorry, modom, but those are our instructions."

"And the reason you haven't been paid," continued Florence, "is because it's so frightfully inconvenient to come rushing round to pay you the whole time, and it's out of our way, and you're usually shut anyway."

"I'm sorry, modom. The rule is that all accounts—"

"Yes, yes, I know. I'm just pointing out that it isn't because we haven't the money we haven't paid you."

Feeling that at any rate she had had a pennyworth of protest, and suddenly remembering that there was a tin of dried milk in the cupboard, Florence rang off.

Jane was standing behind her, mildly entertained.

"Well, Jane, they're such *fools,*" said Florence defensively. "How can they expect me to come rushing round every day, ten minutes out of my way, to pay them a penny farthing?"

"Absurd," said Jane amiably. She was now taking tea without milk anyway.

"Where the hell's the tin-opener?"

But Jane had just picked up a letter from Henry which was lying on the mat, and did not answer. Florence went to wrestle impatiently with the tin in the kitchen. Almost at once she cut her thumb on a jagged edge. A surge of ill temper welled up in her, and then immediately shocked her by its intensity. What was the matter with her? Why should she be affected so strongly by such a trifle? Never before in her life had she felt her nerves and temper and endurance so strained to snapping point by any minor and passing annoyance. I don't know what's the matter with me, thought Florence despondently, pushing back her hair from her face with a damp and yet cold hand. She swallowed again. Her throat was now definitely sore. She could visualize it, pink and rough and burning. Honey and lemon? She saw again the little yellow saucer in which her mother had prepared the comforting mixture when she was a child, tasted again its sweet astringency in the mouth. But there wasn't any honey or lemon in the flat. And besides (as a matter of course) there wasn't time.

She put the kettle on to boil and went back into the sitting-room and got back into bed with her slippers on and huddled the bedclothes round her.

Jane was reading a crumpled sheet of exercise paper, closely and illegibly written. It was from Henry.

"DARLING, I'm so sorry about our quarrel tonight. I am writing this in the bus going home. I *do* hope you'll be able to read it. I'll post it when I get to the house, and then you'll get it tomorrow morning. This is the only paper I have with me." (Well, of course! As if one needed to explain that sort of thing.)

"I am so reproaching myself, darling. You came home tired and wanting a rest and I was horrid. You aren't still cross with me, are you, darling? I'll try to explain." (Poor Henry. You needn't bother. I understand all right.)

"You see, you mean such a frightful lot to me that perhaps I'm silly and over-particular. But it does seem to me that you can be quite, quite perfect. Only sometimes things happen to stop you being so absolutely perfect, and then, because I love you so terribly, I get cross. It's wrong of me, I know. Do you understand, Jane darling? It's difficult to explain, especially with this bus jerking about so." (Probably he hadn't even smiled over that last remark, the poor pet. And what a perfectly appalling view of her character!)

"You see, I am counting so frightfully on this weekend to put things right between us. I think perhaps the reason we quarrel sometimes is because we are both leading rather unnatural sort of lives, I mean seeing so much of each other, and yet not always being together." (I dare say there's something in that.) "It was marvellous when you told me you loved me enough to come away with me." (I never told him that. I suppose he thinks I did.) "Oh, darling! I can't tell you what a lot it means to me. I shall never forget it." (Well, no. Anyway, it wasn't the sort of thing one did exactly *forget*, was it?)

"I was miserable when I started writing this, but now, thinking about how wonderful this week-end will be, I am so happy. Jane darling, you mean everything to me. Without you nothing has any point at all. I wish I could explain how—damn, we have got to the stop. Love-H."

In the corner there was a hasty and almost illegible scrawl:— "P.S.—Will pick you up in car, outside Charing Cross, 12.40."

It was impossible not to be touched by this letter. It was impossible not to be irritated by it; and Jane, gazing with pity at the hastily-scrawled pencil crosses at the foot of the sheet, wondered for the first time whether it had been wise to promise this week-end to Henry, or whether, having promised, it was wise to go on with it. It was a pity that it seemed to mean quite such a lot to him! After all there was no guarantee—was there?—that it would mean anything particular to her? And afterwards—supposing Henry was more in love, more possessive, more sentimental than ever? Supposing it was more difficult than ever to convince him that no human being should have any permanent hold over another? Supposing the hurt she might have to do him would be even more desperate? For a moment Jane experienced a vague and anxious foreboding for Henry's future happiness; then the habits of thought of many years reasserted themselves. After all, Henry must look out for himself. Everybody must look out for themselves. You couldn't shoulder the responsibility of another person's happiness. Her spirits rose again. She flung the letter into the waste-paper basket and buttered himself a bit of toast.

"Poor Henry," she said gayly, "it must be awful to take things so hard."

"It is rather poor Henry, I think," croaked Florence unexpectedly, wondering if, supposing she had such a devoted lover, she would fling his letters quite so airily into the waste-paper basket.

"Why, what's the matter, Florence?" cried Jane, surprised. "Don't you think this week-end is a good idea?"

"No, it seems to me rather a pity," said Florence without pausing to think. Then, recollecting herself, she blew her nose and added hoarsely, "Only don't take any notice of me. Wash it out. I mean I think I only said that because I've got a filthy cold."

"Have you? Bad luck. There was a bottle of Vapex in the bathroom once. But it may be finished."

"It is. I've looked," said Florence.

II

She took three clean handkerchiefs with her to the office. By the time she got there she felt as if her head was stuffed with hot cottonwool.

"Lovely day, isn't it?" said Miss Conway cheerfully. She was dusting her typewriter as Florence entered their room. "I heard it raining in the night, but it's ever so warm again this morning."

"Yes, it is, isn't it?" said Florence wanly.

"Got a cold? Bad luck. Vapex is the thing."

"Yes, I know."

"Got some?"

"No. Not yet. I must."

"Ask the boy to run out and get you some."

"Oh, no. I won't bother."

Florence was diffident of sending out the office boy on private errands, just as she was much more scrupulous than Miss Conway over private telephone calls. Miss Conway, who had left her secondary school at sixteen and had earned her living for six years, had had time to develop a cheerful and healthy contempt for her employers and a self-confident bossiness towards her subordinates that Florence could only envy. She was an extremely good secretary. She never, as Florence liked to do, thought of herself as handling work of any real importance. Without thinking very much about it, she knew that her job was to keep the office records in perfect order and humour her employer's "little ways." When Miss Locke said to her, "This is important, Miss Conway," she was completely unimpressed, but nevertheless registered infallibly that here was something the old girl would be fussy about. Consequently she never forgot, as Florence sometimes did, that the letter must not miss the evening's mail. From long practice she was an extremely quick and accurate worker, and, as she was never self-conscious or nervous, she had the advantage over Florence on both these counts. For about a fortnight after first arriving Florence had believed that Miss Conway had a quite phenomenal memory. She was amazed to find, from moments of odd conversation with her, that she could hardly recall the characters in any novel she had read after finishing the book, or offer any criticism of a film rather than the two standard comments of "ever so good" or "not bad."

It was impossible not to like her, although there was little common ground on which Florence and she could meet. She affected Florence with a curious sensation of mingled admiration and superiority. They called each other Miss Somerset and Miss Conway with great formality, and exchanged remarks on the weather in the mornings.

Florence had not finished the not-so-urgent letters left over from the previous day when Miss Locke sent for her.

"Good morning, Miss Somerset," said Miss Locke rapidly. "Rather a lot of letters today, I'm afraid. To this man—Fraser—'Thank you for your letter. I am sorry that our reader again reports—'" (She paused, seeing that Florence was still flipping over the pages of her shorthand notebook.) "'—Our reader again reports that he cannot recommend your novel—your novel—' Can you remember its name, Miss Somerset?"

But Florence, who had stayed late one evening to read the novel purely out of interest, for it seemed to her a good piece of work, unfortunately could not recall its title.

"It was about the farming family who—" she began helpfully.

"Look it up," said Miss Locke briefly.

Florence scribbled and nodded.

"Now what did I say?"

"'Thank you for your letter,'" said Florence throatily. "'Upon receiving our reader's report we are glad to be able to tell you—'"

"What?" said Miss Locke sharply.

"Oh, I'm so sorry," cried Florence abashed. The effort of concentrating on reading back her shorthand always left her mind an entire blank as to the meaning of the words, "I'm reading from the wrong page. It must have turned over when I blew my nose. It began the same, you see." As always, she was far too profuse with apologies and explanations.

"Well, what *did* I say?" inquired Miss Locke, with an obvious and alarming control.

"'Thank you for your letter,'" said Florence mechanically ("Yes, yes," interjected Miss Locke), "'I am sorry that our reader again reports that he cannot recommend your novel—'"

"Is that *all* I said?" asked Miss Locke suspiciously.

"Yes," replied Florence firmly. (Oh, dear! Once found out, always suspected!)

"'Your novel, whatever it is, for publication,'" continued Miss Locke, faster and glibber than ever. "'Stop. We are therefore returning the manuscript to you—' You'll have to find it, Miss Somerset, I think Miss Stevens borrowed it —'under separate cover.' I'll sign that one myself. Now the next." She paused again, seeing that Florence's pencil was still chasing the flying words.

There were, as Miss Locke reported, rather a lot of letters. It was a breathless half-hour. Florence did not even get time to blow her nose again. She was obliged to sniff.

"Oh, dear, Miss Somerset, you *have* got a cold, haven't you?" said Miss Locke, as Florence, gathering up the sheaf of letters to be answered, got up to leave the room.

"I have rather," said Florence humbly. Then, encouraged by Miss Locke's more sympathetic tone, and feeling that it would be something of a relief to appear intelligent for two seconds, she added, "I wish we could have published that novel—the one I can't remember the title of—about a farm. I thought there was some good writing in it."

"Wouldn't sell," said Miss Locke briefly. "Mr. Charles was dead against it."

"It was an honest piece of work," suggested Florence.

"Oh—honest," said Miss Locke, as though that had nothing to do with it—as indeed it had not.

Florence left the room thinking that in happier circumstances, in a less hurried and less mechanical world—say at Oxford if Miss Locke were a don—they could have had an interesting discussion on the conflicting claims of selling power and artistic merit, how far one should be subordinated to the other, and how, of course, there could be no absolute standard for either, both being subject to temporary prejudice. For she, thought Florence, knows more than I do about selling power; and I (a faintly comforting thought) know considerably more about artistic merit. She was depressed, on getting back to her typewriter, to find it was already nearly eleven.

If she could only have got straight on with the letters it wouldn't have been so bad. She was, however, continually interrupted by the necessity for referring to the files; and the files were not in her room but down a flight of stairs in the ground-floor office. There was, Florence thought, a disproportionate amount of running to and fro and searching involved in checking some tiny detail. Expediency, she decided severely, was here sacrificed to method. It was a wrong principle. As she pounded up the stairs for the fifth time, with aching back and burning throat, it seemed to her that the principle was very wrong indeed.

"Hasn't any one ever thought of having our letters in a filing cabinet in this room?" she inquired wearily of Miss Conway. "After all, most of this department's stuff is quite separate, and it *is* such a waste of time to go running up and down stairs all day."

Miss Conway, knowing instinctively that it was not worth while, seldom bothered her head over the reorganization of office routine.

"All the letters have always been filed together," she said.

"Yes, but why? It's such a waste of time."

"Oh, waste of time!" Miss Conway's tone seemed to imply that one might as well occupy office hours in running up and down stairs as any other way.

"Don't you think it's awfully silly, though?" Florence blew her nose.

"I say, you have got a rotten cold, haven't you? Sure you won't have the boy go out for something?"

"No, thank you. Won't you come with me and ask Miss Locke whether we couldn't have it altered?"

"What, me? Oh, I don't bother myself about it, you know."

"Yes, but it would save such a lot of time for both of us."

"Well, all the offices I've worked in have always filed all their stuff together."

"Yes, but has any one ever *thought* about it?" cried the Oxford B.A. fiercely.

"I wouldn't worry, you know." Miss Conway pushed the carriage of her typewriter across with a sharp ping. "If there's a rush on I ask Miss Smith to look things out for me."

Miss Smith was in charge of the filing office.

"I don't like to do that." (That's all very well for Miss Conway. Miss Smith's a friend of hers. They're knitting the same jumper in different colours and they go and eat sandwiches together for lunch. I can't do that.)

"She's ever so nice," said Miss Conway encouragingly. "She wouldn't mind once in a way." She started to type at a speed that still seemed to Florence faster than one could ever succeed in imagining any one typing.

"It isn't once in a way. It's practically all the time. That's what's always making me so frightfully behind."

"You do get a bit behind, don't you?" said Miss Conway above the rapid clatter of the keys. "But you'll get faster as time goes on, you'll find."

But Florence, who had spent three years and a substantial amount of her parent's money in learning the importance of thinking for herself, was now totally incapable of relinquishing an idea so easily.

"Well, anyway, I shall go and ask Miss Locke," she said.

"It wouldn't be any good your asking Miss Locke."

"Why not?"

"Because it's not her business. Miss Stevens is the only one who could alter an important thing like that, and she'd probably want to ask Mr. Charles. But anyway she wouldn't."

"But *why* wouldn't she?" cried Florence.

"Well, go and ask her, then," said Miss Conway, adding in an explanatory way, "because she wouldn't."

Without being able consciously to analyze character in the very least Miss Conway yet knew instinctively that Miss Stevens would not react favourably to a suggestion emanating from a newish and not very efficient subordinate. She recognized, however, that Florence would never be happy now until she had got this particular silliness off her chest.

Florence, the light of battle in her eye, marched off to knock on Miss Stevens's door.

"Come in," said a crisp voice.

Florence entered and was confused to find Miss Stevens engaged with a tall young man. They were laughing together over some typescript sheets on the table before them.

"Oh—I'm sorry," said Florence uncertainly. "If you're engaged, I—" She began to back out of the door.

"Did Miss Locke send you for something?" inquired Miss Stevens. She was a very neat person with an authoritative voice.

"No. That is—I wanted to see you myself—about something."

"Ten minutes," said Miss Stevens.

Florence returned to her own room and typed a letter with three corrections. At the end of precisely the tenth minute she went back and knocked again.

Thank goodness the young man had gone, although (horrid thought) had she chased him away?

"Come in, Miss Somerset. Sit down, won't you?" There was an underlying suggestion of efficiency even in Miss Stevens' amiability. "That was A. L. Ferguson in here just now."

"Oh, was it?" said Florence, registering a suitable interest, and wondering who the hell A. L. Ferguson might be.

"The detective-story writer, you know."

"Oh, yes, interesting," murmured Florence.

"Have you read his last?" pursued Miss Stevens, who seemed, rather disconcertingly, to be in the mood for light conversation, "I think it's *excellent.*"

"No. Actually I haven't."

"Although I think the one before—*The Margate Villa Mystery*—was the best of the lot."

"Yes, was it? As a matter of fact, I haven't read any of his."

"Oh, haven't you? You ought to try them. I always look out for them."

"Yes. Although as a matter of fact I never *do* read detective stories." It was the simple truth, so it was a pity it sounded both crushing and snobbish. But anyway, thought Florence unkindly, I didn't come here for light chat, with all that work waiting upstairs.

"Well, Miss Somerset, you wished to see me about something?" Efficiency rose uppermost again.

"Yes. That is—I wanted to make a suggestion."

"Oh. Yes?" Miss Stevens' tone was absolutely noncommittal.

"We—at least I mean I—" (better not drag Miss Conway into it perhaps) "seem to spend an awful lot of time running up and downstairs to the filing cabinets. I mean we're always having to go down there to check up things. So I thought—at least, don't you think it would be better—if— since our department's stuff is quite separate, I mean—if we could have a filing cabinet of our own upstairs?" Without pausing for Miss Stevens' comment, Florence, once launched, became fatally enthusiastic and voluble. "You see, then everything would be to hand—and we could do the filing ourself, and it would mean less work for Miss Smith, and then when we wanted to look up something it wouldn't mean looking through thousands of things that have absolutely nothing to do—"

"Just a moment, Miss Somerset." Miss Stevens firmly stemmed the torrent of Florence's eloquence. "I don't think you quite realize that, in a big office like this, *no* department's work is separate in any real sense. All are interdependent and, of course, subject to the head office."

(Poor Florence! How was she to have realized that the independence of her department was entirely the wrong note to have stressed, that it was just the occasional suggestion of this, in fact, in Miss Locke's attitude that goaded to the point of fury her immediate superior, Miss Stevens.)

"Oh," said Florence, with an ill-timed effort at persuasiveness, "but *really*, you know, in practice our work is quite separate, isn't it?"

She waited for an assent that did not come. Instead Miss Stevens inquired, "Have you had any experience of filing yourself, Miss Somerset?"

"Well—er—no, actually not."

"Well, can you say that you thoroughly understand the system on which our filing is worked?"

"I expect I—I mean, it wouldn't be very difficult just to invent a system just for our department. I mean, since we'd be the only people handling it. . . ." The filing system in use downstairs had always seemed to Florence completely inexplicable and arbitrary. Thankfully conscious that it was not her job to understand it she had been accustomed to refer for direction to Miss Smith.

"Invent a system!" Miss Stevens laughed kindly. "I don't think we could run a department on an amateur filing system very satisfactorily."

A boiling sense of injustice swelled up in Florence. It was all very well for some one who sat in a chair and had a secretary of her own to run about for her to dismiss the idea so lightly. It was all very well to suggest the filing would be in a muddle if she did it—

why should it, why in heaven's name should it? She had as much—more—brains than any one who had invented a rotten system. Why couldn't she—why shouldn't she—it was a shame not to listen properly—they weren't giving her a chance—it wasn't fair. . . .

All pretence at a suitably subordinate manner vanished. The perfect secretary (at best an elusive dream) went up in smoke.

"Well, *I* think," said Florence with a reckless and intensely satisfying emphasis on the "I," "that it's a very good idea and you ought at least to give it a trial!"

Miss Stevens raised her eyebrows and there was a nasty silence. At last, in an icy voice, she said:

"Perhaps, Miss Somerset, if you were to occupy yourself with training your memory instead of trying to reorganize the office you would not find that you wasted so much of your time."

This not unmerited rebuke had a quite startling effect on Florence. She bounced up in her chair, turned red in the face, and exclaimed hoarsely: "I don't think it's worth my while. I think I'll be leaving here anyway." Then she blew her nose violently, dropping at the same time a pencil on the floor. It rolled away under a desk.

Miss Stevens raised her eyebrows. "Just as you like, Miss Somerset. I dare say you're wise." She turned away and reached for her scribbling-block. "I'll send your notice in to Mr. Charles, shall I?" She was quite calm and unimpressed.

"Thank you," said Florence, suddenly deciding, a little tardily, to emulate Miss Stevens's collected manner.

"Would you like to leave at the end of the week or the month? You have a right to leave at the end of the week, but it is more convenient for us, of course, if you stay the month out."

"Very well," said Florence, feeling exactly like a dismissed cook, promising grudgingly to "oblige" her employer a little longer.

"So I think that is all for this morning, isn't it, Miss Somerset?" It was the usual formula of dismissal.

"Thank you," said Florence a little meaninglessly, and somehow got herself out of the room (abandoning the pencil). On the stairs she thought, irrelevantly, that she must probably have a temperature.

"I'm leaving," she announced abruptly to Miss Conway. It was quite a bombshell.

"Why, good gracious! She didn't want you to go just because of that silly idea about the filing?" cried Miss Conway, amazed. "Silly" slipped out by mistake, but Florence did not care or notice.

"No. At least, not exactly. I sacked myself actually. I shouldn't think she was sorry. As far as I remember I was very rude."

"Were you really?" Miss Conway, accustomed to a nervous and diffident Florence, was intrigued. "What did you say?"

"I don't really remember." Florence slumped down in her chair, feeling that all she wanted in the world was to lie quite flat and be left alone.

"Well, I dare say you're right," said Miss Conway after a moment's pause, echoing unconsciously Miss Stevens's verdict on the situation. "I don't think—you'll excuse my saying this, won't you, Miss Somerset?—that you're altogether cut out for office work, are you? I expect you've felt that yourself sometimes. You're clever, aren't you?"

She was not being sarcastic.

"They used to think so at Oxford," said Florence bitterly.

"Well, there you are," said Miss Conway sagely, "you've been up to the University, you see. You're different from most of us here. We left school at sixteen and started in the filing office. It's different, you see, for us."

"If what you're suggesting is true, it's the most frightful criticism of a University education."

"Have a bit of chocolate, won't you?"

Florence took the chocolate, not wanting it in the least, and munched it mechanically. Presently she said, "I don't suppose it's altogether Oxford. I expect I should have been a bloody bad secretary anyway."

Miss Conway, profoundly shocked at Florence's language, said, "You're feeling rotten, aren't you? Why don't you go and lie down for a bit and then go home?"

"How can I with all this work? I haven't *begun* yet."

"Perhaps I could help you out with some of it. What is it all?"

"God knows. Millions of frightful letters. I think I'd better not go to the party I was going to this afternoon. I think I'd better stay here and type till midnight."

"Here, let me look at it," said Miss Conway, very properly disregarding this suggestion and beginning rapidly and efficiently to sift the pile in front of Florence. "This can wait—this isn't important—this must go and this and this. . . . You have got a lot, haven't you?"

"Some of it's yesterday's," said Florence, concealing the fact that a little of it was actually the day before yesterday's.

"I'm afraid you've missed the American mail with some of this. Well, never mind. Since we *have* missed it there's no particular hurry now. I wouldn't let Miss Locke know."

"I say, why should you bother? I mean it's awfully nice of you but you oughtn't to bother over it. It's not your work."

"That's all right, Miss Somerset. I haven't very much of my own this morning. Now I wonder if I can manage to read your shorthand? I could easily finish off these for you." Miss Conway picked up all the pile she had sorted as urgent.

"Oh, it's awfully nice of you. But I shouldn't think you possibly could. I can't myself very often."

"Let me look at your notebook. Oh, I think I can read this all right."

"How *marvellous* of you," said Florence. Her admiration of such an extraordinary talent was profound.

"I'm used to other people's outlines, you see. I give Miss Smith a lesson now and then. Besides when you know the work as well as I do. . . ." There was not the slightest trace of boastfulness or superiority in her manner. Just a plain statement of fact.

"Look, Miss Somerset. You lend me your notebook and I'll just finish off this little lot. And while I'm doing it you can be looking out the queries we want and bringing the index up to date."

"It's frightfully nice of you," said Florence gratefully. Miss Conway deftly inserted note-paper and carbon and was immediately away at her usual speed. Sometimes she checked and frowned thoughtfully at Florence's scribblings. The solution (or possibly, thought Florence, a neat alternative?) was never very long in coming.

Presently Miss Conway said, "That book of Fraser's— you needn't bother to look up the title—it was called 'Firm Furrow' wasn't it?"

"Oh, yes, *that* was it. Of course—I ought to have remembered. Wasn't it good?"

"Was it? I didn't read it. I just saw it lying round here one day."

Florence marvelled.

"Can you be sending it down to the mail, Miss Somerset? They like parcels by twelve on Saturdays you know."

"Oh, bother! Miss Stevens has it. I ought to have asked for it when I was there—I forgot."

Miss Conway understood very well Florence's reluctance to re-approach Miss Stevens.

"All right, never mind," she said, and presently Florence heard her telephoning to the mailing clerk, "I say, Elsie, be an angel and get a manuscript called 'Firm Furrow' out of old Stevens, will you, for us? We don't want to stir up the old girl again this morning. You will, won't you? That's a good girl."

Florence thanked her silently for that blessed "we."

Miss Conway's fingers pounded the keys faster and faster, while Florence continued her checking in a sort of trance. She could not as yet realize what she had done, nor whether she was glad or sorry. She thought about how dirty her fingernails were and whether she could stop and buy some more handkerchiefs on the way to the station.

At twelve o'clock Miss Locke came into the room.

"Is it true that you've just told Miss Stevens you're leaving, Miss Somerset?"

"Yes."

"Well, why didn't you come to me about it first?" Miss Locke, her authority slighted, spoke more sharply than was perhaps necessary. It had been unpleasant to learn the news second-hand and by chance from Miss Stevens. "After all, you work for me, don't you, not Miss Stevens. You should have come to me first."

Miss Locke was certainly not prepared for the effect of this speech on Florence, who suddenly, quite without warning, flung the handful of index cards she was holding onto the ground and exclaimed wildly, unpardonably,

"Oh, for God's sake leave me alone for one second. Isn't it sufficient that I'm jolly well going as soon as I can?"

Miss Conway stopped typing. Her mouth fell open. Miss Locke gazed in dismay at the distorted face of her usually meek secretary. The index cards lay on the floor and nobody picked them up.

"Dear me," said Miss Locke at length, mildly (for she was a kind woman, and naturally distressed by the spectacle of so much misery, so much rage), "dear me, Miss Somerset. I think you'll be all the better for a little holiday, won't you?"

"I'm going now—this minute, this second," cried Florence. Tears were now streaming down her face. She knew she was behaving inexcusably and took a savage delight in so doing. "I shan't stay here any longer." She gave her typewriter an angry push. "I can't stand it a moment more. I've loathed and hated every minute—yes, I dare say it's all my fault, don't say so, I know what you think." She gave a savage sniff. It was a lamentable scene.

"She's been feeling rotten all day," put in Miss Conway.

"Perhaps you'd better go home, Miss Somerset."

"I will. I jolly well will," said Florence, and rushed in a blundering and utterly undignified way from the room.

For a moment after she had gone both Miss Locke and Miss Conway were too taken aback to speak. They gazed mutely at Florence's disordered desk, at the typewriter pushed awry, at the littered floor.

"Dear me," said Miss Locke again at length. "I'm afraid she's left things in rather a muddle. What a funny way to behave."

"She's usually ever so quiet."

"Well, well." Miss Locke shrugged her shoulders. "It's rather awkward. I wanted her to do a few urgent letters for me. . . ."

"Can I help you, Miss Locke?"

• • • • • • •

Huddled on the top of a bus, Paddington-bound, Florence shivered and scrubbed at her eyes. Anyway she wasn't going back to the empty flat to think about nothing else all the week-end. She was going to Leslie's party if she died in the attempt.

CHAPTER X

I

"I WONDER WHAT you'll think of Florence now," said Leslie to her mother as they sat in the summer-house on the Saturday morning of the party. "She's an awfully interesting sort of person, I always think. She gets a lot out of things." Her glance strayed thoughtfully to a vivid bed of tulips, while she tried to imagine her London friends in these sylvan surroundings. "You must get her to talk to you about her novel."

"Yes, I'm very interested in it. It's very clever of her to find the time to write if she's working all day."

"Well, mummy, when you care about a thing, you know —I mean *really* care. . . . Besides Florence and Jane take their work in their stride. I mean I'd never describe them as being sort of chained to their work at all. Their real life—I mean their *real* life," said Leslie with meaning, "goes on all the time beside it."

Mrs. Fisher digested these remarks in a kind silence.

"You won't like Jane quite so much."

"Won't I, dear?" Mrs. Fisher's lips twitched, but Leslie detected no amusement in her mother's accustomed interest.

"No. Although I think she's a very sort of *admirable* person in a way. I mean I think she has a quite unusual talent for living. I can't quite express what I mean. It's something to do with going right on her way and never minding about other people at all."

"How nice for her, darling."

"Yes. I don't expect you see quite what I mean. As a matter of fact, I don't expect you will when you meet her either. It isn't very obvious, and people—especially women—don't always like her very much at first."

"Dear me. Well, I hope I shall be clever enough to see it fairly soon."

Leslie glanced sharply at her mother.

"Well, anyway, mummy, you'll like seeing them for yourself, won't you?"

"Oh, yes, dear. Thank you. I shall be very interested to see Florence again. I've hardly seen her since she came to stay here once when she was quite a little girl."

"Quite a little girl? Oh, you mean when she was about fifteen. Oh, but of course she's *quite* different now. She's developed enormously. Mentally, I mean, of course."

"I remember she had very decided views about things then. She was very down on circuses, I remember. Does she still think them so cruel? It was rather awkward at the time, because I had got tickets for you both for Olympia. I had to cancel them."

"Circuses? I don't know whether she still minds about them. But I'm glad you remember her as quite an exceptional person."

"Oh, yes. Quite."

As a matter of fact, all my friends are rather exceptional, thought Leslie, selecting carefully a blade of grass to chew.

"And she used to write long letters every day to a friend. Even while she was here, every single day. Such devotion, I thought."

"Oh, mummy! That wasn't a friend. I mean, she was school games captain," said Leslie seriously. "It was the most *unhealthy* type of devotion. It was a jolly good thing she got over it when she did. It might have warped her whole character." Respecting her mother's innocence, Leslie said no more.

"Really, dear? Well then, as you say, it was lucky she recovered. I remember thinking at the time that it probably wouldn't last. I shall enjoy meeting her again."

There was a pause.

"I think it should be a nice party," said Leslie hopefully.

"I'm sure it will, dear. Although it seems rather a long way for people to come just for half a day, but nobody thinks much of that nowadays, I know. Leslie, I shan't bother to stay with you all very long. I'll just be here to meet them all when they arrive and then—"

"Oh, but mummy! You're *meant* to stay. Darling, really you are. You really must. At any rate, long enough to talk to them a bit. I want you to hear about living in London and things from them all. And see for yourself that they're not just rackety and overworked, but people who—who— well, who *get* something out of life. You will stay, won't you, mummy?"

Mrs. Fisher wondered how long it would take her to begin to feel dead and buried.

"Well, but, Leslie, they'll be wanting to play tennis—"

"You must talk to them while they're sitting out," said Leslie earnestly. "To Jane and Florence, of course specially. They can tell you all about the sort of life they lead in London. It would be sort of helpful, wouldn't it?"

"Very helpful, dear. But you know, Leslie, I'm not trying to oppose your idea of an art-school in London. I think in some ways it's a very good plan. It's just that I want you to be quite sure of exactly what you do want."

"Oh, mummy! I *do* know."

"For instance, darling, I think you'd be sorry afterwards if you went and spent your hundred pounds like that, when I'm quite willing—"

"Oh, mummy, I want to be independent."

Mrs. Fisher sighed. Children on whom one gladly lavished time and money with no motive at heart but their happiness; children who, imagining fetters where none existed, broke away exulting, drunk with the illusion of escape.

"Well, don't let's talk about it any more just now, shall we, mummy? You see I really do want you to have a talk with Jane and Florence. You will, won't you, darling?" Mrs. Fisher dutifully promised.

"In a way I'm sorry Bert and Bill are coming," said Leslie, temporarily relieved. "And yet it's very convenient to have some one living close who'll make up the numbers. I do hope they'll mix."

"I think they're rather jolly boys."

Leslie screwed up her nose.

"Oh—yes—jolly."

"It's rather nice to see two brothers going about together so often and so fond of each other."

"Well, yes. Unless you think that it's just that they're so sort of—well, *ordinary*—that they never get on each other's nerves."

"I shouldn't object to that sort of ordinariness."

"Well, anyway," said Leslie, dismissing the subject, "if they're not very interesting to talk to they can always rally round and pick up balls and carry drinks about and things."

"It will be nice for them to feel they're useful."

Leslie was so sure that her mother was never sarcastic that she did not pay much attention to this remark.

II

Jane and Henry journeyed spasmodically out of London by way of Hammersmith Broadway and the Great West Road. Behind, ahead and alongside streamed all the other Saturday afternoon traffic. They rounded islands, they stopped at traffic lights, they slowed down (occasionally and grudgingly) at pedestrian crossings, they complied with compulsory turnings and avoided No Entry notices. Perpetually they accelerated, changed gear, braked, stopped. Jane was reminded of a dice-game of her youth played with an illustrated and numbered board and small tin models of men (in cycling knickerbockers) and ladies (in long skirts) on differently coloured bicycles. It was called "On the Road to Ripley." Getting held up by traffic lights today was very similar to being counted onto a square marked "Unavoidable delay. Wait two throws." Compulsory loopways would correspond to "Wrong turning. Go back three," and pedestrian crossings to "Road up. Miss one." She began to ask Henry whether he had ever played the game, but at that moment the tram they were about to pass on the inner side stopped suddenly. Henry braked violently, swung round behind it, and accelerated with the intention of passing it on the right. Jane clutched the side of the car. A Green Line bus was charging towards them. There would never be time to pass—would there? Just as Jane closed her eyes for the crash, Henry decided not to attempt the cut-in. More braking— the kind that swayed Jane onto the windscreen and brought her stomach up into her chest.

"Daddy has ruined the acceleration of this car," said Henry sadly.

Jane agreed. She was agreeing with everything Henry said that day. It seemed the best plan. Both enjoyed thus a precarious kind of peace. And really, thought Jane, surprised, really Henry is a dear. She tried to imagine that she was meeting him for the first time—surely she would be most pleasantly impressed? But it was difficult to dissociate him long from her knowledge of him, from the memories bound up in it. She found that she could not think of him simply as a person. He was to her all the time a person who had an effect on her, an effect which was not now what it had once been. Well, anyway, thought Jane suddenly, whatever happens in the end and even when it's all over and I'm in love with some one else—Henry will always be the nicest man I have ever known.

Henry had not the courage to allow his thoughts to range thus recklessly into the future. He marshalled them strictly to order, enclosing them in the small bright room of the present, refusing them the dark and conjectural realms of time to come. He was obsessed by a vague idea that only by such stealthiness could the spider-spirit be tricked into acquiescence. Once make plans for the future, thought Henry, and you challenged this thwarting fate, this power that worked with instruments far more potent than your own will; but if you could (on the sly, as it were) snatch a few bright hours, force yourself, however much against the grain it might be, to blot out all thought of the future—well, then that meant defeat, at least temporary defeat to the spider-spirit, didn't it? "Not heaven itself upon the past has power." A two-thousand-year-old cry.

From this shallow well Henry drew comfort, nor realizing, so cunningly does the human mind disguise its own workings, that by such means only could conscience be lulled.

"I thought, darling," said Henry, "that it would be nicest not to make any definite plans about where we're going. Don't you think it would be lovely just to leave about six and drive off into the country until we saw somewhere we both felt we'd like to stop?"

Jane, not knowing the train of thought that had led to this, thought it the daftest idea she had ever heard of.

"I think that would be lovely, darling," she said. She had a ridiculous vision of themselves driving round and round Berkshire in the search for a perfect stopping-place. Until finally all the country pubs were shut and they were obliged to come back to London, to the Regent Palace.

"I hoped you'd think so."

"Oh, yes, darling. Oh, Henry," said Jane, suddenly touched by the happiness on his face, "it will be fun."

"Darling," said Henry fervently, and meant by it "I'll never love anybody as much as you, I'll never be happier than I am now."

"Darling," said Jane, and meant "I'm so glad I haven't said anything to hurt you yet, because when you look so happy I feel so terribly sorry for you."

III

Claud was not of the generation that reacts favourably to the suggestion that he should travel anywhere by train. He was disappointed not to be able to get hold of the small sports car he shared with three other men in his digs, but he bowed to the justice of it. It was not his turn for it, and on Saturday afternoons it was inevitably much in demand. Yet on Sylvia suggesting to him that he should travel down to Leslie's party by train, he had been frankly appalled. Claud, who would cheerfully take over an unknown make of car and pilot it in the dark through unfamiliar country to any specified destination, seemed unshakably convinced of his own inability to find his way there by train.

"But darling, don't be silly," Sylvia had said, patiently, when Claud, panic-stricken on suddenly realizing the situation, had rung her up a few days previously. "You've only got to go to Paddington and sit in a train till you get there."

"Oh, but darling, it's so difficult. How do I know when there'd be a train?"

"Look at a time-table, of course."

"I don't know where there is a time-table."

"Well, ring up Paddington."

"*Can* you ring up Paddington?"

"Of course you can. Why have you suddenly gone helpless like this?"

"I'm not helpless, darling. Only it all seems so peculiarly difficult."

"You're a big boy, now. You're old enough to travel alone."

"How are *you* going to get there?"

"By car. By family car booked in advance."

There was a jealous silence. Then Claud said, "Oh, if you've got the car, darling, couldn't you possibly come and pick me up at the works and we could have lunch together. . . ."

"No."

"No?"

"No."

"Not even for lunch with me?"

"Not even for lunch with you, my sweet, will I start about five hours earlier than I need and drive right up to town in order to drive back again immediately after lunch to a place twelve miles from where I started from."

"You shouldn't end a sentence with a preposition."

"I expect there's ever such a nice puff-puff for you, darling. Only be sure to ask the guard whether you change at Reading because—"

"Oh, I say, darling! For God's sake don't ring off. I mean this is serious. How can I possibly change?"

"Oh, you won't have long to wait," said Sylvia cheerfully. "Not more than three-quarters of an hour probably. And I expect there'll be lots of jolly slot machines to pass a little boy's time."

Claud did not think this amusing.

"Couldn't you really come up to town for me?"

"I could," said Sylvia brutally, "but I'm not going to."

"Damn you. Why can't you be fluffy and yielding for a change? Oh, I say! I've thought of something though. That settles it. I can't possibly come by train. Isn't Leslie's house miles from the station?"

"Just over a mile."

"Well, that settles it, doesn't it? I mean I can't possibly walk all that way carrying countless things, can I?"

"What do you mean—countless things?"

"Oh, an absolute trunkful of flannels and tennis rackets and bathing-costumes and—well, things."

It was no good. There was no one else in the world who could be so perfectly exasperating in such an appealing way. Sylvia, knowing herself yielding, made a last desperate effort.

"Well, darling, since you've obviously both physically as well as mentally deficient, I will if you like ring up the Invalid Children's Aid Association and ask them to have a bath-chair waiting for you at the station."

"Which station?" said Claud, eagerly. "You see, darling, I've got a terribly clever idea. Couldn't you bring the chair yourself to Reading? Look here, darling, for your sake I will come by train as far as Reading. I know how to get there. I went there once."

He sounded, thought Sylvia, quite proud of himself.

"Oh, Claud! Darling, you are a half-wit. Still I suppose I don't mind coming as far as Reading if you think yourself capable of indicating any particular time you'll be there."

"Say three," said Claud, promptly clinching the bargain. "It's sweet of you, darling. You do see it's really the best plan, don't you?"

"I'll tell you my opinion of the plan when I meet you at Reading," said Sylvia, ringing off.

But when she met him at Reading on Saturday she did not even refer to it.

She had been driving aimlessly about all the morning, and was in urgent need of an outlet for all the seething jumbled thoughts that teased her conscience. A dozen times she had swung, with a sickening lowering sensation, from self-justification to self-reproach. A dozen times she had reinstated her self-respect by argument, only to feel a few moments later the whole carefully erected structure crumbling at the sudden memory of Henrietta's tears.

As soon as she had handed over the wheel of the car to Claud she began to pour out the whole story. It was not very coherent. It was tangled up with self-justification, self-reproaches. "If I'd only realized," cried Sylvia again and again, and then, "if only Henrietta had understood that I didn't mean—" At one moment Sylvia appeared the villain of the story and Henrietta her innocent dupe; the next Captain Fortescue was roundly reviled and Henrietta scolded for leading him on. There was a general uneasy shifting about of responsibility, alternated with violent denials of its very existence. "Everybody *must* rely on themselves, mustn't they?" One fact only Sylvia suppressed. She did not dare tell Claud that she had lied about herself and him to Henrietta. Nobody, she thought, who had not gone through what she had gone through in the course of the quarrel could possibly understand the justification for this denial of the truth. It was, of course, clean against her principles.

Claud listened to all this in silence and with a gratifying appearance of concentration. When she was at last silent he said:

"I say. Just a minute. Did you notice that the clutch was slipping?"

The utter irrelevance of this comment infuriated Sylvia.

"Oh, *Claud*! What *has* that got to do with it? I don't believe you've been listening even."

"Oh, yes, I have, darling. But now *you* listen a moment. Listen to this," and he declutched momentarily and let his clutch in with a jerk.

"Well, what's the matter with that?" demanded Sylvia coldly.

"Can't you really hear how she's slipping and revving up far too much for the pace we're going?" Claud was perpetually surprised at Sylvia's apparent inability to hear defects in the engine. One would not perhaps expect her to be able to diagnose their cause, but surely, surely, unless one was stone deaf one could not help being immediately struck by anything so obvious?

"And didn't you notice your feet were getting a bit hot, Sylvia?"

"I was far too hot all over to bother about a little thing like that."

"I'm not sure that it is a little thing," said Claud. As always, when dealing with machinery, he was serious and imperturbable, quietly disregarding other people's impatience or flippancies. Sylvia fumed while he drew in to the side of the road, stopped and prepared to investigate. "The clutch-housing is very hot," he said. "It may only need adjusting, but I shouldn't be surprised if you had to have it relined. Funny you never noticed anything."

Funny, indeed! thought Sylvia. Men! It's important if the clutch-housing is hot. It isn't a bit important if your sister will never speak to you again. It's important if the engine gets overheated. It isn't a bit important if you have a violent quarrel with your family. Men! She was so annoyed that she forgot how absurd she believed it to be to classify human beings sharply into men and women, as if it wasn't all a matter of infinitely delicate gradations.

"Sorry, darling," said Claud, straightening his back and coming momentarily out of his trance of concentration. "It's a nuisance for you." His voice became serious again. "We'll have to drive very slowly and stop at the garage nearest to Leslie's house."

"You'd have done better to come by train, Claud," said Sylvia, and, feeling that she had scored one point at least, improved in humour.

"I like this better because I have you to myself for a little first," said Claud disarmingly.

It was no good. He was too clever with her when she showed signs of being in a bad temper. Sylvia did not really believe that his insistence on being fetched in the car was due to such touching fidelity; and as for seeing more of her—he had showed interest so far in nothing but the rotten engine. Nevertheless, in spite of herself, her ill humour began to dissolve. After all he couldn't help being like that about machinery. He *really* couldn't help it, and perhaps it was better than being quite incompetent and artistic. He was, she thought sentimentally and secretly, really rather sweet.

Moreover, she had for several minutes succeeded in forgetting about Henrietta, and now, as her thoughts automatically flew back to the subject, she was surprised to find that everything did not look quite so black and wretched as before. Perhaps it was not, after all, such a terribly serious matter. If one looked away from it, as it were, for a little and then looked back one seemed to see it more in proportion. What did Claud think about it?

Claud would not proffer any opinion until he had got the story a little clearer.

"You say your mother will certainly have stopped her going?"

"Oh, yes. Good heavens, yes!" (It was funny. It was only when Claud suddenly asked an extraordinary question like that, that one realized that never having known his own mother must really have made quite a difference to him.)

"And *you* told your mother?"

"Yes."

"Well, why did Henrietta tell you in the first place?"

"Oh, well, because—" Sylvia faltered. "I suppose she thought I'd sympathize. I suppose—you and me sort of thing—although I didn't—but she knows anyway that on *principle*. . . ." It was difficult to explain. "I think it was really a sort of accident she told me," finished Sylvia rather weakly. Claud nodded sympathetically. He was driving the car all the time with scrupulous care.

"What do you think, Claud?" inquired Sylvia anxiously.

"Think? Oh, that when Henrietta comes round a bit she'll be jolly grateful to you."

"I think it will take her a long time to 'come round' as you say."

"Quicker than you think, I expect."

"Then you don't think that I was wrong—wrong on *principle* I mean—to interfere?"

"Lord, no," said Claud, cheerfully. "Best thing you could do."

Sylvia felt comforted.

"You do honestly think so, darling?"

"Oh, yes. Honestly. I mean quite apart from principle and all that."

Without investigating further the insinuations of this rather remarkable statement they squeezed hands and drove on, comforted and reunited in spirit.

"Funny, you know. I'm feeling particularly fond of you today. Can't think why," remarked Claud presently.

"Are you really, Claud? You wouldn't rather I was a motor-car, for instance?"

"No. You can stay just as you are. I don't mind." There was at least a decent pause before he added, "It's a pity about the clutch though. I hope to God there's a good garage near Leslie's."

· · · · · · ·

When Claud and Sylvia, trudging along the road, laden with bags and rackets, looked back and saw Henry's car overtaking them they were so thankful and excited that Henry had difficulty in avoiding running over them.

"Oh, I *am* so glad to see you," cried Claud, "and that isn't politeness. I really mean it."

"Dear Henry. Dear Jane," murmured Sylvia.

They got in at the back. Henry and Jane seemed to have chosen peculiarly large suit-cases.

"Sit on my knee," suggested Claud.

"No," said Sylvia, "it would make a bad impression."

"What's happened to your car?" asked Jane.

"Oh, it's sprained a sprocket-knob and won't be ready till nine. We've left it at King's garage down the road."

Jane was perfectly satisfied with this explanation, but Henry, who had not spoken before, said "What?"

Claud soothed him with a more technical explanation. "Or it may not be ready then if it's a question of relining," he added, "in that case Sylvia has arranged that Leslie should transport us home."

"I shouldn't think Leslie would mind, would you, Jane?" put in Sylvia.

"Good Lord, no! Of course she'll take you anywhere," agreed Jane confidently.

Leslie was waiting at the drive gate and sprang onto the step. She chattered rapidly as they drove to the house.

"Isn't it marvellous it's such a nice day? Why didn't you bring your own car, Sylvia? It is fun to see you all here. Oh, by the way, Jane, you won't forget to have a chat with mummy, will you? She may be a bit elusive."

"There she is now, running round the rhododendron bushes," said Claud. Mrs. Fisher, stately in black and white voile, was moving gently towards them across the lawn.

"She isn't dodging yet," said Jane. Leslie, a little uncertain whether they were laughing at her or at her mother, felt a moment's anxiety. Supposing this party didn't go off quite as she had intended it? Suppose her mother classed her friends in the category of "horrid young people"?

However, on being presented to Mrs. Fisher, all four behaved impeccably.

"It's awfully nice of you to ask us down here, Mrs. Fisher," said Claud.

"On such a marvellous day, too," chimed in Jane.

"And doesn't the garden look lovely?" Sylvia was jealously determined not to be outdone, and having been brought up in the country she knew that sooner or later this had to be said.

Mrs. Fisher's heart warmed towards Sylvia. She decided that she might have misjudged her in the past.

"It really is rather in its prime now, isn't it, Sylvia? That shower last night did it good. Do you share your mother's interest in gardens? Would you like just to have a peep at the rose-garden? It really is looking—"

But no! thought Leslie. This is all wrong. Sylvia and mummy mustn't be allowed too much together, not, at least, if Sylvia is going to be at all interested in gardens.

"We wanted to play tennis, mummy," she said quickly.

"Oh, very well, my dear," said her dutiful mother. "Run away and change."

But before they could run away a bright red sports car drew up in the drive with a loud roar of the engine and much crunching of the gravel. Bert and Bill had arrived.

"Oh, hello," said Leslie, and began to introduce her friends. She had a vague idea (drawn again from modern fiction) that people at London parties never bothered about introductions. However, one had to, more or less, in the country. All concerned seemed to take it quite calmly. Henry and Claud began to look at the car. Bert and Bill stood beaming a general welcome. Wasn't it a wizard day? said their honest smiling faces. Wasn't this party a great idea?

"Now we're all here but Florence," said Leslie.

CHAPTER XI

I

"How MUCH ARE those meat-pies?" said Florence three times to the waitress in the buffet at Paddington. But the waitress was serving out beer and rapid back-chat to the Saturday crowd of men and either did not hear or did not choose to hear.

"Sixpence," she flung eventually at Florence.

Florence looked doubtfully at them. There seemed to be a lot of rather stodgy pastry about them.

"Could I have half one?"

"What?"

"I said could I have half one?"

"Sorry. We don't serve them in halves."

"Oh. Well, how much are those ham sandwiches?"

A red-faced man in a bowler hat jostled Florence against the counter. She moved crossly away. He had spilt some beer down her skirt.

"Fourpence each."

Fourpence! What a price for a small ham sandwich!

"Do you have anything else? Tomato or anything?"

"Only ham and cheese." The waitress was becoming impatient.

"Oh. I'll have two ham then, please, and—and—oh—er— a bath bun."

A very uninspiring lunch. Florence, clutching hand-bag, suit-case, tennis racket and paper-bag, went off to study the indicator. What fun it would be to open a chain of really nice snack-bars at all the big London stations. She would decorate them in scarlet and chromium and serve savouries and toasted sandwiches, all piping hot. White-coated bartenders would hand out the food with quite incredible dispatch. There would be a welcoming smile for old customers, a kindly warning for the tardy. "Your train's whistling, sir. I think you ought to be off." During her slow progress to the indicator Florence became quite entranced with the idea. Florence's Bar, perhaps? or just Chez Florence? And they wouldn't charge fourpence for a small ham sandwich. The prices would be surprisingly reasonable, but in spite of this they would be filled with *nice* people, thought Florence with a shocking lapse into snobbishness. Girls and young men who said "Good morning, George," to the barman as they entered, not men in bowlers who said "Thank you, miss" as they tried to push you out of the way. But as she searched the indicator for her train (and a pretty poor sort of indicator it was for any one who didn't already know the time it went) she suddenly realized with a pang something that had hitherto barely penetrated; after leaving her present job the world was in fact her oyster. She was as free to try her hand in the snack-bar trade as in the millinery, the veterinary, the teaching, or indeed, any other in the world. The realization had in it no exultation. Immediately the snack-bar scheme appeared improbable and foredoomed to failure. Probably you needed ten years' experience of hotel work and a capital of several thousands. Florence knew that she had plenty of enthusiasm and a capacity for hard work; she still hoped, in a slightly crushed manner, that she might have some organizing ability; but the problem of mating these qualities to any congenial form of employment seemed at the moment insoluble. She shifted her suit-case to her left arm. Bother! Now her hand-bag, insecurely wedged under this arm, was slipping out backwards. She put down the racket and paper-bag and performed the rather complicated manoeuvre of pushing the bag forward by putting her right arm round behind her back. A small boy watched her with amusement and a porter immediately volunteered his services. "No, thank you," said Florence. She was not going to spend sixpence on a fifty-yards walk. She did, however, stop at the bookstall and buy a paper, a woman's weekly, price 2d., because two coppers came easily to hand, and because it was a good deal of reading for the price, and because she wasn't feeling in the least intellectual. She was not even so revolted as she would ordinarily have been by the coloured cover depicting a naked and chubby baby tactfully grasping a large sponge. Underneath was printed "Baby Problem Week." Very well, Baby Problem Week let it be. Any problem so utterly remote from her own difficulties might be positively soothing.

But the effect of the perusal of this innocuous little paper on poor Florence was devastating and unexpected. Gradually she felt more and more miserable. It was as if every hint in the paper, every problem cheerily solved (and was there *any* problem the editress didn't consider herself capable of solving, asked Florence angrily?), every anecdote and short story had been designed to enhance her sense of failure. The whole paper was a hymn in praise of women. Women, it seemed, all women, were efficient, reliable, beautiful and intelligent; or at any rate could be if they followed the simple expedients of putting on a clean lace collar for the office every day, remembering the "Chief's" favourite brand of tea-biscuit, massaging arms, face and neck with cold cream night and morning ("My dear, you'll be *shocked* at the dirt that comes out!") and keeping "up" with the newspapers and modern novels. ("It is not really necessary to have read *all* a novel in order to talk intelligently about it" added the paper comfortingly.) In comparison with such paragons men were, of course, rather poor creatures. They were all exactly alike, looked about eighteen in the illustrations, and were treated with a sort of affectionate patronage. It was not necessary to characterize them further. If any more had to be added it was usually

that "He" had a nice smile or that dogs and children adored "Him."
(Florence could not help finding this use of the capital a little blas-
phemous.) Men were left at that. But women and their duty stood
revealed in these pages with an attractive simplicity. Women's job
was firstly to attract "Him" (involving a whole ritual of beauty-care,
"personal daintiness" and knowledge of masculine psychology—
since all men were the same this could be quickly learnt), secondly,
to bring "Him" up to scratch, thirdly to keep "Him" content at home
so that he should not stray after other women (a great deal was
made of this subtle point—"make his home *attractive* to him")—
and finally (particularly, of course, because this was baby problem
week) to discover with every symptom of surprise and delight that
"another little stranger would be knocking shortly at the door of
life." The charming life-cycle then recommenced. "How wonderful
it is to think of your child as a bit of you." And how maddening for
the child, thought Florence, and discovered, crossly, that she felt
nearer tears than laughter.

For however much one might jeer, however much one might
despise that sort of thing, however silly one might think it to talk
as if all women wanted the same things, nevertheless this harmless
little paper gave Florence the most sickening and unpremeditated
attack of a dreadful sort of shut-out feeling. Here was this world
of cosy domestic happiness; here was Jim coming home in the
evenings, here were days spent in running up new curtains for the
spare-room, trying out a new recipe, or giving a little bridge party.
("Don't be too formal, my dears, informal parties are *much* more
fun.") Here was baby having his bath by the fire, here (a little later presumably) were the children going off to school (the "facts of
life" previously explained to them in the very nicest possible way),
here was granny coming to stay, installed comfortably in the spare-
room, told (very tactfully) that there was a writing-desk and easy
chair in there "as I expect you would like some time to yourself."
Here, in fact, was a whole world which Florence, despising, did not,
could not, and would now never belong to. A world in which your
husband brought you home surprise chocolates and praised your
new hat; not a world in which you tried to smash your typewriter
and ran out of the office; not a world in which if you cried it was
your fault and there was no one to comfort you. Even the "Answers
to Correspondents," usually a fruitful source of merriment, seemed

on this occasion devoid of power to amuse; for Brown Eyes wrote from Clapham to say that although she knew lots of boys they never fell in love with her. What could she do? And the answer was, "Don't worry. Perhaps you are self-conscious. Join a jolly mixed hiking club and forget about yourself. Mr. Right will come along one day—perhaps sooner than you think." As though, thought Florence angrily, as though there weren't *lots* of girls that no one ever wanted to marry. Lots with brown, blue, grey, green eyes, all making the best of it, all so bright, so keen on their careers. But I haven't got a career, thought Florence. Her bath bun tasted like ashes in the mouth. Tears rose in her throat, choking her. Could anything be more absurd? Florence Somerset, B.A., crying in the train into a bath bun. Florence Somerset crying because she hadn't got a man to take care of her.

Leslie marshalled them all into the house to change, and then marshalled them all back on to the tennis-court. Now, she thought triumphantly, I've got them all here—except Florence—and they've only got to behave quite naturally and mummy will understand at once what I mean about their being different.

She arranged a four, and felt obliged to include Jane and Sylvia, although she would have liked to play herself, leaving Jane free for Mrs. Fisher to talk to. Well, never mind, mummy could talk to Claud. Although Leslie had only met him once she felt sure that any friend of Sylvia's would be thoroughly modern in outlook. Unfortunately Claud had begun to talk not to her mother but to Bill, with whom he seemed to be getting on surprisingly well. Now what could *they* have in common? Presently Leslie realized that they were talking about cars—or was it aeroplanes? The same thing anyway. Put a criminal, a barrister, a publican and a boy of ten together, thought Leslie, and presently there'll be an animated buzz of conversation and you'll hear the words "four and a half to one back axle ratio," "high-lift overlap camshaft," and "twin down-draft carburettors." (These were the gems that the summer air wafted to her.)

When the set ended Leslie said quickly, "Now let me see. If Jane and I sit out" (so that I can *see* that Jane talks to mummy about London) "that leaves—" At this point Jane sat down and Bert seated himself with determination beside her. He had decided at a glance that this was the girl for him to cultivate on this particular occasion. Nice hair, he thought appraisingly. Nice legs, too.

"That leaves Claud and Sylvia and Bill and Henry—oh, bother! Where's Florence, I wonder? She's late. Was she coming by train, Jane?"

"Yes. Yes, I think so."

Mrs. Fisher wondered what Jane and Henry were doing not to have brought Florence with them. She understood that they were an engaged couple—but even so it seemed a little hard on Florence. Was Jane perhaps a little selfish? She had hardly spoken to her yet, had not, in fact, had an opportunity of searching for the alleged "talent for living." But she seemed rather lively for such a nice but very solemn young man as her Henry. Probably, thought Mrs. Fisher rather unkindly, probably she wasn't so talented about other people's lives as about her own.

Leslie had decided that a men's four would be the safest arrangement for her purposes. Bert was firmly prized out of his strategic position next to Jane and sent on to the court. Leslie seated herself between her mother and Jane, and arrogated to herself the role of conversational umpire.

The four men players dutifully concentrated on their match, driving strongly and accurately and manoeuvring for smashes at the net; but to Leslie's disgust the sitters-out played a poor sort of knock-up game, neglecting each other's openings and only seeming to give half their attention to the business in hand.

"Jane shares a flat with Florence," prompted Leslie.

"That must be very nice for the two of you," said Mrs. Fisher amiably.

"Oh, yes. It's much nicer than digs, really," said Jane. (One point scored, thought Leslie.)

"I wonder what train Florence will catch," said Mrs. Fisher. "She didn't say?"

"No. Breakfast is all rather sordid and rushed when you have to get off to work. There's never time to say anything."

"Is that so? What do you have for breakfast, Jane?"

"Oh, just tea and toast, you know. Florence has an egg usually."

"I think that's sensible," said Mrs. Fisher, registering a good mark to Florence in her mind. "Tea and toast don't seem to me much to do a morning's work on."

"Lots of people, doctors and people, say it's far healthier," put in Leslie.

"Well, it's a great saving of bother anyway," said Jane, and Mrs. Fisher immediately shook her head over young people who sacrificed health to convenience. She became aware of her daughter's urgent gaze and obediently took up the catechism.

"Do you find it expensive living in a flat, Jane?"

Jane became judicial.

"I should say it's slightly more expensive than cheap digs, but of course far nicer. You can't really give any sort of a party in digs. People complain."

"Yes, I suppose that would be a difficulty. (How noisy her friends must be.) Then what do you do about supper?"

Jane seemed surprisingly vague about this important point.

"Oh, I don't know. Sometimes we cook or bring something in, or we're often out, of course."

"Whenever I've been to supper there," said Leslie hastily, "we've had the most marvellous meals."

"Do you and Florence take it in turns then to do the cooking?" pursued Mrs. Fisher. Surely, she thought, there must be some sort of method about these extraordinarily vague and inadequate arrangements.

"No. When we do cook we each do things for ourselves. For one thing, we don't like each other's kind of food, and then we don't often know whether the other will be in or not."

Mrs. Fisher marvelled.

"And do you really find it more comfortable than digs, Jane, where you'd have a nice hot supper waiting for you when you got in?"

"Oh, yes. Really, it's much nicer in every way." Jane suddenly recollected that she was supposed to be giving an enthusiastic account of her life in London. "Really, it's lovely," she said. "It's far the nicest way of living. As a matter of fact, I'm afraid it probably spoils you for any other kind of life."

"I suppose in some ways it would," said Mrs. Fisher, agreeing for the first time with her guest. Bitter disappointment flooded Leslie's heart. Hint as she might, this conversation would not run along the appointed lines. As if it mattered whether one had an egg for breakfast or not!

It was to be hoped that Florence would do a little better than this.

Mrs. Fisher turned to Sylvia and began to talk about gardens again; and Leslie had not the spirit to interrupt them, even though she could hear Sylvia being unnecessarily polite and responsive. Unknown to Leslie, Sylvia was finding a perverse sort of pleasure in an exchange of the pleasant banalities that ordinarily she despised so much. After the events of the morning there was something strangely reassuring in all this talk of rose-gardens and the weather and the local fête.

· · · · · · · ·

The men finished their set and every one stood about waiting to be told what to do next. They were, thought Leslie disappointedly, almost too polite, too well-drilled, too much the perfect guests. She had not exactly wanted them to shriek and break things and be rude to her mother, but it was a little dull to see them behaving exactly like any one else.

Leslie suggested more tennis. She suggested alternatively a bathe. Every one said, "Very nice," and refused to commit themselves to any preference. Things were still undecided when Alice appeared to tell them that King's garage was ringing up about a motor-car. Claud and Sylvia went in to answer the phone.

"Why did you want me to come too?" asked Sylvia, as she found herself firmly led toward the house.

"I thought you looked as if you wanted kissing," said Claud kindly. "And I didn't think you could be the perfect guest much more without bursting."

"As a matter of fact it comes perfectly naturally to me. My brilliant impersonation of a really nice girl is well known in the neighbourhood. A sort of bright docility that goes down splendidly."

The garage was ringing up to say that the clutch would need relining and the car would not be ready for two days.

"Now what about Leslie's running us home?" asked Claud hopefully.

"Yes, of course. Only we shall have to inquire hypocritically about trains."

"I will say this for you, my love. You have a quite extraordinary grasp of the social conventions."

"Yes, I rather pride myself on it. Darling, you can't kiss me here. Your affection is most ill-timed."

"Well, you looked so lonely and peaked. As if nobody had kissed you for years and years."

"Sweet of you to notice it. I think your ears are sticking out more than they used to, Claud. Perhaps you had better wear a shingle-cap at night. I say, I'd better ring up mummy and ask her to have one ready for you tonight, hadn't I?"

"Thank you, darling. You're taking all that part about going back by train as said, are you?"

"Yes. Although, as a matter of fact, you could perfectly well, couldn't you? However, don't. Because I think it would be rather nice to have you, so that I shan't be left alone with Henrietta."

"All right, my sweet. To please you I will come."

Sylvia sat on Claud's knee and asked for her own number, but on hearing footsteps in the hall she hastily sprang up again.

"But darling, why shouldn't you?"

"I don't know," said Sylvia. "I just can't tell you. I just instinctively can't go on sitting on people's knees if housemaids are walking around. It's something to do with my early training, I expect. Damn, now I've told the telephone girl all that. I feel rather nervous of speaking to mummy. I wonder what she and Henrietta said to each other."

Claud reflected again that Sylvia was the most peculiar and adorable mixture.

"I expect Henrietta said 'Oh, mummy!' and mummy said 'Oh, Henrietta!' and then they both burst into tears and said nothing more," suggested Claud.

"Hello, mummy? This is Sylvia."

Mrs. Perry's voice came faint and placid over the wire.

"Oh, is that you, dear? You're at Leslie's, I suppose?"

"Yes. I say, the car has broken down. The clutch is jamming—"

"Slipping," said Claud.

"Slipping, and has got to be done and the car won't be ready for two days. It's a nuisance, isn't it? Look here, will it be all right if I bring Claud back tonight? Leslie is going to—at least I haven't asked her yet, but I expect she will run us back, and otherwise he doesn't know about trains and things, you see. So will it be all right?"

From this slightly involved explanation Mrs. Perry drew the impression that Sylvia, without actually intending anything untrue, meant her to draw; that the young man, Claud, was somehow inextricably stranded in the middle of Berkshire and could only be rescued by a preliminary transportation to Sylvia's home.

"Very well, dear. We shall be very glad to see him. About what time will you be back?"

"Oh, I don't know. Quite late, I expect. We probably shan't see you, I shouldn't think."

"Well, in that case I'll just leave the spare-room ready, shall I?"

"Yes. We might be quite early, you know. But don't expect us till late. I say—what about—I mean, how is Henrietta?"

"She's asleep," said Mrs. Perry, a deep satisfaction in her voice. "Poor little thing, she was quite worn out. I don't think she'd slept a wink all night. She just said, 'Mummy!' and burst into tears as soon as she saw me. So I gave her two aspirins and tucked her up, and she went straight off to sleep. I haven't disturbed her and she hasn't come down yet."

"Oh. Good."

"By the way, dear, I'll just take the opportunity of warning you that I thought it better not to say anything to daddy about this. It was all quite simply arranged. I won't mention names over the telephone. But I just asked Doris to phone up—you know who I mean—and leave a message to say Miss Henrietta's mother was so sorry but Miss Henrietta was a little indisposed and would not be coming to lunch that day."

"Lunch? Oh, yes."

"I thought that was the best way of putting it. However angry one is with—you know who I mean—well, for Henrietta's sake it's best just not to see the people in question any more and forget the whole business as quickly as possible, isn't it?"

"Yes—yes, I suppose so."

"So I really think we needn't bother daddy about it. Henrietta— poor little thing!—sobbed out to me that she didn't want to think any more about it ever again. It was just all a silly mistake and there's no necessity to upset daddy about it. He thinks Henrietta has a bad headache. As a matter of fact, I expect it would be wiser for none of us to refer to it again. It was just all a mistake which we want to forget about."

"Very well, mummy. I'll remember."

"Well, I'm sorry about the car, dear, and I'll expect you and Claud late tonight. Is that it?"

"Yes. Thank you, mummy. Good-by."

"Good-by."

As her mother rang off Sylvia turned to Claud.

"Did you hear that, darling? Lord, I do think mothers are incredible!"

"What did she say?"

"Oh, just not to tell daddy and the poor little thing, and asleep and two aspirins and so on. Obviously she's ready to defend Henrietta against any one. Why, goodness, darling, if I was mummy with her views and upbringing and everything, I should be furious with Henrietta. She's so incredibly inconsistent. Henrietta couldn't have found anything more awful to do according to mummy's point of view; and then she says we won't tell daddy because it would only upset him, and it was all just a mistake, and rings off. Honestly, she's either just a fool or an angel—I don't know which."

"You ought to know more about mother-love than I do, Sylvia. Is that the sort of way it takes one?"

"Apparently. As a matter of fact, I've always thought mother-love pretty nauseating—a sort of emotional hold over your child that stops its developing freely along its own lines."

"Well, this particular development has come in for some pretty firm checking on all sides, hasn't it?" said Claud, amused.

But Sylvia, although reassured, was not yet ready to see any humour in the situation.

"I don't know," she said with a profound sigh, "I don't know. I simply don't know. I never thought I'd live to approve of interference, but—darling, what's the matter? Why are you suddenly so affectionate?"

"Because you looked worried. You're so sweet when you look worried."

"The trouble with you, Claud, is that you need perpetual attention to keep you happy." Sylvia put her arms round his neck and kissed his nose fondly. "Just like a jealous fox-terrier."

"The trouble with you, Sylvia, is"—Claud, hesitating over a choice of insults, was lost. Sylvia's teasing expectant mouth was too alluring to resist. He kissed her suddenly and finished weakly, "that you're much too adorable for any man."

III

"There's a striking variety of costume about us," said Jane.

Leslie gazed at the figures prostrate around her on the grassy river-bank. Henry and Sylvia, although warned, had tiresomely forgotten to bring bathing-costumes. They may have had more important matters to think of that morning, but they were now paying the price for this earlier unmaterial attitude. Sylvia, offered first choice out of an impromptu collection of old suits, had chosen a red cotton garment, which hung loosely in folds about her, the legs flapping nearly to her knees. "I wore that only a few years ago," said Leslie encouragingly.

"I don't see how you could have," said Sylvia, with a slight lapse from her "nice girl" impersonation, since Mrs. Fisher was no longer with them. "It's far too big for me and I'm larger than you."

"That was supposed to be the correct size," said Jane. "I remember distinctly. It was really. It was considered decent."

"This carries decency a bit too far," said Sylvia, mournfully flapping the legs.

"Indecency, you mean," corrected Claud lazily from where he lay in his superior black Jantzen, spread-eagled to the sun. "Modesty is indecency, you know."

"Sorry to arouse your worst instincts," said Sylvia, sitting down with as much dignity as possible beside Henry, who said in a discreet and gloomy undertone, "I didn't notice this female thing was hand-knitted when I took it. You wouldn't like to change, I suppose? Do you think Leslie would mind? Do you suppose she knitted it?"

"Oh, it's all right, Henry dear," said Sylvia soothingly. "It really looks perfectly all right on you."

"Do *you* think this is all right, Jane?" inquired Henry hopefully.

"I think it's lovely," said Jane unkindly, "so *you*, somehow." Bert, who had stationed himself next to her, laughed heartily, and Henry rolled over on to his face and began to bite off stems of grass and chew them. I mustn't be a fool, he thought, I mustn't mind such silly things; damn, I wish I hadn't forgotten my bathing-dress. What a silly laugh that fool Bert has. Bother, thought Jane, how can I possibly remember all the time how sensitive Henry is, although of course he isn't nearly so much with any one but me. As soon as I begin to enjoy myself I always forget. I wonder if Bert swims well. He looks rather nice in a bathing-dress.

This party is beginning to go better, reflected Leslie, every one seems more natural now. I never realized before how polite they could all be. It was quite a shock.

Leslie herself was dressed in a very smart two-piece of blue and white wool. One of the pieces was a diminutive pair of pants, the other a wisp of a brassière, ingeniously anchored fore and aft to the pants by a button and strap. Mrs. Fisher, a little self-consciously broad-minded (she had reached the stage of thinking the bathing-dress of today "sensible" but not the stage of taking it for granted) had said it was very nice, but perhaps Leslie had better not wear it at the local baths. So Leslie had been hoping they might all have kept on their bathing things and played tennis in this sensible and convenient costume after tea; but Sylvia and Henry had been so silly and forgetful, and now they would never want to play in their borrowed red cotton and hand-knitted suits. Leslie was once more struck by the perversity of visitors who would not behave as planned. Natural and spontaneous gaiety was going to be extremely difficult to achieve if people were going to be so overnatural and super-spontaneous as to forget their bathing-dresses.

They all lay sprawling luxuriously in the sun, languidly comparing each other's degrees of sunburn. Bert engaged Jane's attention with a long anecdote about a bathe at Oxford. Jane gathered that he had been up at B.N.C. He was very kindly making the story easy for her with helpful explanations of all the university references she might not be expected to understand. "So another chap from Jesus —that's one of the colleges, you know—and I went down to Parson's Pleasure—that's the men's bathing-place. It was a lovely evening and we thought we'd like a swim. When we got there we met two men who'd been gated soon after the beginning of the term—that means they weren't allowed out after nine, you see—and so I said—" It was a very long story and Jane found it extraordinarily soothing. The conclusion seemed indefinitely deferred, but this she did not mind, for she was quite sure that the story would eventually ably illustrate the daring cleverness of the undergraduates as opposed to the doddering and senile stupidity of the authorities. When, however, Bert told her for the third time that Parson's Pleasure was the men's bathing-place, she was moved to assure him of her comprehension.

"Yes, I know. I was up at Oxford."

Bert appeared as astounded as if women had not yet gained admittance to the University.

"*Were* you? But I thought—that is, all the women I ever saw were so—I mean they went about on bicycles in herds."

"If your college is some way out of the town," said Henry, slightly defensive on Jane's behalf, "a bicycle is the most sensible way of getting about."

"Yes. Although, as a matter of fact, I admit I was too snobby to use one," said Jane, basely refusing his support.

Bert appeared relieved to hear this.

"I say. How very funny. Do you know we must have been up at the same time!" he exclaimed, much struck by the coincidence. "When did you come down?"

"Two years ago."

"So did I!" He gazed at her enthusiastically.

"Didn't you know any women students?" asked Jane kindly, guessing him to be bursting with suppressed astonishment.

"Good Lord, no! I always thought they were—I say, will you think me frightfully rude if I say they always struck me as pretty awful?"

"No. All B.N.C. thinks that," said Jane agreeably, and added, with a disgraceful lack of loyalty, "I dare say they're quite right."

Bert began to produce reasons for this widespread and well-merited opinion.

"They go about on bicycles—and those caps are so awful—and great herds of them used to come to our lectures and take notes all the time—and—and they go about on bicycles—and, I say, don't you honestly agree with me that most of them are pretty awful?" He smiled at her disarmingly, convinced that there must be only one conclusion to be drawn from such a striking list of indictments.

Jane thought him soothing and sweet and artless, and Henry thought him the silliest fool he had ever met.

"I think you're absolutely right," said Jane. "Although if it wasn't so sunny I should probably think quite differently."

"Well, it's jolly decent of you to admit it," said Bert generously.

Henry, feeling that he had had about as much of this as he could stand, got up abruptly, said, "I'm going in," and did so immediately.

"Well, I wish I'd known you were up there when I was up," said Bert, as Henry disappeared into the water.

Nobody copied Henry's example, so that the burst of laughter which followed his reappearance on the bank was general and immediate. His hand-knitted suit, stretching in the water, had nearly doubled its length. The shoulder-straps reached to his waist and the skirt dripped round the region of his knees. Every one except Henry thought this very entertaining.

"How can I swim in this damn silly suit?" demanded Henry. "I can hardly move my legs.'"

"I'm so sorry, Henry," said Leslie. She had knitted the suit herself and consequently did not think the spectacle quite as amusing as the others. "It's only been worn once and it did that before, I remember. I don't know why it should. When it's dry it shrinks back—"

"Oh, it's all right, Leslie," said Henry, immediately afraid that he had hurt her feelings. "It's really very nice. It's only this stretching—" He hastily got back into the water and began experimentally to kick his legs.

Sylvia laughed so much that she got a pain. She lay on her front and pressed her hands to her chest.

"I wouldn't laugh so much if I were you," said Claud. "Let me warn you that your costume will probably be equally comic when you get it wet. That sort of cotton goes quite transparent."

"All the more reason for laughing now," gasped Sylvia.

"I love you," said Claud irrelevantly.

Leslie felt that they had laughed enough.

"Well, I'm going in too," she said, and executed a neat running dive. She was a little surprised and embarrassed at the applause this occasioned. Although she had known every one was watching and felt a little self-conscious, she had meant them all to take it for granted that this was the way one ordinarily entered a river.

"Do come on in," she called out.

They came. Bert and Bill at the same moment with hearty twin splashes, Jane more slowly, feeling the water with an experimental toe, Claud and Sylvia, prancing hand in hand to the bank, prepared to offer helpful criticism of each other's dives.

"Oh, why isn't Florence here!" cried Leslie impatiently, sitting on the bank and stretching her arms streaming with the ivory water. "She oughtn't to miss this."

Bert was instructing Jane in the crawl. They paid little attention to Leslie's wail. Henry had set off on a lone and furious swim upstream. Despite his knitted skirts he was traveling at a great rate, with white submerged face and wet plastered hair. Leslie had her back to the house. It was Bill who said, "Why, look, there's some one coming towards us now. Is that her?"

Perhaps, he thought hopefully, she will be some one I shall want to pair off with. He had not been able to help feeling a little out of it so far. Leslie was a good sort, but she didn't seem to have much to say to him. Old brother Bert was taken up with the Jane girl, the fair good-looking one.

It *was* Florence. She was still carrying her bag and tennis-racket. Her shoes were very dusty. She had walked from the station and had developed a sore heel and a splitting headache. When she saw the river and every one splashing about in it, it struck her that cool water—the cooler the better—was exactly the remedy for all her ills. She broke into a run and began to babble confused greetings from a parched and hoarse throat.

"Hello, Leslie. Hello, Sylvia. Hello, every one. Oh, you do look nice and cool. I'm so hot. Oh, Jane! Jane, you'll never think—I've given up my job. Isn't it priceless? Oh, Lord, I am so hot. Leslie, the maid said you were all out here, so I came. Oh, I do want to get into the water."

"Florence! I'm so glad you've come at last," cried Leslie. "But, darling! Haven't you got an awful cold or something? You sound so hoarse."

"I shall be all right after a bathe. I'm so frightfully hot. You see, I walked all the way from the station—"

"Oh, *why* didn't you let us know what time you were arriving or take a taxi or something?"

"Florence, have you really given notice?" inquired Jane, abandoning the crawl lesson and swimming interestedly towards her friend.

"Yes, isn't it priceless? But I shall be all right after a bathe. Where's my bathing-dress?" Florence knelt down, opened her bag, and began to rummage violently in it.

"Oh, I say, look out, Florence. You're chucking all your clean tennis things out on to the grass."

"Don't worry, Leslie. I say, where can I change? They aren't clean anyway."

"Well, it's more comfortable to change in my room. Look, here's mummy coming. She'll show you the way."

Florence stood up to greet Mrs. Fisher, kicking impatiently at a tennis shoe under her foot. Mrs. Fisher, taking Florence's hot hand in her own cool grasp, gave her a kind welcoming smile.

"It's very nice to see you here again, Florence."

"Yes, isn't it fun?" For some reason, although she was very hot, she was trembling all over. Mrs. Fisher wouldn't notice, would she? But Mrs. Fisher did.

"My poor child! You have got a cold, haven't you?"

"Oh, it's nothing. I shall be all right after a bathe."

"A bathe! Have you got a sore throat?"

"Sort of. It's nothing really."

Mrs. Fisher gazed with solicitude at Florence's reddened nose, feverish flush and slightly bloodshot eyes.

"Poor dear," she said, and Florence immediately sensed in her sympathy the dreaded note of maternal authority. "Before I let you go into the water I'm going to take your temperature."

With such a sensible pronouncement was Florence's doom sealed. If people were going to take any particular notice of her she would never be able to keep it up.

"I'm all right, really, Mrs. Fisher." The assertion was beginning to lack conviction.

"Come along into the house, dear."

On the way in Florence suddenly began to cry. Mrs. Fisher was tactful.

"These summer colds make one feel rotten, don't they, Florence?"

"I do feel rather funny," sobbed Florence.

Mrs. Fisher, with a motherly gesture, took her arm.

"You're going straight to bed," she said.

CHAPTER XII

BERT ASSURED JANE that she was improving no end at the crawl, that she was a wizard pupil and that in no time she would have the complete hang of it.

"It's just a knack, really," he said.

This was meant as encouragement, but had, of course, as always, the opposite effect.

Jane, sated with instruction, looked about for Henry. He was not in sight. He must have swum round the bend of the river.

"Thanks, awfully, Bert," she said. "I think I'll dry off now for a bit anyway."

She clambered on to the bank, muddying her knees, and began to run down the side of the river towards the bend. Bert watched her appreciatively. She was leaving him, but she had called him "Bert." Fancy her being up at Oxford! She *had* got nice legs.

Henry was sitting, out of sight of the others, on the bank, trailing his legs in the water and gazing rather gloomily at a patch of bulrushes.

"Hello, darling," said Jane.

"Hello," replied Henry, brightening.

She came and sat beside him and allowed him to scrub her knees clean with bulrushes and water.

"Do you like that man, Bert?" asked Henry.

"I'd rather be with you," replied Jane untruthfully and bewitchingly. "Why did you go off?"

"He doesn't do the crawl very well himself," was Henry's somewhat elliptic answer.

Jane took off her bathing-cap and shook out her short fair hair.

"Is it very wet, Henry?"

Henry stroked it.

"No. It's sweet and curling up at the ends."

"Darling, it's not meant to be all sweet and curling up at the ends. It's meant to be dry and smooth."

"I like it like this." There was a silence. "Do you love me really?" asked Henry.

"Yes. Yes, of course I do." There was another silence. They might love each other, but they had not apparently very much to say to one another.

"The sun is lovely, isn't it?" said Jane, and thought immediately, How awful that I should be making conversation to Henry of all people.

"How long have we got to stay at this party, do you think?" asked Henry.

"Oh, I don't know. We don't want to go too early, do we?" (Of course, there was this idiotic idea of finding somewhere to stay. If only Henry had had the sense to settle it beforehand.)

"After tea?" asked Henry, persistently.

"Oh, no, darling! I'm afraid we ought to stay till quite six. As a matter of fact, I believe Leslie's expecting us all to stay to supper—"

"We can't do that," said Henry firmly.

"No. All right. But I don't think we can leave too soon after tea, really."

There was another silence.

"Shall we have a race back?" asked Jane gently.

"No. Let's stay here a little longer."

So they stayed side by side without speaking, listening to the shouts and splashes from the invisible bathers around the bend, and thinking their own thoughts.

II

Tea was served on the little lawn in front of the summer-house. Florence was in bed in the spare-room and Jane and Henry had to be fetched, but the others came rushing from their bathe, eyeing enthusiastically the piles of savoury sandwiches and big bowls of strawberries and cream and choice of iced drinks.

"I shall eat Florence's share," said Sylvia in an undertone to Claud. It had just occurred to her that she had had practically no lunch or breakfast. It may have been this, it may have been the bathe, it may have been the relief of hearing from her mother that Henrietta had burst into tears and gone to sleep; probably it was all three, but she had never before in her life felt so hungry.

Mrs. Fisher, dispensing food and drink with a hostess's pleasure in her guests' appetites, said that Florence had a slight temperature, but now that she was in bed was feeling much happier already.

"Funny," said Jane, accepting a further selection of sandwiches. ("Take two, won't you? That's right, take several, they're so small.") "She was quite all right this morning."

"Didn't you notice she had a cold, Jane?" asked Mrs. Fisher. Surely the child must have noticed *something*!

"Yes, I think she said she had a bit of a cold, but she seemed all right, you know."

"Well, I certainly think she ought to take it quietly for a day or two. She'd better stay down here and get good country food and air for a bit."

"Oh, mummy!" cried Leslie, deeply wounded at such tactlessness, "you needn't talk as if she half starved herself in London."

"No, of course I didn't mean that. Jane knows I didn't mean anything of the sort." Mrs. Fisher, sure of her ground, was quite calm and unflurried. "But every one knows that if you're a bit run down it's nice not to have to rely on restaurant food altogether."

"Oh, mummy," said Leslie resignedly.

"Oh, yes, that's awfully true," said Jane agreeably. "I do think after living in London for a bit a change of food is simply marvellous."

"Of course it is," agreed Mrs. Fisher warmly, thinking that Jane had more good sense than she had at first given her credit for.

"Funny her giving up her job suddenly like that," speculated Jane. "Did she tell you why, Mrs. Fisher?"

"No, I didn't ask her anything about it."

"Of course, I know she hasn't been liking it much recently," said Jane, "but—"

"Do *you* work at a job too, Jane?" put in Bert with interest.

"Yes. Nine-thirty to five-thirty and every other Saturday."

Bert seemed enormously impressed. This wonderful girl was not only good-looking but apparently intelligent; and not only intelligent but apparently industrious. She responded in the sort of way one expected attractive girls to respond, and yet she had been up at Oxford. One could teach her the crawl and get up willingly to fetch her still more pâté sandwiches, and yet she worked in an office and presumably earned a salary for it. She was not at all like the sort of girls he usually met, although fortunately she looked like them. One must not lose sight of her.

"Did you come down here by train?" (One could perhaps offer to drive her back?)

"No. Henry and I came down in his family car."

Bert looked at Henry and mentally dismissed him. A nice enough sort of chap, but rather dumb. Went off by himself and hardly uttered. Occasionally useful, no doubt, but hadn't apparently even a car of his own. (In Bert's experience this was an enormous handicap for any man.)

"The grey Austin twelve?"

"Yes. Very family, you know. Your car looks marvellous. What is she?"

The question went straight to Bert's heart. For ten minutes he talked about his red two-seater M.G. He told Jane stories of what he had done in her, flat-out on the Barnet by-pass, and further stories of the average speed he had maintained on a long journey from Great Crosby (on the outskirt of Liverpool) to Bishops Teignton (just the other side of Exeter) and further stories of how he had discovered new and ingenious routes out of South London, saving quite seven minutes on the way to Croydon if one was careful not to go wrong. Had she got a map in the car? Well, he would show her in two ticks. You circled round Clapham Common and crossed the tram-lines at— He had worked it out for himself and it was worth knowing.

One could just go on eating and listen to all this. Jane thought it very nice of him to be so easy to talk to.

"Do you drive yourself? Perhaps you'd like to try her for a bit afterwards, would you?"

Jane realized that this must be a special mark of approbation not to be lightly refused.

"I'd love to. I do drive, but never anything so hot. Look here, you mustn't let me muck her up or anything."

"No, no. Of course you won't. She feels marvellous. You'll get the hang of it in two ticks."

"Is it just a knack?" asked Jane mischievously, remembering the swimming lesson.

"Yes, that's it," cried Bert, pleased at such instant comprehension. "You'll pick it up at once. I know you will."

"It's awfully nice of you."

"No, I'd love to, honestly. Look here, you're not eating anything. I'm terribly sorry. Will you have some of that chocolate cake over there? I know it's awfully good. I've had some. Do!"

"Thank you, I will," said Jane readily.

Mrs. Fisher saw Henry sitting silent and kindly engaged him in conversation. With a heavy heart he politely responded.

"You and Jane were up at Oxford together, weren't you, Henry?"

"Yes. Yes, we were." (If only I could get her away, if only I could smother all these prattling idiots.)

"That must have been great fun."

"Yes. Yes, it was really." (Fun! Canoeing up the Cher together early on Sunday morning, the picnic-basket between them. Walking in Bagley woods, sitting on a fallen tree-trunk to exchange kisses.)

"It must be a wrench when you have to leave Oxford and begin to do regular hours in an office."

"It's all rather different certainly." (Different! God, yes!)

Claud and Sylvia, sitting a little apart, were rather rudely bargaining over their strawberries and cream.

"Look here, Claud. I rather like the look of that strawberry of yours. I won't be mean. I'll give you these two for it." She indicated two smaller berries.

"Funny you shouldn't have noticed that one of yours was green and the other mouldy." Claud caught Mrs. Fisher's eye and hastily lowered his voice. "I'll make you an alternative offer though, if you like. I'll be generous. I won't take more than three of those extremely small ones in the nursery at the side of your plate. I dare say they're quite tasty."

"That's not the nursery, it's the junior scholarship form. Specially selected. However, fair's fair. Give me your one."

Claud regarded her with suspicion. He dipped the strawberry (rather gingerly) in cream and sugar and handed it to her on the end of a fork. "Adorable pig," he said.

"Thank you, darling," said Sylvia, and handed him one of hers.

"And the other two please, Sylvia?"

"What do you mean? What other two?"

"Look here, darling. I won't be hard on you. I'll just ask you to remember you're on your honour as a Girl Guide—"

At this moment Alice arrived with a message to the effect that Miss Perry was wanted on the telephone. It was her mother who wished to speak to her.

"All this telephoning," said Sylvia, slightly startled. "I'm so sorry, Mrs. Fisher. I'm being a frightful nuisance, I'm afraid."

Back across the lawn again, this time without Claud. Probably he would be eating all her strawberries. What on earth could mummy want? Wasn't it going to be convenient to have Claud for the night after all? Bother, just when everything was so nicely arranged. Bother, just when she was beginning to enjoy herself!

Immediately she heard her mother's voice, saying, "Is that you, Sylvia?" she knew something upsetting must have happened. Mrs. Perry was quite shaken out of her usual calm. The story was in consequence a little confused.

"I thought she was asleep in bed the whole time. She must have got up and dressed and gone out without our knowing. And now they've found a loose horse—"

"Do you mean she's *ridden* away?"

Sylvia was visited by an absurd picture of Henrietta eloping romantically and elaborately on horseback.

"They say at the riding-school that the reins are broken. I don't know, Sylvia, I don't understand it at all, but I'm afraid she's fallen off somewhere, but where are we to look?"

"Well, where was the horse?" (One mustn't get upset. One must just be sensible and remember that it was always supposed to be funny when one fell off a horse, and that everything which had gone before had really nothing to do with it.)

"The beastly horse," said Mrs. Perry with passion, "was just going straight back to the riding-school as fast as it could go." She sounded rather as if she thought it should have trotted straight off to a doctor's house and whinnied outside. She had never ridden herself, but was fond of newspaper anecdotes illustrating the intelligence of animals.

"Hasn't any one found her or seen her or anything? I mean there's probably nothing to worry about. She's probably walking sadly home."

"I'm afraid not," said Mrs. Perry, agitatedly refusing consolation. "They found the horse nearly an hour ago. She could have got a lift or telephoned or done *something*. I wouldn't have rung you up, Sylvia, but we're getting so worried, and no one knows which direction she went in at *all*—she didn't say at the riding-school, but they say they warned her that the horse was savage."

"Savage! They couldn't have said that!"

"Well, the man himself says it was a bit hot on the grass —you know I don't understand exactly what they're talking about, but it sounds awfully dangerous to me. They oughtn't to have let her go out alone."

"Oh, mummy—" (Oh, never mind though. If it relieved mummy's feelings to heap blame on poor old Wilson, let her.)

"Your father's quite distracted. Of course I pretend to him I'm not really very worried. But what can we do, Sylvia? If only we knew where to look for her—but then we haven't got the car, you see. But I suppose she wouldn't be on the roads, would she? Where do you usually go?" Sylvia pondered. Probably Henrietta had been in the mood for a really good gallop. She couldn't have meant just to potter about along the lanes. She would have wanted the green upland opening before her, the rough grassy track that led round and up the hill, the wind in her hair, flying clots of earth behind her, galloping hoofs, galloping hoofs. Piggott's Hill. The mile-long gallop!

"Well, I say, mummy. I tell you where we always go when we want to get a really good ride. Piggott's Hill. You know it, don't you?"

"Is that the hill you see on your right going into the village?"

"Yes. At least you see a whole range, don't you?"

"Yes, I suppose you do," said Mrs. Perry uncertainly.

"Of course you do. Well, Piggott's Hill is the—let me see—the end bump but one from the end nearest the village."

"Oh." The monosyllable sounded very unconvinced.

"And you get to it—at least the way we get there on horseback— is—do you know a white gate on the right just before you come to the post-office?"

"I think so."

"Well, you go through there, and presently you take a track that leads off to the left round a little wood—do you know the little wood I mean?"

"Yes," said Mrs. Perry, and Sylvia knew by her voice that she had not the slightest idea. Obviously she had just made up her mind to say yes to everything.

"I don't believe you do."

"Well, I always think it's best to ask, don't you?"

"There won't be any one to ask. This is right off the road. Besides, people don't know the way. They'll only try to direct you round by the road, and that's much longer, and she'd never have gone that way."

"Well, when you've done that—what you said—are you at Piggott's Hill?"

"Lord, no. Not nearly."

"Oh, dear. Well, go on then. You take a track to the right round a little wood and—?"

"No, to the *left*, to the *left*. And that leads you down between a field and the wood to where—oh, Lord, there's about six tracks come in there. How can I explain?"

"Why ever do you go such a complicated way, dear?"

"It's perfectly simple, really. It only *sounds* complicated," said Sylvia desperately. The futility of it all broke over her in a sudden wave. Even if mummy were really listening it wouldn't be too easy to explain, and she wasn't attending properly. She was too agitated over Henrietta and too convinced that she wouldn't understand anyway.

"Look here, mummy. I think I'd better come back. I'm the only person who knows how to look for her."

"Oh, darling, I hate to spoil your party. It *would* be a help though."

"Well, the party's spoiled now anyway for me," said Sylvia unkindly.

"How will you get back home though? There's this bother about the car, isn't there? Will Leslie mind running you over now instead of later?"

"I don't know. As a matter of fact I haven't asked her anything about it yet. I expect I can borrow a car or hire a car or do something. Claud will arrange something, I expect," said Sylvia, taking considerable comfort in the thought. "Or would you rather leave him out of it?"

"Oh, no. No, I don't think so. If we've got to organize a search he'll be useful. After all—this accident hasn't really anything to do with our little upset of this morning has it?"

Poor mummy! One could see the workings of her mind. How horrified she would be if she knew that Claud already knew all about the "little upset."

"Well, anyway, I'll get over *somehow*. Good-by," said Sylvia abruptly.

She hurried out of the house and back to the tea-party. It seemed an age since she had left them ten minutes ago. There was something in her manner that suggested bad news. Claud got up and went to meet her half-way across the lawn. She explained rapidly, adding, "You must come with me, darling, don't let them stop you, I want you with me."

Everybody tried to be helpful, and became very voluble. Unfortunately it turned out that the Fishers' car was down at the garage being decarbonized.

"Oh, Sylvia, what a pity! Otherwise I'd have run you over in no time. It's only about eight miles, isn't it?"

"Twelve. But I couldn't have let you," said Sylvia, suspecting that this was not true as she said it, "I don't want to break up the party—"

"*I* could have run Sylvia over," said Mrs. Fisher regretfully. "Oh, dear—aren't things tiresome?" It was a pity that they could only explain how helpful they could have been in other circumstances.

"Could we hire a car?"

"Oh, no, don't do that," said every one immediately. Somehow such a suggestion seemed to convict them all of a lack of generosity. Every one began to look instead at the two cars that stood outside the front door, Bert's red M.G. and Henry's old Austin.

"I'll run you over," said Bert immediately, and could not forbear adding, "You'll get there quicker in my car."

"It's awfully nice of you. The only thing is it's a two-seater, isn't it?"

"You see, I'm going with Sylvia," said Claud.

"Oh, are you?" cried Leslie. It was a little hard that one guest should retire to bed immediately on arrival and two more should now leave precipitately.

"I'll drive you over," said Henry, who could not now very well say less. He had been listening to this discussion in silence. Somewhere, hidden in some unanticipated concealment the spider-spirit had begun to stir, to stretch out a groping tentacle. Acutely conscious of an inexplicable danger, Henry had tried to avert it by doing and saying absolutely nothing. He had a feeling that with the slightest movement the creature would pounce. Now that these words were forced out of his lips he was nervously aware that he was being trapped in, but how or why he did not have time to realize.

"Thanks frightfully, Henry," said Sylvia, and added, "You won't need to be away from the party so awfully long, will you?"

The creature in the dark recoiled a little.

"At least an hour," said Leslie mournfully. "And what about when you get there, Sylvia? Won't you want a car to help in the search?"

"Well, we think she must be well off the roads, you see. Still, of course, it would be useful, but we could probably get hold of one. Of course Henry must go straight back. I'm terribly sorry about breaking up the party anyway."

"Well, but need Henry go at all?" Leslie felt that she had struck a brilliant solution. Why should more people leave the party than absolutely necessary? It was rather silly for Claud to go, but it would be sillier still to lose Henry also. "Couldn't you lend them your car, Henry? Then they could keep it for the search. Wouldn't that be the best idea? You were just going back to town tonight, weren't you? There's quite a good train at nine-thirty. Or you could both, you and Jane, stay the night. Do! If Jane wouldn't mind sleeping in my room, you could have the little room—couldn't he, mummy?— because of course, there's Florence in the spare-room. And Sylvia could return the car tomorrow. That's much the best plan. Do!"

"Yes, do let us persuade you both," said Mrs. Fisher. "I should love to have you."

"I think I ought to get back to London," said Henry. He stood stock-still and had the strong physical sensation of dodging.

"Oh, no! Must you really? What about you, Jane? Do persuade Henry to stay."

"What do you think, Henry? It might be a good plan, mightn't it?" (Why was he looking like that? Surely they could go away tomorrow instead—or another week-end?)

"Think it out afterwards if you like, Henry," advised Mrs. Fisher.

This gentlest of hints, combined with a slight movement of impatience from Sylvia, suddenly forced on Henry the realization that the final triumph of the spider-spirit, the last renouncement of all his hopes, was to take the bitter form of words put into his own mouth.

"Oh, yes, do take the car, Sylvia," he said. "That will be quite all right."

III

The walnut bed in the spare-room with its white linen sheets and big frilled pillow looked both crisp and smooth. With a sensation of utter relief Florence sank into its soft buoyancy. Now that the waters had met over her head she was drowned and lost, but, secure from the world's clamour, she was floating in soothing green depths where no jar could reach her. Mrs. Fisher's thermometer had shown her to be several points above normal, and as soon as she closed her eyes her mind split into two. Part of it rushed on into a green, undersea, muffled world of water, part of it lagged behind, snatching at the small normal facts of the bed and the room and Leslie's mother telling her to go to sleep. Sleep! When you were under water no movement was brusque, no sound sharp. There was no cackling, no grating, no hurrying throng, no pushing to and fro. Paddington station was all submerged. It was infinitely soothing that you could not hear the trains whistle or the doors bang. The movement of the crowd was smooth and silent like the turning of the tides. The water made the office very dark. As Florence stood there, the greenish glow thickened and darkened to a brown opaqueness. Miss Conway was trying to type, but the swirling water made it very difficult. With a long sigh Florence turned over on her other side, rising far enough up to the surface to know that she wanted to throw off a blanket. Between the thought and the action the green water surged in again. The dull thunder of the waves was mixed up with the noises of a car moving off under the window, crunched gravel and people saying good-by. Then at last the surface of the ocean grew smooth again and spread itself tranquil and shining over the whole world.

It was an age, a hundred years, before Leslie poked her head in at the door and said cautiously, "How are you feeling now?"

Florence, softly dragging herself up from the depths, felt a sudden pinpoint of sharp inquiry shoot into her mind. She was suddenly enormously anxious to know what the time was. It was of vital importance to know how long she had slept. Leslie was asking her something.

"Did you ask me what the time was, Leslie?"

"No, of course I didn't." Leslie laughed softly. She felt something of the protective tenderness that any fully-awake person feels for a sleeper. "I asked you if you were feeling a little better now?"

"What *is* the time?"

"Oh, I don't know. About half-past five, I think. Why?"

"I seem to have slept for such ages." Florence, blinking, relaxed back onto the pillows.

"Only about an hour and a half. Well, how *are* you feeling?"

Florence explored her own bodily sensations.

"Oh, better. A lot better, thanks."

"Good. Would you like some lemonade?"

Florence directed her own attention to her mouth and throat.

"Yes, please."

Leslie rang the bell, and, on Alice's appearing, asked her to bring some lemonade up.

"Going to sleep in the daytime is so funny, isn't it, Leslie? When you wake up you're quite surprised to find yourself existing in the same world, and everything that happened before you went to sleep seems about a hundred years old."

Leslie guessed that Florence was thinking about giving up her job.

"I should think going to sleep was about the best thing you could do," she replied soothingly. "You looked rotten when you arrived."

"Did I?" said Florence, not without interest. She was beginning gradually to absorb her surroundings. When she had gone to bed nothing had been of significance except the sensation of feeling absolutely worn out. Now she began again to notice things. Circumstances and her surroundings no longer dominated her; she began to feel herself in control over them. She studied appreciatively the walnut dressing-table and washstand, the gay curtains and soft carpet, the little table on which a cut-glass vase of yellow roses stood, the writing-desk in the window which displayed a spotlessly clean blotter and shining silver inkstand.

"Am I in the spare-room, Leslie? It's awfully nice."

"Yes, it's all right, but not a bit modern of course. I'm always wanting mummy to put running water in and divan beds. I love modern furniture, don't you? I think it's so sensible."

"It may be sensible, but it's very expensive."

"Is it?" Leslie stared. "But there's so little of it—surely? It *ought* to be cheap."

"Well, it isn't. As a matter of fact I think it's lovely to be in this sort of room for a change. Plenty of space so that you don't need to *save* space, and none of the chairs pulling out and becoming washstands or mangles or anything of the sort."

The lemonade arrived. A yellow crystal jug and glass stood on a little lace mat covering a small silver tray. Florence, pouring it out and tasting it, found it iced and delicious.

"This is divine, Leslie. Aren't you going to keep me company?"

"Well, yes. I think I will, although I've really finished tea."

Florence's eyes strayed to the washstand in search of the tooth-glass, but Leslie promptly rang the bell, saying she would ask Alice for another tumbler.

"Of course you don't know the excitement about Sylvia, Florence. Her mother phoned up to say Henrietta had had a riding accident and they'd found the horse, but not her. So Sylvia and Claud rushed off home in Henry's car."

"Good Lord. But why Henry's car?"

"Oh, you know Sylvia's is being repaired at the garage here, so Henry lent them his because it was convenient for them and he didn't particularly want it. We're trying to persuade Henry and Jane to stay the night if Jane doesn't mind sharing my room."

"Oh. Yes, I mean." (Poor Henry! How would he cope with this? Leslie, in her anxiety to demonstrate her London friends to her mother, was complicating things for them.)

Mrs. Fisher appeared at the door, followed by Alice with another glass. Florence took a guilty pleasure in feeling herself the centre of attraction. She shifted a little higher up in the bed, thinking that this at least showed a sort of polite willingness to be talked to. The necessary interchange of appropriate remarks took place.

"I was telling Leslie," continued Mrs. Fisher, "the inquiries being finished, that I thought it would be so nice if we could keep you down here for a few days. I think the rest and country air would do you good. Do you think you could manage it?"

"It's awfully kind of you. But I suppose I ought to go back to work on Monday."

"Oh, but surely! Really I don't think you'll be fit for it."

"I thought you'd left anyway," put in Leslie airily.

"Yes. But not immediately. Anyway I'd have stayed another week, probably another month." Florence saw the office. Smelt the heavy musty smell of the old files. Remembered with a shudder the scattered index cards on the brown linoleum floor.

"We could write and explain. I certainly don't like to think of you going up to town in this condition. I don't like to take the responsibility for it."

Leslie trembled for the effect of this remark on Florence; but Florence only thought it rather sweet of Mrs. Fisher.

"Are you so very anxious to go back there to finish, Florence? Because it seems to me that, considering your cold and everything, a good long rest—"

"Oh!" cried Florence, reduced by low health and sympathy to a devastating honesty. "Oh, a good long rest! I'd give anything in the world for it!"

"Florence!" cried Leslie, profoundly shocked.

"I thought so," said Mrs. Fisher, deeply gratified.

Florence burst into a sort of hymn of ecstasy.

"Oh, it would be so *lovely* not to have to get up and get the breakfast and rush off every morning to that blasted office. Oh, Leslie, you don't understand! In this heat, you know—and coming back in the rush-hour—and never having time to sew on a button or anything. Oh, of course it's lovely really," continued Florence unconvincingly, "but honestly it would be rather nice to have early morning tea brought to you for a bit, oh, and perhaps breakfast in bed sometimes and a tablecloth at dinner and milk not going sour and things like that."

"Well, I think we might manage all that," said Mrs. Fisher, beginning to like Florence more and more.

"Oh, but Florence! I thought you loved your little flat and *not* having to be in for meals and all that sort of thing. Isn't it *fun*?"

"Oh, yes. Yes, of course it is. Only in this heat, you know. . . . It isn't the *only* thing that's fun. You can think I'm as feeble and inconsistent as you like," cried Florence defensively, "but honestly I should like a *change* of fun for a bit."

"Don't you worry yourself about it any more," said Mrs. Fisher with kindly determination. "A rest in the country is exactly what you want and I shall write myself and explain to your employers. You mustn't dream of going up on Monday. Now, what about another sleep? We've been talking and exciting you, and when you've got a temperature, even a slight one, you want to lie quiet. Look, I'll tuck you up and draw the curtains again and I'll leave these lozenges by your bed. Put one in your mouth now. Come along, Leslie. Florence is going to sleep till supper and see how she feels then. Sleep well, child. Don't you worry about anything. We shall enjoy having you with us, and everything will settle itself beautifully that way."

Luxuriously acquiescent, Florence smiled and closed her eyes. The door was softly shut.

"I've never known her like that before," said Leslie disconsolately to her mother on the stairs. "She must be feeling awfully rotten."

CHAPTER XIII

I

"GOOD AFTERNOON, Mr. Wilson. I dropped in on the chance of a ride. Have you a horse I could take out?"

Henrietta, smelling the familiar stable smell, hearing the familiar stable sounds—the clink of a bucket, the noise of a horse moving about in a loose-box, the piercing whistle of a stable-hand—thought how funny it was to feel so different and find everything so exactly the same.

"Well, now, Miss Perry. If you'd let me know beforehand I'd have kept back Bess for you, but the boy's taken her over half an hour ago to—"

"Oh, Mr. Wilson! Well, what about Polly?"

"Polly!" Old Wilson paused impressively. "Polly's sold."

"Sold!" cried Henrietta, automatically registering surprise and interest.

"Yes, miss. It was like this. A lady came into here Tuesday. Tuesday? Well, now, was it Tuesday or Wednesday? Jim, was it Tuesday or Wednesday the lady come in?"

"What lady, dad?" said Jim, a little sharply, appearing in the doorway.

"The lady I'm talking about, of course. The one that come in first about Polly—"

"I came in to ask if I could take out a horse this afternoon," said Henrietta, "but Mr. Wilson tells me Polly's been sold. Is there any other I could have?" It was against her practice to appeal to Jim to hurry up the old man. She knew that he would do it with a brutality that would make her wince. But clearly something must be done about this interminable Polly story!

"Yes. Lady Winterton's bought her for her little girl," said Jim, ruthlessly anticipating the story's climax. "Can Miss Perry ride the grey, dad?"

"No. Wednesday it was she come in first. I was in the stable, and the boy, he come in and said—"

"I said, 'Can Miss Perry ride the grey, dad?'" repeated Jim loudly.

"Eh? Oh, the grey. Well, now, Miss Perry. There's a lovely ride for you."

"That will be splendid then," said Henrietta quickly.

"Come with me this way, Miss Perry, and I'll show you your horse. There! He's a good 'un, ain't he?"

"Oh, yes! Very nice looking," said Henrietta, no judge of a horse at the best of times, and now only anxious to get away as quickly as possible. "You haven't had him long, have you? Could you get him ready now, do you think? I don't want to be too late home. . . ."

"Ah, you'll have a lovely ride on him," said old Wilson, immovably. "We've only had him—let me see—"

Jim appeared with saddle and bridle, giving Henrietta a look that was practically a wink.

"You'll find him a bit keen on the grass, miss," he said.

"Pulls, does he?"

"Ah, he's a lovely ride," said old Wilson.

"No, he doesn't pull, not really, you know, miss, but he just likes to take hold a bit, if you know what I mean."

"Yes. Well, I feel fairly energetic."

"Oh, he'll be all right, you'll find."

Old Wilson, leaning against the door, watched her departure.

"You'll have a nice ride on him, missy."

"Yes, I'm sure I shall," rejoined Henrietta politely. "I'll be back in about two hours." She gathered up her reins and moved out of the gateway.

"I'm not sure that we did ought to have let her go out alone on that grey," said Jim, more to himself than to his father. "He's a bit fresh for her."

"Ah, she'll be all right," said old Wilson comfortably, "She and her sister, they've been riding here, on and off for some years now. I remember the first time—"

Jim disappeared.

The hoofs of the grey clicked sharply along the asphalt of the road. It was only a quarter of a mile to the turning into the woods. Already Henrietta felt comforted by the movement of the horse, the creak of the saddle, the feel of the reins between her fingers. Her eyes felt hot and puffy as she blinked them in the sunshine. Crying and sleeping! What a way to spend a June morning! Perhaps mummy would let her live in a riding-stable, be trained as a pupil. Then she wouldn't need to think of anything but saddles and watering the horses and brushing her breeches. She would never bother about evening dresses or manicuring her nails again. She just didn't care about that sort of thing. She would just never care any more. She did not want to think about John again at all—ever.

She did not really understand about this, and she did not want to ponder over this sudden change of feeling. It was quite monstrously incredible to realize that if there hadn't been all this fuss she would be with John now. Not that she was going to admit it would have been wicked or anything like that. It was just that it seemed so absolutely incredible. Like something out of a book or in another world.

She did realize dimly that these last few weeks she had been thinking of herself as some one quite different from her normal self, some one much older, much braver, more self-possessed. She had believed that this was the sort of person she was really becoming. This was her grown-up self. Who would have thought that a sleepless night, an attack of nerves, mummy's worried face and the sound of her voice saying, "Darling child!" could have caused this new grown-up Henrietta to collapse, in a fit of tears, into somebody very young and—frightened? It was no good going on refusing to admit it. She had been terribly frightened.

Somehow her love for John, the thought of which had, up till yesterday, thrilled her so much, had been quite spoilt. She couldn't hold it separate in her mind any longer as an exciting and glorious secret. It was a love that had belonged to the Henrietta she had thought she was, not to her real self. She did not formulate this clearly to herself, but she did find herself wondering why her mother and Sylvia and her home seemed now so much more real, so much more solid in her thoughts than John. They didn't, thought Henrietta, really live in the same world at all. You couldn't mix them. And now that mummy's world had intruded on and spoilt John's world she didn't want to see him again for a long, long time.

Probably, she thought, she would never be really happy again. It was too frightful to think of how she had said, "Oh, mummy!" and burst into tears and how mummy had tucked her up and fetched her a dry pillowcase from the linen-cupboard because all that awful sobbing and sniffing had made her own quite damp. If ever mummy alluded to it again she wouldn't be able to bear it. If nobody ever said anything about it perhaps she could just bear to stay at home, but if—

Here was the turning into the woods. Perhaps she ought to have told mummy she was going riding. But she hadn't wanted to see or speak to any one at home. She had woken up and lain miserably in bed for a little. And then she had suddenly thought that if she were on horseback on Piggott's Hill, galloping as fast as she could go, she might succeed in forgetting for a moment how utterly spoilt everything was. She had dressed quietly and sneaked out of the house.

The grey, feeling the asphalt give way to a grassy path, gave a little snort and broke into a canter, taking his rider slightly by surprise. It occurred to Henrietta for the first time that her stirrups were a bit short. Never mind. She would pull up and adjust them in a minute. The grey took Henrietta along the track round the wood faster than she had ever been before. It was difficult to avoid the branches that hung over the path. Twice a bough scraped sharply across Henrietta's cheek. The only way of dodging the beastly things seemed to be to bend low in the saddle; but it was difficult to check the grey when you were crouched down like that. Not that the grey seemed to take much notice of her tugs at the reins, anyway. This was what Jim Wilson called being a bit keen, was it? Funny. He had been as quiet as a lamb on the roads. Oh, here was the place where she ought to stop. Here was the place where one took that track to the right. Blast the animal, thought Henrietta with a sudden surge of temper, as the grey, ignoring her tugging wrists, head low, cantered past the turning down the wrong track. She finally tugged him to a standstill fifty yards down the path. This wasn't riding, this contest of strength, this struggle for mastery between mount and mounted. Keen indeed! The word suggested pricked ears, alert eye, the forward movement of a horse and rider perfectly attuned to their eagerness. The brute has no mouth, thought Henrietta, turning round crossly and starting to walk him back along the path; and now of course the grey chose to think he was being taken home already and made quite a fuss at turning up the right track. "Oh, stop it, damn you," muttered Henrietta. Uncertain of her horse, uncertain of herself, she was holding the reins very tight, and very short, and the grey fretted about, blowing and tossing his head. Henrietta was now convinced that her stirrups were far too short—that was why she was bouncing about in the saddle so badly. Now if the blasted animal would only stand still for two seconds— stand still, can't you?—one hole, two holes—so horribly stiff. Now he was blundering sideways into a blackberry bush. Henrietta's language and temper descended further and further from the Black Beauty tradition. If only the damned horse would stand still for one second—why did they make these leathers so blastedly stiff?—there, that was one side done. With bent head and nervously tugging fingers she wrestled with the other leg. "Stand still, stand *still*—all right, *walk* on if you must," cried Henrietta, desperately applying both hands to the infinitely troublesome task of forcing the steel tongue out of the hole in the stiff, dark leather. The grey, joyfully taking advantage of the loosened reins, broke into a blundering canter and gave Henrietta some nasty moments while she tugged roughly with all her force at the reins and tried at the same time to thrust her foot into the swinging loose stirrup. They came to a lopsided jolting halt; and as they stood there, just at the turn in the path, that led uphill to where the woods fell back and gave place to the open turf, Henrietta realized, with sudden dismay, that she was frightened. She knew it first by a funny sour taste in her mouth, and recognized it further by the fierce determination to go on at all costs that suddenly filled her mind. The image of the mile of open turf that lay beyond the bend danced before her eyes. A mile of open turf! What an exhilarating thought when she was on the back of Bess—dear Bess, who never pulled at all and knew all about stopping at the end in good time to avoid the stony part where the track disappeared into the woods. But would she ever be able to stop this grey, once he really got going? Of course, it was silly to doubt oneself and, of course, it was silly to look for trouble ahead, and very wrong, moreover, to allow oneself to think of one's horse as something one had got to fight against. Henrietta knew all that, knew it and repeated it to herself; and yet, as the grey went at a jogging uncomfortable walk up the path she found the image of all that stretch of open turf perpetually before her eyes. The place where the track was especially rough—and the place where there was a steepish turn—and (with a sinking of the heart) the place where there was that very unexpected dip and the stream. How clearly she could visualize it all—and then suddenly they rounded the bend and it all lay before her eyes, just as she had imagined it. She could even see faintly in the distance just where the track disappeared into the woods, after winding round and up the shoulder of the hill. I'm not afraid, thought Henrietta. I'm just afraid of being afraid, and waited for the thought to bring comfort (which it did not). We'll go very slowly at first, thought Henrietta, and then just a bit faster over that good stretch and then pull up again before the bend. She gave the grey a hypocritical pat, and allowed him to plunge forward into an eager bouncing canter.

Give and take, sit well forward, look out for rabbit holes, check gently but firmly, give and take—oh, Lord, that was a near one! Her nervous and sudden wrench at the sight of the stump lying in the path pulled the grey right off the track into a rut. A stumble brought Henrietta forward out of the saddle onto his neck; and by the time she had recovered her seat the grey was thundering along as fast as he could go with Henrietta tugging with all her strength at the reins and at the same time making desperate attempts to regain a lost stirrup. Clots of turf flew away behind them, the air whistled past Henrietta's ears, a cloud of earthy dust rose in their wake. I must slow up before the turn, I must slow up. Forgetting to keep her hands down, forgetting to keep her toes turned up in the stirrup, forgetting everything that she had ever known, Henrietta pulled with all her might at the reins. They took the bend at high speed with the result that horse and rider temporarily left the track. The rough heather and coarse grass into which they floundered, however, helped Henrietta to pull up, and the lamentable tug-of-war was at last concluded when the grey, still pulling, slackened to a trot. We're going to walk the rest of this gallop, thought Henrietta immediately she was again capable of coherent thought. I wonder if there is a way home by the roads? It was funny to be so puffed and yet to feel her forehead cold with sweat. They walked on. The hot June sunshine was full of little noises, the buzz of crickets in the grass, the barking of a distant dog, the creaking of the saddle. Henrietta, inwardly tense, seemed to see and hear everything with an abnormal acuteness. Was this what fear did to you? But she hadn't been exactly afraid—not anyway at the time they were really going fast. She had been much more frightened in the woods when she was just thinking about whether she would be able to stop the grey, and, funnily enough, she was much more frightened—now. Although there was nothing to be nervous about now, was there? Everything was all right. They would go home quietly by the roads and she would tell old Wilson that she *had* found the grey pulled a bit, but that they had had a nice ride. They crossed the stream in the dip, and Henrietta noticed how distinct the pebbles were at the bottom, and how the tufts of grass grew coarsely out of the mud at the side.

It was funny that when she thought she had decided everything, what she would tell old Wilson about the ride, and how she hadn't been frightened after all, her mind would keep on teasing her still. You always gallop up here. You can't walk all the way. Yes, I'm going to. You're frightened to canter. No, I'm not, but this horse pulls so. If you let this get the better of you, you'll always be frightened. No, I shan't—shall I? I'm never nervous. I never have been before. Well, you're frightened now. You'd better finish this gallop properly and then you'll feel fine. You're turning into the sort of person who's frightened of everything—you'll feel fine once you've done it. . . .

Piggott's Hill on this sunny June afternoon was deserted. There was nobody to see the rider on the grey put her horse to a gallop up the slope that was crowned by the little wood. Nobody to see her frantic tugs at the reins as, faster and faster, horse and rider breasted the slope, nor how the grey charged blunderingly through the stony boulders right into the wood at the top. There was nobody to help when an overhanging bough caught Henrietta a severe blow on the forehead and she fell sideways out of the saddle. Nobody to pick her up and nobody to catch the grey which cantered right through the wood and away down the lane beyond, reins dangling and broken.

II

"Of course they'll probably have found her by the time we get there. Turn right here, Claud."

"Oh, yes, probably. Still it's not a bad plan to go over."

"Last time I fell off I wrenched my wrist."

"Oh, did you? Is Henrietta a good rider?"

"Not bad. She's ridden off and on in the holidays for some time, but she hasn't really had much experience, you know."

"Oh? No."

"If she was walking home or trying to catch the horse it might take her ages."

"Oh, yes, rather. Years."

"Of course, mummy gets a bit excited if we're five minutes late."

"Does she? How funny."

"Yes, silly, isn't it? I suppose she can't help it."

"No, I suppose not."

• • • • • • •

"I hope I didn't alarm the child," said Mrs. Perry. "I wouldn't have alarmed her for worlds as I'm sure there's nothing to be alarmed about really. It's just that she's the only person who knows—"

"Yes, yes, of course." Mr. Perry was determined to reassure his wife. "With Sylvia's help we shall find her in a moment. I wonder where we'd better look. It's so impossible to tell—"

"Yes, of course that's what so difficult. She might be *anywhere*. Still, of course, we shall find her in a moment probably."

"It was funny of her not to tell you she was going riding," said Mr. Perry. "Did you know she was getting up?"

"Well, dear, I expect she woke up and found her headache was gone and thought a little fresh air would do her good."

"It's not like Henrietta to have headaches."

Mrs. Perry looked mysterious.

"No, this was a little exceptional." She adopted a tone of voice which was always instantly recognized by her family as the one reserved for the occasions when she was determined to pass off something tactfully. "I don't think we want to question her too closely, dear, about just why she went out without saying anything. If we're just very kind and sweet to her—"

"Oh, certainly," said Mr. Perry, obediently taking his cue and wondering what there really was behind this business that he was evidently not going to be allowed to ask about. "We usually are," he added mildly.

"Oh, I know. Good gracious, I'm sure we've nothing to reproach ourselves with. . . . I wonder how long Sylvia will be? Shall we walk down to meet them? It might save time."

"Certainly, if you like. Although actually it won't *save* time, will it? If we're going to Piggott's Hill, as you say Sylvia suggested, that's the opposite direction, isn't it? But by all means let's walk. . . ." It occurred to him that his wife would be easier in her mind if she could only be doing something.

"Come on. Let's," said Mrs. Perry. They set off at a smart pace down the road. It was very hot and dusty, but at least it was better than hanging about in the porch straining their ears for the distant whirr of a car on the road. Mrs. Perry was glad they had come. Now that she had persuaded Charles to start out he wasn't looking quite so worried.

"Good Lord, there's mummy," said Sylvia. Claud slowed down, jumped out and politely opened the door to the two dusty plodders.

"You've been quick," said Mr. Perry, sinking down with considerable relief into the back seat.

"Yes. This is Henry's—"

"Darling, I wouldn't have disturbed you at your party for worlds if only it hadn't been that—"

"That's quite all right, mummy. We managed to borrow—"

"You see, I don't know where you and Henrietta go when you ride and it seemed so hopeless—"

"Yes, of course. Well, I can easily show you the way she would have gone to Piggott's Hill. We can take the car to the cross-roads and then strike through the woods—"

"Well, if we go the way she's gone we're bound to find out if there's been an accident of any sort, aren't we, Sylvia?"

"Yes, of course, mummy. We're sure to come upon the—I mean, of course we shall. The only thing is, I don't know that she's gone to Piggott's Hill."

Everybody looked at Sylvia as though she was letting them down by this admission.

"I thought you said you were sure she would have," cried Mrs. Perry reproachfully.

"No, I said I thought probably. She may quite well not have," said Sylvia unkindly. She could not help feeling a little irritated at finding herself suddenly in the rôle of the girl who sapped the party's morale by her base suggestions.

There was a despondent silence, only broken by Mr. Perry pointing out that if they *were* going to Piggott's Hill no one had directed Claud to take that turning to the left.

"Shall I turn back?" asked Claud, slowing.

"Well, Charles, Sylvia now says she doesn't think Henrietta *has* gone there—"

"No, I didn't," said Sylvia crossly. "I said she might not have. As a matter of fact, I think she probably has."

"Well, I'll turn then, shall I?"

"After all, Sylvia," said Mrs. Perry in the tone of one persuading a child, "we may at least meet some one who has seen her or—"

"Yes, *yes*, mummy. It was me who suggested it in the first place, wasn't it?"

"This way?" asked Claud patiently.

"Yes, fork right here," said Mr. Perry, opening his mouth for the second time.

Poor Claud, thought Sylvia. It's a shame to plunge him into family life up to the neck like this. She patted his leg and gave him an inquiring look. Claud, knowing that this meant, "You don't mind, do you? It's all right, isn't it?" replied with a reassuring grin. Presently the road ran into woods and twisted up a hill. They were approaching from the further side the knoll that crowned Piggott's Hill. Mrs. Perry began to scan the woods on both sides of the road with a sort of eager anxiety. Her expression made Sylvia nervously inclined to laugh. At the cross-roads they left the car and struck off up the dusty lane that dwindled into the track that led to the knoll.

"What's that?" said Mrs. Perry sharply.

They all jumped, but it was only a piece of rag.

"When we get through these woods we shall be able to look down and see the track all the way up," said Sylvia.

Horrible pictures raced through her mother's mind at these words. Henrietta, half-way down the hill, lying among the stones. Henrietta at the foot of the hill huddled in the grass. Henrietta crawling on hands and knees towards the stream.

"Hoof-marks," said Claud, pointing to a softer patch in the track.

Everybody gazed intently at them.

"Might be yesterday's," said Sylvia. The tension relaxed again, until Mrs. Perry exclaimed dramatically, "I shall never forgive old Wilson."

"Oh, mummy! She's probably perfectly all right."

But the idea of an accident was by this time so firmly implanted in all their minds that the suggestion that nothing had happened after all appeared a shocking heresy.

"Perfectly all right!" exclaimed Mrs. Perry indignantly. "How are you going to explain where she's been all this time?"

"How on earth do I know? I wish you wouldn't treat me as a sort of—a sort of—"

"Now we're coming out of the woods, aren't we, Sylvia?" inquired her father hastily. Drawing his daughter ahead of the others he whispered to her that she mustn't mind her mother, who was perhaps a little overwrought.

Claud, following with Mrs. Perry, said:

"Sylvia's upset about this, I'm afraid."

"Of course it may be all about nothing," suggested Mrs. Perry reasonably.

At this point loud exclamations of excitement rose from the couple ahead. They had just come clear of the woods, and Sylvia was eagerly pointing out something to her father.

"That's her, daddy. Oh, daddy, you *must* see some one walking down the track there—look!—almost at the bottom. . . ."

Mrs. Perry and Claud hurried to the others, and they all stood there gesticulating and pointing out the distant dot of a figure to Mr. Perry. Now it was his turn to be exasperating. He could not or would not be persuaded to identify the dot with his daughter.

"Of *course* it's Henrietta, Charles," said Mrs. Perry firmly, after casting a single glance at the figure.

"I can just see that there is some one walking there, but why you're all so sure it's Henrietta—"

"I believe—yes, I think—I'm almost sure I can make out her riding-breeches," said Sylvia.

Her father gave her a sceptical look.

"Thank goodness she doesn't seem to have hurt herself," exclaimed Mrs. Perry.

With one accord they began to hurry down the track. Presently they were all running. At first Mr. Perry, toying still with the rôle of the cool-headed doubter unstampeded by mob emotion, lingered behind. But running is infectious; and besides, as they drew nearer the distant dot did seem, more and more, to take on the appearance of his daughter. Soon he was running as fast as the others.

They had gone quite a long way before Sylvia began to laugh, but once she had begun she could not stop. Giggles burst from her at every step. Great sobs of laughter shook her as she dodged round boulders and gorse-bushes. Perspiration and tears ran down her face.

"You're making yourself far hotter," panted Claud.

"I can't help it. Look at mummy and daddy! Mummy's hair!" She struggled silently with herself. "And think of Henrietta's face when she turns round and sees her entire family—"

"Look out," said Claud sharply. "Look where you're going."

Sylvia, suddenly seeing the dip in the path, executed an enormous leap. At the same moment Henrietta, still some distance ahead, turned round and remained stock-still, transfixed by the sight that met her eyes. "Henrietta!" cried Mrs. Perry, and hurried towards her, followed by her husband. Claud was the only one to see Sylvia collapse on the path, her foot twisted under her. Suddenly all the laughter left her face. She went rather white. Claud immediately knelt down by her.

"Darling. Hurt yourself?"

"Yes. . . . My ankle. . . ."

"Let me look."

"Never mind. It will be all right in a moment. Go and see if Henrietta's all right."

"Nonsense. Of course she's all right. Do you think you've sprained it?"

"Feels like it. Oh, Claud, it does hurt."

Perhaps it was not in the best brave little woman tradition to tell him so; but it was very comforting.

"Does it, sweetheart? I'll carry you back to the car."

"Quite in the best magazine fiction style," murmured Sylvia. She gave a surreptitious lick at a tear that was running stealthily down her cheek. "Poor Claud! This is the most awful day for you!"

"Keep still, darling, while I mop you up with this filthy handkerchief. Ankles are hell, aren't they, while they last?"

"I'm so sorry I'm not doing the it's-nothing-really-at-all business better."

"Oh, I should do that after it stops hurting, if I were you. It comes much more convincingly then. Hello, here's your mother back again."

Mrs. Perry's mind did not seem completely at rest.

"She says she's all right, but I don't think she really can be. She doesn't remember much about how she fell off—what's the matter, Sylvia? Can't you get up?"

"She's hurt her ankle."

"Oh, dear!" Mrs. Perry's exclamation was not without a trace of exasperation. "We'd better all go home as quickly—Here comes Henrietta. I must say I'm a little worried about her. Henrietta, Sylvia's hurt her ankle now."

"I'm sorry, Sylvia." (Yes, reflected Sylvia, she did look a little dazed.) "How did you do it?"

"Oh, just running."

"Why were you all running after me like that?" asked Henrietta. "What made you come out here?"

"Well, darling, we were worried when you never came back from your ride and Wilson rang up to say they had found your horse loose—"

"Oh. It's not late, is it? I spent some time looking for my horse, I know, but I've only been out about an hour, haven't I?"

Mr. and Mrs. Perry exchanged renewed glances of anxiety. An hour!

"Well, never mind all that now," said Mrs. Perry briskly. "Let's all go home as quickly as possible. Can you walk to the car, Henrietta?"

"Me? Walk? What do you mean? Of course I can."

"Well, I can't," said Sylvia. She was not, of course, being intentionally annoying, but she did not sound exactly sorry about it.

"Do you mean you've *really* hurt your ankle, Sylvia?"

"Yes, it is really a nasty sprain, Mrs. Perry," interposed Claud hastily. "I think if she puts an arm round, my neck and the other round Mr. Perry's—"

In this manner, with Sylvia half carried, half hopping, and Henrietta lagging dreamily behind, the unconscious target for a battery of worried glances from her mother, the hot and anxious party returned to the car. On coming in sight of the road everybody was equally appalled to see a large picnic-party unloading from a car that stood near to their own.

"It's the Lovelaces," said Sylvia. "Quick!"

Instinctively and with one accord the whole party dodged behind a large chestnut-tree. Nobody thought this funny. For one moment at least every one was in entire agreement. A meeting involving inquiries, sympathy, expressions of regret, explanations and all the long-drawn-out, delaying ordinary politeness would require was too horrible to contemplate.

"It's not that I don't like the Lovelaces," said Mrs. Perry, apologetically emerging from behind her tree as the clear merry voices inquiring about the whereabouts of beauty-spots and thermos flasks mercifully died away into another part of the woods, "but I just felt I *couldn't* meet them—you don't want any one but the family when—"

Nobody except Claud noticed his adoption.

They drove back to the house in silence, and on reaching home Mrs. Perry insisted on sending Henrietta, apathetically protesting, straight to bed, and telephoning for the doctor.

"I don't like that sort of dazed look. I'm afraid she must have fallen on her head. I wonder if I ought to give her anything? Better not perhaps till the doctor comes. A knock on the head is a nasty thing."

"Concussion, I expect," said Claud.

"Concussion, yes. I expect you're right." Mrs. Perry seemed to find considerable comfort in giving this name to it. "Poor dear! I expect it gave her a bit of a shock too. I must go and see if she's quite comfortable—"

"How's the ankle, darling?" asked Claud, when he and Sylvia, who had sunk into the first chair she saw, were abandoned on the porch.

"Swelling," said Sylvia grimly, "and hurting like hell."

It was no good. She jolly well wasn't going to behave well about it. Let mummy worry as much as she liked about Henrietta. Henrietta had been very tiresome and naughty—yes, tiresome and naughty. (Sylvia found a sort of savage relief in applying these adjectives to her sister's conduct.) She had come out of the whole thing very well. The end of it was that the whole house was running round her with hot-water bottles and eau-de-Cologne. And—and—(the normal conclusion to this train of reflection was of course "And nobody is paying any attention to me," but Sylvia was not always as honest with herself as she imagined. She thought instead, "And I shouldn't wonder if my ankle isn't pretty badly sprained," and nearly believed herself.)

Fortunately Claud behaved in exactly the right way.

"It's awfully swollen, isn't it? It must be hurting frightfully. Listen, darling. You don't want to sit here with every one tripping over you. Let me help you up to your room. You can lie down and have a drink or something, and the doctor can see your ankle when he comes for Henrietta. How's that? Look, put your arm round my shoulder and you can hop up the stairs."

It was lovely to be made a fuss over. Lovely.

"Now you lie down on the bed," said Claud, "and keep your leg quite still for a bit. Wait a moment. I'll take off the coverlet."

"Ever so domesticated."

"There, that's right. Comfortable? You do look sweet lying there. At least, as a matter of fact, your face is quite filthy. Shall we wash it?"

He seemed quite taken with the idea, pouring out water in a basin and finding a sponge and towel. Sylvia had never had her face so carefully washed before.

"Shall I comb your hair now, Sylvia?"

"Yes, do. I must say I'm seeing a new side of you, Claud. I say, since you've gone all helpful, do you know what I'd really like?"

"What?"

"To be read aloud to," said Sylvia, luxuriously shutting her eyes. "You know, some really good trash. There's a pile of magazines over there—find me some genuine rubbish and that would be heavenly. All I want at the end of a perfect day like this."

Claud began to look through the magazines.

"Would you like a serial called *Dreams May Come True*?"

"I believe I read a bit of that. Is that about the girl who has a hundred pounds left and means to spend it all on a week at Monte Carlo?"

"I don't know. There's a picture here of a girl in camiknickers flinging some money at a man in evening dress and saying, 'I wouldn't touch a penny of it if you went down on hands and knees to ask me.' Would that be it?"

"I forget. But anyway read it. What's the synopsis?"

Claud settled himself comfortably in the window-seat. Sylvia composed herself for absorbed and luxurious attention.

Mrs. Perry was surprised to find them thus half an hour later. Dinner and the doctor had been (as usual) announced simultaneously. He had reported favourably on Henrietta. Slight concussion—rest and quiet for a few days—and was just coming along to examine Sylvia's ankle.

"Oh, mummy, it's nothing," said Sylvia amiably. "It's really nothing at all."

"Nonsense, dear, it's quite a nasty sprain," said Mrs. Perry. "I've been quite worried about it."

"It's nothing, really, mummy."

"Brave little woman," said Claud in an encouraging undertone.

"Dr. Dawson is just coming along to look at it. You know he *does* relieve my mind a lot about Henrietta. . . . Oh, here you are, Dr. Dawson! You saw my husband? Poor Sylvia's got *such* a painful ankle. . . ."

CHAPTER XIV

I

WHEN LESLIE SAID something about Henry's playing in this next set he pretended not to hear. He edged Jane away round the side of the summer-house and there confronted her desperately.

"Why did you tell Leslie you'd stay the night?"

"Well, darling, it was so difficult to refuse. How could I? With every one listening and saying 'Do!'"

"I refused," said Henry grimly.

"That only made it more difficult for me. How could we both insist on such frightfully pressing engagements early tomorrow in town?"

"You're usually pretty good at thinking of excuses," said Henry bitterly.

It was unnecessarily unkind and absolutely unwarranted. But the shocking thing was that Jane didn't get in the very least annoyed. With a particularly winning gesture she put her hand into his, and said, "It's horrid, isn't it?"

Henry suddenly saw a vision of himself in the years to come. Often angry, annoyed, feeling badly about something; and then Jane would put her hand in his, or pat his shoulder or kiss his ear, and, utterly unresentful of all his unkindness, slip in a word of sympathy that would suddenly prick the balloon of his anger. Well—it wasn't a pretty picture. He felt a sudden revulsion from such a vision of himself. It was wrong to be angry. It was always silly to lose one's temper. But the causes that made him lose his temper weren't silly and he wasn't going to allow Jane to make him believe they were. Nobody who allowed himself to be "managed"—"managed"—hateful word!—was going to keep his self-respect for very long. Their quarrels might end in bitterness, but the after-taste of this sort of episode could be, he knew, more acrid still.

If only one could ever put anything one felt into words. If only he could explain something of this to her—perhaps, he thought anxiously, it would clear up things between them. Perhaps if she understood why he got angry, instead of just wanting to soothe him when he did, everything would be all right.

He played thoughtfully with her fingers.

"Jane. Jane, do you think I'm terribly wrong to mind about this so much?"

"Wrong? Darling, you know I never know what you mean when you say 'wrong' like that. I suppose you can't help minding."

"And *you* don't mind?"

"Well—we can go away tomorrow just as well, can't we? Or—or another week-end."

"So you do really think I'm wrong?"

Jane sighed. "Honestly and truly, Henry, I don't see what wrong and right has got to do with it. I don't mind as much as you do, but that's not to say you're wrong, is it? We're simply different."

"So when I get angry—and try to make you do something—or agree about something—you never think I'm in the right at all?"

"I never think anybody's 'in the right,' as you say, about anything, Henry. Or in the wrong either for that matter."

"So there's no use in getting excited or—or angry—about anything? Anything in the world. Is there?"

"No," agreed Jane immediately. "No. There isn't." Her hand still in Henry's she raised her eyes to his, smiling. There was sun and laughter in her eyes, joy on her lips and brow. She was as carefree as the day, as heartless as the sunshine, as elusive as the breeze. Henry, taking both her hands, stroked them thoughtfully. He felt the smooth warm skin, the little wrinkles over the knuckles, the pretty polished nails; and all the time he held her hands she was slipping away from him; dissolving, he fancied, back into the lovely inhuman sunshine and wind of which she was made.

"Funny hands you've got, Jane," he said, closing his fingers suddenly on hers as if to hold her prisoner a little longer.

"Funny?"

"Yes. Small and white and fragile-looking."

"Glycerine and honey and Cutex nail polish."

"Is that so? Is that what makes them look as if they needed—protecting?"

"Protecting?" (Poor old Henry. There simply wasn't time to allow him to get sentimental just at that moment.) "Yes, that's the effect we girls aim at. But fortunately, you know, they don't."

"No, I know they don't," said Henry gently. "Not the least little bit." He added surprisingly, "Jane, I must have been awfully tiresome recently, getting into tempers the whole time and that sort of thing. I'm sorry."

"Oh, darling—it's nothing. I mean you haven't really. I mean I know when it's hot one gets snappy over nothing. . . ."

"Nothing? No, I suppose not, really."

"Not really," said Jane lightly.

There were no words in which he could voice the deepest conviction of his heart and mind—the knowledge that a sense of right and wrong were for him as necessary as the blood that ran in his veins, as the air he breathed. No words; and even if he had been able to find them he would not have wished them spoken. If Jane believed all their quarrels were about nothing, then that was all there was to be said, because, however much they might talk, they were not using the same language.

Henry raised her hands to his lips, kissed her fingers, and released her.

"Shall we go back to the others?" said Jane.

"Yes."

It was the only one of their quarrels that had ever ended gracefully.

• • • • • • •

"I say," said Bert, rollicking up to Jane like a nice dog, "what about trying out the car now? Would you like to? That is, if nobody wants us to play tennis or anything."

After that nobody liked to ask them.

"As a matter of fact, we were beginning to think about supper," said Leslie.

There was a general pause. Henry looked at his watch and said, "Seven o'clock." It sounded just a little sepulchral. There was another silence and into Leslie's head flashed the thought—This isn't at all what I meant the party to be. Every one suddenly seemed to be afflicted by a recurrent attack of polite indecision.

"Well, what about just a twenty-minute spin? Just up Dover Hill? Back before half-past? What about that?" said Bert eagerly.

"Yes—do, if you'd like to—do," said Leslie. Because she was thinking, Silly fool, what does he want to go rushing out in his car for now, she took care to say it particularly nicely; and Bert triumphantly escorted Jane to his M.G. in high spirits. Jane threw a backward glance at Henry. He was twiddling his racket and did not seem to notice. I hope it's all right, she thought, as she had thought so many times on leaving him, I hope he's happy and doesn't mind; and then the reaction came, the feeling that recently had been following stronger and stronger on this initial consideration—well, anyway, *I'm* going to enjoy myself. I can't be always bothering about what I'm saying and doing. "This is fun," she said, smiling at Bert, and squeezing herself happily into the driver's seat. I do like some one who enjoys herself, thought Bert appreciatively. He devoted himself eagerly to the task of showing her the gears.

"We'd better play tennis till they come back," said Leslie, and then was more than a little disconcerted to find that, in some extraordinary way, the party had now dwindled to three—herself, Henry and Bill.

"Every one seems to have gone," said Bill tactlessly.

"Where *is* every one?" said Leslie. It was absurd to feel so abandoned. Nobody seemed to have said good-by and left in the normal way, and yet every one had suddenly disappeared—Florence in bed, of course—and Claud and Sylvia had had to rush off—and mummy had wandered off indoors, but then of course one hadn't expected (hadn't, if the truth be told, exactly wanted) her to stay—and Bert and Jane—but they were coming back. . . .

"I say, before we start, could you tell me what time there's a train back to London?" said Henry.

"Oh, Henry! Must you really go?" (She knew it! Once some one started it, every one left. Absurd phrases about sinking ships flashed through her mind.)

"Yes, I'm afraid I really must."

Leslie divulged the information reluctantly.

"There's one at nine-thirty and one at eight."

"Thanks. That will do splendidly. The eight o'clock one, I mean."

All right, go then, thought Leslie. I don't want to keep you. But a glance at Henry's face made her regret her unspoken ungraciousness. Dear Henry! There was something appealing about his brown eyes and stiff untidy hair. He was so obviously a nice man. It was almost painfully obvious.

"Bert can take you to the station," said Leslie gently. (If Bert was going to amuse himself and disorganize the party by taking out Jane in the car he could make himself useful by taking Henry afterwards.)

"Oh—we won't bother him. What about this game? Shall we play?"

"Yes, let's. What a nuisance we're only three. We might ask mummy, of course. . . ." Her voice was apologetic.

"Do you think she would? Shall I go and ask her?" said Bill willingly.

"No, I'll go. I don't know quite where she'll have got to," said Leslie, and left Henry and Bill to drive balls rather aimlessly at each other, while she went in search of her mother.

Mrs. Fisher was glancing over the cold buffet supper arranged in the dining-room. The cool and silence of the house was by no means unwelcome to her.

"Well, one thing, there'll be plenty to eat, Leslie. I hope you're all still hungry. Have you left the others playing tennis?"

"No. There aren't enough of us. Please do come and play, mummy."

"Me play? Oh, but I should have to change and—why, where are all the others?"

"Jane and Bert have gone out in Bert's car and so there's only three of us."

"Well, but, my dear, you know I'm not up to your standard. And besides I was meaning to—"

"Oh, *please* come, mummy. Every one is sort of standing about. Please come."

There was a note in Leslie's voice which her mother had hardly heard since Leslie was a little girl. She responded immediately, however. Immediately and handsomely. She said yes, very well, she would like a set. She said she would be changed in a moment. She said it was nice of them to ask her.

Leslie went out happily and told the others her mother would be very pleased to play.

"We ought to have asked her before," said Bill.

"Oh, no. I don't think she wanted to play till just now," said Leslie confidently.

It was a funny set. Bill and Mrs. Fisher, surprisingly enough, beat Leslie and Henry. It was not at all good tennis. Bill dashed to the net at the earliest opportunity and would remain there, more or less in the middle, enthusiastically trying to intercept anything and everything in or out of his reach. When he was successful Mrs. Fisher congratulated him warmly. When he had tried and failed to reach a shot he would cry, "Yours, partner!" in a stentorian voice, and Mrs. Fisher would chase as hard as she could go to either end of the back line. Leslie was inclined to resent this unorthodox manner of play, and consequently sent a good many of her own shots out. Henry seemed to be trying, but he did not play well. Mrs. Fisher and Bill won 6—4 and were rather pleased with themselves.

"That was wizard," said Bill. "Let's have another."

"I'm afraid I must go," said Henry. "I mustn't miss this train."

"Bert and Jane have been a long time," said Leslie. "They ought to be back any minute. Perhaps if you started to walk you'd meet them. Oh, no! They said something about going to Dover Hill though, didn't they? If they've gone to the top I shouldn't think they'll be back just yet."

"I don't want a lift to the station," said Henry. "I'd like to walk and get—" He suppressed the phrase "get some exercise," which had been on the tip of his tongue, as being, in the circumstances, both unconvincing and vaguely insulting, and substituted "get cool."

"Just as you like," said Mrs. Fisher kindly. "You'll have nice time to change and walk there."

Henry went off to change in the house. In the cloakroom he took his note-book out of his pocket and, steadying it against the rim of the washing basin, he wrote in pencil his last letter to Jane.

"DARLING,—I think you're quite right about explanations being so silly. It isn't that I think you're in the least wrong or I'm in the least right about anything, or that I shan't always love you as much as I have and do now. Only I do see that we're too different ever to be really happy together, so there isn't anything more to be said, is there?—HENRY.

"P.S.—Will you bring the car up to town and leave it outside the office on Monday some time?—XX."

It was rather awful, thought Henry, tearing out the page and slipping the note-book back into his pocket, to have to end a letter like that with a reminder about the car. But then things were like that. One couldn't abandon one's parents' car with quite the same grand gesture that one might one's own. And the kisses that he had refrained from adding to the letter and then had added, on impulse, to the postscript would make it all right. Jane wouldn't mind. Jane never minded about anything.

For a moment he stood touching the cold, smooth rim of the washing basin, looking with a sort of meaningless attention at the smears the soapsuds had left round the plug-pole. It was funny that, while for the past three years he had not had a wish unconnected with Jane, now he didn't want anything from her, or indeed anything in the world at all except just one thing: to get away before she came back again.

He picked up his bag and went quietly and quickly out to say good-by.

II

"Sorry," said Jane, as the gear-lever grated sickeningly into second.

"Too fast," said Bert. "Now take this change into third much slower. You'll get the hang of it directly. There—that was much better."

Bert was delighted with his rôle of instructor; not only did his instructee show enthusiasm and a touching deference, but she had eyelashes which curled up and back and hair of really rather a nice sort of colour.

"She's marvellous to drive," said Jane; and indeed the M.G. was rather marvellous; when you pressed the accelerator pedal, even ever so lightly, her red nose instantly bounded forward with a rising hum of delight; or she would purr along the road at a "cruising-speed" of fifty, roaring silkily past all the humdrum family cars jogging along in the gutter. It was exhilarating to think that so much power, so much reserve of energy, could be controlled by a foot in a canvas tennis-shoe on the accelerator and a careless bare hand on the wheel. Jane's hair was blown straight back from her head, her light silk dress fluttered back against her body, her lips, slightly parted, tasted the strong current of air that bore against them. There was not a thought in her head beyond the ecstasy of speed.

"You handle her jolly well," said Bert. The admiration in his voice was not, of course, for her driving, but for her self. Indeed honesty compelled him to admit, "For a first time."

"You must drive now," said Jane, slowing to forty, "and take her really fast."

She slowed up and stopped—not quite as near to the side of the road as she thought she was.

Quite a pleasant little business ensued of trying to crawl over and change places without getting out of the car.

"This is grand," said Bert, feeling once more the satisfactory solidity of the wheel in his fingers. "I say, I wish we didn't have to go back, don't you? I wish we could go on and really try her out and then have supper later somewhere, don't you?"

The correct ingredients for perfect happiness were, he felt, at the moment in his grasp—a good car in exquisite running order and a girl who (in spite of her strange intelligence) belonged quite evidently to the type of girl he liked.

"Yes, I wish we could," said Jane truthfully.

"Still, I suppose one must more or less do the polite thing and get back, I suppose?"

"Oh, yes! Yes, one must—definitely," said Jane, suddenly recalled by the hopefulness of his voice, to the realities of Leslie's party and of course—Henry. Henry in whose car she ought now by rights to have been, heading for some unknown destination, holding hands and trying so hard to regain their elusive Paradise; Henry who would be waiting for her when she got back; Henry who would always be waiting for her when she got back from anywhere. . . .

"What's the time?" asked Jane regretfully.

"Half-past seven. Later than I thought."

"Blast. We must hurry."

They did.

"I can't understand people who are nervous about cars, can you?" said Bert, as a cyclist whom they had just passed turned to shout some indistinguishable remonstrance over his shoulder at them.

"Oh, well—old people, you know," suggested Jane with a vague tolerance.

"Oh—old people!" said Bert, dismissing the subject. "I say, since you like cars, would you care to come out one evening and we might go and have supper at some roadhouse or something? It would be rather fun, I mean, if you'd like to."

"I'd love to," said Jane readily, thinking, rather unkindly perhaps, what a nice restful evening it would be, and how she would be able to do all the conversation and entertainment required of her on her head, so to speak.

"That's grand," said Bert; "that's splendid. Which day shall we make it? Next week?"

There was an agreeable discussion about the day, followed by the pleasant business of interchanging addresses and telephone numbers. They had also to tell each other their surnames.

"That will be grand, then," said Bert for the fifth time as he swung the car up the drive.

· · · · · · ·

After Henry had said his good-bys and gone, Leslie murmured something about changing for supper and went off, leaving her mother and Bill in sole possession of the court.

"That was a grand set," said Bill. "You and I must play together again, Mrs. Fisher."

"Yes, I enjoy a game now and again," said Mrs. Fisher. "That will be the last for today, I'm afraid. We'd better pick up the balls. . . . Oh, thank you so much, Bill. I believe the sixth one went over into that flower-bed—over there—thank you."

"I mustn't tread on your flowers," said Bill, stepping gingerly.

He was a nice boy, thought Mrs. Fisher.

"What about these chairs? Shall I take them in or anything?"

"Oh, thank you so much. Don't try to carry them all. You can't possibly. The others can be brought in later."

"No, no, I've got them," said Bill, staggering under the weight of six deck-chairs.

"You must come and play again soon, you and your brother. The court doesn't get played on enough, with only Leslie and myself here."

"I'd love to. We'd simply love to. Bert's awfully keen to get into the club first this year. I think he has quite a good chance, don't you?"

"I'm sure he has," said Mrs. Fisher warmly, trying to recollect anything of Bert's play and wondering what club he meant. "And what about you? Do you play for them?"

"Oh, no, I'm not as good as Bert," said Bill simply. "I say, I wish our court was in as good condition as yours. Ours has got moss all over it."

"Well, you must come and play on ours as often as you like," said Mrs. Fisher. "Leslie and I will be very pleased to see you. And if Leslie isn't here—she may be going away, you know—*I* shall be very pleased if you will use it whenever you want."

"Going away?" said Bill. "Is she going to stay with friends or something?" In his experience when girls went away it was to visit friends. Either that or the winter sports.

"No. She wants to be in London for a bit," said Mrs. Fisher.

"In *London*? In the *summer*?" cried Bill incredulously. He gazed around him, at the peaceful garden, at the evening sunshine slanting across the grass, at the glimpse of river-water between the trees, and drew a deep breath. "Gosh!" he exclaimed, "if I had the chance of the summer here instead of stewing all the week in an old office like I have to! . . ."

"She wants a change, you see," said Mrs. Fisher, half apologetically. She was thinking how pleasant it would be if Leslie had a companion like this nice boy to keep her happy at home.

"Oh, well," said Bill, with an effort at tolerance, "I suppose there's something in that. I suppose really every one wants what they haven't got."

Leslie, coming back across the lawn to rejoin them, heard this last remark of Bill's; and thought scornfully that it was just like him to be producing platitudes by way of conversation.

· · · · ·

When Bert and Jane finally came to a standstill again outside the house, Leslie came out on to the porch and said: "We're having supper."

It was not, of course, exactly intended as a reproach. Nevertheless Bert and Jane immediately both apologized, and, having done so, felt considerably drawn to each other by a mutual consciousness of guilt.

"Oh, Jane," continued Leslie, "by the way, Henry's gone. He wanted to catch that earlier train. He left this note for you—it's about the car, I think."

Jane took the rather crumpled little bit of note-book paper (carefully folded and marked Jane) and decided not to read it immediately. It might contain reproaches, or something she couldn't be bothered to cope with at the moment. However, as she shoved it, unread, into the pocket of her sweater, she was reassured by catching sight of the two hasty pencil crosses at the foot. Probably it was all right if he had put those in. Henry was so sentimental about that sort of thing. Two pencil crosses really seemed to have some meaning for him.

III

Much to all the Perrys' surprise, dinner, when at last they sat down to it, turned out to be a very pleasant sort of meal. Sylvia was mildly astonished at Claud. He had never had a real family life of his own (she had often envied him for it), and disapproved, she knew, in a general sort of way of the parent-child convention. How did it come, then, that he seemed to know all about getting up to ring the bell at the end of each course—not too promptly, in case Mr. Perry should think he was being hurried, but a few minutes after the head of the family, the carver (and unfortunately also the slowest eater) had laid down his knife and fork; about pleasing mummy by saying chocolate ice was his favourite pudding; about listening (with apparent interest) to daddy's golf stories and admitting that, though he hadn't had many chances of playing since he had been working in London, it was a grand game, and his handicap was 14.

"Good Lord, is it, Claud?" said Sylvia. "I always thought you were just quite hopelessly bad—like me. But 14's quite good, isn't it?"

"Yes, of course it is—very good," said Mrs. Perry. "Better than daddy."

Sylvia tried to catch Claud's eye, in order that they might enjoy this joke together. But he was busy handing the salt to Mrs. Perry.

"I didn't know you really liked golf, Claud."

Mrs. Perry reflected that her daughter did not really seem to know very much about this agreeable young man. She did not know he liked chocolate ice; she did not know what his handicap at golf was; she probably had not noticed that a button needed sewing on to his coat. The child was spoilt. She didn't properly appreciate Claud's attentions, didn't seem to take very much notice of him altogether. Mrs. Perry, accustomed to take seriously the comfort of her menfolk, was shocked.

"I should like a game with you some time," said Mr. Perry.

"Thank you, sir. I should enjoy that."

"Well—how about tomorrow?" said Mr. Perry heartily. "Quite a good course here, you know—ever played on it?"

"No, I should like to. But I say, you weren't expecting me—I don't want to plant myself on you—"

There was an instant chorus of dissent from the Perry parents.

"Very glad to have you," said Mr. Perry.

"But, of *course* you are to stay the week-end," cried his wife. "We were expecting you. Directly Sylvia phoned about the difficulties about the car and everything I said, 'Well, of *course* Claud must stay the week-end.'" She believed this heartily as she said it.

"It's awfully good of you," said Claud, recognizing at once that the moment had come when polite protestation should topple over into cordial thanks.

"I don't know why I've never thought of offering you a game before," said Mr. Perry. "If I'd known you were a keen golfer—there's always Saturday afternoon."

Sylvia sighed to see her Claud, Claud with his precious Saturday afternoons, transformed into a keen golfer.

"You ought to practice more yourself, Sylvia," said Mrs. Perry, thinking, in a kindly way, that the child was getting a little left out of all this.

The retort, "I loathe the beastly game," rose, not unjustifiably, to Sylvia's lips. It was true. She did loathe golf, and Claud had never said a word about the game recently. If he'd really wanted to play he'd have said so, wouldn't he? And now mummy and daddy were trying to spoil their lovely Saturday afternoons together by suggesting horrible family games, insinuating that she had been keeping him from playing up till now. Claud wouldn't really enjoy it. Of course he wouldn't. Hot resentment mounting within her, she challenged Claud across the table with a look. His eyes met hers with the special intensity that she felt, perhaps foolishly, was for her alone. There was nothing but good temper and merriment in his glance, together with a touch of that expression that she was accustomed to describe to him as "looking disgustingly pleased with yourself." Darling Claud! He was so pleased at getting on so well with her family. Pleased and just a little provocative. "There you are, you see, it's quite easy. I know how to manage them." Well, she wasn't going to be grumpy just to show him how clever he was. Besides, now that she had decided not to be cross, it *was* rather nice that Claud should be friendly with them like this. Pleasanter really than always whisking him away from the family. Easier and simpler really if he could drop in to a meal sometimes like this. And of course the family would never really absorb him, because he would always want to be with her most, just as she would always—always (shocking as the admission might be, because one shouldn't ever talk like that really)—want to be with him.

It was only a moment since her mother had spoken, but the pause was long enough for all these thoughts to rush through her head; long enough for her to decide, half unconsciously, to reject one standard of honesty and accept another.

She smiled and agreed with her mother.

"Yes, I ought to practice more. I will, as soon as this sprain gets all right."

· · · · · · ·

Before she went to bed Sylvia went in to say good-night to Henrietta. Henrietta had been to sleep, woken up and drunk a glass of milk, and was now asserting once more that there was absolutely nothing the matter with her. She was perfectly all right.

"Do tell mummy I'm *really* all right, Sylvia."

"Yes, of course I will. But anyway, it's bedtime now. We're all going to bed." The phrase suddenly touched a chord in her memory. That was what mummy used to say when they were children, awake in bed after they should have fallen asleep. Whether Henrietta remembered this or not, she appeared reassured. She sighed, turned over, relaxed and murmured:

"Mummy talks as if I'm ill. It's so silly."

But for once Sylvia did not agree with her sister about her mother's silliness.

"Well, you've been giving her a shock or two. You oughtn't to mind her enjoying herself a little now fussing over you."

Henrietta shot her sister an inquiring look. It was a new thing for Sylvia to be telling her how to manage her mother.

"It was nice of you to come and look for me," she said. Sylvia smiled. It was so like Henrietta to slide off at a tangent at the merest hint of a scolding. Sylvia laughed, and suddenly recognized the utter futility of preaching "intellectual honesty" to a creature like Henrietta, to whom beguilement was the breath of life and other people's approval the only breathable atmosphere.

"What are you laughing at, Sylvia?" murmured Henrietta drowsily.

"I was thinking that you're so damn lucky. You chose so precisely the right moment to fall off a horse and bang your head."

"Did I? This has been such a funny day."

Sylvia contemplated her sister with admiration. A drowsy contented smile curved Henrietta's lips. Her head was nestled comfortably into the pillow. Her mother had just brought her a glass of milk. Her sister was about to tuck her up and ask if there was anything else she wanted. Secure, surrounded by care, love and affection, she was about to drop asleep in her own home—and probably, guessed Sylvia, very glad to be there. Judged by all the standards on which she had been brought up, she had behaved about as badly as she possibly could. Nobody was going to reproach her. Nobody was ever going to bring it up against her. Everybody was, in fact, going to take especial care never to refer to it again; and if anybody ever did, even by so much as the slightest hint, they were going to feel a tactless, heartless brute.

At this point in her reflections Sylvia gazed down at her sister and reflected, charitably enough, that she wouldn't have her changed for anything.

"How's your head, now, Henrietta? Let me tuck you up. Is there anything else you want?"

"No, thank you very much. I'm quite sleepy. Good night, Sylvia darling. I do hope your ankle's all right tomorrow."

"Good night, darling."

When she got back to her own room she found Claud sitting on the window-sill.

"Your father has lent me a pair of pyjamas," he said. "But may I borrow a sponge from you? I didn't like to ask him."

She gave him a sponge and they lingered together, talking at the window. Claud arranged a chair for her to rest her swollen ankle on.

"Claud, I had no idea you were the sort of man who's good at— well, at picking up the knitting-needles granny drops and that sort of thing."

"Didn't you? Perhaps you don't bring out the best side of my nature, darling."

"Perhaps I don't."

They held hands.

"This is a nice house," said Claud. He looked out at the dew-drenched lawn and the darkening huddle of trees. "I think I should like to live in the country like this and come down every morning to a breakfast of kidneys and bacon and devilled game and say, 'James, will you tell Stevens I'll be riding the new roan this morning?'"

"Yes, and in the evening you could come back and say, 'James, will you ask Stevens to brush my breeches? I fell off the new roan several times this morning.'"

"Yes, and the next day I could say, 'James, will you tell Stevens I'll be riding the children's pony—the smaller one—today?'"

"No," said Sylvia, "I should like to live in quite the most extraordinarily modern flat. You know, with even one's tooth-brush built in, and all the lighting incredibly concealed."

"Not entirely, surely? Wouldn't that make it rather dark?"

"And I should have furniture not 'made' but 'expressed' in Hungarian ash or Canadian sycamore, and a bath you walk down into and a shower-bath of green glass. And whenever I felt cross I should give orders for it to be entirely redecorated on the spot."

"Whereas, of course, what we're likely to have," said Claud, the "we" slipping out unconsciously, "is the basement of a converted house. Two rooms and a woman in three times a week."

"Yes, and the gas-cooker outside in the passage, so that the saucepans have to be kept on the hat-rack."

"'Look-out,' we shall say to our friends, 'that's not your bowler, that tomorrow's stew.'"

Neither of them appeared depressed by the prospect.

"The bathroom will be on the top floor—five flights up," continued Sylvia.

"Yes, and we only share it with six other tenants."

"But even if it is only a small flat," said Sylvia, with as much nauseating sentiment as possible, "it will nevertheless be a *home*."

"Besides, it won't be a flat if the bathroom's upstairs, and the kitchen outside," Claud pointed out.

"Inside it would be so clean and gay and tidy," said Sylvia in a sprightly voice, "with bright little pictures—framed magazine covers perhaps—on the walls and rosebuds on the curtains."

"Yes, and all our friends going away would say, 'What a *homey* atmosphere. Did you notice the forks?'"

Their laughter was followed by a moment's silence. Then Claud said softly:

"Darling, you are going to marry me, aren't you?"

"Oh, darling. Do you think I'd better?"

"Oh, I do. I think you had better really."

"All right," said Sylvia, striving, rather unsuccessfully, for casualness. She added, with an awkward little laugh, "Sorry to sound merely obliging. Would you like me to be more romantic?" For some reason she was trembling.

"You are romantic," said Claud eagerly. "Romantic and obliging and adorable—an extremely fine combination. I am so frightfully glad you're going to marry me. I was afraid you wouldn't."

"But Claud! You didn't—I mean we didn't—at least hasn't it only just—oh, well never mind," said Sylvia, giving it up. There were so many things one couldn't say. One couldn't say, "Surely you knew I would?" because that sounded plaintive and idiotic. One couldn't protest, as one ought to protest, that they had agreed on a temporary attachment and wasn't it rather a risk to make it more permanent, because the very sound of the callous calculating phrase "temporary attachment" seemed to jar with the June night, with the words of love that rose in their hearts. One had better perhaps pretend that the idea of marriage had only just occurred to them both, but that, reasoning it out, they found it practicable and workable; and Sylvia, the more conscientious of the two, did try hard for a little to believe that this was what happened. Claud, however, seemed to be suddenly forgetting all his principles. He knelt beside her and covered her hands with kisses. He said he was not good enough for her and never would be. He said he couldn't imagine himself marrying any one else. She was the only woman he'd ever wanted or ever would want. He said he'd work frightfully hard for her and swore he could make her happy with him. He said she was wonderful, adorable and sweet. He said, finally, that he had four hundred pounds a year, and they could live on that, couldn't they?

IV

Henry went back to London in a third-class smoker. Stifled by its warm mustiness, he let down both the windows and drank in with relief the undercurrent of coolness that was beginning to thread its way through the evening air. The train was a slow one. It stopped at nearly every station, but Henry was grateful for every pause. It broke the current of his thoughts, it was some distraction to watch the few passengers get in and out. He was going back to an empty house, for his parents were away for the week-end. When he got back it would be too early to go to bed, and when he woke up tomorrow morning it would be too early to get up. Tomorrow he must make himself wash and dress and have some breakfast. He must make himself go for a walk in the park, and go out to lunch somewhere. How long would all that take? Could he make it fill up the whole day?

Never in his life had he so suddenly come to an end of everything. He had said good-by before, but always with eyes turning towards the future. He had been sorry to leave his old school, but there had been all the excitement and interest of going up to the University. He had hated the idea of coming down from Oxford—and yet the prospect of work in London, with Jane taking some job there too, had beckoned alluringly. Now, thought Henry flatly and finally, there is absolutely nothing to look forward to. As if in sympathy with his thoughts the train stopped. He gazed out of the window at an advertisement of Oxo and told himself that he must learn how to forget. A girl passed by the window. Immediately he thought that she had hair rather the colour of Jane's; only Jane's was prettier. And then he found that he could not think of the colour of Jane's hair without the whole of Jane, her ways, her voice, her laughter, crowding into his mind. She was so much at home in his thoughts that he could not immediately turn the key on her, so real to him that, by comparison, she dimmed all else. For three years she had been the ultimate meaning of all he had said or done or thought. No effort of the will could now shut out from his thoughts that lovely visitant. He could not leave her behind him even though he had said good-by and come away. He could not forget her because she had become a part of himself. Even to comfort himself he could not belittle in his mind all she had meant to him these years he had known her.

He was profoundly miserable; and yet, curiously enough, he grew slowly conscious of a feeling at the bottom of his mind that had nothing to do with unhappiness. He was half surprised and half ashamed to discover that somewhere within him lurked an odd sort of feeling of relief. He thought: I shall never be more unhappy than I am now; I shall never really care about anything again. Each reflection brought a surge of misery with it; and yet somehow, as the wave retreated, he knew that some faint grain of comfort had been left lying in his mind. Musing over his wretchedness, he stumbled on the thought, No one will ever be able to hurt me so much again, and saw, dimly, that there was comfort in this and would be more comfort in the days to come. Without admitting it to himself he yet had a glimmering of self-knowledge. In the depths of his mind he knew that somewhere in his misery there was freedom, there was an escape. A nervous strain of which he had only been half conscious, but which nevertheless had been steadily increasing, had suddenly snapped. He thought, without knowing why: I shall never believe in the spider-spirit again, and half saw, and yet edged away from the thought, that herein lay his consolation. It was only after further brooding, further agonizing memories of Jane, of her voice, of the gay, careless, hurtful things she had said, that he suddenly put his finger on the key to his only comfort—Anyway, I chose this for myself. No one but myself has forced this on me.

To this thought he constantly returned, while, all the way back to London the rhythm of the wheels mocked him with a bitter reiteration. "Anybody right about anything," chattered the wheels, speeding faster over the metals. "Anybody right about anything." The rhythm quickened till the wheels could hardly spin out the words fast enough, quickened till Henry wanted to scream to them to stop, they could never keep up; and then, with a jarring of the brakes, a jolting and clanging over the points, the train would slow up for a station, and the maddening chatter would subside; but only to be changed to a slower, heavier rhythm—"We're *different, different, different.*"

"Oh," thought Henry, touching the very bottom of his misery as the train clanked finally into Paddington station, bringing him back into the city he had left with such high hopes that morning. "Oh, I shall never really forget. Nothing will ever be really worth-while again."

But even while his heart assented to this his intelligence told him it would not always be so.

CHAPTER XV

I

THE NEXT MORNING Florence's temperature was down to normal. Mrs. Fisher insisted that she should have breakfast in bed. She then allowed her to go and sit in the garden, luxuriously tucked up in the hammock, and thoughtfully supplied with three large clean pocket-handkerchiefs. Leslie, coming to sit with her, found her enormously restored and very cheerful. She was studying a letter.

"I say, Leslie," she said. "Your mother's being very sort of kind and helpful. Do you know this Mrs.—What's-her-name? Burton, it looks like."

"Oh, the woman with the little girl? Yes, I've met her."

"Do you know what this letter is about? She's writing to your mother to ask if she knows of any one to coach this child for a year. Apparently she's to go to school when she's thirteen, but they don't want to send her away before then, and they live in the depths of Devonshire or somewhere, where there isn't a decent day-school. She thought I might like to take it on."

"Oh. Do you think you would? It would be rather cutting yourself off from everything, wouldn't it?"

"Well, yes, it would. But I think it would be rather a good experience, you know. What's this child like—do you know?"

"Oh, sort of ordinary, I think. I only saw her once."

"The mother says, 'My little girl, Jessie, is unusually intelligent, but I am afraid is not altogether an easy child to teach. She will not work unless she is interested.'"

"Sounds lazy to me," said Leslie unkindly.

But Florence already took a proprietary interest in little Jessie.

"Oh, no! Not necessarily. As a matter of fact, a child is often quite right to reject things when they're not presented to it in the right way."

Leslie, who had not kept abreast of modern educational reform, found this surprising.

"She went to school once, I think," she said, "and was awfully unhappy or ill or something. I can't remember which but anyway I know it was a failure."

Florence found this slightly vague information definitely encouraging.

"Oh, I *do* sympathize with her if she didn't like school. You know, Leslie, it's always the worth-while child that won't fit in. I have the greatest sympathy with any one who's unhappy at school, because I can remember it all so well."

"But you weren't unhappy, were you, Florence? I remember your being quite sorry to leave."

"No," admitted Florence regretfully. "I can't say I was unhappy *all* the time, really."

"I rather liked it," said Leslie, tolerantly.

"Of course the whole system is quite wrong," said Florence, dismissing the subject. "But anyway—about this child. I should say that good coaching would do a lot, wouldn't you?"

"I don't know. I've only seen her once."

"The curriculum of a school is usually far too fiddling. How can you keep a child properly absorbed if you're always switching it off algebra and shoving it on to geography, or snatching it off English to bother it about French verbs?"

"I don't know," said Leslie truthfully.

"When it gets interested in a play of Shakespeare's or some poetry or something it shouldn't be fussed about with anything else all the rest of the morning," declared Florence. "Now if *I* coach it I shan't divide up the books it does into sections. I shall let it go straight ahead and finish. I mean I don't mind if we do nothing one week but read the *Faerie Queen*—and George Eliot all the next—and Shakespeare all the next—"

"What about maths and things? I suppose it's got to pass into this school at the end of a year."

"The mother says it's bad at maths, but good at history," said Florence, studying the letter afresh. "As far as I remember I was pretty bad at maths myself. Do you remember what one did at twelve in the maths line, Leslie?"

"Fractions?" suggested Leslie.

"Fractions? I rather forget about them." She paused thoughtfully, but succeeded only in recalling a dirty exercise book with large red crosses marked against all the answers. "I think I shall start her on simple interest. It's more practical really, and I can be looking up about fractions and things in the meantime."

"Oh, yes," said Leslie comfortingly.

"I'm glad she's good at history. Shows imagination, doesn't it? I hope she's keen on literature too. As a matter of fact, it's much better not to separate those two subjects. I shall teach them together."

"I think it's marvellous of you to take such an interest," said Leslie. "I should have thought after living in London on your own you'd have been bored to tears by the prospect."

This was the sort of remark that endeared Leslie to her friends. It afforded such a splendid opening for explaining that one was far too interesting a person ever to be bored.

"No, as a matter of fact the idea rather attracts me. Education is so frightfully important, you know."

Leslie did not know. She had always taken it more or less for granted that one had to go to school. She was a little impressed by Florence's enthusiasm.

"Well, anyway, I'm sure mummy will be frightfully pleased to hear you want to do it. Here she comes. We'll tell her. I wonder where Jane has got to. She wandered off some time ago. I've hardly seen her since breakfast. Oh, mummy! Isn't it marvellous! Florence says she'll do the coaching job."

Mrs. Fisher settled herself in a deck-chair beside them.

"I'm glad the idea appeals to you, Florence."

"When will Mrs. Burton want her, mummy?"

"I shall have to write to her. Of course," added Mrs. Fisher, after a slight pause, "of course she will have to meet you and discuss matters. I don't know, for instance, whether she has asked any other of her friends whether they know of any one suitable. I believe—" she groped for suitable words—"I believe Jessie isn't everybody's child."

Florence, recognizing the tactful drift of these remarks, hastily assented.

"Oh, of course. I know it's only an idea. She's probably got dozens of people in mind—"

"I expect your degree, would be an advantage."

Florence was refreshed by this novel point of view. After nearly a year's work in an office, she had become quite unused to thinking of her degree as any sort of an asset.

"I think I should enjoy coaching," she said.

"I wonder you never thought of taking it up?" suggested Mrs. Fisher.

"Teaching, you mean?" The enthusiasm died out of Florence's voice. There seemed a world of difference between coaching and plain teaching. "I don't think I should make a very good school-mistress."

"You're not a bit the type," said Leslie, displaying once again her admirable faculty for saying the right thing.

"You'd find the routine tiresome?" suggested Mrs. Fisher.

"No, not exactly," said Florence. She sought for words which would convey delicately that it would not be a deficiency in herself but a deficiency in the school which would unfit her for the profession. "I don't think I could stand all the humbug and hypocrisy," she said finally.

"Oh?"

"Florence," said Leslie, rushing enthusiastically to her friend's support, "thinks schools are all wrong. She has all sort of theories about education."

Mrs. Fisher looked a little doubtful. She seemed about to say something, changed her mind, and contented herself by merely asking Florence if she had ever had any experience of teaching.

"No," said Florence, "actually I haven't."

"I see. Well, Florence, I'll certainly write to Mrs. Burton and ask her if she'd like to meet you and talk things over."

"Thank you very much, Mrs. Fisher. It's awfully good of you. There's—there's no harm in trying, is there?"

Mrs. Fisher was touched by the note of appeal, the demand for reassurance, that suddenly broke through Florence's self-confidence.

"No harm at all," she said warmly. "I think myself—" she paused and dismissed firmly from her mind Leslie's hints as to Florence's "theories"—"I think myself you'd be an excellent person for the job."

"Where's Jane got to? Do you know, mummy?"

"Somebody has just rung up on the telephone for Jane," replied Mrs. Fisher. "I think it's Bert. Those two seem to be getting on very well together. What will Henry say? You told me they were engaged, didn't you?"

"Oh, Henry and Jane aren't silly over that sort of thing," explained Leslie airily. "They don't only go out with each other—do they, Florence?"

"No. At least Jane doesn't. She knows lots of other men. I don't think Henry goes about with other girls much."

"In that case I should prophesy disaster," said Mrs. Fisher.

"Oh, no—why?" Leslie reflected that her mother could never really grasp the fundamental idea of love without possessiveness. "I mean—if you really love a person—you want them to do whatever will make them happy, don't you?"

"Perhaps, dear. It depends on your character. It's a very high ideal."

"Oh, I call that just common decency," said Leslie.

"Here's Jane coming. She shall have my chair. I'll go in and write some letters. I won't forget your Mrs. Burton, Florence."

She smiled at Florence and left them.

"I think your mother is sweet, Leslie."

"Yes, she's very kind. Of course she doesn't really understand people awfully well, you know—but she's terribly kind."

Jane arrived and flung herself full-length into the deckchair.

"I think," she said, "that I could lie in the sun in a deckchair for a week in perfect content."

"I wish you could," said Leslie, and could not help adding, for it seemed to her that nobody had been paying much attention recently to her particular problem, "I've had quite enough of it."

"I dare say I should get disagreeable by about next Friday," said Jane. "Start complaining that the chair creaked or something like that."

"Jane," said Florence, "what are we to do about the flat?"

"Do? Why, will you be away for long, do you think?"

"Yes. You see, there's the prospect of a coaching job. I'll tell you all about that in a minute. It looks as if I might not be back in town for a bit."

"Oh, Lord," said Jane lazily. "What a nuisance." She stretched herself luxuriously, selected a blade of grass and put it in her mouth.

"Poor Jane!" said Leslie with her ever-ready sympathy. "You'll be all alone."

"Oh, it wasn't that I was thinking of," said Jane truthfully. "I was only wondering about the rent and things. Still, it's paid up to the end of the quarter, isn't it? Damn, though, that's quite soon."

"I think," said Florence, "that you'd better—really—find some one else to share as soon as possible." As she spoke an odd little pang shot through her. She remembered signing the lease. She remembered painting the bookshelves blue one Saturday afternoon. She remembered how, if the bath-water was running, you couldn't hear anything on the telephone. She saw Jane's tin money-box standing on the mantelpiece, dusty sunlight, books, the bowl of bulbs that never came up, the bright orange cushions on the green divan. "You'll be able to find some one else, won't you?" she finished.

Jane selected another bit of grass and said she thought she probably could. She chewed the blade for a moment and then suggested an old schoolfriend, Joan Carfax.

"I thought you didn't like her much," said Florence. (If she hadn't known that jealousy was impossible between two enlightened people, she might have recognized the feeling.)

"Didn't I? No, I remember I didn't very much. But I think she'd be quite nice to share with, you know. In a way I think it's better not to be particularly fond of any one you live with."

Florence received this in silence. During all her friendship with Jane it had never ceased to amaze her that any one with such a capacity for inspiring affection should have, apparently, so little need for it.

Leslie did not want to pursue the subject of Joan Carfax. She could not help feeling that one obvious suggestion remained to be made. She did not like to mention it herself. But surely, either Jane or Florence, knowing that she was planning to come and live in town, knowing that the object of inviting all her London friends to a party was to help them persuade her mother, surely one or the other of them would think of suggesting that she, Leslie, should take Florence's place at the flat. They might, she thought, at least suggest it, even if she replied that she was really looking for a studio. Even if she decided against it because she wanted, really, to be quite alone.

But Jane and Florence had both completely forgotten Leslie's schemes.

Tentatively feeling her ground, Leslie said, "But what about Henry, Jane? You'd better marry and then he could come and share the flat."

Jane had not needed to try very hard not to think of Henry. It was easy and instinctive for her to avoid things that might hurt.

"I'm not going to marry Henry," she said. "We've broken it off."

Leslie and Florence, telling themselves that there was really no need for embarrassment, sat awkwardly silent.

"I expect it's a good thing," said Florence at length. She could not help wishing that Jane had told her first, instead of just casually mentioning it in front of Leslie. Moreover, the shadow of Henry's unhappiness touched her for a moment, weighing on her spirits and blackening the sunshine.

"Good thing," said Jane, drowsily blinking up at a tree. "Better to find out in time, not really suitable for each other, always be good friends, etc."

"Will you always be good friends?" asked Leslie. She could not help being interested, although at the same time she was afraid it was a little vulgar of her.

But all Jane said was, "No, I shouldn't think so," and Leslie could guess nothing from her voice.

A moment later she was eagerly comparing her sunburn with Leslie's. And, when Leslie, moved by some vague idea of distracting her, for girls who have just broken off their engagements should, she felt, be distracted, even if they showed no apparent need for it, suggested a bathe, Jane assented eagerly and offered to go and collect their costumes and towels.

"What do you think she thinks about it all?" asked Leslie, curiosity getting the better of her as she saw Jane wave a bathing-dress encouragingly out of the window to show she had found it. "Do you think she minds very much?"

"She minds a little when she thinks of it," said Florence, slowly. "So she doesn't think of it very much."

Leslie found this admirable.

"I think that's so sensible, don't you, Florence? Don't you think that shows a much more—much more sort of controlled mind than people used to have?" She paused and then added, "All the same, I don't think I shall tell mummy. She wouldn't understand how simple and pleasant that sort of thing can be."

Jane reappeared with the bathing-dresses, Leslie joined her, and they ran off together to the river, leaving Florence to her thoughts in the hammock.

They were not unhappy thoughts. Indeed Florence was surprised to find herself so cheerful, when yesterday (she did not mind admitting it now) she had been extremely miserable. It was partly that her cold was better, partly perhaps the gentle swinging of the hammock and the sun warm on her closed lids. But there was more to it than that. Florence's thoughts turned idly towards Mrs. Fisher's unknown friend with her unknown little girl. It might all come to nothing. Probably the mother had already found some one; and yet, curiously enough, the mere idea of something possibly in store for her released some secret spring of happiness in her mind. It was not just one particular hope. It was a feeling that had once lived constantly with her, but had of late, almost without her knowledge, stolen away. Something to look forward to. Could the mainspring of happiness really be summed up in so commonplace a phrase? Florence, searching for something more profound, could only come back regretfully to the same thing. Regretfully, because it seemed to her wrong that human beings should be so foolishly constituted. Regretfully, because she believed that every one should have what they want, and she did not like to admit that happiness could not be so obtained. It would be wrong, surely it would be wrong, for happiness to lie only in unfulfillment? The sun was very warm. A bee buzzed languidly round her head. It ought not to be so; and therefore, concluded Florence with dreamy satisfaction, it could not be so. Dismissing the subject, she allowed her thoughts to slide away happily into the future.

II

"How much do your clothes cost?" asked Claud, pencil poised. Sylvia reflected.

"It depends. For instance, last year I bought a fur coat. At least, when I say 'bought' the family subscribed a good deal. Well, I suppose that brought it up to about a hundred and twenty last year."

Claud laid the pencil down again on the grass beside him.

"Well, I shan't put that down," he said, rolling over onto his back and blinking at the sun, "because it just looks silly."

"Oh, no, darling. Don't put that down, of course. You didn't ask me what you thought you ought to put down. You only asked me what I spent last year. Well, that's nothing to do with it, is it?"

"I hope not, my sweet."

"Besides, I've got a fur coat now. I shan't want another for ages. I've got a lot of other clothes, too. I wouldn't put anything down if I were you."

"I've put down ten pounds," said Claud. "That's for raffia for both of us."

"It isn't what will be our current expenses that worries me," said Sylvia. "Look, Claud—isn't that a fascinating pattern of leaves and grass on my elbows? Whenever I see people shopping it always strikes me how incredibly cheap things are. I mean bread, for instance. You get an absolutely whacking loaf for threepence. What I do think will be awkward is getting the furniture and stuff."

There was a thoughtful pause, ended by both Sylvia and Claud hitting on a simultaneous solution.

"People will give us things, won't they?" from Claud.

"Of course wedding presents help a lot," from Sylvia.

"Well, leaving out clothes and furniture," said Claud, "the budget looks rather good."

"Let me see," said Sylvia. She scanned suspiciously the rather dirty little piece of paper. "What about laundry?"

"Oh, yes. I'm always being asked for that at the digs. But I thought you were going to be the little housewife ever so busy in soapsuds up to the elbows."

"If I got in soapsuds up to the neck I couldn't wash the sheets."

"Oh, sheets and things, of course. Does one have clean sheets often? I don't think I ever do at the digs."

"Oh, you must sometimes. You probably don't notice."

"Yes, I expect I do," agreed Claud, amiably. "It doesn't seem to be a thing one does notice very much."

"We'd better practice not noticing a lot of things, I think," said Sylvia, scanning the list, her eyes wrinkled up against the sun, legs waving in the air. "According to this we mustn't notice there being no electric light or gas in the flat."

"I didn't put that down on purpose. We've allowed such a lot for food that there ought to be plenty of odd shillings over for the meters."

"Oh, I see. I know it looks a lot for food, but I don't think it can really be too much."

"How did you decide it?"

"Well, I know what mummy allows every week for the house-keeping. That's for four of us. So I halved it. And then I halved it again."

"Why?"

"Well, because it was too much," said Sylvia simply.

Another thoughtful pause.

"Yes, but there's something you've forgotten," said Claud, with the usual satisfaction that such a discovery brings. "Your mother has to cater for the maids too, hasn't she?"

"Oh, yes, of course." Sylvia was refreshed by this heartening discovery. "Two maids and part of the gardener. He eats a lot, I'm sure. That's nearly seven people really. Oh, well, I'm sure what I've put down is more than two-sevenths of what she spends."

"And of course it's—" Claud suddenly stopped.

"What were you going to say?"

"No, it doesn't apply to us."

"Yes, but what were you?"

"Well, I was going to say it's cheaper for numbers. Only of course that doesn't apply."

"Well, it applies if you think of two people living cheaper than one, doesn't it?"

"I dare say there's something in that. Of course I'm in fairly cheap digs at the moment. Only we ought to have something a little better than that."

"We ought to have a better bathroom, anyway," said Sylvia, remembering Mrs. Wilkins' rusty geyser and patchy walls. "But then you must be living pretty cheaply at the moment, aren't you, Claud?"

"Well, I suppose so. I don't know. Certainly the digs are good value. The only thing is—well, you know I live quite nicely on my salary, but I don't have a penny over."

There was the longest and most thoughtful pause of all.

"Well," said Sylvia at length, "I suppose that just goes to show that a flat for us two would be much cheaper than you alone living in digs—as well as being nicer of course."

"Yes. It'll have to be, won't it? Cheaper, I mean. Of course," he added, quietly conscious of extreme heroism, "of course, I could give up my share in the car."

"Oh, of course," agreed Sylvia, cheerfully and immediately. She added, "All this talk about meals and things has made me hungry. Shall I go and see if there are any little chocolate cakes left?"

"Yes, do. That is, if your ankle doesn't hurt to walk on."

"Oh, no. It's practically all right today. I say, we shan't have to have any doctor's bills, shall we?"

"No. If you're going to have appendicitis or anything for goodness' sake have it now at your parents' expense."

Claud, left alone, picked up the little list again, flicked a squashed ant off the side, and, after a moment's reflection added "Laundry? Odd shillings" at the bottom.

"Darling, I've been thinking," said Sylvia, returning with a plate of cakes. "You know I can't help wishing you got more out of this. You know, I do feel marriage ought to be a partnership of two independent people—don't you? I think any other tie than inclination is so degrading." She knitted her brows and bit largely into a chocolate cake. "I wish I knew more about the price of things," she continued. "Take these cakes, for instance." She stopped to lick a crumb off her cheek. "In a shop they'd cost about tuppence each. Made at home they work out at less than a farthing. I asked Mary just now. But the point is I don't know whether it's worth paying a cook about forty pounds a year in order to get chocolate cakes at a farthing. That's just the sort of thing that worries me. Another thing. I wouldn't mind a bit having some sort of a job when we are married. But you see I should have to be trained first. Well, would it be worth paying quite a lot for training and then starting at a low salary, when all that would entail paying some one else to do the housework at the flat and feeding in restaurants?" Exhausted by this speech and by these problems, Sylvia finished the last mouthful of cake, lay back and exclaimed, "You see, I don't like to feel you're getting absolutely nothing out of it except making your salary do for two instead of one. Turn your face over the other way, darling. You'll be getting your sunburn uneven again."

"No. I want to look at you," said Claud.

It was by such unexpected remarks that he could always move her, in spite of her own disapproval, even half against her will.

"Darling," said Sylvia fondly. But although she stroked his hair she would not drop her argument. "Don't you think it's rather a poor bargain for you, Claud?"

"No," said Claud sleepily.

"But, darling, it is. It looks as if you'd just have to support me as well as yourself."

"Well?"

"Well, that's all wrong, isn't it?"

"I dare say it is. I suppose it is, if you mind."

The slight emphasis on the "you" caused Sylvia to sit up and contemplate his prone figure with suspicion.

"Don't *you* mind, Claud?"

"No, of course I don't. Why should I?"

"But don't you think it's *wrong*?"

"I dare say it seems wrong to you. But you can't expect me to feel strongly about it, can you?"

"Why not?" shot out Sylvia.

"I've told you. It doesn't affect me. No one," continued Claud in sleepy satisfaction, "minds having some one dependent on them. It's only the one who's dependent who minds." He closed his eyes as if dismissing the subject.

The suspicion that she was being deliberately provoked increased rather than diminished Sylvia's indignation.

"If I didn't know you were doing it on purpose, Claud, I'd say that that was the most immoral thing I've ever heard any one say."

Silence.

"I suppose you positively *like* the idea," cried Sylvia.

"Yes. Yes, I do rather."

"Flatters your male vanity, I suppose?"

"That's right," agreed Claud amiably.

"Well!" said Sylvia disgustedly. With as much dignity as possible she rolled away from him into a patch of shade. She took another chocolate cake and munched in an aloof silence. Presently she said, "And suppose I ever want to leave you?"

"You'll have to ask me for the train-fare, darling."

"Well, I shan't." An idea struck Sylvia. "I shall save it out of the housekeeping."

"I see. I shall get nervous if I'm given herrings more than three times a week. Is that it?"

Sylvia, too happy to remain indignant, giggled. "If I fall in love with some one in Edinburgh you'll be lucky if you get anything but bread and porridge for weeks before I finally go."

"You won't be able to help giving yourself away, you know," Claud warned her. "I shall be able to calculate exactly where you're going. Bread and porridge—as far as Edinburgh. Herrings and no marmalade—the Midlands. The usual, without chicken or cream—somewhere near home. I shall be able to track you instantly. That's to say if I want to."

"All the same, Claud," protested Sylvia, "I do think the idea of being dependent on you is beastly." She felt that although she might consent to put up with such a state of affairs, she could not allow herself to do so without pointing out first that the position was morally a false one.

"You'll get used to it," said Claud kindly. He added annoyingly, "You didn't worry about it until you thought of the word 'dependent.'"

"Oh, nonsense. It's the idea I dislike. I think it's all wrong."

"Darling," said Claud patiently, "what's the good of tearing yourself to bits about it? It can't be helped, can it? Since you haven't—" He stopped.

"Haven't what?"

"Well, I was going to say haven't any money of your own."

Sylvia's expression suddenly changed.

"Claud!" she said seriously, "will you answer me something truthfully?"

"Yes."

"Well then—" She paused. "Did you think—I mean are you surprised. . . ." Her voice trailed away. "Look here," she said bluntly, "do you think I ought to have some money of my own?"

"Well, it's not exactly 'ought', is it, darling? I might have expected you to have a dress-allowance, or something like that."

"To go on after marriage?" persisted Sylvia.

"Perhaps. I certainly wasn't counting on it or anything like that, you know."

"No, no, of course not. But you wouldn't have objected?"

"Objected? No," said Claud truthfully. "After all, it's quite usual, you know."

"Quite usual," repeated Sylvia thoughtfully. There was comfort in the phrase.

"Well, anyway, what was that all about, darling? We needn't bother about it, need we? Since you haven't we shall be perfectly—"

"Yes, but you see it's like this. I think I could have."

"What do you mean? Good Lord, you don't want me to go to your father and ask him—"

"No, no. You needn't be alarmed. It's quite different. It's—it's rather difficult to explain."

Claud waited patiently.

"Some time ago," said Sylvia. She broke off. "Well, it wasn't really some time ago. It was only the other day. Only somehow such a lot seems to have happened since."

"Well?"

"Daddy said he wanted to talk to me. Well, after a lot of preamble it turned out that he wanted to say that if I ever married he would settle something on me. I can't remember exactly how much. But it was quite a lot."

"That was awfully kind of him," said Claud.

"Yes. Yes, I suppose so. Only I didn't think of it like that, you see. I—I refused."

"Oh. Why?"

Sylvia lost herself in a tangle of explanations.

"That's just it. I can't quite explain. Do you know at the time I thought I was doing it from quite high motives? But afterwards I wasn't sure. I didn't think I ought to take the money when I didn't really believe in any of the things he believes in. I couldn't bear his being so generous. It made me feel awful. I—I knew he wouldn't approve of us. . . ." She stopped and threw a glance at Claud. It was a desperate appeal for sympathy and comprehension. He did not fail her.

"Darling," he said, sitting up and taking her hands, "I think it was perfectly sweet of you to feel like that. I—I do understand. It—it was partly my fault, wasn't it?"

"No, no, it wasn't your fault. I didn't mean you to think—"

"I don't," said Claud instantly, "but I think you've been perfectly sweet and marvellous about everything. Darling Sylvia, you've gone quite pink. My funny sweet. I do understand—really I do."

"Oh, darling, how *comforting* of you," sighed Sylvia, gratefully abandoning her confused explanations. "Oh, Claud, I do love you."

"I love you too."

The noise of the gardener's barrow on the path behind them postponed further endearments.

"So you see it's like that," concluded Sylvia, "and as a matter of fact, they don't disapprove of you at all. They were quite pleased when we told them, weren't they?"

"Oh, I thought they were awfully nice about it."

"So you see, I don't see really why I shouldn't—I mean daddy was really awfully sweet. He said he wasn't going to believe I meant it."

"I think he's a very nice man," said Claud.

"So I just told you so that in *case*—suppose he *did* say something to you—now you understand anyway why I said 'No,' don't you?"

"I believe he's going to be rather tactful about it," said Claud comfortingly. "As a matter of fact, he did murmur something about having a business talk with me."

"Oh, darling! We shall be *rich*, shan't we?" cried Sylvia enthusiastically.

"Shall we? You say you can't remember—"

"Well, anyway, quite a lot. . . ."

"I hope it wasn't—well, of course it wasn't *more* than I have?"

Sylvia giggled triumphantly. "No, I don't think so. But anyway, enough to make me quite—oh, quite, quite independent."

"So after all," said Claud, "the herrings will only indicate a lack of imagination."

"Don't let's have herrings at all. I don't like them much, do you?"

"Well, what shall we have?"

"Oh, don't let's have many puddings or silly things like that. Let's have savouries and fruit and cheese instead."

"All right. As long as I have a good breakfast."

"Oh, dear. Do you really want bacon and eggs and barbarous things like that?"

"Yes," said Claud firmly, "I do."

"Don't you think it would be nicer to have a Continental breakfast in bed?"

"No, I don't."

"What a pity. I always think just rolls and coffee in bed are all you want. It's so nice to lie in bed afterwards and think you needn't get up just yet."

"Yes. You have plenty of time to lie back and look at your husband getting up and think, 'I wonder why he bothers to dress and go to work. It's so much nicer here. Funny of him.'"

"Darling, do you really want me to be in the hall to hand you your umbrella when you go?"

"Certainly. There's a lot you've got to learn. I'm not going to have you get slack. You'll have to put out clean socks for me and put studs in my dress-shirt and ask me if I've had a nice day, and pour out glasses of sherry for me when I get back and buy quinine for me when I catch cold and—"

"I certainly shan't. Not any of those things."

"Well then, I think you'll be a perfectly rotten wife." Claud took her hands. His eyes were shining with tenderness and affection. "I don't see what's going to be the good of you at all. If you don't turn out better than that I shall have to take you back to the toy department at Selfridge's and get you changed."

"I expect they'll say they can't do me again at the price. I expect they'll say they 'can only get an inferior article now at a slightly higher price.'"

"I expect they'll say—" Claud paused and finished rapidly, "That you're the most adorable, wonderful, sweet person they've ever seen. I expect they'll say that I'm the luckiest man they've ever met. I expect they'll say—"

"Shut up, darling. Darling, shut up. You—you mustn't really think I'm wonderful—"

"Yes, you are. Be quiet. What do you know about it? You can't judge. Now say after me, 'Claud, I'm wonderful.'"

"Claud, I'm wonderful."

"There! I knew you'd admit it if you gave it a moment's thought. The trouble with you is that you don't know the first thing about yourself."

"Yes, I do."

"No, you don't. It's lucky you've got me to decide things for you. Women need a man like that."

"Indeed? And what have you decided on?"

"A beautiful wedding," exclaimed Claud annoyingly. "The bride in white satin and never had the bells of the old church rung so merrily and squadrons of Girl Guides cheering, and just like her mother, isn't she, and that's the clergyman who christened her, and orange-blossom and champagne."

"Is there a bridegroom present at this ceremony?"

"Somewhere in the vestry, I believe, but nobody really notices. He doesn't matter."

"Yes, he does," cried Sylvia absurdly. "He matters terribly."

"Darling! All right, we'll have him there. We'll order him down from town for the day, and pay a shilling more to have a carnation in his buttonhole."

"After we're married, Claud, are you going to have many of these fits of decisiveness?"

"Now and then. When I think you need it. When I think you don't know what you want."

"I always know what I want."

Claud looked at her with a sceptical tenderness.

"Well, you don't know everything about yourself. I know something about you that you don't."

"What's that?"

"You're faithful," said Claud triumphantly.

"How do you know?" Faithfulness was not a quality of which Sylvia altogether approved. She was not going to admit to it too easily.

"I just do know. You are." He kissed her. "I like your being faithful. Please go on being faithful. You will, won't you? Say you will—please."

"Darling! How can I promise something—"

"Oh, *please*, darling. Say you will. I want to hear you say it."

"But, Claud, I don't believe—"

"Oh, my sweet, what does it matter what you believe? Say what you feel."

There was a pause.

"You do *feel* faithful, don't you?" The absurd earnestness of Claud's inquiry melted all Sylvia's resistance to a wave of tenderness.

"Oh, darling, I do, I do. I feel most frightfully faithful."

"That's all I wanted to know."

Completely satisfied by this splendid compromise they kissed adoringly.

III

After lunch Leslie, finding her mother gardening alone, tried to lead her tactfully up to the question of living in town.

"Which of the people at the party did you like best, mummy?"

Mrs. Fisher reflected. "I think they were all very nice, dear. Bill is a nice boy, isn't he? He was so charming about helping with the chairs and net after we had finished playing."

"Oh, Bill! Do you like Jane, mummy?"

"Yes, I think she's a very attractive little thing."

Leslie was not quite sure whether she was getting anywhere or not.

"You do think—you do see what I mean—you understand now what I meant when I said my London friends were different from the girls who just live at home here?"

Mrs. Fisher thought of Florence sobbing that she did feel rather funny; of Jane gleefully going off to drive Bert's car just as they were going to have supper; of Henry, glum and monosyllabic, leaving suddenly, saying that he would walk to the station. She had an idea that more lay behind all this than Leslie saw. All that she said, however, was, "I think they're all very nice young people."

"Yes, but they're *different*, aren't they?" persisted Leslie.

"Yes," agreed her mother, "they are a little different." She was thinking that the old-fashioned word for this difference would have been selfishness.

"I knew you'd notice it," said Leslie. "And now you do see—don't you—why I want to go and live in London for a bit?" Impatiently she watched her mother snip off the withered head of a pink and drop it into her gardening basket. "It's not really a life here, mummy. I don't feel I'm getting anywhere with my painting or anything. You know I can't help thinking that the only really possible life is one that widens out and out all the time."

At this confident assertion her mother sighed, laid down her basket, and said resignedly:

"Very well, dear. You know I haven't ever really opposed your suggestion that you should go to London. It's just that I wanted you to be sure you really know what you are doing."

"Oh, I know that all right. I've thought it all out. Really I have, mummy."

"Perhaps you took the opportunity of having a chat with Jane and Florence this morning about the cost of living in town?"

Leslie was a little taken aback. Jane and Florence had been asked down as demonstrators of a wider and freer mode of life, not as mere financial consultants.

"Well—I was talking to them the other day when I had supper in town."

"Oh? About how much a week do they spend?"

Leslie racked her brains. She had not been prepared for her mother to come so soon to practical details. It had never occurred to her to relate intellectual escape to financial freedom, and to pass so rapidly from one to the other betrayed, she felt, a slight lack of sensitiveness. Feeling, however, that some effort towards the practical was required of her, she managed to recall a few of Jane and Florence's pronouncements.

"They said you mustn't forget having your shoes repaired and toothpaste and that sort of thing."

"Yes, quite. Did they mention any actual figure?"

"Well, I know they said they never seemed to spend money on what you think would be the big things. Jane said it all seemed to go on sherry and oranges and bus-fares."

Mrs. Fisher silently resolved to have a talk with Jane and Florence herself.

"You didn't ask them what was the minimum they thought you could live on—I mean live on decently?"

Leslie, fidgeting under this catechism and vaguely resenting the word "decently" suddenly decided that her mother was being over-helpful.

"Oh, mummy—I don't want you to bother about that." (Immediately she had said this she felt better.) "I'll work it out for myself. I'll find out all about it by doing it. I've got that hundred pounds. I'll—I'll adjust my scale of living to make it last as long as possible." As she spoke she felt sensations of capability and independence flow comfortingly back into her.

"I thought you said once that it wouldn't be any good going up to town unless you had at least a year at the art-school?"

Leslie, feeling trapped, tried to sound confident rather than annoyed.

"Well, of course, even six months would be something."

"What about the art-school fees? Could you manage even six months with those to pay?"

It was very nasty of Leslie to dislike her mother at that moment. Nasty, but natural. The young woman of independence vanished. The disappointed child turned on the author of its disappointment.

"Oh, mummy!" Baffled pride suggested an angry change of tactics. "Why don't you say if you don't want me to go? What's the good of pretending to encourage me and then—" Leslie turned away and kicked crossly at a stone on the path.

Mrs. Fisher sighed. The prickliness, the defiance, the silly, silly pride! Trying, but at the same time faintly touching. The pathetic confidence that any escape from present circumstances spelled freedom. The yet unshattered illusion that things could ever be as you wanted them in this world.

"Darling, you know you shall do as you like," said Mrs. Fisher (and knew once again that old familiar thought of Leslie's childhood, I'm spoiling her. I'm making things too easy for her.) "Of course you must let me pay the art-school. I want to. I'm sure it will be money well spent."

"I wish I didn't have to ask you," said Leslie. She was conscious of having behaved very badly, but could not for the life of her achieve yet a proper simulation of gratitude.

Mrs. Fisher scaled further heights of heroism.

"You oughtn't to mind, Leslie. After all, you have a right to some sort of training, haven't you? Every parent expects to do something of the sort for each of their children."

Leslie, forcibly struck by this point of view, cheered up noticeably.

"It's awfully sweet of you, mummy. I don't," she added handsomely, "see why you should."

"Yes, it's quite right that I should give you training and help support you for a bit," declared Mrs. Fisher. "Every one ought to have a start in the world."

"I'm so glad you think so, mummy."

In such a tactful manner was an extra allowance proffered and, with equal delicacy, accepted.

"I'm sure it will be good experience for you, Leslie."

"Oh, mummy, it really is what I want. A start, you know."

"Yes, dear. Of course."

Neither of them was so tactless as to broach the question—start to what?

"You see," said Leslie, who, now that she had got her own way, wanted to be sure that she had got it for the right reasons, "you see, I've never lived any life but this. It's a very nice life, I know," she added generously, "but I do feel that I've had enough of it. I want to go right away—now—and start another, more of my own."

"Yes. Of course you did go away to school, Leslie."

"Oh—school!" said Leslie scornfully. Obviously that hadn't been a life of her own either. "School did me no good at all," she explained, casually disposing thus of five years of her twenty-three. "Unless I go away at once and start some sort of life of my own I shall never be any good. At painting or—or anything."

"No, I can see that once you've decided on a thing you don't want to delay. Only don't you think you'll find July and August in London a bit hot?"

Leslie looked surprised.

"Oh—oh, when I said 'at once' I didn't mean exactly tomorrow."

"Oh, I see. When did you think of going?"

"Well—the art-school begins its term again at the end of September."

"Oh, *September*," said Mrs. Fisher, relieved. Seeing that Leslie was looking a little discomforted she added hastily, "That's a much more sensible idea."

"Well, it would be rather silly, wouldn't it, to rush up to London just the wrong time of year? After all—after all, every one would be away, wouldn't they?" The original ending to this remark in Leslie's mind had been "the country is so lovely now"; but she had rejected this as an unworthy consideration.

"September will be much more convenient," agreed her mother. "You will have plenty of time to find a nice place to live in. I'm sorry you don't like the idea of Aunt Sybil, but you say you'd rather be on your own, do you?"

Leslie hesitated.

"I've been thinking it over," she said cautiously, "and perhaps it would be better to share with some one."

"I should be much easier in my mind if you were with a friend. I'm so afraid you would find it lonely all by yourself."

"Oh, as long as I had my painting I should never be lonely. But I think it would be far cheaper to share."

"Yes?" said her mother encouragingly. "Is there any one you think you might like to live with?"

Leslie hesitated again. "Well—it did just occur to me—some one like Jane, for instance. You see, if Florence isn't going to be in town any more—"

"Jane. Yes. Well, that is a possibility," said Mrs. Fisher, reflecting that, of the two, she would much prefer her daughter to be sharing with Florence. "What does Jane think of it?"

"I don't know. I'm not sure that she hasn't another friend in mind. I—I haven't asked her."

Mrs. Fisher, glancing at her daughter's eager troubled face, took a long shot.

"Would you like me to suggest it to her? I can understand it's a little difficult for you."

Leslie's face, clearing instantly, belied her casual assent. "Well—if you like, mummy. You might just suggest it vaguely, mightn't you? As if you thought it would be rather nice to have me sharing with some one you knew."

Mrs. Fisher suppressed a smile and replied that she would certainly look out for an opportunity of broaching the subject. Then she sighed and dismissed regretfully from her mind the solid comforting figure of Aunt Sybil and all that Aunt Sybil so reassuringly stood for—a comfortable house, regular meals, some one to look after Leslie if she were ill.

"Oh, mummy, it will be fun," cried Leslie ecstatically. Her thoughts, joyously releasing themselves from all practical considerations, bounded forward unrestrained. Abandoning the body that remained still most solidly present in her mother's garden, her mind raced off and away towards the glamorous ever-widening reaches of the future. Nothing, she felt, could ever hold her captive again. Henceforward the sun would rise on a new world, lighting up a landscape more wonderful than any she had known. She was standing on the threshold. She could go forward as she pleased. The distant peaks, to which she had raised her eyes in longing, were hers for the scaling. She would adventure further and further; and always, she thought, she would be conscious of some definite purpose in her life. Because at last, at last, even if she were a little late in starting, she was going to do what all the others had done. She was going to begin a life of her own.

FURROWED MIDDLEBROW

Made in the USA
Middletown, DE
24 July 2020